Running
from
Love

Teal Rose

Acknowledgment

I dedicated this book to my best friends and sisters, Noura and Ebony. Thank you for inspiring me and being there for every step of this bumpy ride.

Thank you to my amazing editor and friend, Tori Moore. Thank you for checking in on me and feeding my ego.

Thank you to anyone who helped to push me to release any of my labors of love! And to my readers and new followers, the best is yet to come.

Peace, Love, and Keep Beyoncé in your heart!

Content Warning

This book contains the mention of suicide, light BDSM, cheating, manipulation, and abusive situations.

But mainly, this story is about redemption and finding one's voice.

Contents

Prologue

Present day

Clomp

Clomp

Clomp

I knew I looked like a madwoman as I ran down the streets of New York City with my five-year-old twin boys strapped to either hip while each of them broke my eardrums with their sobs. Golden-blonde locs were a wet mess on top of my head, piled up in a bun from my shower. My purple crop tank top and sleeping shorts were plastered to my honey-brown skin. Worst of all, my sneakers were soggy from the water that dripped from my short, thick legs.

I passed a couple of international affairs offices and hotels that shared the long avenue. Typically, this part of the city was filled with people buzzing around at all times of the night, but tonight, it was eerily deserted, and I had never been so thankful for that.

Clomp

Clomp

Clomp

I prayed no one spotted me and took a video of me. The paparazzi would love to get ahold of that video. It would be a disaster. As I ran from Fifth Avenue to my Tesla parked on Park Avenue, my brain raced right along with me. Who thought it was an excellent idea to park my car a block from my home? Oh yeah, me. I sighed.

As I approached my Tesla, I saw the lights when I unlocked the car with the key fob. I rushed to put my babies, Teodoro and Tris, in their car seats. As I jumped in the driver's side, I gave them the snacks I stored in my armrest. Putting the Teterboro Airport address into my GPS, I peeled out into the late-night traffic. I hit the number for Allison Johnson, my assistant and best friend, on my dashboard.

"Hey, Jasmine. How—" Allison answered.

"Hey, Allison. Sorry for cutting you off, but I need you to call and get my plane ready to go as soon as possible! I need to get out of New York tonight. Tony, Wren, and Gabe are coming to New York to see me, and that can't happen, Alli… Think about the kids!" I said loudly.

"O-Okay, do you want me to get—" Allison stammered.

"YES! Get me whatever, however! No matter the cost."

"Okay, I will call you back in the next fifteen minutes with a plan."

"Make it ten minutes, and I'll give you a bonus," I pleaded.

I wasn't usually abrasive with Allison, but home training left my brain. I could hear her roll her eyes as she said, "Sure thing, boss lady."

"Sorry, I just need you to do this for me," I pleaded into my phone, my heartbeat pulsing in my throat as she hung up the phone.

I hated driving in New York. On a good day, I was an okay driver, but tonight, with my nerves on edge and my babies in the backseat, I shook uncontrollably. I was acting on autopilot, unaware when I'd entered I-95 until Allison called me back ten minutes later. That was when the glaring lights of the cars snapped me back into reality. It impressed me that she was able to get the pilot to leave in the next thirty minutes.

I could finally breathe after I ended the phone call with Allison. My babies were fast asleep when I looked back at them. The tightness in my eyes eased. I gave the gear selector two tugs and waited for the gray steering wheel icon to appear and activate the self-driving function of my electric car. I took a deep breath, lifted my chin, and repeated my affirmation: "I am strong and capable, and I can make it through anything!" I recited it five times before my car veered onto Industrial Avenue and drove into Teterboro Airport in New Jersey.

Luckily, there weren't any lines at the entrance gates, and I could get onto the tarmac where my plane awaited. I woke the twins and watched as they dragged their little feet to their seats. I gave my keys to the concierge with a courteous smile and requested he return the car to my storage. I thanked the gentleman and boarded the plane to the last place I wanted to go: Nashville, Tennessee.

I shuddered and sighed because it meant I would likely run into my ex-fiancé, which would be a fate worse than death.

As I made myself comfortable in my seat and watched as the twins fell back to sleep, I wondered if I was making a mistake and acting out of selfishness and the usual Jasmine tendency of being scared as shit of the unknown. You would think that someone like me, a thirty-time Grammy award winner, would not be afraid of anything. But you would've guessed wrong. That's why, instead of overcoming my problems and difficult situations, I ran. Because all I had in life was me, my kids, and running, that was all I got in the end, as my fellow diva, Queen B, once sang. My eyelids grew heavy, and when my phone rang, I looked at the screen and prepared myself for the interrogation I was about to receive.

"Hey Jassie, I heard you were leaving New York early, and you were heading here. Is that true?" My mom asked me in her deep southern accent.

"Allison called you already?" I asked. Allison worked like she was the president's personal assistant. I'm glad she got to my mom first. That just means less explaining I had to do. At thirty years old, you would think I knew how to handle my mom, but that was easier said than done.

"Allison called me asking to get your old room ready because your place won't be ready until tomorrow morning," she said. I bit back my typical snarky reply. My mom and I finally reached a point in our relationship where we were more open with our feelings after everything that took place recently. My mom continued, "You could have called me yourself and asked."

I bit back a sigh that was trapped in my throat. Yes, my mom was right, but right now, my patience and nerves had hit an all-time low. Breathing through my nose, I spoke in my most calming voice.

"My beautiful mother, may your grandsons and I please stay at your home until they set my place up tomorrow? I didn't predict I would run out of my home at midnight." I could hear her eyes over the phone, banging around her sockets as she rolled them, with her famous half a smile on her face as she shook her head.

"Well, if you weren't doing some mess, you wouldn't have to be running out in the middle of the night with my babies," she said teasingly.

"You're right, Mom. I promise to do better."

She paused for a second before agreeing that we could stay until my home was ready. I quickly thanked her and hung up because I feared it would have sent her into a religious sermon if I stayed on the phone.

I found the spare clothes I usually kept in my closet on the plane for emergencies. They were old, apparently, because I jumped for five minutes trying to get into my jeans before finally calling it quits. Throwing my damp clothes back on, I huffed and returned to my seat with them still clinging to my skin and prayed I wouldn't get sick. I quickly covered myself and my babies with the lavender-scented sheet and pillow onboard and tried to sleep.

Part I

Hajime ni[1]
Six years ago

---

1 In the beginning in Japanese

Chapter 1

Jasmine

Absentmindedly, I tapped my foot to the sound of the current performer's beat. The bustle of both my crew and the one from the award show buzzed around me as I stood still. I clenched and unclenched my fists with each of my breaths. Allison came to stand next to me, and I opened my mouth to speak. Allison arched one of her perfectly manicured eyebrows at me, so I stopped and closed my mouth.

"You're almost out of the hustle and bustle," she said.

"And not a moment later." I rolled my neck. "One last performance, and I'm done."

Allison hummed her agreement and busied herself with straightening out my wardrobe. I folded my arms to hide the slight tremor of my hands and thought back to how I got to this point in my life.

It all started at Johnson Magnet School in the heart of Music City. I was in the eighth grade, and similar to my best friend, Samantha Field, I was an active member of our school's music program.

At thirteen, I was skinny as a pole and wanted nothing to do with singing until Samantha "convinced" me to try out for the lead position in the school choir. Until then, I had thrived in the shadows. While in the background, I played the flute and hid behind all the super tall kids in the band.

See, I had figured out how to make it through life without problems. I kept my head down and spoke to no one except Sam. I met Samantha when I was in second grade when she decided the class bully was going to regret picking on us. You can only imagine how a four-foot girl looked standing up to a group of boys twice her size. She had big balls, which she attributed to her being Black and Irish. After that, Sam stuck beside me through thick and thin. When my dad passed away from cancer at ten, it was like I lost a part of my soul. My parents were my world, but I was a daddy's girl. Whenever I needed anything or just wanted to vent, I sought him out first. Luckily, I had Sam to help me through this time because my mom broke down in front of me. There were days I had to spoon-feed my mother because she was so depressed, and other days, I was helping her go through her hourly panic attacks until she found her relief in liquor. After that, Sam and I made a pact to always stay together no matter what we were going through.

Samantha always had unique plans for me. This was no different from any other time. It was almost Thanksgiving of our eighth-grade year, and Mr. Bran, our band teacher, had prepared us for our winter concert. Samantha, my ride-or-die, walked into the band room and sat beside me.

"Ugh, this blows! I hate practicing in this cramped room with everyone packed together," she complained while she tossed her curly cherry-colored hair over her shoulder. Samantha looked like a dwarf in the chair. Yesterday, her lime green nails shone against her fawn skin, but today she'd replaced them with a polish that resembled the apricot color of the setting sun. I eyed her enviously as she scooted to the end of the chair. Sam was well-developed for an eighth grader, and sitting next to her made me slouch a bit more in my chair.

"Well, we have a month left of school, then we're free. I can't believe we will be in high school next year," I blurted out enthusiastically. The idea I would be one step closer to freedom excited me.

"I know, right!? Gosh, new year, new boys to date," she replied with a dreamy look on her beautiful face.

I rolled my eyes. "We haven't even made it to high school yet, and you're already thinking about guys."

"Well, I'm preparing for my future husband."

"You're what?" I looked bug-eyed at her.

"Yeah, I decided I want to be a stay-at-home mom. I can help cheer for you from home whenever you become a famous singer!" She wiped at the mist on her pink-colored upper lip with the back of her hand.

"You're not serious, are you? What about college?" I looked at her as if she'd lost her mind.

"Yes, I am, and my second goal is to get you famous. It's not fair to have such a beautiful voice just to hide it from the world," she declared as she stood up from her seat. "Come on. I have something to show you."

I never wanted to stir the boat with Samantha, so I followed her into the hallway. We were near the open double doors to the choir room when she shoved me through.

"Hey," I yelled as I rubbed my now sore arm. Samantha had heavy hands, sheesh. "Why did you push—"

"There you are, Jasmine," Mr. Bran's wife, Mrs. Bran, said. She was the choir teacher.

I froze when I looked around, and everyone in the choir stared at me. My face felt about a hundred degrees, and I got nervous because everyone's eyes were on the straggler, aka me.

"Hello, Mrs. Bran. S-sorry, I tripped and fell into your classroom. I will leave now," I stammered. The straightened edges of my hair being pressed started to kink up as I tugged on my loose black uniform.

"What do you mean, leave? Aren't you auditioning for the solo for the winter concert?" she asked with glee. Everything gleamed on Mrs. Bran, from her wild electric blue hair to her pink Crocs. One thing about her, she sure loved her colors.

"I-I you must be mistaken, Mrs. Bran. That list must be wrong. I play the flute!"

"Flute, smoot! I have your name right here." She showed me where my name and two other students had been listed on the paper. "I already told Mr. Bran you and Samantha will be in here with me for your audition, and he had no choice but to nod and agree."

"B-But I can't, Mrs. Bran!" I was positive I'd turned green around the gills. "I didn't even practice a song."

"I know, Jassie, you can sing your favorite song, Emotions by Destiny's Child," Samantha stated as I stared a hole into her back as she avoided me. She knew I would kill her if she looked my way. "Yes, Ms. Bran, that's what she'll sing. She knows it like the back of her hand."

"Speaking of backhand-" I started to say, but she had the nerve to pin me with a guilty look.

"Would it be okay if Jasmine auditioned with just us in the room?" Sam asked.

Mrs. Bran tapped her foot on the polished wooden floor and nodded.

"Okay, ladies, let's line up outside the door so that I can watch Jasmine's audition." Mrs. Bran scurried the rest of the choir outside.

When she was out of earshot, the wretch, Samantha, leaned over and said, "Please do it good, Jassie. The winter concert is going to have a talent scout there. This can be your big break!" She beamed.

"I don't want to be famous. I just want the money to have a big house and not work a nine-to-five," I whined, but she wasn't taking no for an answer. "Fine, but I'm not that good, Samantha. You think way too highly of me."

"Yeah, get up there and show us your marvelous voice," she whispered to me. "And don't mess it up or else," she growled as she balled up her fists, and I cringed because Sam could fight.

I blew out hot air and walked up to the mini-stage. Mrs. Bran was in the middle of the room, and Sam was in the back. From my position, I stared face to face with Mrs. Bran. I grabbed my hands to steady them and found something to focus on: Mrs. Bran's teal polka dot glasses.

Sigh! Out of all the things to stare at, you choose her glasses!

I cleared my throat, stood up straight, and counted to three. On the third count, I let out a melody that took me away to the most secure place, my room. There I was, tucked away from the harsh reality of school, the world, and my mom's unbearable need to control my life ever since my father passed away. I channeled all my fear of the future, my lingering grief over my dad's death, and my disappointment with life.

When I was done, I opened my eyes, and everyone stood with their mouths agape. Mrs. Bran had her tiny mouth wide open in awe. Sam beamed, and some girls from the choir gathered by the door, astonishment written all over their faces.

And there I was, standing there with my face, feeling like someone pushed it into the fire.

"Jasmine, that was so unearthly beautiful. There are not too

many times I am left speechless, but today you achieved it." She stood up and clapped like a madwoman. "You got the part. I will even let you pick whatever you want to sing."

"What? Me? Mrs. Bran, are you sure about this? I'm supposed to play my flute twice this concert!" I shouted and heard some girls in the hallway snicker.

"I have never been so sure of something in my life! You're going to be amazing, and you might even catch the ear of Mr. Garrett, the talent scout," she beamed.

Every year, Mrs. Bran tried to get Mr. Garrett to sign one of her choir girls to the record label In The Loop and make them a successful star, and each year, she failed to impress him. The ongoing joke was that Mrs. Bran was in a talent contest with herself, and she kept losing. But Sam and Mrs. Bran were so determined to prepare me for this concert that I spent an extra hour every day with them, sequestered in the choir room after band practice, much to my mother's dismay.

It was the night of the winter concert, and I had run to the bathroom about ten times in the hour leading up to the show. I didn't even know how it was possible. After all, I hadn't eaten anything that day because I was so nervous I would mess something up in front of everyone, especially Mr. Garret.

My mom, who was against this "talent show," was now on pins and needles. I looked over at her; she had on her signature white head wrap that she fought to keep up because her hair was short. I wasn't sure why she was nervous because she'd said a million times, "Ain't no talent scout going to want a skeleton on stage, rattling her bones." So, I didn't know why she bothered.

We met Sam and her parents at their seats when we entered the auditorium. They were both dressed in the same color as Sam's gray dress. Sam and I walked toward the backstage, where everyone had gathered. The air behind the stage was so thick you could choke on it. Everyone paced around with a fake plastered-on smile. After a while,

I fed off the energy.

Samantha noticed and grabbed my shoulders, which prevented me from bouncing. "Hey, Jassie, you're going to do fine. Quit worrying. You have the voice of a goddess," she praised me, and I looked at my best friend. Even though her words comforted me, they added to the churn of my stomach.

I mistakenly swiped my hand through my hair, and it caught one of my tight curls. I'd forgotten I had to forgo the silk press for this week because I knew it wouldn't last a day with the sweat I produced.

"What if I make a fool of myself, Sam? What if-"

She cut me off. "What if, what if, what if..." Sam sighed. "Stop with the what-ifs and show those lame people what they've been missing in their lives."

"Which is..." I went on skeptically.

She shook her head. "Your beautiful voice, Jas! Snap out of it. You're up after the band finishes."

I nodded as she left. I went to warm up my vocal cords.

Twenty minutes and two bottles of water later, I waited on the side of the stage with Sam before they called my name. I thought I was relaxed and ready until I looked into the auditorium and saw it was a full house. Mr. Garrett was seated in the front row with his pink suit on.

What a way to stand out.

Sam exited the stage next and came to stand next to me when the announcer called my name. I was frozen in my spot. Sam whispered, "You got this," right before she shoved me hard enough to get me on stage.

I found my mother, who was fussing with her head wrap, and Sam's parents in the audience, which made me relax. Surrounded by all the lights and people, I wanted to choke, but I looked back at Sam from my position on the stage, and she had the widest smile. When I looked back out at the audience, my mother smiled when she turned and looked at me. I trembled as I saw her beaming like a Cheshire cat. Her smile was probably meant to bring me peace, but it was just creepy.

The announcer seemed to sense my hesitation and repeated my name, which shook me out of my little daze. I don't think I'd been this nervous since I spoke at my dad's funeral. I proceeded on rickety legs, and when I got to the microphone, I turned to see Mrs. Bran give me a thumbs-up from the side of the stage. The background music started, and I pictured myself in my room at home dancing. I sang my best version of Love Gives You Wings by one of my favorite artists, Treasure. Midway through the song, I started to sway and dance to the music as I lost myself in the song.

It wasn't until I heard the music stop and listened to everyone applauding that I realized I had made it through the song without dying or choking. I looked into the audience, and my mom was beaming. At that moment, I knew everything would change.

I rushed off the stage, and Sam pulled me into a bear hug.

"OMG, Jassie, you were amazing! I can see your name in lights." Sam swept her hand over her head. "Jasmine Grant, Grammy-award-winning singer!"

"Sam…," I shook my head. "I don't even know if I did well."

"You were amazing, and if Mr. Garrett, with his loud suit, doesn't see that, then he's a dweeb," she pressed on.

"Well, geez, cut me some slack!" Mr. Garrett and my mother walked up to me. "You must be Jasmine Grant. You, dear, have an amazing voice. I spoke with your mother, and she told me your dream is to become a famous singer."

I think I almost broke my neck as I spun toward my mother. "Oh, yes, Mr. Garrett. We talked about how performing at this concert could help her career." My mother's smile was painted on to the point you couldn't tell her apart from the Grinch.

The heck? She told me I was wasting my time and didn't have what it took to become a singer.

"*I think with a great vocal coach, we can make you the next big thing,*" *Mr. Garrett beamed. "I want to invite you to come to our vocal camp this summer. It's free, and at the end of the camp, my boss and I pick two individuals to sign with our recording company, In The Loop Records. So how about it?"*

I jumped as Sam and my mom yelled, "Yes!"

"Well, that's nice 'n all, but I think I need to hear it from Miss Jasmine's mouth. So, what do you say?" Mr. Garrett turned to me.

I became hyper-aware that we were now the focus of everyone's attention. It was so quiet that I could hear the soft chatter from the audience. The weight of everyone's eyes on me as they waited for my answer strangled me. Unfortunately, I glanced at Sam, and I watched as her mahogany eyes widened as she slightly pleaded for me to say yes. My mom had the same expression as Sam's, but I could tell my mom's mind was far away from this little backstage.

I felt a single bead of sweat run down my back and gathered enough strength to form a single sentence.

"Mr. Garrett, I will gladly accept the invitation to your vocal camp, and I will win that contract." My voice was unsteady, but I played it off.

If Mr. Garrett cared or knew that I made that statement to appease my mother and Sam, he didn't show it. Instead, he said, "Excellent. I will get your mother's information and have her sign off on some paperwork. Camp starts the last week of May. So, you will have until then to be ready to go."

"I will, Mr. Garrett."

Little did I know that day was the last time I would have the chance to be a carefree, introverted thirteen-year-old.

I spent my next six months of freedom with Sam, but my mom made it difficult. When all three of us would go shopping, Sam and I found outfits I loved, but my mom would chastise me and tell me she wouldn't buy them. I ended up just giving in to my mom's demands because I didn't want her to have a panic attack, a habit she picked up after my dad's death. I knew it was wrong, but after my dad's death, everyone abandoned us, and I couldn't live without having any family in this world. But after a while, it took a toll on me, and Sam noticed it. Sam made it her mission to build my confidence up with pep talks and wrote me affirmation notes. I appreciated them, but I couldn't tell her that the pep talks made me feel like I would never see her again. In the months that led up to camp, I noticed Sam became uncannily distant and wouldn't tell me what was bothering her. I tried to get her to open up, but she said it was nothing. I left it alone, but I'd end up wishing I had pushed harder.

The vocal camp was the most intense time of my life. Some days, it was so stressful that I couldn't breathe and became dehydrated from sweating because of the stress-induced state I was in all the time. Until then, I'd lived my life in the shadows and tried to stay behind Sam. But I couldn't hide at In The Loop's vocal camp. The moment I stepped foot onto the vast campus they rented for the students, I no longer had time for myself, much less for Sam or my family.

Within the month and a half that I was gone, I learned that people my age could be as cutthroat as adults. Each week, we were picked off, one by one, until ten of us survived. That's when I became the target of bullying because the other kids believed Mr. Garrett gave me preferential treatment. Their words didn't affect me until I overheard some of the girls whisper about me giving Mr. Garrett blow jobs, and that's the only reason why someone such as myself would ever make it this far.

First, ew, and second, I wasn't desperate!

Their rumors and hatred fueled me to push myself harder. After I won the contract from In The Loop Records, my life went from dull and routine to hell in a handbasket. The only saving grace was when the record label hired Allison to be my personal assistant. They didn't know that she would become my wingwoman after a year. I was in awe when I saw the petite woman with umber-colored skin and ice-colored hair that made her green eyes stand out. But it was her compassionate spirit that sealed the deal for me as she swooped down to carry me as much as she could. I really don't know how I would have gotten through the first year of showbiz without her advocating for me.

I spent most of my free time during high school in the studio. It became so bad that I ended up swapping school for a private homeschool teacher, Ms. Crane. Sam and I barely had time to talk, much less see each other in person. Even when Allison scheduled some time for a video chat with Sam, my mom cut the time down to a ten-minute call. We spent our short time on our choice of video chat app and never talked over five minutes.

I was so consumed with my record deal and constructing my fan base. My mom took it upon herself to be involved in every aspect of my contract, but not in a good way. She picked my songs, clothing, and everything in between. It wasn't until the second year of my career that she all but blocked every attempt for me to interact with Sam, and when I confronted her about it, her simple explanation was, "Sam understands you're busy. Build your career now and then have friends later." It became too much to fight her since she completely controlled my contract. So, I gave in.

I didn't notice the signs of my best friend's mental state until it was too late.

I perfectly remember the day when I got the news Sam had committed suicide. I was fifteen, and it was a bleak day in Los Angeles. I had woken up in the new home my mom purchased for us with my money from my first album. It was the first day I'd had off since I started my journey as a singer. My mom was already up and in the kitchen if I went by the noises outside my room.

She heard me approach, turned around, and I could see her eyes were puffy and red-tinged. I had only seen my mother cry a handful of times. The last time was when my dad passed away from cancer when I was seven. Since then, she had shielded her emotions from me and the world.

"Mom, what's going on?" I asked calmly.

She fidgeted with her cross pendant before she mumbled, "I have a letter from Sam for you. Before I- I tell you—" She paused and then fumbled with the letter. She already had her cup filled to the brim with coffee and what I assume was her favorite alcoholic beverage, a disturbing hobby she took up after my dad had passed, along with controlling my life. I guess that's her way of coping with things instead of seeking help.

When she handed it to me, I looked up to see tear streaks on her cheeks, and the sight of my mom upset genuinely mystified me. She didn't cry in front of anyone, let alone me.

"Wow, something must be really wrong for you to be crying in front of me." And I wished I could take back the words instantly when I saw the hurt in her eyes. "I'm so sorry, Mom. It's been a long night, and I woke up on the wrong side of the bed."

"It's okay. I have to make a call. Be right back." My mom got up and scurried into her room.

I sighed. I mentally kicked myself and promised to make it up to my mom later. The letter was open when I grabbed it. It was on the typical pink paper Sam always bought; when I opened it, I could smell the faint whiff of her citrus perfume.

Dear Jasmine,

I'm so proud of you and all your accomplishments in such a short time. It was a dream to see you become the biggest star I knew you could be, which you will. But I will guide and cheer you on from the stars. Please understand what I did was none of your fault, and I forbid you from mourning me or beating yourself up. I want you to carry on flying up those charts and winning a Grammy every year. Push the envelope and break records. Fall in love and have amazing sex. I want YOU to live your life and be free. I will always love you and will be watching from the stars.

Love you to the moon and back,

Sam

I read the letter ten times. I turned the letter over to see if the words "I got you" were on the back. It suddenly became too difficult to breathe, and my head pounded along to the beat of my heart. I abandoned the food my mom had given me and ran to my mom's room. I found her on her bed, a dazed look on her face as she stared out the window.

"Mom, I-I don't understand this letter," I stammered, even though I knew perfectly well what this letter meant. I sat next to her as it became too difficult to stand. "This seems… but I… Mom."

"Jasmine, Sam fell into a deep depressive state after you left, and it took a toll on her." She sighed and wiped away the tears from her face with the sleeves of her shirt. "Her mom mentioned she got involved with a guy she loved, and they broke up a couple of weeks ago. She didn't tell her parents because they wouldn't accept the guy. She was flunking school and started to use a new drug that altered her thoughts. She was skipping school, sneaking in and out the house. Her parents tried to get her help, but she kept everything in until it got to this point. She tried to reach out to you, but you were preoccupied with your new album. She ended her life two days ago. Her mom is planning a small funeral for her this weekend."

Nothing made sense, but everything made sense at the same time, if that was possible. I neglected my friend and left her to deal with whatever she was going through by herself. I sulked all the way to my room and remained there for the rest of the day.

"I'm sorry, Jas," My mom said while she grabbed her dainty wrist. "I thought giving you guys some time apart would allow you and Samantha to focus on both of your futures. Jas, I'm sorry I-"

"I hate you," I muttered to her. My mom stumbled for a minute. Her brown eyes, which mirrored mine, were red-tinted, and if she had a lighter complexion, I knew she would be red.

I stumbled out of her room as her voice drifted off into the distance. Samantha was gone, and I could have stopped her from going off the edge. I was too self-absorbed with my own world that I neglected the one person who made everything worthwhile. Even though my room was two doors away from my mother's, it took me a while to get to the room. Especially when she kept calling my name up until I slammed the door so hard that the framed picture of Samantha and me on the last day before the In The Loop records camp started shattered as it connected with the floor. Without a second thought, I swiped the items off of the table next to the photo. I watched as unopened bottles of perfume and the discarded jewelry from the night before went sliding along the brown hardwood floor. I stood there with my arms at my side as I trembled.

I looked down at the frame, which stared back at me, broken, like me, into a thousand tiny pieces. Shame washed over me as I forwent picking up the shattered photo frame to throw myself onto the large white platform bed and stare at the teal tray ceiling. I lost track of the time, but soon enough, my body couldn't produce any more tears, and the darkness of the night lulled me to a restless sleep.

I became a shell of myself in the days before her funeral. I cried and moped around the house. My mom tried to get me to eat, write, or study, but I couldn't do it. When the weekend of the funeral arrived, I all but zoned out the entire weekend, and when it was time to leave, Sam's mother gave me some of her ashes and the art piece she'd made for me. I placed her ashes and the portrait she drew of me on a shelf in my room. It reminded me that life is fragile and that I took my best friend for granted.

My mom and Allison, thankfully, forced me to go to therapy for my sanity. For the following six months, I focused on closure and how I would move on, which was hard since I still carried the guilt for not being there. My mom and I attended therapy as well, which was harder said than done. But eventually, we found ourselves back on reasonable terms. When I was strong enough, I gave Sam's ashes to the sea in my ode to her. As her ashes hit the water, I felt the sky open up. The warmth of a beam of sunlight washed over me.

"I know, Sam. You always loved the water. It only feels right to place you somewhere you loved." I said out loud to no one in particular during our trip to France.

When I turned seventeen, life took another turn, but I was too far into my career to question anything. My mom and the company's creative director quarreled over my body because while I was still that skinny little girl from Nashville to them, the public preened over my new curves that had finally shown up. I went from a size two in jeans to a size six. My nonexistent breasts filled out to a C-cup. It appeared as if I gained curves overnight, which made everyone believe I'd had surgery. My PR rep came out and denied the allegations. It was because my creative director, Mike Thomas, and my personal assistant had increased my calorie intake and pushed me to work out every day. Plus, puberty had finally kicked in.

Later that year, my mom decided she would have even more control over my schedule and projects. Allison hated this idea, but she couldn't convince my mother or Mike otherwise. I didn't have any say in it either. My mother made sure of that. But I wasn't going to take it lying down. I pushed the envelope and took an interview to be rebellious. It didn't work out well for me. I wrecked the whole interview and made myself look incompetent. So, from then on, I did what I do best: stayed in the background and let her dictate everything for me. My mom took that and ran with it. Soon, she had a hand in everything from my boyfriend down to what type of albums I released.

It wasn't until my twenties that I started to slowly break away from my mother. I went behind her back to participate in photoshoots, interviews, and performances that would send her into a heart attack. I still remember the slack jaw and my mom's dark brown eyebrows touching her hairline when I showed her my Hustler photoshoot. She was rendered so speechless that, for the first time in my life, she spun around on her pleather kitten heel shoes and left, muttering that "the devil got into her." I smiled at her and waved every time she wouldn't agree with something. Allison would just shake her perfectly straight, bright blue bob and tell me I was going to get her fired someday.

To that, I just replied, "Bless your heart! Do you think you can get away from me that easily?" She would just shake her dainty head some more and tap her stilettos. As she continued on whatever task she abandoned. But then I was left with my thoughts and all the bravado I once had crumbled. I would find myself apologizing to my mother by going to church with her the following Sunday. You could see her smile from LA when she saw me in the pews with her, and that made things a bit better.

The sound of someone snapping their fingers brought me back to my current reality.

"Hey, spacey, you were about to say something, and you zoned out," Allison said.

"Oh yeah, that. I am bored," I said, snapping out of my daze.

I stood there as I waited to perform my latest hit song, Stalking Ass, featuring Liz the Goat, on the side stage at the Grammys. My team stopped bustling around as they snapped their necks in my direction. But I didn't care because it was true.

Allison, who was always by my side, looked at me. I saw her turn slightly green and plead, "Please get through this performance. After this, you're retired. You don't have to worry about it anymore. You don't have any kids, and you're single. So, you'll be free."

I looked at her as if she'd gone mad, and she rolled her eyes.

"Of course. I will not mess up my last performance. I'm so over this, and I'm ready to be somewhere on my yacht in the middle of the ocean," I whispered.

Allison looked at me with her large green eyes full of pity. I knew I could tell Allison anything because she'd been my personal assistant since I began my journey as an artist at thirteen. Now, at twenty-four, she had seen me through more hardship than any family member or friend.

At times like those, I was lucky she was around to deal with the mess of the music industry.

"How about we go back to your house, order takeout, and binge-watch the first season of American Gods on Starz?" she spoke with enthusiasm.

"Sure, that sounds fun. Plus, my mom won't be in town this week. So, you can stay over if you want and keep me company," I rushed out as the last performer got offstage. My crew hurried to set everything up.

"Sounds like a plan. I will call Wayne and make the order for an hour and a half. That gives us time to leave and return to your place."

"Yes, please, I want to leave ASAP after this," I said as she used her phone to place our order.

As soon as she and the other team members were gone, the countdown clock started. I took a deep breath in and stepped out on stage as soon as I heard my name. The harsh lights turned on, and I performed as if I was thirteen again, like when I had to prove to everyone that I was still that girl. Liz joined me for our newest song, and my lifetime achievement performance was done in twelve minutes. *THANK GOD!* I hugged everyone and told my team and Liz's team that we had done a fantastic job. I accepted my performance award with my four-minute speech about hard work and a consistent grind that would get you everything.

Or a mother who controlled your every move.

I ran off the stage to my dressing room. I dumped all the stuff I had brought with me into my bag and jumped into my custom Rolls-Royce Phantom that waited for me outside.

"To the house, my chocolate Adonis," I commanded playfully to Mr. Jackson, my personal driver.

"Anything for you, Queen J," Mr. Jackson replied in his

baritone voice. I swear, if it were a different time, I would have asked Mr. Jackson for a record of his voice. I once told him I'd hired him because of his voice. He told me I had to quit flirting with him before he told his wife. I laughed hard because Mr. Jackson was around sixty years old, but he moved around as if he were in his twenties.

"Thank you, Mr. Jackson. I am exhausted mentally and physically." My eyes drooped lower as I yawned. "I hope you don't mind if I fall asleep on you for the ride back."

"Not at all, Ms. Grant. Rest. I will get you home in one piece," he said as I slipped out of this realm for the thirty-minute drive.

I awoke when the car stopped at my home. I felt a bit more energetic since I'd left the show. As soon as I opened the black glass doors to my home, Allison pulled up. I gave Mr. Jackson a tip, as usual, before I headed inside.

"Right on time, Allison!" I yelled and flapped my arms wildly at her.

"Yes, sorry, some of us had to pick up the food and drive in traffic." She rolled her eyes, but not before I saw a grin break out on her face.

"Yeah, yeah, excuses, excuses," in the most New York accent I could muster up. I let out something between a laugh and an evil bark for the first time in a month. I covered my mouth instantly as Allison shook her head. We entered my home, I placed everything out in the movie room, and we got into our pink matching PJs I got when we took a mini vacation to the Alps cabin retreat. We started American Gods on Starz. After only one episode, I noticed Allison knocked out on the sofa.

I shook my head as I rubbed my hands along my arms.

"So much for movie night." I turned off the screen and tucked her in for the night. Once Allison was out, she hardly woke up unless she had to use the bathroom or she wanted to cuddle with someone.

I huffed as I shuffled to my bedroom. I bypassed my California king bed and walked out to my suite's covered balcony. The cool Los Angeles night greeted me as I sat on the black and white oversized reading chair. I took a deep breath of fresh air and closed my eyes. It was my peaceful last goodbye to my hectic career as I started my new journey.

My eleven-year career had finally come to an end. Finally, I'd woken up, mentally slapped myself, and finally taken back my life from my mother and In The Loop records. When I stepped out of the artist role, I could breathe. My last album and tour were fantastic, and I winged most of the performances during my tour.

That drove my creative director crazy, but guess what? I didn't care. That tour earned me over one billion in revenue and had been nominated for a slew of prestigious awards.

When my mom found me in my home after I announced my retirement late last year, she tried to force me into another album before I gave it up for good. So, I'd pulled something Sam would do if she'd still been here with me. I stripped down to my underwear in my backyard and jumped into my pool. The tip of my mom's ears turned slightly pink, and she called me rude. I just looked up from the pool and smiled widely at her screwed-up face, and said, "Good." She turned and stomped away, and that was the most freeing thing I had done for myself since I was thirteen.

When I got out of the water, I took a deep breath as the water washed away my sins and came out reborn to the world.

I hated to dwell on the past because I knew I had only lived up to half of what Sam wanted for me. Despite that, I was glad to have learned all the beauty secrets, filming secrets, and ways to hide from the paparazzi. I'd achieved accolades and fame. But I wanted more, and I wanted to choose the life I lived for myself.

I wanted to fulfill the side of me I kept hidden from everyone. The side that yearned to burst out of my skin every night I was alone in my bed…

"Hey, Jas," Allison yawned as she dragged herself into my room. "Sorry for ruining our relax and chill night." She jumped into my bed and under my covers.

"It's okay. We were both worn out. Get some rest, Alli," I voiced, but she was already snoring lightly.

I left the room, careful not to wake Allison, went to my hobby room to view Samantha's portrait of me, and said a brief prayer. No one remembered today was her birthday but me and her parents. Even after all these years, I remembered my best friend. I knew she was up there as she watched from the stars.

I returned to my room and slid in beside Allison. I closed my eyes and prayed that my first day of retirement would turn my life in the right direction.

Part II

E poi c'era Celeste[1]

---

1   And then there was Celeste.

Chapter 2

Jasmine

Six Months Post-Retirement

Why was I a glutton for punishment?

You would think I'd learned my lesson after I destroyed my last womanizer by dropping it on the floor. But I had the urge to touch myself so badly that I couldn't wait until I got to bed. So, stupidly, I decided to use my sink as a footstool. With one foot on the counter and the other planted on the floor, my golden toy swallowed my sensitive clit, and I convulsed because the setting was too high. One minute, the stupid thing was in my hand, and the next, it was on the floor, buzzing. When I picked up the toy, a crack ran from the base of the toy to the top. I let out a string of curses as I dumped the toy away.

I felt as if someone was trying to claw their way out of me, and it all came out when I opened my mouth.

"I'm so fucking horny!" I yelled to no one but myself.

It'd been six months since I'd retired, and I hadn't done much. I spent my days in disguise as I tried to visit different places on my bucket list, which sucked because I hated covering my locs. But that wasn't enough. I wanted to start this new part of my life with a bang, and my expectations hadn't been met. I couldn't blame anyone but myself since I was afraid to put myself out into the dating world.

I walked into my lonely bedroom, hot and bothered. After dressing for bed, I decided that my ruined womanizer wouldn't damper my mood. I threw myself on my bed and grabbed my dildo out of the bottom drawer of my nightstand. The urge to rub one out built in my core. Dildo in hand, I continued with my next step, which was the tricky part — finding something that would set the mood. I turned on my computer and searched for something to help me find my release.

I'd always felt ashamed of my desires. I wasn't a virgin by any means. The last "boyfriend" my mom hooked me up with bored me to tears. It became the same repetitive dates, lackluster conversations, and aimless kisses. But I played along until we decided to split ways. No one knew about my desires, not my two ex-boyfriends and especially not my mother. She would cast holy water on me if she ever found out. But as hard as I tried to do the Christian thing, I couldn't help it. I had tried to watch regular porn with a girl and a guy having sex, but it didn't get a rise out of me. It bored me to death. I'd tried lesbian porn to see if I would like that. Nope, same results. The only thing that got me in the mood was bisexual porn. Just the thought made my body flush with desire. Finally finding the perfect video, I angled my dildo to my entrance and turned the volume up on my computer—and then my doorbell rang. I could not hold the internal scream of frustration.

Who the hell is it?

Mood dampened, I angrily paused the video and hit the view of my cameras. Allison's heart-shaped face staring into my camera was like an ice-cold shower.

I slammed my laptop shut and stumbled to the door to open it because I knew Allison, and she wouldn't go away until she knew I was either dead or not here. Plus, there's the fact that she had a key and the code to my door.

Welp, she helped me inadvertently kill my mood.

As I reached for the door, I wondered if I should tempt fate and pretend I wasn't there. I peered through the peephole, and from my angle, it was hard to see her. I snickered in my head and turned to walk away to hide until she was gone. Then the door suddenly opened and collided with my back, sending me face-first to the floor. Luckily, my hand broke my fall.

"I knew you were hiding from me!" she exclaimed instead of helping me up as I turned over on the floor to face her. Allison stood with her hands on her slender hips.

"Well, hello to you too, Allison. It's Sunday morning. I wasn't expecting anyone. Unless you've come to take me out." I huffed and got up. "Which, from the looks of it, you almost succeeded."

Allison angled her head and sighed the deep kind of sigh you felt in your spirit. "Well, next time, open your door, and we won't have problems. I'm still your elder."

Only by five years, but I didn't say that out loud. My running joke was Allison was twenty-nine going on eighty. That always earned me an eye roll.

"I brought a friend of the family over for you to meet. She lives in New York, but some of her clients from her firm live in LA, so she travels here for work. I told her I was your assistant, and she begged me to meet you. Her clienteles are elite, Jas. She knows things about the upper echelon here that I couldn't even fathom knowing. I'm ashamed. She lives on a different coast and knows more than me." Her green eyes were wide. Allison fiddled with her black Anime t-shirt and black shorts that hugged her umber-colored skin.

"How about we go to the new café around the corner?" she asked.

Okay, I won't lie. I was intrigued because someone with more resources than Allison is absurd. Allison could find you golden fairy poop if you asked her.

"But Allison, it's Sunday, and I look like shit," I whined. I wasn't in the mood for an impromptu meet and greet.

"You're being super dramatic. You look amazing as usual." She gave me an incredulous look and waved off the insult. "Go change into some shorts and a shirt. It will be maybe thirty to an hour tops. My treat. What do you say?"

I stared at Allison with her chartreuse eyes, which always were my weakness.

"Okay, but she better not be a talker!" I yelled out as Allison jetted back to her car.

"Meet you there in a few!" She called out before she hopped into the vehicle with the slack-jawed passenger.

I sighed and turned to stomp up to my room. I grabbed the first thing I saw in my drawer: a pink T-shirt and my camo shorts. I looked like I stepped off the plane from Nashville as I tugged on the garments.

Lord hammercy! If my mom could see me now.

As I headed back downstairs, I headed to my Land Rover with my bodyguard, Bruno, in tow. We arrived at the café twenty minutes later because someone decided to drive five miles per minute on the backroads. Bruno and I entered the pink and blue colored quaint café called Café Sucré. The pink and blue theme from outside continued inside with the pink walls and blue trim. The inside of the small café reminded me of my tours in Paris when I noted white bar stool tables that were typically found there. I looked around to find Allison, but I heard her before I'd seen her. Her laughter was so loud it vibrated around the tiny Café. It almost made me jealous. The only time I heard Allison's lofty laugh was when she was with me or her boyfriend of seven years, Wayne.

"You guys are cutting up in here," I threw out once I reached the tiny table for three. Bruno sat at one of the empty tables beside us, and I sat in the empty seat at the table.

"OH MY GOSH!" Allison's friend jumped up and ran over to

hug me. "I'm your biggest fan. I know you hear that a lot, but I truly am. I have been to all your concerts and know all your songs, even the deep cuts that didn't make your album." She had a twinkle in her eye, which made me slightly uneasy.

I always had trouble with this type of praise. I never knew what to say or worried I would say something stupid. The last time I was in the same position, an interviewer had said, "You're Jasmine Grant." I'd stupidly responded, "Thank you." When I'd left the stage, Allison was gracious enough to hold back her laugh until we were in the car.

"Ah, thank you," I said meekly. "What's your name? Allison told me you're from New York but have some highly affluent clients who live here in LA."

She giggled. "Yeah, the name is Sage Ashford. I work for a private assistant firm that handles the bigwigs out here and in the Midwest."

Sage was so beautiful, she put me to shame. She had skin the color of obsidian, a smile that sparkled against it, and looked like she could walk the runaways of Paris.

"Okay, I'm jealous. Your job sounds amazing. So, tell me more about what you do?" I asked, and her eyes lit up. She was a talker, that one. She told me about her job and how she was relatively new, but she'd worked her way to the top. I learned she was a Southern girl like me and her transition from the South to the North. By the time she was done, my eyes were dry from gawking at her lips as she moved from one topic to the next.

I cleared my throat to interrupt her politely because Sage was approaching thirty minutes of talking nonstop. Allison knew that meant I was reaching my people limit for the day.

"Guess what?" Allison said. She didn't wait for our response as she continued. "My cousin Roeshall and her husband found a second wife."

I choked on the French vanilla cappuccino, my favorite, that

Allison ordered for me.

"Excuse me?" I said. My forehead wrinkled. "When did they decide on that? Wait, so they will live together? And share? And you're okay with it?"

I had so many questions and not enough time or energy to ask them.

"They're having a union ceremony next month! And yes, of course, I'm happy. This is what my cousin always wanted, and as long as she's happy, I'm happy." Allison said and smiled. Sage had a dreamy smile on her face.

Her cousin is an amazing, sweet person and this development derailed my entire train of thought. "A what?" I said as I caught up with the conversation.

"It's a ceremony for polyamorous couples. My cousin is in a Polyamorous relationship, and she had one. It was so beautiful. She has a wife and three husbands." Sage explained as a sigh fell from her lips.

My eyes blinked rapidly as I turned to Allison, who struggled to keep a straight face. Her cousin had three husbands and a wife. I rubbed the back of my neck.

Three husbands and a wife! God, I wonder how that would work...

"JAS!" I jumped when Allison yelled my name. I felt like I'd gotten caught with my hand in the cookie jar. I knew the tip of my ears and nose were faint pink from the heat I felt on my face. I couldn't tell this lady I was picturing how three men and two women would play out in bed.

"Where did you go, Jas?" Allison chided, and I turned away from the group.

Sage turned to me with a playful smirk against her perfect skin and stated, "Don't worry about it. I always wonder how they work out, but they get it done, honey. But it's nothing compared to some of these clients out here."

"What do you mean?" I asked.

"Oh, the one-percenters out here are freaks. I have a couple of clients who have signed up for this exclusive club. It's by word of mouth only—you have to be vetted. It caters to their every desire." She took a sip of her expresso.

I should have minded my business, but what Allison said next zeroed my brain in on the tail end of the conversation. "Oh yeah, you're talking about Club Celeste. I heard some of the PAs talking about it in hushed tones. Anyone who has been caught speaking about the club has gotten fired and exiled. But I caught the tail end of a conversation. You pay a yearly membership fee, and they set up a doctor's appointment with some elite doctor, and when everything comes back clean, you pay your dues, and you're in."

By then, I had abandoned my now cold cappuccino and scone. I kept cool as I stared at Sage's mouth as if I would miss out on the information that fell from her lips. My ears picked out the important information and committed them to memory.

"Yeah, you can't even pay the dues yourself or accept the invite. It's done through a courier service no one has ever heard of and by cash only," Sage continued.

"Wait, so how do they know if the shit is legit? Seems sketchy to me," Allison responded.

"You would think so, but it's legit. I have flown out here twice to sign up two clients," Sage continued. "It's crazy, but I would pay to get in for a night." She sighed as a dreamy look appeared on her face. "Anyway, it's getting late, and I have to be up at the crack of dawn to return to New York. My cousin's baby, Nixon, is turning one year old."

"How nice," I muttered, still highly engaged in the previous conversation. Sage got up and gave me a bear hug.

"Sorry, I would kick myself if I didn't get two hugs out of this," Sage said as she glowed.

"It's no problem. Let's take a picture together."

"I would love that!" She nearly broke my bones when she pulled me for another hug.

When she let go, I fixed myself with my mind still on Club Celeste. In my mind, the thought was like the old Windows screensaver with the words bouncing off the side of the screen. What if I inquired about a membership? I was considered one of the one-percenters, so why not? For research purposes, of course.

I was in such a daze that I hadn't realized we had taken the photo. I saved it and airdropped it to her phone. Sage thanked me and said goodbye as we walked to our respective vehicles.

"Alli," I called her right before she closed her car door.

"Yeah?" she said.

"Get me an invite to Club Celeste," I demanded. I knew I sounded impatient. But the sexual frustration from earlier returned, making my tongue sharper than I intended.

"Your mom would kill me, and you—"

"My mom doesn't own me, Allison. She may have railroaded her way through my career, but I'm calling the shots now." I straightened my back. "Please, can you get me that invite? I want in."

Poor Allison nodded her head. I hated being curt with her, but sometimes she was too good. After getting home, I ran upstairs to my bathroom, showered, and wrapped up in my bed.

I felt the hot heat pooling in my core at the thought that maybe I could live out my fantasy, even if it was for one night. I could tell Allison wanted to lecture me about this club. I could almost hear her voice say, "Jasmine, this isn't like you," or "Jasmine, you're beautiful, and you don't need this club to find someone," but fuck it.

Ping!

I rubbed the bridge of my nose and picked up my phone. This better be fucking good because I was tired. I looked to see the nickname

I penned Allison with when I took her to the Whisper Club, a male strip club, in Paris and gave one of the dancers a hand job.

Alli if ya nasty

> I can get you in if you truly want.

> Of course, I do. I wouldn't have asked if I wasn't serious.

> I will get you the invite tomorrow. Have your money ready.

> How much is the fee?

> A million if I remember correctly.

> Cool. I will call my accountant tomorrow.

> ...I love you, Jas. You're so gorgeous and fabulous.

> You could find someone for yourself.

> Are you sure about this?

> Yes. GN, Alli. Love you, get home safe!

I put my phone on Do Not Disturb and threw myself back into bed. I should've felt bad about doing this, but I didn't.

When I got the invite two days later, I decided to apologize to her for being snippy with her; she didn't deserve that. But then, to make matters worse, I lied and told her I had changed my mind after I got the invite. She sighed and said she would support me no matter what. When she left, I was on my way to pick up the million dollars in cash without a second thought.

As instructed, I returned the invitation with my preferences on the back, which took me some time as I wrote on a piece of loose notebook paper my perfect combination. One hour and several glasses of wine later, I sent the form attached to the invite back through one of the freelance personal assistants that I used from time to time when Allison wasn't available because I couldn't face Allison after I lied to her. I wanted two tall, dark, handsome bisexual men who were experienced in BDSM to carry out my fantasy. Well, that's a maybe on the BDSM thing.

Damn, maybe I filled it out wrong. I thought as I tossed the old paper with all of my outlandish options and the invite into the bottom drawer of my dresser.

Well, I couldn't cry over spilled milk! My mom's favorite idiom rolled through my head. That stopped me for a minute. Freezing in horror, I realized I was thinking like my mother. I shook my head and shuddered. What was next? Stomping around as I ran people's lives?

I tugged on the light blue sleeping shorts and shirt and shook my head. Nothing good would ever come from those thoughts.

It took way too long for the okay from Club Celeste. I was on pins and needles as I waited for the confirmation text. I started to get antsy and had all sorts of crazy thoughts, like was my money fake, or did I have some sexual disease I didn't know about? That would be my luck. The latter would have been laughable since I had only had sex with one person before, and it was cut and dry. So, when the text from an unknown number came through stating, "Access granted," I cried and threw up simultaneously.

I dodged my mother's nosy questions and Allison's efforts to hook me up for two weeks. Allison probably thought I was lonely in this big house and needed someone to help fill it up. I mentally rolled my eyes. Like I was some handmaid wife. My mom, though, was on a different tune. Her antics had ramped up about a hundred notches. She'd told me she could smell my eggs drying up from Nashville. It was now that I was ever so glad she moved back to Nashville when I turned nineteen because if she told me this to my face, I'm sure I would have cursed her out.

But that was okay. Once I got to live out my fantasy, just once, this Friday, then I would be set for life.

But four days later, I thought I was having a mini-stroke. I received the location, but I wasn't sure I could go through with it.

The day before, I treated myself to one of the most exclusive spas in LA. I booked a hotel, which, now that I thought about it, was stupid on my part since I was twenty minutes away from the club's location. I was ashamed to admit that I looked rough in the beginning, and by the time I finished, I felt like I could perform a concert—

Well, let me not get too carried away.

With a shaky hand, I picked up the small bag I'd packed for tonight's event and dropped it on the bed again for the sixth time. The soft clicking sound of the old analog clock I bought three years ago reminded me for the thousandth time that I was running out of time. If I didn't leave in the next ten minutes, I would be late to get ready at the hotel before I went to the club.

I can't believe I thought I could do this—it's worse than performing.

I took several deep breaths and willed myself to grab my bag and head out. I barely reached the car before dropping into the front seat and starting the engine. I wasn't used to being in the driver's seat. So, I knew I had to pull myself together. I had five minutes left. I took a paper towel from my armrest and wiped my forehead and mouth. I looked down at the paper and nearly laughed because it was so damp, I could clean the car with it.

You got this, Jasmine.

Yeah, sure, it was just sex. I mean, I have sung about it in many of my songs. I even had sex before. Granted, it was only a handful of times and lasted maybe four minutes each time.

I mean, but who was counting?

As I pulled into the hotel, I got out and let the valet take my car. It took me a good twenty minutes to get to my room. Once I was left alone, I regretted reserving the presidential suite. I was supposed to be lowkey, but I had to go big. I could have kicked myself, but there wasn't any time for that now. I dashed into the blue and white bedroom and quickly got ready. Since this was going to be a one-time thing, I was going to go all out. I twisted my locs down, put on the wig I'd brought, and glued the black curly wig down so Jesus himself couldn't remove it. I applied my makeup using my performance latex foundation because it was sweatproof. I used it to cover the small tattoo of the peace hand symbol on my hip bone I'd gotten when I was eighteen in England. I applied red lipstick and winged eyeliner. I poured myself into the red leather mini dress that fit me like a second skin and fastened some simple diamond earrings to my lobes.

I threw on my red stilettos, stood in front of the mirror, and blinked a couple of times. Even in my music career, I would never have worn something like it. The dress was sexy and made me feel warm all over. I fixed my hair in the mirror and tugged on it to make sure it was secured. I'd brought a red mask because I wanted to be sure this wouldn't come back on me. I wouldn't want my fans to know I had to pay for my sexual habits.

Okay, Jas, time to put on your big girl panties. You spent a million dollars for some dick, and now it's time to cash in on it.

I grabbed my purse with my red lipstick in case I needed a refresh. I didn't trust the club to protect me, so I brought my own condoms in different sizes. It may have been a bit overboard, but I had to because I had experienced visual changes from my birth control. I found that out the hard way when I woke up one morning, and it looked like everything in my room was doubled. Allison rushed me to the hospital when she found me holding the wall to get to the bathroom.

I glanced out the window and saw the moonlight bouncing off the pool's reflection. Even though I knew what I was doing was sinful in the eyes of God, I sent a prayer for protection. Hopefully, the guys weren't serial killers, as I remembered the countless murder investigation shows I binge-watched.

Okay, Jas, let's get folded. It's only one night!

I sucked in my breath and power walked to the valet to retrieve my car before I could get any ideas of backing out. I took a moment to take in the warm air of the Los Angeles night. I took a deep breath, jumped in my car, and stole one last look at the hotel before leaving the parking lot. The ride to the club was filled with winding paved roads that led to homes with plush forests in between them for privacy the further I drove up into the hills. I eventually pulled up to a black metal gate with armed security, and my back stiffened.

What did I get myself into?

That was the first thing that ran through my mind when I rolled down the window to speak to the security guard.

"Confirmation text and invite." He was a burly man who, from my position, had an AK-15 and a handgun on him. He was so jacked that if he wanted to hurt me, he could have smashed my window and dragged me out in one swoop.

"O-okay," I stammered as I rifled through my small purse for the items he demanded. I held them out, and he took them from my hand.

He grunted, walked over to the other guard, and handed him the information. When he turned back to me, he had a pointed look on his face with his eyebrow cocked as if he were judging me. I turned my hot face back to look at the gate and only turned back when he returned.

"You're good to go, ma'am," he grunted as he turned to walk back to his spot.

The gate opened, but I stared at the guy who watched me as if he wanted to scold me.

Yeah, screw you, guy!

I made sure to give him the finger… when I was out of his sight.

I drove my car through the gates surrounded by tall cherry laurel bushes that hid the property until I reached the club. Here, in the middle of Hollywood Hills, was a vast modern black mansion. Someone had planted white peonies around the mansion. I guess to give the gloomy mansion some warmth. The mansion made the one I lived in look like a one-bedroom apartment in New York City. That's when I noticed that the entire first floor was made of floor-to-ceiling glass, and what looked like an orgy was occurring on the dancefloor.

Sheesh, it's only eight o'clock.

The lights from the room allowed you to see the outline of bodies grinding together. I couldn't determine who the people were, but I knew I would probably recognize a few folks if I entered that room. I dropped my car off with the valet. I walked the small distance to the club door and stood with my hand on the black knob.

Okay, now turn the knob in one, two, and three.

I opened the pitch-black double door, and two things greeted me. First, the soft beat of the house music enveloped me at the entrance. Secondly, the lady at the front desk, located right in the middle of the most impressive foyer I've ever seen. The foyer had white floors, red walls, and a colossal white statue of Eros in the middle. She was an older lady with silver hair and a green tweed suit, and she wore White Diamonds perfume like a second skin. I held back a choke when I was in front of her.

"Hello, Ms. Grant. It's a pleasure to meet you." She smiled, but it looked like she was struggling to do so.

"How did you-" I stammered.

"Oh, I know every one of my clientele. Don't worry, love.

Nothing gets by me, though," she said and winked. "Hopefully, you found us without any trouble," she continued as if I wasn't there standing with my mouth agape.

"Yeah, thank you."

"So, we found the perfect match plus a surprise bonus for you since this is your first time here. We have set you up on the top floor. I hope everything is to your liking and you enjoy your time here at Club Celeste." She smiled and handed me a keycard. "You'll find your room with your guests at the end of the hall. You can use the elevator or the stairs to get to the third floor. Room number seven. Alfie will escort you to your room."

I thanked her and took the keycard. The guy named Alfie was an older gentleman as well. His white hair was combed back, and he wore a gray sports suit straight out of the twenties that made his pale skin look sickly.

"Ma'am, are you ready?" he said. The croaky sound of his voice made me wince.

"I can find my way to the room myself," I said after clearing my throat. "If you don't mind."

"I will show you to the stairs and the elevator then," Alfie said with a thin lip smile. His dark brown eyes sparkled.

I turned to the lady at the desk. "Thank you…." I quickly read her name tag. "Ms. Edina."

She said welcome and gave another hard smile before I shuffled off behind Alfie. He pointed me to the stairs and the elevators, which were located around the corner from the front desk, next to each other. I told him thanks, and he turned on his flat heels and walked away.

I didn't trust my legs on the stairs, so I used the elevator. I would have hated to fall down the steps and bust my ass in this palace. I would have to move out of LA. I hit the third-floor button, and the elevator jerked before it ascended.

When the elevator doors opened, I took one shaky step into the long white hall, and the white marble tiles from downstairs followed me. As I walked along the hall, I noticed different pastel paintings of various men and women of all different shapes, colors, and sizes lined the stark hall. Soft classical music floated from the speakers. There was a faint moan from a nearby room that almost made me feel flushed at the thought of what may have caused the sound.

I got so caught up in willing myself to put one foot in front of the other that I almost walked past my door.

I started to shake and felt acid rise in my throat.

Okay, it's now or never, Jas. What are you going to do?

I turned on my heels and decided I couldn't do it. I mumbled to myself like a madwoman.

What was I thinking? I wasn't made to be this type of person. If my mother could see me now!

I can see her with her hand on her hip and the cruel smirk she reserved only for me when I did something she didn't agree with, as she scolded me and weaponized my dad's death to keep me from exploring my needs and desires.

Then I stopped in the middle of the hallway and wondered what I was doing. I'd spent too much money on this experience to cower because of my wayward thoughts.

I took a few deep breaths and turned around on my heels as I clicked right back to room number seven. While I fumbled with the keycard and the solid black door, I reminded myself that I could play my way through this night and scratch it off my bucket list of having wild, hot sex with two chocolate Adonises.

Finally getting the door open with a click, I pushed it open and walked through. I looked up, my eyes widened, and my mouth dropped almost to the floor.

What in the hell?

Chapter 3

Jasmine

I had the wrong room number. That was the answer. I checked the black and white keycard to see if the lady at the front desk gave me the wrong card.

Nope, it had the number seven on the card.

The room seemed small with the three half-naked men in the powder blue wall room. The room held an oversized king-size bed with white linen. The small seating area had a small blue sofa and chairs with a plush white carpet big enough for someone to sleep on, and had what I assumed was their clothing on it. There were two other doors in the room, which I assume were the closet and bathroom. The vanilla lavender scent drifted through the room, and warm white lights made the room feel intimate.

And then, of course, there were the three men dressed in silk black boxers…excuse let me rephrase that three **White** men dressed in silk black boxers.

"So sorry, I have the wrong room," I croaked out as I turned on my heels to walk out the door. The sound of my high heels on the white marble floors ricocheted in the large room.

"How do you know this is the wrong room?" one of the guys with an eyebrow piercing asked. He moved from the king-sized, white, wingback bed in the center of the room and walked towards me. His black boxers stood out against his sand-colored skin.

Make that eyebrow, nose, and lip piercings. *I wonder how many piercings he has?*

"W-Well," I stammered and cleared my throat. "I asked for two tall, dark, and handsome men. I-"

"Wren, am I tall?" the same man asked another of the trio.

"Yes, Tony," he answered, looking at me with the lightest gray eyes I'd ever seen. They looked abnormal against his pale skin.

Are they even natural?

"Gabe, am I not handsome?" Tony asked the last guy, who looked like a cross between a football player and a model.

"Don't push your luck, Tony," he grumbled. As I got caught up in Gabe's forest green eyes, he smirked when he noticed me gawking at him.

I snapped my eyes back to the baby-powdered blue walls. First, before anything, I was a Southern lady, and that was how I tried to leave, using my Southern charm to save the last of my wit.

"Well, gentlemen, there seems to be a misunderstanding. So, I'm going to leave now," I told them with my head held high and a slight tremble to my chin.

I turned and grabbed the silver doorknob. But before I could open it, one of the guys stood over me and leaned on the door. They were so damn tall that I had to let go of the door handle, turn around, and crane my neck to see which one it was. The one they'd called Tony kept the door shut over my head.

"You're going to waste that sexy dress and hot mask just to go home? I always had a dream of fucking with a mask on. Haven't gotten the opportunity to try… well, not with a woman, that is," he claimed, and someone snickered from behind him. I folded my arms as my face grew warm.

"Are you holding me hostage?" I asked with some bravado, but inside, I was shaking like a leaf. I knew I was curious about Sage's cousin and her motley crew, but I didn't think I was ready for that. Three dicks at the same time. God, I could hear my mom's judgmental voice now.

"No. Tell me your name, princess, and I might let you go," Tony said, and I made a mistake and looked into his light green eyes.

"M-My name i-is… Kitty," I stammered, and I immediately mentally slapped myself. Out of all the names, I chose Kitty.

"Well, that's not your real name, but I will accept it for now," he replied, and I shoved him back because his presence was clouding my judgment. I should've made my way downstairs and back to my hotel room to lick my wounds, but his eyes held me captive. I wanted to feel his eyes roam all over my body. Just the thought alone had my clit throbbing.

"I think we're a little melanin deficient for her liking. Isn't that right, Kitten?" Wren, who moved to block the door behind me, was shorter than the other two. Despite that, I had to crane my neck to look at him as well.

Perks of being short as hell.

A warm sensation swept through my face as I shook my head. I had never been with a white man before and definitely hadn't expected to see them in the room I ordered. I tried to move back but bumped into Wren, flush against his front. His thick, long dick was sandwiched between my cheeks, and I wanted to move, but Tony closed the gap between us. My head was going to explode as the mandarin and cedarwood scents mixed with the lavender of the room, which smelled so good it made the throbbing between my legs grow more intense.

Get ahold of yourself, Jas.

I mentally cursed my pussy as I felt my thighs become wet with my essence. Just my luck for not wearing underwear. How the hell was I supposed to use reason when I had a big dick sandwiched between my ass and another one pressed into my stomach?

I chided myself, but that didn't make any of this situation better. I needed to get ahold of myself and get back home.

Yep, that was what I needed to do. Find a safe and familiar lay. But that was easier said than done when you were forming a new river between your legs. But here I stood trembling like a leaf rooted to the spot as if they took my legs away from me.

"What's the safe word?" Tony asked.

"What do you mean safe word?" I asked.

"A word you would use if we've made you uncomfortable or if you become too overwhelmed," Gabe explained.

It made me feel a little better that I could stop at any time—just a bit though. I mulled over the request, and I had picked the craziest word to use as my safe word, "Impossible."

They all nodded.

"Go easy on our kitten here. If we breathe too hard, she might jump out the window," Gabe mentioned as he came to stand next to me, boxing me in against the powder blue wall.

How was I supposed to respond when these human towers had me cornered? My legs were like jelly, and my neck hurt from straining to look at them.

"I must be crazy, but I think we've found the one girl in LA who doesn't know who we are," Wren said.

Tony smirked, and Gabe cleared his throat.

"Kitten, I'll give you one more chance to change your mind. You can either stomp back downstairs and go back home, or you can let us fuck you until you can't walk. The choice is yours," he said as he grabbed my clammy hand and kissed it.

And how did I respond? By almost biting a hole into my lower lip as I moaned.

Fuck me. This might be too much for me. This is like the advanced stage of sex when I've barely scratched the surface of being a beginner.

I wished I had thought it out better because what I said next was enough to make me want to smack myself.

"I-I've only had sex with one other person. It's impossible to have sex with all of you guys," I choked out, and I instantly regretted opening my big mouth.

"So, you're a newbie. That's even hotter. I'm going to enjoy breaking you in." Tony smiled as he leaned in. "So, Kitten. Yes, or no?"

I blamed my pussy for the words I said next because, between my sex-fogged mind, the feeling of two dicks squashed up against me, and my essence that threatened to run down my legs, I spoke the first word that came to my mind.

"Yes," I squeaked out. I decided to bite the bullet and allow these men to cater to my needs.

I mean, it's just one night. What harm could it do?

Tony stepped back and turned me towards Gabe. He hoisted me over his shoulder as I scrambled to grab a hold of something. Defeated, I settled on keeping my dress from riding up over my ass. *Damn short arms!* My dress was *not* made for me to be thrown over someone's shoulder. I thought as I shivered from the cool drift in the room that slipped between my thighs.

"Wait, put me down! I can walk," I yelled and slapped Gabe's back.

He chuckled. "Soon, Kitten," he said.

His arm that held me slid up my thighs. Before I could scold him, he dropped me on the plush white bed. One of my breasts became dislodged during my manhandling, and I moved to push it back in place, but Gabe stopped me.

"The dress is coming off, anyway. Wren, take off her dress so we can see how soaked she is." It was then that I noticed the large bulge in his black silk Tom Ford boxers. He smirked.

This one has got some enormous balls on him.

"I-" I wanted to deny it, but Tony cut in.

"My little Kitten, I saw you were leaking down your thighs. No use in denying it."

They wouldn't even allow me to stand up as they maneuvered me up and out of my dress. There I was, butt naked as the day I was born, in front of three men. Three fucking desirable men that looked about ready to devour me. Maybe I'd lost my mind—No, I'd definitely lost my mind because I got wetter by the way Gabe's blown pupils glided over my body.

He lifted my chin with his hand and smiled. "Take me out, Kitten. I want to see how those tiny hands fit around my cock."

My heart was on a marathon run as my trembling hands slowly touched the taunt V-shaped muscles by the band of his boxers. Just the feel of his soft smooth skin under my fingertips sent a shiver down my spine as I anticipated what lay beneath Gabe's boxers. I looked up to his eyes and saw the excitement and desire that shined in them. All of it for me, who up until today had never truly experienced anything remotely close to the three men in this room. I bit my lip and pulled his boxers off in one swoop.

And I nearly poked my eye out when the waist of his boxers sent his dick flying to his defined stomach. He had a body that was made for fucking. Well defined abs, broad shoulders for mounting, and full pink lips that I wanted wrapped around my aching nipples. His long, muscular thighs tensed when I grazed them. But none of that mattered right now as I sat with my mouth open and wide-eyed at his cock. It was enormous and angry as it took its rightful place above his navel.

Holy fucking shit! Is this man human?

He grabbed himself at the base and squeezed. His hand pumped over the veiny member. My eyebrows became one with the lace of my wig, and my mouth dropped open even further.

"Good girl." He took my chin so lightly in his hand that I almost didn't realize he did it and peered into my eyes. "It won't bite you, but I will. Now show Daddy how well those soft, pretty little hands wrap around me."

A whimper from my chest let loose, and I fought the battle between being defiant or sliding his big dick into my mouth. I thought the latter may very well split my mouth open. Slowly, I reached up to wrap my shaky hand around his cock and slide it down to the base. He was so thick that my hand couldn't fit around him.

He'll split me open for sure.

I'd only given head once with my ex, and we never did it again because he told me it made him feel ungodly. I bit my lip at the thought of showing these men I was that inexperienced. It made me feel jumpy.

"No," I blurted out loud by mistake.

"No, what?" Gabe repeated with a cocked eyebrow.

Tony laughed from behind me.

"She's my twin, Gabe." He chuckled at the joke.

"Please don't wish that on her," Wren warned from beside me.

As I turned my head, Gabe grabbed me by my chin and pulled me into a kiss that I could only explain as a freefall descent into the black hole like Alice in Wonderland, but the black hole was Gabe. His spicy, woodsy scent washed over me and went straight to my core as I felt myself drench the sheets again. With every nip of my lips and every sweep of his tongue inside my mouth, it was like he wanted to memorize everything about my mouth.

Gabe kept dragging me deeper into that hole. His kisses were like a drug, and I wanted more of them. His fingers went on to explore the small curve of my stomach and over my mound until he found my engorged clit. He pinched and teased my bud until the warm sensation washed over me as I moaned through my first release. He pulled his fingers away abruptly. My lip trembled from the quick release, and his pupils were so blown that I couldn't see the green anymore. They were pure black. I knew if I had a mirror, mine would be identical. My heart was not merely thumping. It banged against my chest like it wanted to implant itself into Gabe's chest. I was afraid to admit that it was the first time coming from someone other than my fingers or toys.

Fuck me, I should run. Run as far away as possible and lock up my pussy. Maybe move to Serbia and change my name to Glenda.

"Fuck, that was hot," Wren whispered from behind Gabe. I hadn't noticed that he'd moved.

Gabe rubbed two of his thick fingers into my dripping core and sucked his wet fingers. He moaned, and I swear I couldn't breathe anymore.

"Did I tell you to come, little Kitten?" He grabbed my chin.

My bruised lips were nonfunctioning, so I shook my head.

"Use your words, or I won't let you come again," Gabe demanded.

My tongue rolled around my mouth as I found the word to barely squeak out, "No."

"You won't do it again, will you, Kitten?" His eyes bore into me.

"No, I won't," I whispered.

"Good, because I would hate to punish you on our first night together."

Gabe gave me a look that told me he wasn't joking.

I nodded yes but stopped short and answered, "Yes."

"She's learning well," Wren continued. "Grab her, Gabe."

Gabe slid his long frame behind me and placed me between his legs. I could feel his hard cock, which bored into me like a steel rod. His large, calloused hands slipped down my legs and grabbed me by the back of my knees. I had been attempting to keep my legs locked because I was too ashamed to allow them to see my arousal that had soaked the bed. But of course, I was finding out, slowly but surely, that I couldn't hide from these men.

Gabe opened me up so wide that I couldn't hide my wet spot anymore. Tony used one finger to trace the fading marks from the middle of my thigh to my wet lips that were left behind from my essence.

"Our little wet Kitty." He licked his lip, and I caught the shiny flash of his tongue piercing.

He kissed the center of my thigh. A bolt of desire that hit my core made me whimper, and my walls clenched. The feeling of Tony's soft plush lips smirked against my thigh made my swollen clit throb. He bit lightly on my right inner thigh, right next to my outer pussy lips. I hissed as he licked over the bite, which took away the stinging pain. Tony kept going until he made it to my dripping wet pussy. He stared at my soaked core. Wren's icicle stare was locked onto my breasts, which Gabe kneaded and pinched at the brown sensitive buds. I became self-conscious. Here I was, spread wide for a group of strangers.

"I think you have the most beautiful pussy I've ever seen."

I knew I shouldn't, but I glowed at Tony's words. All common sense exited my brain when he spoke. He swiped his flattened tongue against my pussy entrance up to my swollen clit. A scream that came from the pit of my stomach ripped from my throat. The gentle vibration from his vibrating tongue ring added to the fiery sensation. I hadn't experienced being eaten out before, so without thinking, I tried to push Tony away from my sensitive core with my hand.

He barely budged, but he looked at me with a condescending smirk as if he were daring me to stop him again. The heat in my face grew as I realized I was so out of my depth. But that didn't stop Tony. He muttered something in another language to Wren, who shuffled off somewhere, and when he returned, he asked me to put my arms around his neck. My body responded as if it was on autopilot, and I placed them around his neck. I heard Gabe swear when I barely brushed against his erection.

Jesus, did he get even bigger?

I was so lost in my foggy mind that I didn't notice the handcuffs until I heard the soft click of them locking.

"Hey!" I croaked out. I sounded as if I had eaten a baby frog.

Tony grabbed my face and turned me towards him. "You're not allowed to stop me from what's rightfully mine anymore."

The gall of this guy. "I-I don't even know y-you."

"Meh, semantics," Tony pointed to the bite mark left behind. "See, I knew you belonged to us the moment you stepped into our door, my little Kitten, and now I've marked you so you and everyone else will know you're ours. So, now we got you locked up so you won't hit my pretty face again."

He must be on drugs. That's the only explanation for his answer.

"I d-didn't consent to handcuffs!" I blubbered, but even I could tell my claims were frivolous.

Gabe ran his tongue from my shoulder to ear. I shuttered, and he whispered, "You wanted light BDSM, and we're taking it easy on you tonight. Next time, not so much."

I whimpered when he sucked on my earlobe as if that settled things, which it didn't. But Tony returned his devil tongue to my pussy when I opened my mouth to protest. He latched onto my swollen clit and gently bit down on it. It wasn't painful, but the act pulled a curse from my mouth. This time he sucked and licked it until I screamed, and my legs shook with the need to come.

Do you know what the fucker did? He pulled away. Gabe and Wren stopped caressing me, and like the manic that I had become, I sobbed and whimpered. My wet red mask was stuck to my face. They took their sweet time returning their attention to me, and when they did, it only took a couple of minutes to get me back to the cliff.

Tony said sternly, "Not yet," when he slipped a finger into my pussy, I clenched down and groaned.

Really? Get yourself together, Jas. I'm supposed to be running the show, not them.

Tony was a psycho. He entered another thick finger, and I was full. His fingers moved in and out as he continued to suck on my pussy lips and my engorged clit. Wren nipped and sucked on my painfully tender nipples. A streak of wetness ran down my cheek, and I couldn't hold it anymore. I came so hard that I shoved my pussy into Tony's face, and he withdrew his fingers to lap up my release. The beads of sweat multiplied as I was doused in warmth as my orgasm rolled through me. I'd never come so many times in my life. My body grew weak and tired as I collapsed into Gabe's hard body.

Wren chuckled, "Tsk, Tsk, so impatient."

Tony rose from between my thighs and spoke something in an unfamiliar language. The other guys responded—I think. It was all confusing and way too much for me.

"What are you guys saying?" I barely got out.

"Deciding whether I should punish you for coming without my permission," Tony's tongue cleaned up the remainder of my essence. When he had his fill, he said, "My sweet little Kitten. Do you know how fucking good you taste?"

"N-No," I stammered out.

"Open up, Kitty."

I followed his direction, too tired to fight back, as he placed his fingers into my mouth. Before he could respond, I swirled my tongue around his wet fingers and tasted my sweet and salty release. He removed his fingers from my mouth and replaced them with his mouth. This kiss was possessive, a claim on me and my soul. His tongue ring vibrated against my tongue and the soft palate of my mouth. Tony slipped a finger in and out of my still warm, drenched pussy, and as he pulled away from our kiss, his fingers left me as well. I knew it sounded crazy, but I missed his fingers inside of me.

I could barely keep my eyelids open, and my legs burned from the awkward position. I closed my eyes for a second and regathered myself after falling apart too many times. But when I opened my eyes, nothing could prepare me for what I saw. Tony took his wet fingers and shoved them in Wren's mouth, and Wren grabbed his hand and greedily stuck them into his mouth. I watched as his tongue wrapped around Tony's slender fingers. When he made sure every last bit of my essence was gone, he released Tony's fingers with a wet pop and kissed Tony.

Wait, everything is happening way too fast!

It was too much to process. As I watched, Tony and Wren shared the most passionate kiss. Their tongues peeked out as they both warred to get into each other's mouths. Watching these two beautiful men in action sent a sharp bolt of desire to my core. Tony shoved Wren's pants down and stoked him. Wren's breath hitched as he moaned into Tony's mouth.

Gabe's thighs and mine were wet with my essence.

Fuck!

Wren pulled Tony off of him and asserted, "I got the first dibs on our little Kitten."

Tony smirked and nodded.

"You like the show, Kitten? You must have since you're leaking all over yourself." Gabe whispered, and before I could respond, Wren dropped to his knees and pulled Tony's cock free. Wren wrapped his hand around the base of Tony's long cock and started to tease the leaking angry head of Tony's cock.

"Holy shit!" My eyes were going to pop out of their sockets. I never thought I would meet someone with piercings on their dick. His cock was as long as Gabe's but not as thick. He had vertical metal knobs on the underside, straight through his tip, and horizontal piercings that ran along the underside of his cock. I sat mesmerized as Wren stroked and teased Tony with his mouth and hands. He made it look so effortless as I saw a slight smirk on Wren's gorgeous face.

Where did these guys come from?

Tony smiled as he removed his cock from Wren's mouth. "Meet Tony's stairway to heaven, aka my Prince Albert and Jacob's Ladder piercings. Have you ever seen a pierced cock, my little soaked Kitten?"

I tried to be nonchalant as I gaped at his appendage. "No."

"Wren, get it ready for me, baby." Wren, whose cock I hadn't seen yet, took his tongue and licked Tony from the base of his cock straight to the tip. He took the big pink tip, licked the pre-cum off, and sucked it. Wren's big hand stroked him while he devoured Tony's cock all the way to the base, while Tony threw back his head and moaned his approval. Gabe reached over, placing one of my legs over his thigh, and rubbed my overstimulated clit.

Tony grabbed Wren by the hair and shoved his cock further down Wren's throat. Wren was a professional because he held onto Tony's hips, preventing him from moving. He turned slightly and looked into my eyes as he slowly pushed Tony out of his mouth. My body reacted to this bold move, and I came on Gabe's fingers. My arms ached from the handcuffs as I turned slightly to watch Gabe lick off his fingers.

He didn't speak but licked his lips and kissed me soundly. The sweet and salty mix lingered on my tongue. Someone ran a finger up the length of my pussy, causing me to whirl around. Wren had stuck the wet digit into his mouth and moaned.

"You taste like heaven, Gattina[1]," he praised.

"What does that mean-?" I asked, but I stopped myself when I saw him roll the condom on his cock. My mouth went dry, and my voice got caught in my throat. He wasn't as long as Gabe and Tony, but Wren was just as thick with a piercing that came out of the tip of his cock and the underside of his tip.

He's going to split me in half!

He must have seen the half-bugged look on my face because he

---

1   Kitten in Italian

leaned over and whispered, "I would never hurt you, Gattina. I promise pleasure always...well, and only the good kind of pain." As he planted kisses from my ears to my mouth, Gabe moved from behind me, and that's when I noticed he'd freed me from the cuffs. I rubbed at my raw wrists as I tried to soothe the pain. Wren kissed me until he laid me out on the white silk sheets of the bed, and I wrapped my arms around him as I arched into him for the sweetest kiss that rendered me weak in the knees. Wren's thick cock nudged at my entrance, and I stiffened against his body.

God, if I make it through in one piece, I will attend church... one day.

He kept kissing me while Tony found my swollen clit and caressed it. Wren's cock inched into me slowly. Not wanting to be outdone, Gabe broke my kiss with Wren, and we both moaned our disdain for the action. Gabe greedily took over my mouth and marked me again. I was so wired that I didn't remember when Wren finally slid home, just the absolute feeling of being stretched. I begged him to move because I knew I would die if he didn't. Wren appeared to be the gentle one in the trio as he moved all the way out of me until his tip was at my entrance, then back in at a slow pace. All while they kissed, caressed, and stroked me over and over along my overheated skin until I fell apart. I dug my nails into Wren's arm. If he felt it, I wouldn't have known because he didn't even flinch.

I guess I'm leaving my mark on them as well.

Wren must have taken that as a green light because he quickened his tempo as his cock attempted to break me open. The sweat from his body combined with my already sweaty skin. As he leaned closer, he engulfed me in his spicy scent. Our moans became my new hit song as he whispered how good it felt to be inside me. The friction inside me built to a crescendo as I clamped down on him and met my release.

Wren cursed, stiffened, and let out a deep grunt as he placed his weight on me. Without thinking, I hooked my legs around him, not wanting to let him go, even though he was softening inside my fiery core. After a minute, I let go of him, and he leaned back without breaking our connection, and I instantly missed the warmth of his body. Locked in my own world, I didn't notice that he had leaned over until he softly bit me on the silky flesh below my clavicle. I whimpered.

Wren kissed up the curve of my neck, leaned over, and whispered in my ear, "I think I want to keep you, Gattina." He gave me a quick, chaste kiss and slipped his soft dick out of me.

"It's my turn, Kitten," Gabe proclaimed as he rolled me on top of him in one swoop. "I will probably explode the second I'm inside of you, baby. So, I want you to ride me and take what you need from me."

My legs were rubber as I looked down at him from my position, unsure if I could even stand, much less ride him.

I mean, how do you ride? I've only ever seen it done in porn videos.

Seeming to sense the minor turmoil brewing in my head, he took my face and turned it to him. "Can you do that for me?"

Could I? It was a great question.

I grabbed his cock and expelled a deep breath when my hand met the smooth surface of the condom. I lowered myself onto him slowly. He was huge, and I felt a stinging sensation in my core as I stretched to accommodate him. I didn't think I could go further without him tearing me apart. But Gabe was determined to be fully inside of me. He grabbed my hips and surged the rest of his massive cock into me. He was so deep. It was as if he were touching my throat. A string of curse words escaped my mouth. It took a minute, heck, two minutes, to adjust to his girth. I hadn't even moved, and my next orgasm threatened to take me out. I was so tired I could have fallen asleep right then on my wobbly knees.

Gabe grabbed me and thrust into me as if his life depended on it. In the distance, I heard a deep raspy voice that I couldn't believe was mine shout, "Yes, fuck me like that, Gabe." My breasts bounced to the rhythm of his pace.

Thank God my wig glue was top-tier because I was drenched in sweat. My poor mask had become a second skin at this point. Like a synced clock, Gabe stiffened and growled out his release, which set me off as I came so hard I almost passed out. I slumped over, and Gabe held me against his beating hot chest. Running my hands over his soft skin was calming, as what I deemed the drug high kicked in, as my eyelids drooped lower and headed off to cloud seven.

"Were you going to give Wren and Gabe some of my tight little pussy and not Daddy Tony?" He teased as he lifted me up from Gabe's warm body. Gabe winked and smiled, which made me melt into an even bigger puddle.

I whined when he placed me on my stomach next to Gabe. "On your knees, ass up, and hands are optional."

I can't. I'm too weak. I thought to myself as I sat there with my essence leaking onto the bed.

Tony gave me a slap on the ass that woke me up.

"You bastard! Who do you think—"

He cut me off when his fingers plunged into my wet pussy. He removed them and swirled his fingers with his tongue, cleaning off my juices. Drying them off, he coated his fingers with some lube that Gabe retrieved from their discarded items on the sofa. His deft fingers circled my unclaimed entrance as a whimper tore through my throat.

"Hey, I—"

Too late, I thought as he eased a slender finger into my puckered hole, and I clenched down on his finger.

"Hold still, Kitten. I'm going to put you to sleep." He added another finger to my rosette. "Relax, Kitten, it will feel better soon."

I trembled as my tight muscles stretched to accommodate him. His fingers crossed and curled inside of me, which had me arching my back for more as I got more comfortable. The feeling of being stretched back there made me forget Tony was the devil, as he wasted no time plunging his cock into my pussy. I squeaked. Unlike Wren's piercing, everything glided on my walls and hit my spot easily as he fucked me and fingered my ass with no mercy. He was possessed like he'd found gold in my womb. The piercings were weird but strangely comforting. I couldn't even make out anything besides his declaration that I was his because all I could hear was the pounding of my heart in my ears.

My body clenched down, and I came and yelled without thinking, "Yes, Daddy!" I'd never even called my last boyfriend that, much less a stranger.

What the hell is wrong with me?

Of course, Tony heard and replied, "Yes, my good little whore. I'm your daddy." As he quickened his pace, I had to cling to the sheets with my ass in the air, my body still pulsing with the pleasure of my last orgasm.

Every time I thought he would relent—he gained more energy. He sent me over, crashing into another orgasm that had me seeing black dots in front of my eyes. Tony didn't stop. He did finally stop finger fucking my ass, leaned over, and whispered, "You're ours, little Kitten, and no one else can have our pussy." He went still behind me and grunted in my ears, signaling his release. I went crashing into another orgasm, but this time, I had nothing left. No strength, no words, or any energy. With Tony still on top of me like a weighted blanket, I slipped into dreamland right after I felt someone clean me with a damp cloth and said, "I think we've found our girl."

Chapter 4

Jasmine

The Aftermath

Dear Diary,

Hello, my name is Jasmine Grant, and I'm addicted to three men I barely know. It all started six months ago when I paid for sex instead of finding a boyfriend. I'm a sex addict, and here is my story.

I realized this was a bad idea—scratch that, a horrible idea—to begin with. Why would I think someone whose sexual experience, until now, had been to lie still while the guy thrust inside of me would ever make it out of this experience unscathed? I came in mentally stable and stumbled out, barely alive. When I woke up in the early morning, it was a mess of tangled legs and arms flung over me haphazardly. I was sandwiched between Gabe and Wren, whose morning woods threatened to poke through my stomach and back. Poor Tony's long muscular arms stretched out over Wren's hip and mine.

It took me several attempts to remove everyone's limbs from

my body. Gabe was the hardest because every time I got free, he would grab me by the waist and pull me back. After several attempts to break free, I tiptoed to the bedroom and got dressed. When I was almost to the door, I turned and looked back at the trio. An ache in my chest and a stupid voice in my head told me to crawl back in there. When I got back to the hotel that morning, I spent the rest of my hotel stay rehabbing myself since they'd left me sore enough to limp the entire day.

I shook my head. I didn't even know those three men. But I couldn't deny that they left a mark on me.

Literal fucking marks! As I examined the shallow indent of their teeth marks they had left behind.

In the first months after our first encounter, I tried not to think about them, but that was easier said than done. I failed miserably to lock the memory of that night in the back of my mind for my "self-care" time, which had been almost every day since that Friday. Sometimes, even twice a day, or if I was bored, three times a day because I couldn't stop thinking about them. Some days, I had to mentally slap myself to stop my mind from straying to room number seven. But when I touched something metal, it reminded me of Tony and Wren and their piercings, and it sent my hand down my panties. Gabe's deep, sexy voice in my head sang praises of me being a good girl, sending my body crashing into a climax. But nothing was better than the real thing. It was like my body had a mind of its own, and it wanted another repeat with Gabe, Tony, and Wren. Every week, I would tell myself, "Just one more time." But that time never came. That's how I would end up reserving our room, week after week. Room number seven had officially become our home away from home, even if it was only in my mind. The little powder blue room of pleasure is what I used to save any information I needed for our meetings. I long suspected Ms. Edina had become used to my reservation text with my specific wants, as I always got a quick reply as if she was waiting for my text.

I no longer lived in the real world filled with responsibilities and obligations. I was beyond dickmatized, like someone had once coined. Dickland was where dreams come true, and your fantasies held you back from reality. Even now, when I received the text from the club confirming room seven, my body flew into overdrive. It was as if I turned into my custom Rolls-Royce Boattail car and purred to life from that text. All it mentioned was to be there at the same time and place, which turned me on.

A fucking text! I really needed help.

I found myself in our room at the end of the hall on the third floor like clockwork. I no longer needed to be coaxed into staying and being subservient. Even when I tried to act out, either Tony or Gabe dealt with me swiftly over their knees. Wren, my big softie, left bite marks on me as my punishment, which I loved. His bites were always harsh, but he brought me to my knees when he licked and kissed them.

By the second month, I realized I was in trouble when we were finishing our second round for the night and winding down. Wren had carried me into the large soaking tub in the blue and white bathroom. Gabe had prepared the tub with my favorite citrus bath bomb and lit vanilla candles they had brought for me. I was sitting between Tony's legs as he worked the knot out of my shoulders. I was in serotonin heaven when the next words slipped out my mouth.

"How did you guys meet?" I asked as the words tumbled out of my mouth before I could think.

I mentally slapped myself because I tried to make sense of what I asked. I knew it was wrong for me to pry since I was still, after all of this time, sitting in a bathtub with my blue silk mask on.

Tony stopped massaging my shoulders, and I let out a small whine when he removed his fingers. He placed my hair in a messy top bun and rubbed his hands up and down my upper arm. The contact sent a slight shiver down my spine.

"Okay, a story for a story?" Tony asked. He was always finding small ways to get a glimpse of who I am.

I bit my lip and rubbed my hand over my wet forearms under the water.

"Okay, a story for a story, then," I said as I gave in.

Tony kissed my neck, and I moved to sit between Tony and Gabe. Gabe placed his arm around me, and I leaned in. My hand found his earlobe instantly as I tugged on it slightly.

"Well, Gabe and I grew up together. Our families had been friends since they came over from Italy in the fifties. So, I had no choice but to fall in love with Gabe." Tony chuckled. I heard Gabe sigh, and I could tell, even without looking, that he rolled his eyes playfully.

"I think the love is only on one side," Gabe said as he flicked water at Tony. We chuckled when Tony fussed with his short jet-black hair.

Gabe kissed my forehead and continued the stories. "He's right. Our families were thick as thieves. Tony and I are brothers. No ifs, and's, or buts. Our families did business together. So, we were together every day."

"My family did business with Gabe's and Tony's family once during the early stages of our business and maintained a long-distance business relationship that turned into friendship. We were in the Bay area until my dad said we needed to move for the business. We packed up and moved to Los Angeles when I was twelve years old in the seventh grade." Wren paused with a dopey smile on his face.

"He captivated me. I knew LA would be different for me, but I didn't realize it would be a total one-eighty. I was being bullied for being the outcast and newcomer." He stopped to shake his head. "They called me everything they could think of, abnormal freak or mutt, my favorites because I'm half Japanese and Italian and way too nice. One day, Tony walked in like the badass he was and defended me from a bunch of snobby bullies. That was the first time I met Tony, unofficially, and the last time I felt alone. And he wouldn't keep his hands off my ass, either. He introduced me to Gabe, and the pieces fell in line."

I leaned over Tony to grab Wren's hand under the water. In return, he gave one of his lopsided smiles that made me want to kiss him.

"After that, they were inseparable." They chuckled together. It was the cutest thing ever. Gabe continued, "I met Wren after Tony twisted my arm and dragged me to our country club and introduced us. I'm glad he did because I gained another brother that day."

I turned to look up at Gabe. He was the quiet, more pensive one of the group. So, seeing him be so open with his feelings made my heart beat faster. He smiled at me and dropped a quick kiss on my nose. I turned back around as my insides became liquid. I wanted to snatch the damp blue mask off my face right now.

"There's my big softie," Wren said. "Gabe is the protector, even though we can protect ourselves. He's never been this open with anyone outside of us or our families."

I wish I could say the warmth in my face was because of the pure happiness that filled the room, but it wasn't. Dread filled in my body as I stiffened in Gabe's arm. He sensed the change and rubbed my shoulders.

"I know you mentioned it a couple of times, but you guys never explained why you decided to share your life?" I said. I had always wondered why they decided a Polygamous relationship was right for them, but I never wanted to approach the subject because it was personal. I tried my hardest not to go down that forbidden path.

"Well, we were very close to one another, and we did everything together. I think during our first time we shared a girl together. We enjoyed ourselves, and if I'm not mistaken, we always shared from that point on. It just felt right." Tony said.

"Plus, it helped us filter out the weeds," Wren said with a smirk.

"Weeds?" I said.

"Yeah, the girls at our college that only wanted to get to fake date us to get to the head honcho, Gabe. All the girls wanted Gabe but didn't want us because he was the "celebrity" on campus. Since his family's name was reputable." Wren shook his head. "Soon, we would run through them, and they would run away, saying what we were doing was perverse. As if we didn't live in LA." He rolled his eyes. "We are a package… 'Take us or leave us' is my motto."

"I'm glad we started this journey together. It strengthened us. Our future is so fucking bright. Especially with our Kitty by our side," Tony said as he tugged playfully on my ear.

"Especially since we have you, Kitty. We can buy a mini-mansion and fill it up with kids." Wren grinned. He knew kids were my weakness. "Okay, now it's your turn."

I was so surprised by his statement and how they all were beaming from speaking about one another that I forgot to come up with something…anything to say after their confession.

Tony reached over to tug on the mask, but I slapped his hand away unconsciously. He looked hurt but shook off the emotion.

"I'm so sorry I—It was a knee-jerk reaction," I said. I shook even though the water in the tub was warm.

"No worries. I shouldn't have touched you without permission." Tony said sadly.

I opened my mouth to say something, but instead, I reached out to tuck a strand of hair back into his ponytail. He grabbed my hand and placed a kiss in my palm. I knew he was being sweet, but my reaction left a bitter taste in my mouth. I wanted to curse myself out for Tony.

"Wait, one more question!" I said. The guys groaned. "There's three of you, so I get three questions. Okay, how come Tony and Wren are Bisexual? What about you, Gabe?"

Gabe chuckled, "I love that my brothers found love between them, but I always prefer females. I don't mind getting a hand job or a blow job from a guy…I mean, a mouth is a mouth."

There's something about a man who's not afraid to protect his family and love them unconditionally. I think I sank a little further into

Gabe at that.

"Don't get too comfortable. It's your turn now." Gabe teased.

"Wait!" I exclaimed as I scrambled to keep the attention on them. "What are the major future goals for you guys?"

They were all silent. A pensive look on their face told me they figured I was stalling, which I was.

Wren sighed but replied, "Well, we plan to combine our family businesses and work together."

Gabe and Tony both nodded their heads to back up Wren.

"Yes, that's the ultimate goal. We're basically running our families' business right now. So, we're giving ourselves a couple of months to figure out a company plan for combining our businesses, and then we're going to present it to our families, who essentially make up the board members since they gave us full range of the companies." Gabe said.

"That sounds manageable. Are you guys scared they won't give you their blessings?" I asked because I was thoroughly interested in their plans.

"Yes and no," Tony replied, "We're hopeful it will go our way, but that's just us being confident. Our families are willing to hear us out, but only if we have a solid business plan, which we have just started to work on."

"Ok, now it's time to pay the piper, Kitty," Gabe said as he pulled me a little closer to his side. "A story for a story. That's the deal."

I thought maybe they would let it slide or forget, but I have no such luck. Instead, I told them about my passion for fashion.

"I was never into fashion until I got invited to a fashion show. I was in awe of the opulence of the show. The gowns, makeup, and the excitement of the shows." I said with a half smirk on my face. "I always said if I wasn't an… accountant. I would be a model."

My shoulders slumped down, and my eyes found the gold frame with the painting of a beautiful Asian woman who was hunched over a golden chaise as her female lover pleasured her from behind. The portrait was so intimate it could make a nun blush.

"I can see you being a model, Kitty," Wren said. "You're beautiful with your mask on, but I bet you're gorgeous with it off."

"Thank you" was all I could manage to reply as we showered off and went to bed—Well, they went to bed, but I couldn't because my mind was still in the tub with them as they sang my praises. Praises to someone who still, after two months, had yet to even take off her mask. That night, I chewed my bottom lip until it was raw and stifled my voiceless cry into the pillow.

My daily habits changed as well.

During the week, I scrambled to figure out what I would wear to entice them and to keep them from yanking my mask off. Soon, I learned that, along with being totally naked, they loved me in anything red or white. Soon, I got tired of the same wig. So, I bought different styles of wigs and wig glue by the dozen and stored them in luggage that was always ready to go on Friday. It consumed me to the point where if any of my post-retirement gigs interfered with my Fridays, I would cancel them. Allison would scream bloody murder when she learned about me canceling my engagements and asked me if I had lost my ever-loving mind.

Yes, I have Allison. Glad you finally noticed.

Every Friday, the sex improved, if that was possible. I learned a lot about how to please myself and them in the three months we were together. Wren introduced me to giving a proper blow job. Now, I could almost fit them in my mouth without gagging to death, and they had me in positions that had me thanking God I kept up with my yoga workouts. Tony made use of the black leather bondage chair in our room that had me questioning whether I was human, as it had my thighs on my chest with my hands handcuffed with the black handcuffs below the seat. The way your body reacts to praise should be studied. There was something about it that set me off, unlike anything else. I'd never known someone saying I was a good girl or that he loved how I took his ropes could bring me to my knees. It made me wonder how a group of twenty-five-year-olds learned all of this.

Gabe introduced me to being tied up, whether it was frog-tied, hog-tied, balled-tied, or spread-eagle cowgirl style. If there was one thing I learned, Gabe loved me tied up. I would never forget the night he boxed-tied me. Gabe tied two smooth brown ropes across my chest and knotted my hands in a folded position behind my back. The ropes were tight but not enough to cause pain.

I laid in the middle of the bed, thoroughly weak from Gabe's slow tortuous game. He punished me for calling his bluff last Friday by withholding my release until I cursed him out. He just chuckled and finally gave in. Now I was here with the blue silk sheets stuck to me like a second skin, and my breasts were tender from the damp ropes that crossed on top and under them. With every tug of my arm, the rope dug a bit deeper into my skin under my breast.

I was about to ask Gabe to release me from the bondage when I turned to see Wren and Tony. I knew they had snuck off to the small seating area, but it wasn't until now that I heard their cacophony. It was my new favorite sound from my loving duo. With Gabe's help, I turned to view them, and the sight was beyond magnificent. Wren and Tony were in their own love nest as I watched their hands stroke each other's dick. Their pink tongues peeked out as they both kissed each other senseless. It was beautiful to watch and hear them. Wren made the sweetest noises when he was about to release, while Tony's low grunts sent tingles down my spine. Wren's hold on Tony's dick was firm as Tony chased his orgasm by pumping into Wren's hand. Tony appeared to have a death grip on Wren's redden dick as he gasped and sighed with each stroke of Tony's firm hands.

Gabe came back to the bed to release me, but I stopped him. Our conversation drew Tony's attention as he slowed down his pace on Wren, who had his head thrown back and looked ready to cum all over

Tony's hand. I didn't want to stop them from their time together, but I wanted to see them unfiltered. I rarely got to see them alone as they always found a way to incorporate me into their time together.

"Wait," I said with my eyes still trained on my two lovers. "I want you to fuck Wren." My voice rang out in the room.

A half-cocked smile touched Tony's face.

"You want me to destroy our little Wren, Kitty?" Tony asked.

"Yes." I returned as he stopped his torment of Wren. "I want you to fuck Wren. I want you to act as if you were alone together."

Wren looked at me with his silver lustful eyes. A dopey smile formed on his face.

"I'm about to cum, Kitty. I don't know how much longer I got left in me," Wren said in a low, husky voice.

"Please, Wren," I begged.

Wren nodded, and I couldn't help the warmth that pooled in my stomach. My heart was knocking on my ribcage as I thought of the vision I always wanted to reenact. Gabe helped me sit on the side of the bed with my restraints still in place. Tony grabbed one of the white chairs from the table where we usually eat and placed it in front of me. Gabe took a seat next to me.

"Gabe," I said. "You know I love when you touch me, but I don't need any help right now."

He raised one of his black eyebrows, "Okay, I will watch you then," he said as he made his way to the empty blue armchair in the seating area and turned it to watch me with his hand on his semi-erected dick.

"I want Tony to sit on the chair," I spoke with a slight rasp in my voice. "Hands on the seat of the chair, and don't move them unless I say so."

I bit my lip so hard I thought I broke the skin. I had never been so bold to give orders, but I was more than comfortable with them, and I wanted this more than anything.

"Wren, lube Tony. I want you to ride him," I instructed them with glee. "If you remove your hands from the chair, Wren is going to stop. Do you understand?"

Wren broke out into a chuckle while Tony raised his eyebrow at me.

"I understand, Captain Kitty," Tony said. His face was flushed coral, and his light green narrow eyes twinkled.

As excitement heated my already tender core, Wren lubed up Tony. The slip of his hand down Tony's already red hard dick made my clit throb. Tony moaned a bit while he never took his eyes off me, and my face flushed with pleasure.

"Will you join us, Kitty?" My sweet Wren asked.

"No, I want to watch as you fall apart tonight," I said with a smile.

Wren groaned and muttered, "You'll be the death of me," as he straddled, with his back toward Tony's front. Inch by inch, Wren glided down Tony's long dick as I sat on the edge of the bed, unable to touch my lovers. I watched Tony disappear into Wren until he was fully seated in his lap.

"Remember, Gabe and I aren't here. It's just you two in the room," I said.

My voice was just above a whisper as I felt all of the warmth drift to my core.

Wren planted his feet firmly on the ground and held himself in his hand. Leaning over, he spat on his thick dick. The clear white liquid coated his enormous head as he used it to help stroke himself. He maneuvered himself to the top of Tony's dick and dropped himself down to the base. The greedy sound of Wren's tight hole sucking Tony filled the room. With each time he landed in Tony's lap, Wren whimpered and tightened his grip on himself. From my angle, I could see how red Tony's arm was becoming as he fought to grab onto Wren and take control.

"Don't you come before Wren and I come, Tony!" I said.

Wren whimpered as he locked onto me. My eyes, although filled with lust, held adornment in them. Wren's usually large, hooded eyes were narrowed onto me as he continued his deep strokes on Tony. The damp rope bit into my skin every time I unconsciously reached out to touch myself or them. Gabe chuckled in the background as he watched me struggle with his ropes.

Sadist!

I was burning up and drenched in my juices. I sent a slight prayer to whoever would listen, thanking them for my thick thighs as I found the right angle to rub my throbbing little nub. Every time Wren whimpered, my thighs choked the little bud, which brought me closer to the edge.

I would have come all over the bed if Wren hadn't cursed in his deep voice, which drew my attention. Red splotches lined his soft, pale face to his wide chest. His free hand braced his knee, and his straight dark blonde hair was skewed. Wren's strokes slowed down as he fought to not cum. Tony, with his hands still on the chair, found a way around my rule as he jackhammered without mercy into Wren. The muscles in his svelte legs rippled. Tony sounded possessed as he told Wren how good it felt to be inside him.

It was beautiful, messy, and fucking sexy.

"I think I'm…" I started to say, but the words got stuck in my throat.

The heat that simmered in my core ripped through me, and I dropped to my elbows. My breath was shaky, and the dark green bangs from my current wig stuck to my wet forehead as I dropped my head back and closed my eyes. The bed dipped, bringing my eyes up to see Wren boxed me in on the bed as his soft, sticky dick lay on my stomach.

"Did you enjoy the show?" Wren asked breathlessly. His face was still slightly red from his last orgasm as he kissed my jaw.

"I did…It was nothing short of beautiful." I said as a lone tear fell from my eye.

"You're crying?" Gabe asked as Wren wiped the lone tear.

"It's tears of joy." I cleared my throat. "I've always wanted to watch you guys alone, and I'm thankful for the opportunity."

"Kitty, all you have to do is ask, and we will give you the world," Tony said as he stood and tugged lightly on my earlobe.

Gabe and Tony released me from my restraints. With my hands finally free, I was able to reach out to run my fingers over their silken skin. Call me crazy, but when I'm with them, I can't keep my hands off them.

I could live like this forever.

After that night, Tony and Wren tag-teamed me until my voice was nothing but a hoarse whisper, and my negative thoughts were mute. They wore me out so good, physically and mentally, I would limp out the next morning. But like the sex fiend that I had become, I would still masturbate that day when I walked through my front door the next morning. They made me want to learn how to handle them since they were all different. Gabe was a Voyager who loved to watch, something until this moment I never thought about but loved to experience. When he was ready to take control, he was front and center. Tony was the dominant explorer who always found new ways for us to play. And Wren was a pleasure seeker. He went above and beyond to make sure my needs were met.

My Google search became my fantasy research. It was filled with sites on hand jobs and sexual positions. The heat over my face when I browsed through those sites was like fire. I got to a point where I would be the tower in our Eiffel Tower. I was in between two of my guys while they took turns watching.

During our third month, I decided that I still wasn't ready for anal play because a part of me was petrified. Every time I would get the urge to try it, I chickened out because the thought of them together inside me at once sent me scrambling. They would rip me apart because they were so large. But Wren brought me anal plugs to help me get used to it. It was so good to have those little plugs in place as I got slammed in the back of my throat with one of my guy's dick while another fucked me from behind, sending the person in front down my throat a little further.

I bit my lip and moaned out loud at the memory. *God, I couldn't wait until Friday…*

Someone cleared their throat in the background and spoke nervously. "Are you okay, Ms. Grant?"

Chapter 5

Jasmine

My eyes snapped open as the rush of heat swarmed my face. Oh my God, that was the sixth time I'd zoned out that week and made a fool out of myself.

I looked at my nervous accountant of eleven years, Mr. Christopher Black, and his assistant, who looked ready to bolt from the room. Mr. Black was a petite man with a hawk-like nose and always smiled when he was nervous, like now. His wheat-colored skin looked pale as he sat stiffly in his chair. His assistant, Jordan, mirrored his nervous smile, except his tan suit clung to his skinny frame as he fidgeted with the tablet in front of him.

"I'm so sorry. My stomach is acting up, and I think I'm coming down with something. Are we done here?" I asked and prayed that they believed it. It'd been six months, and I was still zoning out.

"Oh gosh, I'm so sorry, Ms. Grant. If I had known, we would have canceled our monthly meeting. We're finished anyway."
He looked almost relieved that I claimed it was a stomachache and

not me almost coming during the middle of my account management meeting.

"It's no problem. This is important, especially when it comes to my money. How is my Real Estate Investment account? I'm excited to see if it's grown more from last month."

"Well, everything is perfect on that account. Your real estate company hit an all-new high of two billion dollars! As we figured in our last meeting," He beamed and pushed his yellow thick-rimmed glasses that were perched on top of his nose up with his pointer finger.

I knew I shouldn't, but I couldn't help the wide smile that stretched across my face. "I didn't think we would make it, but we did."

"Yes, If I may suggest either selling some of your assets or investing some in a mutual fund," he stated gingerly.

"Let me think about how to proceed with that. Can you resend the statements? Thank you again, Mr. Black."

"It's no problem. The pleasure is all mine." His assistant hurried out, leaving me in a cloud of his musky scent. I cringed. His team was the best in Los Angeles, so I put up with it. I avoided his questioning gaze and made small talk with him. After five minutes of me fumbling over my words, Jordan returned, confirmed he resent the statements, and scurried off before I made a fool of myself again.

How embarrassing was that?

I acted like a teenager who couldn't stop thinking about sex. I shook my head as I jumped into my car. Mr. Jackson waited for me in front of the building in downtown LA. I thanked him for waiting and slid the partition up as he pulled off into traffic. The ride would be short, but I needed to clear my mind, and the best way to do that was to take in the scenery of the busy LA area and relax.

But of course, that's easier said than done, as my mind was too busy with my Friday relief day coming up. That was what I called it now since it was the only thing or time I was relieved from my wayward thoughts. Even though I was distracted with my Friday relief day, other things scared me more than being dickmatized. It was Wren and Tony's animated faces when they spoke about their childhood stories and families. It was the midnight conversations with Gabe where we stayed tangled up in each other's arms, talking about nothing and everything in the same sense. I learned about his great relationship with his parents. Must be nice. It was when he massaged my shoulders until I felt he would melt into my skin that I realized I was on a slippery slope, and I didn't think I could come back.

Or when they wore me down enough to go to the special leather kink event orgy party in Club Celeste lobby.

I decided I wanted to wear something special for them, so I had a custom baby pink cut-out split thigh bustier leather Cami bodycon dress. I forwent my panties. The dress hugged my curves and fit like a glove. My nerves were set on high because I thought my breasts would fly out of the bustier since it was basically a bra that was held up by two straps of fabric between the bra and the skirt. But after I tested the dress out, they passed the "jump on the bed like a madwoman test." I paired the daring dress with clear pink stiletto heels, a straight blonde wig, and pink nails. My pink cat mask was placed firmly, covering half of my face.

I fumbled with the dress all the way to our room, but when I opened the door, the guys turned and stared at me. It was well worth the struggle. Their eyes roamed my petite, curvy body, and I felt my face flush under their gazes.

"Fuck me…" Wren said, his pale face turned pink. "Kitty, I'm rethinking this party. Who the fuck needs an orgy party when we can have one right here?"

They all looked so good. I was wondering if this party was a mistake as well. Wren was dressed in a black mesh see-through shirt that he paired with leather pants that hugged his muscular legs. Tony had on the same leather pants, but he paired them with a red leather vest with no shirt on. It made his warm ivy-colored skin pop against the bright red color. His statuesque, lithe body was made for leather. I wanted to run my tongue down his smooth chest. But Gabe…

I don't think anything, or anyone, could've prepared me for what Gabe had on. I expected this from Tony, maybe even Wren, to wear what Gabe had on. But not Gabe, who stood with his arms across his wide chest with a blue, leather, full bodysuit. The bodysuit had a mesh center that allowed you to see Gabe's chest and stomach. There was a zipper in the crotch area so he could pull himself out.

I wasn't going to look, but I noticed they were all hard in their leather ensembles. Tony noticed me looking and threw me a crooked smile.

"You like what you see, Kitty?" Tony asked.

"You know I do," I said. "Or I wouldn't be here now, would I?"

I raised an eyebrow at his surprised face. Honestly, if you told me I would be this bold, I would have laughed, but when I'm with my guys, I feel like I can be me.

"Okay, I surrender," Tony said as he held up his arms.

I smiled as I walked over to them and hugged them each as they took turns coping a feel.

"Now, this dress…" Gabe had started to say but I cut him off.

"Aht Aht," I said while shaking my head. "The party started half an hour ago. We should make our way down now."

They all groaned out loud—while I groaned internally as well. But at last, we made our way down to the large dancefloor room after we locked our room up. The typically white room was turned into a dark bedroom, or so I would have called it. The room was black from the abstinence of light from the windows. Red and blue strobe lights highlighted the bodies on the dancefloor. The lavender scent that always greeted me in the club was replaced with sandalwood and citrus. Everyone was in their own little world as they danced to the DJ's selection of house music. It was then I noticed that either you were dressed or naked as the day you were born. I gawked at the crowded dance floor and slightly lost the bravado I once had upstairs. Sure, I was brave, but I'm not sure I was ready for public nudity.

Sensing my mini nervous breakdown, Gabe took my hand and said, "Hey, you don't have to do anything you don't want to do. The same rules we set upstairs apply here." He kissed the back of my hand.

"Yes, no pressure, Kitty Kat. We just want to show you a good time." Tony said.

"I know you're right," I said, shaking off the last bit of nervousness I felt. "I'm fine. Let's get some drinks and hit the dance floor. I want to see how badly you guys dance."

That earned a chuckle from all of them as we shuffled to the bar and ordered our drinks. Three dry martinis for me and about four whiskey shots for the guys. After we guzzled our drinks down, we stumbled onto the dancefloor. The buzz from my drinks allowed me to forget I had to entertain dancing with three different men at the same time or that I recognized several big stars who forwent their masks. But I guessed I would manage.

I stood in the middle of Gabe, Tony, and Wren as I honed my dancing skills. My arms were thrown over my head as I whined and wiggled my waist to the thumping beat of the house music. The guys were holding their own as I watched them match my pace. At that moment, I couldn't help but feel lucky that I found these special men. I wanted to give all of my guys some time. So, I made sure to turn to each of them and gave them my typical two-step dance. Their hands embraced my curves as I swayed and glided to the music. We were dancing for thirty minutes when I noticed the DJs switched, and the new DJ was chatty as he interrupted the music to call out several different clubgoers.

You know one thing I hate is being put on the spot.

So, I angled myself between Gabe and Wren, thinking I could hide, but I just embolden them. I knew I made a mistake when Gabe and Wren's hands started to touch and caress me, leaving tiny fires that only they could put out. Their hands started something I was fully sure they had intended to finish right here on this dancefloor. Their scents mixing in with the scent of the sex-filled room had me resting the back of my head on Gabe's chest while we swayed as one to the upbeat tempo. Tony, who had stepped away to use the bathroom, came back. I saw him lick those plump pink lips and whisper into Wren's ears. A mischievous smile planted onto Wren's beautiful face, and his light gray eyes sparkled.

Wren leaned over to Gabe and whispered in his ears. Gabe bit back a smile, but not before I caught it. I opened my mouth to tell them to stop whatever they were thinking of, but I was too late. Tony's fingers found my chin as he gently turned my head towards him. His lips landed on mine, and I felt him bite and nibble on my lower lip. I let my tongue sweep his mouth as I tasted the lingering spice essence of his whiskey shot. My heart was already beating fast from all the dancing, but when Gabe and Wren's hands moved over my tender, heated flesh, a bolt zipped down my body to my clit that was begging to be touched. As they kissed and caressed my soft honey-brown skin, I lost sight of the two dozen people who were surrounding us.

"Oh yes, pink dress is living my dream right now!" The DJ announced over the sound system. "I think I may call you Ms. Pink Pussy, meow."

Did I care? No

Should I care? Maybe

I was about to ask if we could leave when Gabe's thick fingers found my wet folds. I stiffened and released Tony's lips from mine.

"Kitty, no one can see you, nor do they care what we're doing. Look around you," Wren said in a husky voice.

Could I be as adventurous as the other couples?

I turned my head as I noted the dancefloor was filled with people either dancing or literally having sex on the floor. There were small groups and large groups all clamming to each other, and I found myself oddly turned on by the scenes in front of my eyes. Their moans synced with the beat of the music. The room smelled like uninhibited desire. No restraints or judgment, just the chance to live out your wildest dreams.

It was then that I realized Gabe's large hand was resting on my naked mound. Waiting for the green light to shatter me into pieces. I bit my puffy bottom lip and decided to take a chance. I placed my small hand over Gabe's large one and pushed it back to my wet folds. Gabe wasted no time finding my little greedy tortuous nub that waited for its fix. I wanted more though, as Gabe caressed, pinched, and stroked the swollen nub with no mercy. The friction from Wren's mesh shirt rubbing against my tender breast and Tony's exploring mouth as he rained kisses down my neck and shoulder should have been enough. But, as I mentioned, I was greedy. I grabbed Wren's hand closest to Tony and shoved his thick fingers on my entrance.

"Oh, we have a very naughty pussy in the crowd tonight." The DJ announced to the heated crowd.

I paid him no mind because, at that exact moment, Wren stopped rimming my entrance and plunged two thick fingers into my drenched core. If I could fly, I think I would have right then and there as Gabe and Wren's fingers teased me. I started a new dance to the music the DJ started playing, but this one would take me over the edge. Wren and Gabe worked in tandem as they mimicked their speed slower when my back started to arch off Gabe's mesh center and faster when I was able to curse them for slowing down. Tony released my breast from the bustier as he pinched and rolled the brown buds. I finally had to shove his laughing face into my breasts so he could give them the attention they truly wanted— his mouth. Tony smirked but complied. I loved an obedient Tony. That was the last thought I had before Wren reached down and stuck my free breast in his mouth. Gabe was nibbling and kissing my neck and earlobes while never losing momentum on my clit. My guys sped up the pace as I felt myself tethering over the cliff.

"Oh, Ms. Pink Pussy is about to blow!" The DJ cheered on. "Don't ease up on her, guys."

The heat pooled into my belly, and I squeezed my eyes shut as my orgasm ripped through me. My legs shook as the orgasm continued to roll through my lifeless body, leaving me no option but to lean on Gabe and Wren. In the distance, the group of couples' moans reached a feverish pitch, leaving me wanting more as I held onto Wren. Our sticky, hot sweat from our dancing, the stuffy sex-filled room, and my last orgasm should have repulsed me, but it emboldened me even more.

"It seems everyone is meeting the mile-high club except me, but who's up for round two!" screamed the DJ as I turned my face up towards Wren to place kisses on his chiseled jaw.

Who's up for round two? Me.

The DJ's words ping-pong in my head, canceling out the rational part of me that would have been halfway to my house by now. As I gave Wren one last kiss on his lips and turned to Gabe, my hands drifted down the soft mesh center, down to the zipper that held what I needed. He shuddered under my hands as he knew what I was seeking.

"You sure about this, Kitty? We can always go back upstairs and finish what we've started." Gabe asked.

"I can't wait to go upstairs. I want you…all of you guys now." I said as I unzipped Gabe's dick from the confines of his bodysuit. He sprung out red, hard, and angry as usual. He was already leaking his sweet and salty precum I was used to tasting. My mouth watered as I grabbed him by the base of his thick veiny dick and dragged my tongue over the slit. Tasting the sweet tangy essence of him, I moaned while Gabe shuddered and groaned.

Trembling from the excitement of what I was about to do. I let go of Gabe, and his mouth twisted in a frown.

"I'm not done, baby," I said in my raspy voice.

I turned towards Tony, opening his leather pants and releasing his cock free. He was already leaking and ready for me. The thought alone had my sensitive clit throbbing to the beat of the song playing around us. I swiped the precum from his big leaking head with my thumb. My greedy tongue reached out and licked the sharp taste of Tony that hit my tongue. Tony bent down and devoured me with a kiss. My tongue sought out the softness of Tony's mouth. My hand traveled down to stroke his hard cock using some of the precum that was left. He groaned in my mouth as I tightened and fastened my strokes on his long member.

"Ms. Pink Pussy is no pussy! She's taking control," the DJ said in the background. Several of the patrons cheered me on. One of them even shouted, "That's right!"

I should have stopped, but I couldn't. I was too far gone in a fog of lust to even care about the others around us. I broke away from Tony's kiss and asked him, "Did you bring a condom?"

Tony groaned and shook his head no. I slowed my strokes, causing him to whimper.

"I brought one…just in case…of course…not that I thought-" Wren said. His face turned pink. I let go of Tony and gave him a chaste kiss that silenced him.

"Thank you, baby," I said while I bit my lip.

I turned to Gabe with the condom Wren had produced. I'm not an expert on putting on condoms, but I was tonight as I rolled it on Gabe's thick, long member and pinched the tip. I did a once-over to make sure it wasn't rolling up.

"Tony, I want you behind me while I fuck Gabe," I said.

All three of my men's eyebrows raised in surprise. But they didn't complain or say a word as I threw my arms around Gabe's long neck and climbed to straddle him. Gabe dropped kisses on my chin to my neck, pulling a deep sigh from me before I slowly lowered myself onto him. The stretch I used to be scared of now became my comfort as I slid down to the base of his dick. Tony held me from behind, kissing and caressing my burning skin as I waited for my body to adjust. Tony's cock was nestled in between my ass, just waiting for me to give him the green light to take my other entrance. Not tonight though. Wren unraveled himself from his pants and was stroking his thick dick.

"That's right, Ms. Pink Pussy, take what's yours!" The DJ yelled. "If you got it, flaunt it, honey. Come on, Ms. Pink Pussy, ride him. Make 'em feel that Pussy power."

Gabe widened his stance and moved closer to Tony, boxing me in and giving me a little more support. I started my slow, steady pace on Gabe's cock as my pussy gripped and sucked him in every time I rolled down to the base. The deep rumble of Gabe's and Tony heightened my already oversensitive skin as I took what I needed from them. Over and over again, I ground and plunged my needy pussy onto Gabe's cock. Feeling Tony's cum smeared on my back and not in my mouth made me whine a bit. But in true fashion, Tony swiped some and fed me the intoxicating essence. The gentle stimulation from Gabe as I rode him made my clit throb. The pelts of sweat dripped from my back and lubricated the nonexistent space between Tony, making me glide effortlessly. The burning sensation intensified as I started whimpering and grinding on Tony and Gabe. Tony teased and pinched my painful pebbles, causing my pace to slow down as I reached the edge.

"Come on, Pink Pussy, don't be a tease. Give us what we want to see!" the DJ said.

My eyes shuddered open a second to see everyone in the room was watching us and were either touching themselves or their partners. Tony whispered in my ear, "Come on, my beautiful Kitty, give your audience what they're waiting for." His soft lips latched onto my favorite spot behind my ear, which made me lose my mind. My back arched, and my legs burned as my pace started to slow down.

"I n-need," I tried to stumble out but couldn't, but Gabe took notice and abandoned my wet buds to grip my soft, curvy hips. Tony's hands traveled along my overheated skin until he found my throbbing clit as Gabe started to plunge faster into me. I was lost by then. My breathing shuddered. The arms that once held on strongly around Gabe's neck had gone lax. Tony pinched, teased, and circled the tight nub relentlessly. The crowd's moans and cries overpowered the music the DJ was playing. Wren moaned my name as wet, warm liquid hit the side of my exposed stomach and breast. That was all I needed. I cried out my release and clenched down on Gabe, causing him to curse and spill into the condom. My head fell onto Tony's chest as I went limp in between them. Tony grunted, and his hot cum painted my back and my skirt. They held me there as I listened to our heartbeats, making melodious beats to back up the thumping song that was playing out from the speakers. When I felt our hearts slow down, it was then I noticed the cheering from the crowd.

"What a way to end our night! Ms. Pink Pussy gave us a stellar performance. Give her a round of moans and applause." The DJ said as the crowd did just that. There I stood in the middle of the room with everyone applauding and me just waving a little while trying to hide my burning face in Gabe's chest.

The DJ took pity on me and started his wind-down session. The smooth, slow-tempo music made it easier to hear everyone around us.

That's when reality set in, and Gabe lifted me off his soft cock.

"You're full of surprises, Kitty. I never thought you would have done something like that," Tony said.

I pushed the pink curly wig I donned over my ears to hide the scorched tip of my ears. Never in my life would I have thought I could, or would, ever have sex in front of three people, let alone several dozen people. Singing and dancing were one thing, but this was a whole different situation in itself.

"Hey, don't do that, Kitty," Wren said when he disposed of the tissue he cleaned our cum off of me with. "Quit living in your head and tell us what's going on, my love."

I stopped fidgeting with my pink leather dress that had now

been turned into a bra and skirt since the straps broke. My mask, which was drenched with sweat, was now damp on my skin. My mouth was open, and my breath caught in my throat. Wren never called me that before. The nickname was very intimate and caused me to feel warm all over. I blinked a couple of times, placing a chaste kiss on his cheek before I responded back.

"I never thought I would ever do something like this. I'm just a bit embarrassed is all, but not at the same time. I don't know how to explain it. I just felt liberated," I said as we left the dwindling party. I was reckless, and the thought that my mask could have slipped off and gave everyone a glimpse of my full face made me mentally smack myself.

"You shouldn't be…did you see everyone cheer you on? You were amazing," Gabe said. "If I didn't know any better, I would have said you were a performer."

I stumbled in my steps as we made our way back to the elevator. Tony caught me before I went colliding with the wall.

"Are you okay?" Tony asked. His eyebrows were drawn together, and his forehead wrinkled with worry.

I took a minute to gather myself as the guys made sure I was okay enough to walk.

"It's nothing, I'm okay. Let's get back to our room." I said, grabbing onto Tony's arm as we continued to walk towards the elevator.

I was relieved when we got back to the room, and we went to shower the night off our skin. They left me in the bathroom while I finished up my nightly routine. Once alone, I was left with my thoughts about tonight. As I stared into the vast bathroom vanity mirror, I couldn't help the smile that crept up my puffy lips, and there was only one thing that filtered through my mind.

You're a bad bitch, Jasmine Grant.

Chapter 6

Jasmine

I remembered when shit hit the fan.

It was our sixth month together, and Tony and Wren had long since fallen asleep. Gabe and I couldn't fall asleep, and we were talking for about thirty minutes about nothing when my slip-up occurred.

"My parents asked me how we were handling all the girls the other day." He laughed, but I didn't find that funny at all.

I gave him a pointed look. I couldn't tell you why because, until now, they knew very little about me. My identity was still an enigma to them, as I still worked hard to evade their questions.

"And how do you handle them?" I asked with a little more attitude in my voice than I wanted. I turned away from him and played with the gold Venetian mask I donned to match the gold see-through chemise that Gabe bought me.

"Are you jealous, Kitten? How could you when you have been playing coy with us?" he asked crossing his muscular arm. Gabe continued, "We've told you about ourselves, but we always get a half-ass response from you when we ask you anything."

I had to clamp my mouth shut and tuck my head down so he wouldn't see the anger in my eyes.

I couldn't even be mad at him.

They gave me so much insight into them I could look them up and probably learn all about them, but I hadn't because I loved to learn about them straight from the horse's mouth.

"You're right, Gabe. I'm sorry. It's just, I had a tough week." I got up to go to the bathroom so I could put some space between us.

But Gabe followed me into the bathroom. "You want to talk about it?" He wrapped his long arms around me from behind. I automatically laid my head on his smooth, firm chest. My hand ran over his arms as I kissed his naked upper arm.

Something about being in his arms always made me do stupid stuff without a second thought, like almost slipping and telling him I was a singer. "You know, it was some comments made by some of my fans… I mean people in my workplace. You know, the misogynistic men in my business." That was mistake number two I made. The first time since we had started our horizontal tango arrangement. I looked to see if Gabe had caught on to my slip-up, but if he did, he didn't let on.

"Yeah, the men in corporate America can be assholes like me," he winked, and I laughed.

"I love your smile and your laugh, Kitten." He kissed the top of my head and moved away from me, and I instantly missed his warmth. "We want more. We have been dancing around the subject for six months now, and frankly, I'm tired of waiting. The guys want to wait forever until they've worn you down, but I can't. When we joined Club Celeste, we made a promise that if we found our fourth, then we would stop coming to the club."

I lowered my head down towards the sink. The thought of our time together ending had tears burning in the back of my eyes, and I had to bite my lip from the sob that wanted to break out.

"I want to, I really do. The way you guys make me feel is indescribable. You, Wren, and Tony have given me something that I don't think I'll forget. You guys have given me freedom to be who I want to be. That means more to me than anything. Could you give me until the end of next month, and I will tell you everything?" The lie left a bitter taste in my mouth. I wanted to run to the toilet and empty the contents of my stomach into it.

"Until next month, and by then, I want us to take this relationship outside of Club Celeste," he stated and walked back to the bed. Then he halted and turned back to me. "I know I mentioned this before, but Tony and Wren are my brothers. I have always protected them and helped them, even when they claim they didn't need it."

He shuffled from foot to foot and rubbed his neck with his hand. "We've never felt this attached to anyone, and I don't want to see them hurt. They don't deserve it, and neither do I."

With that, he turned away as I stared at his retreating figure and bit my lip.

As I closed the door to put some space between us, I turned on the water to drown out my soft cries. I knew my time was up after next month. There was no way around it. My mom was not having it either. When I mentioned Allison's cousin Roeshell's engagement, my mother pinched her eyebrows together as a choking sound escaped her as she muttered, "That's just ungodly." Like a coward, I just sat there and held my head down while my mom quoted bible verses about perversion.

I hated that Tony and Wren always mentioned us advancing our relationship. It made my heart weep at the thought of not seeing them again. I remembered when they first brought up the topic. It was three months into our arrangement, and Gabe went to grab us some food from downstairs since he lost the bet on who would have to go downstairs.

I was in my favorite spot, tucked under Wren's arm. My legs were entwined with Tony's as we watched Suicide Squad.

"We're planning on buying a mansion soon," Tony said, his light green eyes sparkling. I don't think he remembered, but he'd mentioned the mansion before.

"How exciting!" I said as I set my focus on him. I took his hand into my free hand and played with the black commitment ring he wore that matched Wren's identical ring. "I know this means a lot to you guys."

"It does," he said. "Maybe I can convince you to come over…"

"We want you to see your future home," Wren said.

My heart hammered in my chest as I laid my hand on Wren's cheek. I untangled myself from my guys, instantly missing their warmth, so that I could face both of them.

"I would love to, but maybe when things are more permanent with us, then I can come over and tour your oversized man cave," I said with a chuckle. "I know you and Wren love to decorate. What plans do you have for the space?"

Tony and Wren grinned as I watched them speak about their new home. Wren's eyes were glazed over, and a breathtaking wide smile broke out when he wasn't speaking. His normally pale skin had a rosy tint to it. While Tony's arms flailed in the air as he went on about some details of the home.

Honestly, I wasn't listening to them because I was too caught up with doing my favorite thing, watching them. Tony and Wren had the ability to take the most minuscule subject and turn it into something grand. As I continued to watch them, I couldn't help the smile that crept up onto my face nor the way my heart squeezed in my chest. It was greedy of me, but I wanted this all to myself. Their smiles, tears, and everything in between.

When Gabe was present during their attempt to get me away from Club Celeste, he would just sit back and watch silently like an alpha watching his prey before he strikes but he never pushed anything until now.

This time, it was final, like the bathroom walls were going to box me in and crush me. No more half-assing or stringing them along. When Gabe said something, he meant it, and I learned that in the beginning when he asked me to name one thing I wanted right now. I said I wanted the Serpenti necklace from Bulgari that Wren had shown me the week before. I nearly died when he slipped the fifty-thousand-dollar necklace around my neck. I don't think I've taken it off since then.

I couldn't go back out there now. So, I waited until I heard Gabe's soft snoring and tiptoed to get dressed. I was almost to the door when I heard Wren's sleep-filled voice say, "Bye, Kitty."

I stopped in my tracks as I cursed at being caught. But when I looked back, Wren's eyes were already closed. It was as if he knew I would slip out. Which led me to believe they probably guessed I would. I should have left it alone, but the need to ask grew inside of me.

"How did you know I was going to leave now?" I asked.

"You think we didn't know you sneak off sometimes in the middle of the night," Wren said with his eyes still shut. "If we tried to stop you, Kitty, you would just run away from us. But if we let you go freely, you will always come back to where you belong."

I came to a stop in front of my house a little after midnight, which jolted me out of my flashback. Even though our conversation was just a week ago, it seemed like it was just yesterday. As I breathed a sigh of relief at being home, I threw my shoes off and stripped down naked. The cold marble was a comfort to me as my bare feet hit the ground. It was the best feeling ever.

"Girl, put back on your clothes! I birthed you naked, but that doesn't mean I want to see it now," my mom scolded.

I yelled, of course, because why the hell would she be in my home with no notice?

"Quit all of that yelling. I had to fly myself all the way out here to see if you were alive or if the government had put a chip into those

COVID vaccines that you took and got you under mind control." She shook her head.

God, someone shoot me now! This is a cruel and unusual punishment.

"Well, I'm alive and well, mom." I tested her. "So maybe you can catch an early flight back."

She cocked her eyebrow and tilted her head.

"Sorry, ma'am," I apologized quickly. I was too old to get whooped, but I didn't want to tempt fate.

My mom wore her typical get-up, which was composed of her ankle-length skirt and a turtleneck shirt with a vest over it. My mom never changed, and her motto was, "God never changes, so neither do I." But a turtleneck was a bit much for the warm LA winter. I shook my head.

"I told Allison to come over so we can have a talk," she stated. "I called her just before you blinded me, and she told me she was on her way."

I mentally rolled my eyes and sighed. Allison was probably frightened when my mom called her. Now I had two messes to clean up.

"Now put your clothes back on. It is a sin to walk around naked like some hussy." She fanned me away.

One, two, three, four, five, six, seven, eight, nine, ten… breathe in and out… make it through this visit, and she's gone for another six months… Hopefully.

I grinned, which I knew looked as if I were sneering at her. I could—should have said something back, but what would be the point? My Mom always has something to rebuttal. I clenched my hand and started towards the stairs, but Allison blasted through the door when I'd almost hit the bottom step. She yelled, "Oh my God, you're out to blind me, Jas."

"Last time I checked, this was my home." I really needed to

change my locks. "So, I can walk naked in my home if I want to," I muttered to her, and she just shook her head.

I ran up the stairs, dumped my clothing in the laundry bin, put on some shorts and a tank, and headed downstairs with a grim face as I entered the gateway to hell for me. And it was only Monday.

How the fuck will I get her gone by Friday?

I walked into the family area. My mom was cutting up like she just told the funniest joke in the world, while Allison looked like she wanted to be anywhere but here. I folded my arms and tapped my foot. My mom didn't stop laughing, so I cleared my throat, and they turned to look at me. Allison had a huge, help me look on her face.

"Oh, you found your clothes, Jas. Great, come sit down." Allison eagerly patted the seat next to her.

"Oh, ha," was all I could get out. I slumped into the chair next to Allison and across from my mom.

Allison was usually all smiles, but she turned to me with a sad face and said, "Jas, I'm worried about you. You've missed out on your interview with DJ AM and your In the Loop charity performance. Even though you don't need them, you still need to appear reliable."

I sighed. So, that was what the meeting was about. "I'm sorry, Allison. I promise I will attend the next event you sign me up for," I continued. "I'm sorry. I'm in a bad mood, and my focus hasn't been here lately—"

"Lately… Do you mean for the last couple of months? You have been avoiding me. You have been gone sometimes all night, you don't have time to hang out with me, and you have been distant." Allison said as she stared down at her folded hands.

I felt bad about sneaking behind Allison's back. She was the only person who would understand and be in my corner. But as I sat there in front of her, the cold sensation of disappointment washed over me.

"I totally understand, and I—" I stopped. "Wait, how do you

know I was out all night?"

"Well, your mom called me one night, and she mentioned you were going out frequently on Friday nights. I told her you were just exploring the city at night." Allison must have seen the confused expression on my face because she stopped talking.

"I still have access to your cameras. So, I can view when you leave and come in." My mom looked at me, and I turned my confused look to my mother. "For safety purposes, nothing more or nothing less. I'm glad I did. What's going on, Jasmine?"

My face was hot, and my mouth was like sandpaper. "You've been spying on me through my cameras, Mom?"

"I was checking to make sure you got in safely when I noticed you were leaving dressed up in interesting attire and coming back disheveled. Of course, I'm worried about you." She folded her arms. "You're a single woman living in this big house alone."

"Whatever she's doing is nothing dangerous, Ms. Grant. Right, Jas? Plus, she's a responsible adult." Allison looked at me, almost pleading with me to play along with her.

I was beyond livid. My palms were slick, and my heart thudded in my ears. I understood where my mom was coming from, but it didn't make it hurt any less. She had a right to be concerned. Heck, I had a right to be worried. Because along the way, I'd lost myself when I tried to have my cake and eat it as well. The conversation with Gabe the other night was coming back to bite me in the ass.

"So, are you going to tell us or not?" My Mom asked.

I snapped out of my head.

"I'm enjoying life, Mom, just like any twenty-four-year-old. I go to a club and dance the night away," I lied.

"You're better than that, Jasmine. I raised you to be a Christian woman. What can you find in the club? You should be in the church, finding a husband," she stated.

I blanched. "No, thank you, and I'm not alone."

"So, you found someone to go out with?" Allison asked. She had gone quiet. But as I looked at her, I knew she was trying hard to fight back tears. Although I'm not new to club life, Allison and I did everything together—she was my ace. Even now, when I prepared to tell another lie, I cringed and looked away from Allison. So that I could hide the shame I felt inside.

"No, I'm happy by myself," I grunted out the lie. It was the best I could come up with.

My mom sighed.

"So, what about love? Marriage? What about giving me some grandbabies? I deserve to have some grandchildren I can spoil." My mom questioned me.

The guys want kids as well…

"See, there she goes," my mom smirked.

"I'm sorry. I have a lot on my mind." God, I couldn't have come up with another reason.

"Well, I'm tired." My mom sighed. "So, let's put a pin in it for now."

They said goodbye, and Allison left after asking for the millionth time if I was okay. After I reassured her for the umpteenth time that day and set a girls' night out for us, I watched as she left my house and felt beat down. When I arrived home earlier, I'd wanted a nap, but now I needed wine.

I may need to buy some more to get through this week.

Well, at least I wouldn't focus so much on Friday. That was wishful thinking on my part.

My mother mentioned every day that she wouldn't leave until Saturday. It was to the point I could finish her sentences every morning. It was always, "Let's go to this place because I'm only here until Saturday."

Now, I couldn't say it had been all bad. We got to knock off some of my post-retirement visits to some of the local museums, which ended up being fun. But she wouldn't leave me alone for over five minutes after we got back to my house. I couldn't masturbate in peace or get ready for Friday. Speaking of which, I planned on buying her favorite Ace of Spades Champagne in the hope she would devour it, and then I could sneak away. I prayed it worked out because I thought I might combust if I couldn't make it to my guys.

Friday arrived way too fast, and I was sweating like a hooker in church. My mother had turned in for the night after I gave her the champagne. It was easy, too easy, but I rolled with it. I got ready for the night and grabbed the guy's gifts I'd purchased. It was mostly because I felt guilty for stringing them along for so long, but it really wasn't my plan for this to last this long. I used the side door to leave and parked my car outside of the cameras' view so I wouldn't be caught leaving my house.

When I got to our room, the guys were already there, and I handed their gifts to them. For Tony, I got him an appointment at the elusive Perry Harrell tailors in downtown LA. Usually, you have to wait months to get an appointment, but I made a promise to Mr. Harrell that I would gift a signed photograph for his charity for the appointment. For Wren, I had to search a bit for him, but I ended up finding custom cufflinks from Dior. For Gabe, I was able to get my hands on a signed hockey stick from Gardie Howe. They seemed shocked and thankful as they took turns hugging me and kissing me. I glowed as I watched them fawn over their gifts and gave me a replay of their week.

I think it would be impossible to choose a favorite because they all held a special place in my heart.

I switched spots in bed every week so that I could be next to each of them. Tonight, I was wrapped up in Tony's long limbs. It wasn't until midnight that everyone was asleep except for me. I don't know how long it had been, as I was lost in my thoughts until I heard a knock at the door that caused me to come back to reality. I ignored it, but the knocking continued, and the guys shifted. I got up and snuck to the door before the person could knock again. What was so important it couldn't wait until the morning?

I opened the door, and Alfie from the front desk was there.

"Hello, Miss. May I speak with you in the hall?" His croaky voice asked.

"What's this about?" I jumped, not having heard Gabe as he snuck up behind me.

"It's a personal matter—" Alfie explained.

"It's okay, Gabe. I'm going to step into the hall." I kissed him and pulled my robe tighter.

I signaled to the clerk to the alcove in the hallway.

"Madame, we have a message for you." He handed me the note and was gone down the stairs in a flash.

I opened the note, and I thought it was something about my car. But it was a handwritten note with three words: "Come Home Now!" There wasn't a signature, but I knew my mother's handwriting from anywhere. Oh, for fuck's sake. I already dreaded leaving them in the middle of the night, but now, to go home to face my mother would be torture. Gabe stood in the doorway waiting for me as I returned to the room. I walked past him and back into the room wordlessly. I could tell he was worried.

"Is everything okay?" he asked. Everyone was up by then.

I shook with nervousness. My mother, being sober enough to notice me gone and she knew where I was, surprised me. The champagne didn't work. I thought she would have guzzled it down until both bottles were gone.

But, of course, nothing was simple for me as I shoved the note into my purse.

"Oh yeah, something came up, and I have to run." I scrambled as I tossed my phone in my bag. I moved around, consciously avoiding their penetrating stares.

"Maybe we should follow you to make—" Wren said, but I cut him off. I didn't need them being mixed up in this, nor did I want them to see what car I drove.

"I'll be okay, Wren. Really, you guys go back to bed." I stated.

I went to the bathroom to use it before returning to the mess that awaited me. When I returned, they all sat quietly with their clothing on.

Fuck, Fuck, Fuck!

"We're walking you to your car," Gabe said.

"That's unnecessary, really," I pleaded.

"We get you're not ready to come clean about yourself to us yet. But this seems odd…even for you." Tony stated.

My stomach turned inside out. My hands became clammy.

"It's nothing. It's family problems." I grabbed my things and kissed them. They looked pensive and like they wanted to give me an earful. But they remained quiet.

I was so careful about leaving because I was sure they would follow me and figure out who I was. Even though I knew I should come clean to them. But I couldn't bring myself to go through with it, at least not now, not before I was sure my mom wouldn't go off the deep end. When I entered my house, it was dark except for the kitchen. It reminded me of when I got caught sneaking in from my first party I attended with Allison. As I approached the kitchen, my mom spoke with Allison. Her tone was laced with disdain.

My mom had dark circles around her sad red eyes. In her hand I noticed the invite from Club Celeste and the paper with my selections I scribbled on that I chucked into my drawer. She looked at me with her mouth turned down, and I instantly felt the heat of shame blossom on my face.

"Is this who you've become, Jasmine Grant?" She looked about ready to cry, and I knew this wouldn't be easy. "You've been going to a sex house every weekend? Are you prostituting?"

"N-No," I stammered.

"Allison said you might have been exploring different nightclubs. But I went to search your room and found this invitation to this club and this sinful paper… 'butt plugs, a maybe'…" She said as she shook her head. "I had dragged Allison away from her fiancé to help me figure this out. Paying for sex!" my mom emphasized.

The way she said it made me feel dirty. There's nothing wrong with being a sex worker and having specific needs, but my mother was always the judge of God.

"I'm sorry, Mom." My voice had all but given out. "It's not how it seems."

"Then how is it, Jasmine? Because I can't understand it." Fresh tears rolled down her face. "I raised you better than this. You are better than this." She slammed her hand down on my table. It made Allison and me jump. "What would your father think if he were here now? His one and only child prancing off to a sex house at night."

My legs threatened to give out as I held onto the back of the chair.

"If you would let me explain—"

"Jasmine was caught up and didn't have time to tell us about the person." Allison finally spoke up. "But it seems she found someone she loves, and we should be supportive of her, right Jas?"

I hadn't felt the tears until I looked down at my shirt, which was soaked and clung to my chest. I hung my head down in shame, unable to meet my mom's harsh gaze. I heard Allison's question, and I wanted to scream out yes as my best friend tried to smooth out the situation. But no words formed in my head.

"I've raised you to be a Christian woman, Jasmine!" My mom continued on her tirade. She hiccupped. "What will your future husband think? You wanted to be perverse and have sex with any Tom, Dick, and Harry?"

"She won't go back. Problem solved. Will you, Jas?" Allison pleaded. I felt bad for Allison. She hated to be in the middle of my mom and I's shitstorm.

I sighed and shook my head no.

"How long?" my mom asked.

"Six months," I whispered.

"Six months! And how many men?" my mom probed. "And don't give me any bullshit answer."

How much should I tell her? I chewed on my lip. Her red eyes held shame in them. I had never seen my mom look at me like that before, like I was a stranger to her.

"The same three men the whole time. I—"

"Three men? Three? At the same time? You could have an STD!" her voice became shrill.

"Everyone got tested, and we test every two weeks."

"I can't even talk about this anymore," my mom waved her hands in front of her face. "You're not going there anymore."

The chair scraped across the floor, and it made my skin crawl. My mom dragged herself up the stairs, almost as if she weighed a ton, and I followed Allison to her car before she left. She gave me a sympathetic look and apologized after telling me my mom had found out the location of the club through my car app. Left alone in the foyer, I let out a sob that made me grab my chest because I was ashamed, but not for the reason my mother thought. I shuffled up to my room. My feet felt like lead, and I flopped down and stared at the ceiling when I got to my bed. I needed to end things. It had been a good run, but I knew deep in my gut I had to end it. I did not mean for it to last that long. After six months of the best time of my life, I finally got to know three men I liked.

I love them, not like them...

Did I just think that? I didn't even know where that thought came from. I didn't love them. They didn't know me because I never told them anything, and I barely knew them. I didn't even know about that type of love. I was inexperienced, and I'd failed miserably.

I cried for myself, for having to leave the guys, for the shame I brought to my mom, and for the mistrust I placed in Allison. I soaked the pillow with my tears, but I didn't change it. The hair from my wig stuck to my face, and my skin was wet with tears. I fell asleep after a while with a dream filled with Tony, Gabe, and Wren and my mom's shame-ridden eyes.

Chapter 7

Jasmine

I slept and binged on snacks the week after my mother left. Allison called and checked up on me every day until I told her I wanted to be alone. Somehow, that offended her, and she stopped calling me. She then only texted me to see if I needed anything. Typically, I'd never drank alcohol heavily, but that week, I'd polished off four bottles of Blanc wine that had cost me too much to waste.

Unlike the other Fridays, this one would definitely destroy my spirit. It was almost as if I had a meeting with the Grim Reaper, and the bastard took my soul and left me here to walk the earth empty. My insides twisted as time started to count down. Whenever I thought I could get away with the guys, the memory of my mother's shameful eyes reminded me of why I had to stop my arrangement.

I arrived at Club Celeste earlier than usual because I couldn't bring myself to stay in the house anymore. Sneaking out was easier this time because my mom went back to Nashville, and I changed my password to the security cameras and sent a text to Allison saying I was turning in early. I tipped back the third cognac I'd got from the mini bar downstairs in the orgy room. *It's the last soiree. Wish I could enjoy myself.*

"Well, for what it's worth, family is everything, and they're right!" my drunk companion stuttered as he tipped the Vodka shot down his throat. "N-N-No matter what. Families is all we's got."

My face was feverish, and my eyes were red before I got to the club. So, I could only imagine what they looked like now.

"Thank you, my friend." I signaled for another drink and knocked it back. "You're right. They know what's best, and I'm breaking it off." I hiccupped.

I stood up and stumbled a bit as the liquor started to hit a little too close to home. After a few seconds, I got two bottles of water from the bar and took myself to the room. The guys would be there in the next hour, and I didn't want to be too out of it for the conversation I needed to have.

Shit, it's really ending.

That was all I needed—one more night—and I could finally let them go to find some model girlfriend, and I would find my Christian husband. No more zombified Jasmine, but back to the old post-retirement Jas. Back to traveling to places and doing things that I hadn't been able to do during my career. No more masturbating three times a day from the memory of my guys. Back to dull Jasmine with her head in the clouds and her closet filled with disguises that would remind me of my time here. I would be thoroughly satiated enough for me to make it through my life once the night was over.

When I entered the room, I polished off the two water bottles and used the bathroom to freshen up. Since it was our last night together, I went all out and wore something I'd been wanting to try out for a while now. It was a red open-cup bra set with a crotchless panty garter set. I paired it with a red lace top, thigh-high stockings, and my red stilettos. I should have been ashamed to have my breasts all out, but the slight buzz from the liquor gave me an ego boost.

I was saying goodbye, so I wanted to do it right.

I dropped some Visine in my red eyes, as I prayed I wouldn't cry or sweat too much because I only had enough latex makeup for my face and not enough to cover the small tattoo because I ran out the house without grabbing the new vial of makeup I purchased. So, I put a skin-colored band-aid over it and applied several layers of foundation until I couldn't see it. I placed my red Colombina mask from our first night together. I stepped back from the mirror and viewed myself. Not to be egoistical or anything, but I looked fucking sexy.

I wasn't sure how everything would work out, but I knew one thing—I was beyond a nervous wreck. As I paced the floor of the room, rubbing my sweaty hands, I wondered what would happen if I ran away with them, leaving everything and everyone behind. I sighed and shook my head, that wouldn't work. I couldn't leave Allison and my mom behind—they were my only family.

I could not make my mind up, but one fact remained. I was ready to get fucked. No foreplay, the bath we always have afterward, or staying up afterward to talk that I'd become accustomed to. I wanted something quick so I could rip the bandage off. I shouldn't, but I wanted them—correction—needed to give them a part of me that no one had ever had.

I was scared, but I wanted it more than anything else.

The door to the suite opened and closed from beyond the bathroom door, and Tony's chirpy voice yelled, "Honey, we're home!"

My heart clawed out of my chest when I heard them. Unconsciously, my essences coated my folds, and my nipples hardened. I stood there for a good minute before my lungs finally gave me enough air to respond. "Yeah, give me a minute." My clammy hands gripped the doorknob.

Jasmine Grant, you have to let them go. You go in there and take charge.

I took a final deep breath, squared my shoulders, and opened the door. I snuck behind Gabe and hugged him from behind. His signature Bergamot scent enveloped me in a warm embrace. He grabbed my hands, pulled me closer, and kissed them. Normally, the guys always took control. But tonight, I wanted to take it from them.

"Holy shit," Wren whispered from my side.

I unbuckled Gabe from the back and pulled down his pants, setting him free. "So, what happened to hello? How are you? My name is… It's just take off your clothes, huh?" Gabe said as he chuckled.

"Yep, Tony and Wren strip now," I demanded. Tony, who had since moved from beside Gabe to behind me, finally found his voice.

He croaked out, "You're glistening already, Kitten."

I grabbed Gabe around the base of his cock and started a slow-paced stroke. Gabe let out a low grunt of approval, and I felt encouraged. I kept my pace, adding pressure to my strokes, driving him to drop his head back. My fingers itched to play with his dark curls, but I refrained from doing so. I let go of him as I swiped the pre-cum that leaked from his cock with my fingers. Finally, he turned around, and I saw his green eyes were almost black. I pushed the ball of guilt down my stomach, and I stuck my finger with his pre-cum in my mouth and moaned. I was going to miss the taste and smell of him.

His eyes roamed my body, and I shivered under his stare.

Before this could turn into something more than what I could control, I dropped to my knees in front of my three forbidden loves. I pulled Wren on one side of me, Tony on the other, and Gabe with his eyes still on me in front. I turned my head to Wren's cock, and I licked both my hands, grabbing Tony and Gabe's hardened dicks.

"Feed me your cock, Wren," I demanded.

I peeked up to see his gorgeous face had turned scarlet. One of my eyebrows was raised, and my mouth was slightly parted as I waited for him to remember we were waiting on him. I cleared my throat, and Wren came back to this realm. He stumbled but finally placed himself in my mouth. *Perfect!*

As I hollowed my cheeks, I sucked down Wren's cock, taking him into my mouth until he was in the back of my throat, which caused him to curse. My hands worked in tandem with the pace of my mouth. I pulled off of Wren as I felt his hands reach out to grab my head, and I switched him with Tony, ensuring I winked up at Gabe. Tony, unlike Wren, was ready and greedy. His hand found the back of my head and had me gagging on his cock. The metal piercings on his cock rolled over my tongue smoothly. I worked them repeatedly, pushing my hands and mouth to bring them to their limits.

It wasn't until my jaw threatened to lock that I pulled myself off Tony, who had hogged my mouth for himself. He groaned, and I grabbed his hand when he reached out to put me back on his cock.

"No," I said as my bottom lip quivered, but I tried not to cry as my emotions were everywhere right now. I leaned back on my wobbly knees, anchored my arms around Tony, and let him pull me up for a kiss. As I swept my tongue in his mouth, I took possession of him and made him realize he was mine as much as I was his. He moaned, and I followed suit when either Gabe or Wren started to eat my dripping wet core from behind. Whoever it was sucked my wet lips and my sensitive nub, and I moaned into Tony's mouth as he played with my tender beads.

God! How am I going to let go?

Wren came around and kissed me on the cheek down to my abandoned nipple. It dawned on me that Gabe was feasting on me. Wren and Tony possessed me like I was their last meal. I let go of Tony, grabbed the back of Wren's hair, and looked at his blown icy eyes. Fuck, he looked so amazing. I moved to share the same possessive kiss with him. My free hand found its way into Tony's hair and locked us in a three-way kiss. Six lips, four tongues, and hands were everywhere as we moved as one. We were a bundle of energy. And when Gabe slipped his mouth over my clit, I fell hard. As my knees gave out, I thanked

God Tony grabbed me, or else I would have fallen on my face. I let out a string of curse words. Gabe had a wicked tongue that brought me to my knees.

The little voice in my mind kept telling me that I was losing control of the situation, but I couldn't help it. I told myself no kissing, but here I was getting kissed on both lips while I crumbled—literally—in their arms.

"I want to ride you, Tony." His eyes darkened, and he bent down to capture my lips again, but I stopped him. I pushed him onto the bed and crawled on top of him. I took him in my hand and lowered the condom onto his stiff cock. Wren helped me onto Tony's cock by holding him to my entrance while I lowered myself inch by inch as he stretched me out. He grabbed my hip and moved, but I stopped him.

"I want Wren to be behind me." If a pin had dropped in the room, you could have heard it.

Tony groaned. "I wanted to have your anal cherry."

"I know, but you wouldn't be gentle," I stated as I dropped a kiss on his lips.

Wren turned my head and gave me a kiss that had me clench down on Tony. He hissed.

Wren answered breathlessly. "I'm honored, Kitten."

Gabe grabbed the lube from the nightstand. When he returned, I looked up to see Gabe's pensive eyes, like he knew my plans. I beckoned him with the curl of my finger. He cocked his eyebrow and moved beside Tony on the bed. I looked into his eyes and said, "I want you to fuck my mouth." I sounded crude, completely unlike the typical demure Jasmine everyone loved.

Impatiently, I started to ride Tony, but he burrowed his hands into my hips, pulling me back down to his base and preventing me from moving. Wren's hands opened my ass to display my rosette. From behind me, I heard him lubing his thick dick as he got ready to enter me. I locked one hand onto Gabe's thick erection. I prepared mentally for Wren because I knew it would be a tight fit. He angled himself at my entrance and began pushing past the tight ring of muscle.

The metal passed my entrance as he slipped into me inch by inch. With each inch, I squeezed Gabe's cock and Tony's chest. My face contorted. He was halfway in, and it was way too much. Gabe hissed, and I realized that my grip on him was too much. As tiny beads of sweat rolled down my back, I slumped over when Wren was finally in, and I regretted it. The full feeling left me panting. When the pain finally became dull, I muttered, "Please move before I die." They moved, and the pain of the stretch gave way to pleasure. The glide of the metal piercings mirrored one another as my guys worked to bring us to our peak. My sloughy hand was becoming weak as my slow-paced stroke on Gabe became harder to maintain. Defeated, I dropped my hand as Wren and Tony touched and kissed my sticky skin. My head found Wren's equally sweaty shoulder. Gabe turned my head and stuffed himself into my mouth. He grabbed the back of my head and fucked my mouth relentlessly. The corners of my mouth protested as he maneuvered himself, but I didn't stop him.

All I heard were our grunts, moans, and Gabe's rough voice as he praised me. "You're such a good girl for taking all of our cocks at once." I clenched down as I deep-dived over the edge. The small blue room was a scented haven of sweat, sex, and lavender. Wren delivered a sharp smack to my ass. I moaned and slightly gagged around Gabe's cock. It was as if he fed off my orgasm because I was blessed with his salty taste in the back of my throat and on my tongue as he came in my mouth. I lapped it all up as he removed himself from my mouth. Tony and Wren took that time to speed up their pace, and Gabe kissed me until my breath had left my lungs.

I couldn't form a word as my vision became spotty.

Wren leaned over and trailed kisses up and down my neck and shoulder. Wren shocked me when he said, "God, this is my tight little hole now, Kitten." I don't know how I managed, but I slipped into the deep end and clenched down so hard on them again that I swore the metal piercings would break through the thin walls separating them. Wren stilled, grunted, and lightly bit down on my shoulder as I felt his hot cum fill my ass and drip down my cheeks onto Tony's thighs. Wren pulled his soft cock out of me, and I slumped over Tony a bit.

"I'm not done yet," Tony said into my ears.

As I held my weak body up on his chest, he grabbed my hips and plunged into me like he was on fire. I knew I should have stopped him, but my soul had temporarily left my body, and Tony must have sensed it as well. He had dug into my sweaty hips as he struggled to get a hold of me. He gave up, flicked something onto the floor, and sat up, wrapping his arms around my waist.

Finally, he got a good grip on me. My weak body pressed into his as he thrust his dick into me. I lost every single brain cell when he dropped me onto his lap repeatedly. All I could do was yell, "Fuck! Yes, Daddy," endlessly.

He went rigid under me, and I overheard him mutter, "I love you, my beautiful Kitty."

I screamed my release, and I couldn't hear anything over the sound of my heartbeat in my ears. Black dots swirled in my vision, but my lips kept moving. I held onto Tony as I tried to come back to earth. When I did, I discovered the words I continued to mutter repeatedly with my mouth.

"I love you guys," I repeated.

It took me a couple of minutes before I gained enough sense. My hand flew to my mouth, and I looked wide-eyed at a smiling Tony.

It was like a light switch flipped on. I hopped off of Tony and rolled off the bed. It took me a minute to get my legs to work.

Tony and Wren kept asking if I was okay as I panicked. Gabe was in the bathroom. All I could hear was the shame in my mom's voice ricocheting in my head, which made everything worse. I was a royal fuck up.

Somewhere in the background, someone mentioned something about the condom, but I choked as I stared into Tony's concerned face. I grabbed my dress and purse and hightailed it out of the room half naked. I slipped on the dress before getting to the first floor and jumped into my car. I didn't stop until I heard the locking sound of the doors to my house. I slumped onto the floor and cried until I fell asleep in front of my door in a puddle of sweat and tears.

I'm a royal fuck up.

Part III

giorno corrente[1]

---

1   giorno corrente- current day

Chapter 8

Gabe

Six Years Later

Our monthly meetings have been the same for the past four years. We came in, and they told us how our latest venture had tripled our net worth. *Same ol' shit, just a different month.* I wasn't sure why we attended other than to congratulate our employees, check our offices, and then go home. I pinched the bridge of my nose and exhaled loudly so that everyone in this meeting knew I was bored. These days, my attention span was shorter than my temper. I had no one else to blame but myself.

The medium-sized conference room, which was once painted a dull brown, was now a neon yellow colored room to promote idealism and joy amongst our employees. That's what Tony had harped on when I gave him full range to help the associates pick out a color. When I returned to the office, I nearly went blind at the color. *That's what I got for leaving Tony alone to decorate.* I mentally rolled my eyes. With its bright, extremely padded white office chairs, I guess I could see why the employees loved going in there to work.

"Mr. Sabino, is it okay to proceed with this deal?" Michael asked. Michael was one of the company's project managers for six years, working on our latest venture. When his father retired, he was ready to step up to the plate. He was loyal to our business and has been a valuable asset, just like his father. His slightly pudgy body was stuffed into his blue suit while everyone wore denim and business-appropriate shirts. His brown hair was slicked back with a whole tub of gel. I spoke with him about dressing comfortably once, but he simply shrugged and said his father would disapprove.

Everyone turned to look at me. My face grew warm at being caught not paying attention. I peeped a glance at Tony and Wren. They openly rolled their eyes at me.

"Yes, of course, Michael, you have my blessings to proceed," I said quickly.

I rubbed the back of my neck as I tried to remember what he was speaking about before.

"Great! I will work on it after this meeting. Let's move on," he said. "With their acquisition, we will add another two hundred units."

Oh, that's what we're talking about.

I nodded at Michael, and he proceeded with whatever he was talking about now. My eyes wandered over to the new secretary for our finance floor.

She was beautiful, to say the least. Her skin color reminded me of topaz. The curls in her chestnut brown hair were pulled back into a high ponytail. Her tall, lanky body suited her. Her ample ass made up for her flat chest. She was gorgeous and intelligent, and as much as I wanted to like her, she just didn't do it for me.

When I cracked my knuckles, it sounded loud in the room since everyone's focus was on Michael's presentation, except for me. The action caused Michael to turn to me, and I offered him an apology and for him to continue.

How did I get to this point? How did the one thing I had worked towards since I was thirteen become just another mundane chore?

Well, it started when Tony, Wren, and I thought we could wing our way through our business proposal to our parents after our time at Club Celeste. We were in a bad place mentally after Kitty ran out on us. We had to reevaluate our plan after we got back into a better place and weren't screaming or blaming each other. Which took about a year, give or take. By then, we knew to stick to the original proposal plan, to let me lead and let the pieces fall into place, which wasn't easy since we were still working out our distrust over the Kitty situation.

My parents, who had always been supportive and knew we would be successful in our family businesses, gave us the reins after our planned proposal. My mom made it known that I was no longer Gabriele the bambino, but I was Gabriele Sabino, CEO of Sabino International Investment Capital. The title made me gleam for the first time since Club Celeste because I'd worked my ass off day and night for this since I was thirteen, and I could finally reap the benefits.

My pa fully trusted my business ideas whenever I pitched him an idea. So, when I told them we wanted to combine our companies, which would make us even larger and put us under one umbrella, he said it was a perfect plan. Sabino International Investment Capital, Russo Intel Inc., and Costa Oil and Transportation would become SCR Enterprises.

That was a week before our proposal dinner, and Tony's and Wren's family got wind of it. Of course, they weren't as big fans of the proposal as my pa was, but they agreed to hear it out.

One week later, we were ready to bring our offer to the other families. They agreed on a Friday night dinner instead of our usual Sunday dinners, and we accepted. I waited until everyone ate and was lounging around to give my speech.

"So, you want us to give up our family business? So, your company can grow, and ours look like failed ventures?" my Uncle

Russo said. He was never one to hold back.

"Zio," I started. Uncle was what I'd called him since our families had been friends since our great-grandparents were children. "It's nothing like that, and we want to combine everything but have our separate departments. Sabino would still be over commercial real estate, Tony would still be over technology, and Wren would be over oil and transportation. We wouldn't work under the Sabinos commercial real estate. We will get a new name and outlook for the businesses."

Uncle Russo rubbed his full gray beard as he took in everything. We had to get the board's approval, which was comprised of our parents, to move forward.

I sighed and turned my head to my pa. He had his arms folded over his small potbelly. "Gabe, your mother and I trust you—"

My mom cut him off. "Wholeheartedly," she huffed out with a smile that lit up her small, hazel eyes.

"Yes, wholeheartedly." He moved to hold my mom's hand. "It seems like a lot of work to combine and get everything situated. You guys deserve to live a little. Chase some skirts and maybe find a woman to give us some grandkids. We're not getting younger. Right now, the business is basically on autopilot. Take advantage of it."

The Russos, Costas, and my mom nodded and grunted their approval. I held back my sigh because our parents, especially my mom, would make a big fuss about it if I didn't.

"Yes, I understand, and you're waiting on some grandkids, but right now, I have to secure their future, as you did for me, Pa. It's the circle of life. I promise you that once we combine, it will only take a month or two to smooth things out, and everything will return to normal. We won't tie ourselves to the office," I said while I stared into eyes that mirrored mine.

"How about we give them a test trial and see how it goes? We will disband if everything hasn't smoothed out in a year or two," Mr. Costa said. "Wren and Tony, are you fine with combining businesses?"

"Yes, I think it would be best to combine and start pushing out our next rollouts," Tony spoke first.

"I agree with the guys. I won't say there won't be bumps along the way, but we are a united front and will tackle them as they come. The quicker we act, the quicker we can join you on your next yacht adventure." Wren said as he smiled at his parents.

There was a long pregnant pause until, finally, Uncle Russo, Tony's father, spoke. "We will give you until the end of the year to get everything together and reassess it later. I'm in."

After five minutes of holding our breaths, the Costas, Russos, and my parents agreed to the merger.

That was five years ago. It seemed like forever since we'd had to sit down on that fateful Friday and pitch our idea. Thankfully, everything went as we planned because there were times I didn't think we would make it. We spent most of the quarter completing the details and smoothing out legal kinks in our goal of merging. What should have taken us four months to achieve only took us a month. But that was because I thought like my pa and had started the process under my father's nose before I asked for his permission.

"Well, Mr. Sabino, Mr. Costa, and Mr. Russo, that's all the updates we have for this month. Do you have any questions?" Michael asked, jarring me back to the present as he wrapped up the meeting.

Slowly, I shook my muddled brain and stretched.

"No, I think you went over everything thoroughly. But I would love everyone to have a great week," I stated, and everyone scurried off to their departments.

When they were all gone, I turned to Tony and Wren. I had waited for a week to bring up this opportunity for us to diversify our portfolio. This new venue would allow us to get our foot in the entertainment door business. But I had to convince the guys to get on board. They were in love with the passive income life, but they didn't realize that I had a little in with our family friend, who was retiring.

"So, now that we're alone, we can talk freely before we run out of here."

"Shoot," Tony said, placing his foot up on the conference table.

"I have a business opportunity for us. Now, before you guys moan and groan about it, just hear me out." I rolled my neck and heard my joints crack. "You remember Mr. Brine? He owns In the Loop Records. They're known for producing several big-name stars like Jasmine Grant, Lady J, Blue, and others. Well, he's retiring, and we could buy it as a side business. We have a couple of non-linked LLCs. So, we could funnel money into one of them to purchase the business from him. How about it?"

Wren and Tony stayed silent. I wanted to snap them back to reality, but I decided against it. "How much work would we have to do for this side gig? And can we passively control it?" Wren asked.

"So, we're strictly buying to become the board members. But the artists on this label are basically independent. So, they have complete teams for themselves. It would be like this business. We come in monthly or whenever something big happens, and we approve or not approve it. They have a CFO and a CEO. We might have to work a bit until we switch out the CEO. But not for long because I already have someone picked out for the role. I gave the financial report to Michael, and he's looking over it right now. But I trust Michael. He would run the numbers correctly."

"Let's think about it and talk about it after our dinner date with Rose." Tony rubbed his pinched brows and rose from his seat.

I cringed because we were supposed to go out with our latest "girlfriend." Rose Carson was the latest in our failed string of girlfriends. She was the daughter of the CEO of the biggest brewing company in the West. Rose was beautiful with her rosebud pouty lips, creamy soft skin, strawberry-colored hair, and modelesque body. But as much as she was pretty on the outside, she could be downright nasty at times. She was what I called an entitled princess, and everything somehow revolved around her. Wren loved to pamper her and appease her every desire because, in my opinion, he believed that would make her stay. He would bend his back to make her happy. I mentioned that spoiling someone doesn't make a successful relationship, but it flowed in one ear and out the other.

Tony was impartial to Rose. Over the last six years, his demeanor had changed slightly. He would still be the same Tony we all loved, but sometimes you could hear or see the hurt that lingered still. He spent a year taking his loss out with alcohol and then another year in Alcoholics Anonymous.

In the six months we'd been together, he tried to cater to her, but, like myself, it could be overwhelming. Rose would ask us to do things we were uncomfortable with, and Tony and I would be adamant about not proceeding with her demands. But Wren would go behind our backs and do it, anyway.

Me, I barely tolerated Rose. Everything about her set off my barely-there patience. Her voice was like nails across a chalkboard, and she needed to be involved in every aspect of our lives. It drove me insane. One day when I tried to placate her by allowing her to join us at our monthly company meeting, she derailed the meeting and tried to change our minds about some of our business plans. That was the first and last time Rose was allowed in our building. I made sure Wren understood that. The only good thing she brought to our relationship was she was good at getting us the latest gossip around town.

I gathered my things from my tiny office and headed toward the lobby to leave for the day. After six years, someone still had a hold on me, I thought as I passed the front desk clerk who loved the scent of either citrus or vanilla but never a combination of the scents. She brought a new scented item to work every week, which made the only time I came to work a pain in the ass. It was as if she purposefully wanted to annoy me.

The building was nestled in with the shopping centers of Studio

City, slightly nestled off Laurel Grove Road. I drove that day because I wanted to take the long way home to clear my busy mind. Driving through the colorful shopping centers and looming palm trees until the road turned into the comfy subdivisions along the way to the Hills had always been my favorite route. My mind continuously roamed to a place I hated to remember. It was that one voice that kept me crazed almost ninety-five percent of the time. That "what if" voice that kept drawing me back to six years ago, when I stupidly gave six months of my soul to someone who I barely—scratch that—didn't know. Every night we were together, we stayed up, and I foolishly told her about my life just for her to give us nothing in return. The shit still haunted me even six years later. But what could I expect when I couldn't even see her entire face since she never took off her mask?

That was my fault for being too trusting. *Idiota[1]*.

I won't make the same mistake twice. So, I stepped back and let the guys be in charge for once.

And now I live with the reminder of her like some teenager almost every day. Everything that reminds me of her sets me off. It pissed me off.

I was fucking disgusted by the time I arrived home, which I shared with Tony and Wren, and stomped up the marble stairs to my bedroom. I prepared for a miserable time that night because of the dinner. I headed to the shower to relieve myself before Rose could get any ideas.

I shuddered.

Walking through my black and white themed bathroom, I headed for the black-tiled oversized shower. As I stepped into the hot water, I filled my hand with body wash and grabbed my cock. My mind, the stupid part of my brain, automatically drifted to the first night with Kitty. Her small brown hand that could barely wrap around my cock, her wide-eyed stare when she realized how big I was, and the look she

---

1   Idiota- Idiot

gave me when I was deep inside her pussy.

Shit.

I quickened the stroke on my cock as I squeezed and teased my thick base until my balls squeezed, and the hot eruption of cum ran down my hands and into the drain as I remembered the sweet, salty taste of Kitty's pussy. Her citrus lavender scent that engulfed me every time we spooned.

I leaned onto the black-and-white marble tile wall under the showerhead and stood there. The water drenched my whole body, and I swiped my long, curly hair out of my eyes. I looked down at my semi-hard cock and sighed. I got out of the shower with my towel wrapped around my trim waist as I sat on the bed and listened to Tony and Wren arrive and get ready for our dinner date with Rose.

The next part was something I loathed. I had become accustomed to it because it was the only way I could get a good release. I felt like a user, and I hated that feeling.

I sent a quick message to Tony, and in five minutes, he arrived in nothing but his typical black skinny jeans, no shirt, and his black piercings.

I shook my head. Tony was the only person who could help finish me off because his mouth reminded me of Kitty's. Tony already knew what I needed as he dropped to his knees in front of me, removed my towel, and I grabbed the back of his head with my hand. I pushed him to the base of my aching cock and thought about how fucking amazing it was when Wren taught Kitty how to suck dick properly.

I pictured her the first time she had the balls to do it. Her eyes observed every tic in my muscles and jaw to see if she was doing it right. Her soft whimpers were like a massage against my cock. I slammed into Tony's wet mouth repeatedly as he took my abuse. When I remembered Kitty's need to kiss the tip whenever I pulled out of her mouth, I yelled her name out like a lunatic. I felt my ball sack tighten, and I emptied the last of my cum. Tony swallowed it all as I pulled him off my cock with a pop.

Fucking embarrassing, even after all this time.

"I-I'm sorry, Tony." I looked at the Jean-Michel Basquiat painting with guilty tears in my eyes. I hated that I felt like I used Tony. He deserved better than my weak sorry.

"It's okay." Tony smiled as if we were talking about the weather.

Tony walked out of the room as I slipped onto the bed. As I looked at my soft dick, I got angry again. I folded my arms together, thinking I shouldn't have had to go through it. I had been with other women after Kitten, but I always felt disgusted afterward, as if I had cheated. I didn't understand any of it, to be honest. But I kept putting on a blank face and pushing on.

Even though life kept power kicking my ass into the next week.

After I got dressed and headed downstairs, I heard the dreaded doorbell. I tried to put on the best front for Wren's sake because it would be a long night with her. Someone, probably Wren, let her in, and I immediately had to suck in a deep breath before she drowned me in her sweet perfume. She wore it like a second skin and wanted everyone in Los Angeles to smell it. I prepared myself for her intrusion into our home.

I walked into our navy blue dining area and stopped. That was my first mistake. I felt Rose jump on my back, her pointed nails digging into my shoulders as she clung to me. Luckily, the white marble tile wasn't slippery, or I would be face-first on the floor.

Be nice! Be nice! For Wren's sake, at least.

"Gabby, Baby! I missed you," she squealed in her nasal voice.

I suppressed my sigh and said, "Hello, Rose. You seem to be in a good mood."

"I'm always in a good mood when I'm here with my boys."

I tried to dodge her kiss but was unsuccessful. She kissed me right on the lips, and I fought to keep my emotions in check. Tony, already seated and ready for this night to be over, looked over and smirked. Rose continued her attack as she set her eyes on Tony. She leaped into his lap and kissed him.

"Tony the bear!" she yelled as Tony's smirk slid off his face and slid onto mine. "I've missed you, baby. We should cut out some time for me, you, and Wren tonight. After dinner."

Our housekeeper entered the dining room and announced dinner would be served in the next five minutes. I sat across from the lovesick couple, Wren and Rose. An irritated Tony sat next to me, and I'm sure we looked like the poster children for the forlorn crew.

Our housekeeper placed plates in front of us, and I concentrated on my food as if it were the most critical thing in the world. Rose and Wren were speaking as if the world would end if they stopped. Wren, of course, had opened his mouth and told her about our plan.

"So, we're planning on buying a record label," Wren spilled.

I looked at Tony, whose face pinched.

"Oh my God, really? Which one? Are you sure?" Rose asked as she nearly sent her plate to the floor.

"It's, um… Gabe, which one was it again?" Wren turned to me and asked.

I hated to talk about business opportunities before we solidified them, and Wren knew that. It was one of my pet peeves.

I sighed, and I gritted my teeth. "In The Loop records."

"Oh, I've heard of them before. My dad had a commercial deal with one of their artists. What was her name?" Rose stuck her tongue out as she racked her brain. "Oh yeah, it was Jasmine Grant. She was so quiet and seemed uncomfortable doing the commercial. Daddy told me he wouldn't work with her again. You know what? I don't think you should do it."

Jesus!

Tony and I sighed at the same time. I pinched my nose and bit my tongue. I couldn't sit there much longer as my Rose patience had run out.

"Why, babes?" Wren asked.

"Bad vibes and all. I'm psycho, you know." She nodded.

"You mean psychic, right?" I asked as I stared at her.

"Oh right, Gabby baby." She gave us her maniacal laugh. "I'm so sorry."

"Yeah, right," I gave her a pointed look. "We're going to buy it. We decided on it already."

I knew I was being vindictive, but her placing herself in our business irked me.

"Trust me, don't do it. Listen to me, Wren." She gathered him in her arms.

"You know what? Why don't we revisit it, Gabe? Tony?" Wren looked at me.

I wanted to hit him in the head. He never told her no or declined her advice.

"No, we're bidding on it, and we're going Wednesday to meet and learn the ropes from Mr. Brine at his office," I stated.

"Fine, Gabby baby. Can I be—"

I cut her off. "No."

"What? I hadn't even finished asking my question. Tony, baby, please?"

"No, it's not possible to allow you to work for us. It's not good to mix business and pleasure." Tony is always saving the day.

"Fine, but I'm fantastic at makeup." She pouted. Literally, I wondered if I was indeed talking with a twenty-eight-year-old and not a thirteen-year-old.

"You're being very modest, babes. You're amazing with makeup," Wren cooed.

Okay, I had had enough. I needed to leave before I told Wren to grab hold of his dignity. I knew we were struggling to find a partner, but we weren't that badly off. I excused myself and headed back to my room… to sulk and stew in annoyance. Everyone knew that was my norm after our dates because she had pissed me off.

If I could just find someone to fuck, that wouldn't turn my stomach inside out. I could survive, but that's easier said than done.

Wednesday morning came faster than I expected, and to be honest, I was nervous. This would be something out of my comfort zone, but Tony and I were excited to see how it would benefit us. Wren, of course, was content to take up sides with Rose. It was like she bewitched him, and we couldn't remove his head from her bony ass. And I wished I could have said I was exaggerating. Rose and Wren were holed up in his room and were cosplaying rabbits from Monday until last night.

Unfortunately, Tony and I had to hear her screaming because Wren didn't understand the concept of closing a door.

I rolled my eyes and shook my head as we walked into the spacious office. Everyone had their own semi-private offices. The walls were painted a soft white with a blue carpet that had music notes etched into it. The employees had opened the shades, and it bathed the entire office in sunlight. It must have been a busy day because everyone was shuffling around in droves. As we continued to move further into the buzzing office, we found Mr. Brine speaking with a couple of employees.

"Gabe, Wren, and Tony, nice to see you guys. How are your families?" Mr. Brine warbled.

Mr. Brine had on a bright yellow shirt and white cargo pants, making him hard to miss. He puzzled me because he was too relaxed for work. Mr. Brine looked good for sixty-five. He was a little round in the middle and shorter than Wren. But he kept in line with all the younger employees.

"Good afternoon, Mr. Brine. Everyone's good. We're ready to

dive deep into your business," Tony declared, and we all nodded.

Mr. Brine wasted no time going through his business. His voice was peppered with his southern accent as it echoed throughout the office. You could tell he was passionate about his profession, and he took it to heart. He gave us his speech, which I'd heard a million times, about how he started his business, carried his family from Nashville to LA, and lifted his family from the brink of bankruptcy. When my pa and I had lunch with him, he never failed to mention it to us. We would just sit and nod every time.

Mr. Brine's office was like him, big and full of life. His light green and bright white walls popped, bringing color into the office from the outside. His wood desk was planted in the center of the room. The desk was about the size of a small bathroom. He sat with his hand on his stomach as he continued to speak about his business. After thirty minutes, Mr. Brine got us out of the bright office and took us on a tour.

What I loved about his company was everyone seemed to be closely knit. I noticed he stopped to talk and introduce us to everyone, including the cleaning lady for the building, Ms. May. She had been with the company for over twenty years and was adamant Mr. Brine was the best boss she'd ever had. We took her at her word.

"Mr. Brine, do you know when Ms. Grant is coming in? I brought something for her family," she asked.

"You know Jasmine has a mind of her own. She's supposed to meet with me soon about some business matters. But I will make sure she stops by to see you." He gave her a nod, and we moved on.

"Ja mata ne[2], Mr. Brine," she called out. Wren returned the parting phase in Japanese, and they bowed.

"Jasmine Grant is very beloved around here. When she retired, we lost a piece of our family, but I understood," he said as he continued

____

2 Well, see you later in Japanese

to make his rounds.

"Well, we can't wait to meet her. If you and Ms. May love her, then we know we will as well. Plus, who wouldn't want to meet the infamous Jasmine Grant." Tony smiled.

He led us to all the artist's personal offices. Mr. Brine noted he wanted every artist to feel like they had an area of their own in the office. Every artist had a small or medium size room, while Ms. Grant had the most prominent corner office with floor-to-ceiling windows that wrapped around the backside of her office. She'd recently renovated her office, it seemed, because it was modernized with recent white modern furniture and silver accessories. As I admired her portrait from a magazine shoot, I felt drawn to her as if I knew her from somewhere.

Maybe in some past life.

I shrugged off the thought and followed Mr. Brine. After seeing the busy common area and a few conversations later, we were back in his oversized office. My phone vibrated, and I fished it out of my pocket. It was a text from Michael, our CFO at our other primary business. I had asked him to crunch the numbers for me on Monday, confirming that everything looked good.

Sadly, nothing was ever simple for us.

Mr. Brine had told us he had several offers on the table and that if we wanted it, then we had to bid high, which was not a problem since money wasn't an issue.

Three hours later, we parted ways and told him he would have an offer by tonight. We had already discussed keeping everyone except for the CEO. We had someone in mind but needed to clarify some details.

Tony and, eventually, Wren were all excited.

"Okay, Wren Costa, chair of the board of directors of In The Loop records. How do you like your new title?" I asked as I amped him up.

"Actually, it has a fantastic ring to it," Wren noted as he smiled like a goofball. "Did you see that picture of Jasmine Grant? Her breasts are amazing. You know how I've been feeling about breasts lately."

We laughed.

"So, you're saying my boobs aren't big enough for you?" Tony acted hurt as he bunched his nonexistent boobs together.

I rolled my eyes. Some things never change. Tony and Wren will make a joke out of anything.

As we exited the parking lot, I glanced back at the medium-sized brown building that stood out from the glamorous shops on Melrose Avenue. I smiled and silently prayed for us to win the bid. We filled the car ride back with laughter and light conversations as usual when we were together. I hated to spoil the fun, but I wanted to bring up something that seemed important for all of us to figure out.

"Wren, we have to stop telling Rose about our business affairs. She could be a liability if things go south with her. Plus, I think we should stop seeing her. She is not a good fit for our family," I explained.

"Here we go." Wren had a pinched look on his face, and he went quiet. "You don't like her because she doesn't remind you of—"

I cut him off before he annoyed me. "No, it has nothing to do with that. Rose is not a good fit for me personally. How about you, Tony?"

"Wren already knows my objections to Rose. She's the reason I won't sleep in his room anymore." Tony rolled his eyes. "She's insufferable, and you're only dating her because you're afraid of losing yet another girl and another opportunity to start a family. Even though we could adopt."

I pulled into the garage. Wren jumped out before I could park the car and slammed the door so hard the car shook. He was about to enter the house when he turned back and opened my door.

"Not everything is about you, Gabe. I like Rose. She is kind in her own way… and we have a love for fashion. She's okay with me."

"You're okay with having an okay relationship. But I'm not," Tony stated, and he appeared frustrated.

"She's coming between you and Tony as well as you and me, Wren. Is she worth it? We can find someone else." I stated.

"And what if I don't want to start over? It seems like every time we make progress with someone, we regress." He sighed. "We will never find anyone."

"It will be okay, Wren. Let's talk about how we'll discuss breaking it to her." Tony gave him a small smile.

Wren seemed as if he were contemplating taking our advice. He shook his head.

"I'm not breaking up with her, and that's the end of that, and fuck you guys." Wren left us there.

Tony and I sat there for a minute. Wren had done a lot to prolong her being with us because he wanted to pretend to be happy. But we had to put an end to this sometime soon. I couldn't speak for Tony, but I was tired of pretending to be happy, and if shit didn't change, then maybe it was time to rethink the arrangement we made. That pained me to even think.

"I back you one hundred percent. We need to break up with Rose. It's not fair to her or us. She deserves to be happy," Tony concluded as we headed up the stairs.

As we turned towards our rooms and turned in for the night, I sent a group text to Mr. Brine, Tony, and Wren, telling him we were prepared to offer two billion for the company.

You have to spend money to make money.

Chapter 9

Jasmine

"Oh shit, you're so tight, Jassie. You like this, don't you?" Gregory ranted as he gripped my hips like I was a Kawasaki bike.

One…

Greg changed from a snail's pace to a rabid horny dog as he fucked me from the back.

Well, tried to fuck me. If this is what you called it…

Two…

I made the same tired and played-out attempt of a moan that signaled I was about to "come".

"Yes, baby. I'm about to come all over your dick." I cringed deep inside when I uttered this.

This is what my life has resorted to.

Three…

Greg squeezed my breasts roughly. I was sure he was trying to squeeze the tissue out of them as he held on to them for dear life.

Four…

Greg stiffened as his sweaty body stilled against my back. I gagged. Luckily, he couldn't see that I contorted my face or the number of times I rolled my eyes.

I faked another moan and yelled, "I'm coming!" He had about one more stroke, and then he was a goner.

Five…

He squealed his release. He sounded like someone stuffed a hog down his throat and left it there. I tried not to sigh, even though it was on the tip of my tongue.

Just pitiful.

Everything was routine with Greg. So much that I already knew once his alligator-like hands left my body, he would roll onto his back. Then he would yank off the condom with that sickening wet pop sound and tie the end. Sure enough, his side of the bed dipped, and I heard the condom before he threw it on the floor.

Absolutely disgusting.

That wasn't even the worst part. Greg would always reach down, grab his boxers, and wipe his dick off. I heard him fumbling with cleaning himself, and then he threw the boxers down on the ground with a thump.

He's repulsive. This is the punishment I get.

I sighed and got up to use the bathroom. Every week, it was the same thing. Greg woke up horny in the middle of the night, lasted around five seconds, and then it was over. He came, and I was left with a second-degree burn in my vagina. Thankfully, he liked to do it on his side because he had "old hips." His words, not mine. It was a damn shame because he was fine as hell but had the personality of a broken cardboard box.

How did my life become this way? Oh yeah, I remember it like yesterday…

As I thought back, I remembered how foolish I was after waking up with a bad back from sleeping on my marble floors that last

Friday with the guys. My mother told me to come home after I told her about stopping everything at once and my need for a quiet vacation. I should have said I was at home, but I was lost. Next thing I knew, I was on my private plane and headed to Nashville faster than you could say stop. I thought I would be okay if I returned home for a week or two, but it never came.

It started a month after I left my home in Los Angeles. My stomach churned, which turned into me emptying my stomach contents almost every hour. I became so weak that I ended up flying back to Los Angeles and going to see my doctor, Dr. Weston. She was one of the top black female doctors in Los Angeles, and I was more at peace with her than anyone else except for that day. She had me run a bunch of tests and walked back into the room, smiling from ear to ear. I stared at her in shock when she said the words.

"You're pregnant, Jasmine. Congratulations! I can give you a prescription for some prenatal vitamins, and then you have to follow up with…" She trailed off as she looked at her computer. "Dr. Johns, your OBGYN."

I couldn't quite understand. So, I stared at Dr. Weston as I hoped she would tell me it was a joke.

"Earth to Jasmine," she waved her perfectly manicured hands in front of my face. "Come in, Jasmine." She laughed, but nothing about the situation was funny.

Suddenly, my mind worked again, and I blurted out, "You're joking, right? I can't be pregnant. How?"

Logically, I knew *how* I got pregnant, but everything felt rushed, and I couldn't comprehend anything. But, of course, my doctor had jokes. "Well, I'm no doctor, but it starts with—"

I held my hand up to cut her off abruptly. Not because I was trying to be rude but because I got the urge to throw up. I barely made it to the bathroom before I heaved up the soup that I'd had thirty minutes ago. When I returned to the room, she was concerned that I might have hyperemesis gravidarum, which is intractable vomiting related to my hormone levels. She told me I needed to go to the hospital for treatment. She pleaded for me to take the ambulance there, but I told her my chauffeur, Mr. Jackson, would take me. I may have been still in shock, but once I sat in my seat, everything started to tumble out my mouth. Thank God Mr. Jackson was on the receiving end because if it were anyone else, my news would have been sold to the Gossip sites.

He simply stated, "I will look after my God-grandchildren," as he redirected his route to head to the hospital.

He was such a sweet man, but I cursed him out in my head. Honestly, I'm thankful he was there and not someone else that didn't care about me. Mr. Jackson got me to the hospital in record time as he swerved through the LA roads. I had to grab onto the "Oh Shit" handles above the door. When we arrived at the hospital, he parked the car and went with me to the hospital. Once inside, Bruno, my bodyguard, who had driven in a separate car, was waiting for me at the reception desk. He had a deep frown on his face until he saw me and gave me his signature half-smile as he greeted me. The hospital staff were in a frenzy as they ushered me to the celebrity maternity suite. Mr. Jackson and Bruno fussed over me until I got settled into my suite and changed into my hospital gown.

If I wasn't embarrassed enough, I had to call my mom, whom I heard hiccup, and sigh through the phone as if they were right in front of me. I guess she started her winddown time early today.

"Look at what you caused, Jasmine," her words were slightly slurred. "You're pregnant, and you don't have a man!"

"It's not the end of the world, Mom." I tried my best to appease her.

"No, but you just made your life a lot harder than it should be. Are you going to find the father?"

I chewed on my lip as I thought about her question.

"No, truthfully, I don't know if I could find them if I wanted to," I said.

My mom just muttered, "What a mess."

After five minutes of calming her down or waiting until whatever she had drunk kicked in, I was finally able to get her off the phone.

When Allison got there, I wanted to jump out the bed and hug her, but I opted to wait until she reached the bed. When she did, I hugged and kissed her. She had bought me some things from my house so I wouldn't have to wear the hospital gown all the time and my tablet. I didn't give her a second to unpack my things for me when I started to relay everything that happened, and she just dropped into the seat next to me and gawked at me. When the shock wore off, she asked me what I wanted to do about the baby and that I should keep it, but she would support me in any way possible. I knew she had a deep love for kids and wanted to have a big family herself, so even thinking about abortions was a major thing for her. I looked at her and asked if she was senile before I could stop myself since this wasn't a time for joking. That earned me a pointed stare. The thought had never even crossed my mind to have an abortion. I knew the risk. But as I sat there with my best friend— I took comfort in knowing she would support me even if her views didn't align with my choice.

I'd made my bed, and now I had to sleep in it.

But other than the initial shock of being pregnant, deep down in the corner of the dark part of my mind where I kept my time with Gabe, Tony, and Wren, a deep peace settled inside of me as I knew that I would have something permanent to remember them by, not just fleeting memories. A gift that I wasn't expecting, but I was highly grateful for it.

Yes, I knew it sounded self-obsessed, but I wouldn't apologize for it, and yes, I should have contacted them, but I didn't think I should saddle them with my responsibilities. I would be okay with a baby. *If only it was that easy.*

I was amped up about the baby until Dr. Johns hit me with the biggest news when she came to visit me in the hospital for my prenatal visit. She told me I was having twins, and I nearly passed out in the hospital bed. When I received the two black and white sonogram pictures, it was like a dam had broken, and the little makeup I decided to throw on that day to make me feel better was ruined as I sobbed and wiped at my face. I knew from those pictures I would never love anyone or do anything for anyone as much as I would for them. As my need to protect and nurture them tripled.

My pregnancy left me in a trance as I tried to work out the next steps in our future. For the first three months, I stayed in and out of the hospital as I became a human projectile, as Allison and I coined the nickname for me. I would wake up, and within thirty minutes, I was vomiting whatever liquid my poor body had inside of me, which wasn't a lot. Allison would be so scared that she abandoned her then fiancé to stay with me almost every night. When I threw up more than four times in one day, Allison would rush me to the hospital. The nurses on the unit would take bets on when I would show up again.

My mom would call me every hour, surprisingly. I think my mom becoming a grandmother changed her—a bit. She stopped drinking excessively and started therapy during my second trimester. To Allison and I's shock, it actually worked for her. When she came to stay with me to help me out because I ditched the nausea for heartburn. I became a walking ad for those chalky calcium tabs and coconut water. While I sat around the house, my mom busied herself with cleaning my house because it was too dusty, which I found hard to believe since I had a maid, and buying every toy she could find online. I wanted to complain that she was already spoiling them, but when her brown eyes sparkled, I couldn't bring myself to bust her bubble.

It was a little after my third trimester had started and my mother had to go back to Nashville for a church event that I realized that I missed her like crazy. Allison was only able to come over after work, and I was left at home. I was left during the day to hobble down to my kitchen and ransack the pantry for snacks. I gained almost twenty pounds when they left me alone. Soon, I was just a small ball that would huff and puff whenever I had to walk anywhere. The private nurse my mom insisted on getting while she was away would just shake her head and say, "Ms. Grant, you're eating just to eat," as she fussed with the equipment she brought over. She reminded me of my mom when she fussed.

When Teodoro and Tristano Grant were born, it was the happiest moment of my life. As I looked down into their beautiful little smushed faces, I couldn't help but think someone had given me the best gift. *The perfect names for my perfect little boys.* I wanted to start their name with their dad's initials, so they could have some connection to him.

When I got a good look at them, I knew I made the right choice. Their heads were full of thick black hair that surrounded their chubby little faces. *That's why I had heartburn twenty-four seven.* I held my breath until they opened those big light green eyes. They were Tony's twins through and through. Teo and Tris wailed when the nurse removed them from me to clean them up. But she didn't even flinch as she carted them off to the nursery.

My mom's eyes popped wide open when she saw her grandchildren were the color of warm ivory. She stood there for about five minutes and shook her head. Of course, she had to add that I needed to put them in the sun for a while. I thought I might have bitten through my lip that day. Of course, she apologized later and said it was wrong to mention that. I just forgave her because I knew she was just surprised.

You know what I learned? That postpartum was a bitch.

My postpartum depression was no joke. The first month, I walked around in a daze as I tended to the twins. I neglected the things I loved to do, such as my spa days and painting. Allison would pull me out of the house, but I barely had enough energy to get out of the car when we reached our destination. We would have to turn back and go back home.

It wasn't until my mom found me standing at the kitchen sink, water softly dripping from the overflowed sink as I stared out the windows that lined my kitchen, that she, thankfully, stepped in to help me as she pushed me to go get therapy. It took almost six months before I started to feel like myself again. I thanked my mom for everything she had done for me – until she introduced me to Gregory.

Gregory Simmons attended my mom's church in Nashville, and she introduced us one Sunday evening a couple of months after I left LA for an extended vacation in Tennessee with her. My mom complained about how she wanted me and the boys, who were just seven months old, to attend church with her, and I gave in after several failed attempts to convince her otherwise. It wasn't until after the service, when I had to search for her, that I found her speaking passionately with Greg. Their heads were bowed as they whispered to each other. I should have known she was up to something.

Greg was gorgeous with his dark brown eyes, faded haircut, chiseled jaw, and willowy body. He wore a blue suit that matched his smooth, dark brown skin and blue penny loafers.

I mean, who wore penny loafers anymore? I digress.

But he was kind, so when he asked me on a date, I gave him a chance.

When we got home, my mother pleaded with me to give him a chance for the boys' sake, even though I had already agreed to anyway. But I let her believe she had some say in it, which, in the end, she did.

On our first date, I realized it was a "hell no" for me within the first ten minutes. Greg talked about his job as an accountant like it was the only source of happiness in his life. When I tried to switch the conversation to anything other than accounting, he returned with something tied to the profession. I had never seen anyone tie drawing and accountant duties together, but Greg did. That's how our typical "dates" went, although I would call it more of my free food night. *Did I mention how I love food?*

Six months later, Greg proposed. I thought it was a joke, but he was serious. I always imagined that when the time arrived, we would have a quick engagement, with Greg just buying a cheap ring and handing it to me so I could put it on my finger. That was the plan we came up with when he moved to LA six months later. But that was wishful thinking on my part. Greg invited everyone we knew to my mom's home for a dinner party, and when the time arrived, I stood stuck like a deer in headlights in the middle of my mother's tiny brown living room with my then thirteen-month-old twins clutched to each side of my legs. My mom and everyone had all but gloated in the tiny space, and I felt the remainder of the cocktail shrimp making its way back up my throat as I hurriedly choked out the yes so I could find the bathroom before I threw up. For the remainder of the night, I walked around with a fake wide smile to match my fake being excited for the engagement mood for the rest of the night, which made my cheeks, jaw, and brain hurt for the next couple of days. Every time I would bring up any issues with how he was handling our arrangement, Greg would mention how it worked out for both of us and how I was overreacting. He would harp on, saying, "You would get a stable man in the home for the boys, and I will have the family I deserve. Just because we have an arrangement doesn't mean it can't be fun for us."

Fun for who? I wished I asked.

How could I win? By delaying the inevitable since then. Every year or mention of a wedding, I either wasn't feeling good or had to travel somewhere for an extended period of time. *Petty, I know.* Greg would ball up his fist and storm off to his musty office every time we approached the subject. I knew what I was doing was wrong and wasting time, but I just couldn't bring myself to sign the papers or start planning anything just yet.

The boys' peppermint infuser caused me to sneeze, which stopped all of those old memories from running rampant. Nothing good would ever come out of bringing up old news anyway. They were long gone, and I have left them in the past. The only things that mattered now were my babies as I watched them sleep, wild like their father. Tris had one of his legs off the side of the bed, and the other leg was straight. Teo mirrored his brother. Even in sleep, they acted alike. I smiled as I lay down in between their beds. We had tons of room for them to have their own bedrooms, but they were adamant about sharing a room.

When I looked at them, I knew everything would be alright. I usually retreated to the boys' room after I cleaned up because it was the only place I found peace away from my current situation. The twins were why I stuck it out and stayed with Greg's arrangement. He tried to be a good father to my babies, and that was all that mattered to me. For the past five years, Greg had helped me raise the boys. At first, they wouldn't allow Greg near them. It was a tough battle since they would run the other way when Greg would appear. But when they turned two, they became more used to having Greg around. He started to help them with their homework, taking them to school when I couldn't and playing with them when they allowed it. My boys were happy, and that sustained my personal happiness. That was the only thing that kept me going all this time, and I was fine with that as I finally fell asleep with Tris and Teo on both of my sides.

The following day, I got up and buzzed around the kitchen. I made cereal for the boys and oatmeal for Greg. I thanked the person who made instant anything because I could burn water.

"Mom, Teo said Mr. Greg is taking us to school today." Tris shoved a spoonful of his cereal in his mouth.

I shook my head. My kids refused to call Greg Dad after they saw him grab me in the pantry when he thought no one was around. I stood there for what felt like an eternity as I processed what had happened. My hands that gripped the shelves hurt, and I had trembled so hard that the bottles of water on the shelf shook slightly. After that horrible event, I lied, saying we were playing around and that Greg didn't hurt me. But I didn't think they believed me, and that became another setback in their bonding with Greg. It took almost six months, when the twins turned two, for them to warm back up to him. Since then, Greg had become a somewhat decent stepdad to them. Every Saturday, I found them going out to play together, which would be the only time I would smile at those moments.

"Yes, Mr. Greg is taking you to school today," I told them, ready for the fight.

Tris pushed his long hair out of his tiny face and said, "Mom, we wanted you to take us today."

Greg flopped down in the seat after he rushed down. He landed a kiss on the corner of my mouth, and I bit my lower lip as my mouth instantly turned downward. "Good morning, my love."

"Good morning, Greg. I made your favorite oatmeal," I told him. Greg started calling me "love" out of the blue a couple of months ago. I kept reminding him this wasn't going to be a marriage of love but convenience. He'd shrugged and said he would change that one day at a time.

Good luck!

"Thank you." He smiled. "How are my boys today?"

"We're good, Mr. Greg," Tris grumbled as he looked down into his cereal.

"It's Dad, guys. Come on," Greg pleaded.

"We like Mr. Greg better," Tris stated.

Oh God, I wanted to laugh, but I kept my face straight and said, "Boys, what did I tell you about being rude? Do I have to take away your games from you again?"

"NO!" they shouted in sync.

"Alright, apologize now."

"Sorry, Greg," they mumbled. I raised my eyebrow at them. "Sorry, Mr. Greg." They quickly corrected themselves. They knew better.

I didn't raise them to be rude to anyone, especially adults, even if it was Greg. I didn't want to force them, so I let them call him Mr. Greg until they were ready to call him Dad.

"Did you guys pack your stuff? Remember, we're going on our family trip to Amalfi for the weekend."

"Yes, we're ready," Tris answered for the both of them as they abandoned their breakfast and clambered to gather their things for school.

Once Greg returned, he went straight to his home office.

Meanwhile, I got to work.

Besides the personal stuff, I had been doing really well. Allison had booked me some interviews over the years. I had two movies that came out about my life, which was odd because I didn't know the individuals who made the movie, but I still benefited. A win in my book. I still did a concert here and there if I felt up to it, which hadn't happened in a while since I had the boys. I hated being away from them. Plus, I kept them out of the limelight because I wanted to protect their privacy and give them a normal childhood.

My real estate side business continued to thrive even after I sold some properties when the value skyrocketed. The company was worth over two billion dollars. That meant I was a multi-billionaire. I loved the sound of it. I still hadn't told my mother about the business. You could call me a coward, but I preferred not to have my mom in every aspect of my life. I'd already given her access to my relationship and career and look at how that turned out for me. When she came to me about the possibility of investing in real estate, my eyes popped out of my head. But I told her I would have to think about it because I didn't need the money, but as good faith to her, I brought her a new home in Brentwood, Tennessee, that she rented out instead of moving into. I finally agreed, and we had a smaller business together that we hadn't done anything with yet.

Anyway, I was on to bigger and better things.

I struggled to figure out how to increase my net worth when I realized I needed to change my mindset. So, when the opportunity to purchase the record label arrived, I threw my bid in. The plan was to place myself on the board of directors. It must have been destiny because this was the perfect timing and opportunity. It meant not only would I own my masters, which I hadn't realized I didn't own, but I would have over ten established artists doing well, and I wouldn't have to do the legwork. Nothing more than an "okay, I'll approve that" or a "no, I won't" was required. I submitted my highest and best offer on Wednesday, and Mr. Brine said he was waiting for another offer to come in and then he would let me know.

So that was why I treated everyone to a weekend in Italy for Thanksgiving. We would enjoy the blue water and the fresh air. It would take my mind off the offer and give the boys some bonding time with Greg. I accidentally stubbed my little toe on my bed, lost in my thoughts, and cursed which sent the water down the wrong way. I threw my hand over my mouth as I spat out the water that I was drinking all over my luggage.

In the back of my mind, I could hear Greg, "Oh, you were just watering the luggage," as he would have laughed while I stared at him like he'd lost his mind.

I rolled my eyes as I mentally beat myself up. He was taking over my mind.

This is what dreams are made of.

I lounged on one of the chaise chairs on my yacht, which I'd named Celeste. Allison thought it wasn't right to name it after the club, but the club gave me so much more than a sexual outlet.

I soaked up the sun in my two-piece Chanel bathing suit and was minding my business when Debbie Downer, aka Greg, waltzed over to me.

"Babe, maybe you should put on something more modest. The boys are here. You don't want them to get the wrong impression, do you?" Greg asked.

I bit my tongue. Greg had been irritating me since we left. First, the helicopter, which we took to the boat to avoid the paparazzi, was too loud and too small. Then the boat was too large, and we'd spent too much money. Mind you, it was my personal yacht, not his. Finally, it was the bathing suit.

Greg sometimes reminded me of my mother, except she wasn't that bad.

"Greg, my sons won't think nothing of it. Look at them." I pointed to Tris and Teo, who were engrossed in their Nintendo Switches. "They're worried about their games and playing around. You should do the same."

He cocked his head and shook it before he disappeared into the cabin. He probably went to tell my mother.

Christ, give me strength! I don't want to fight while I'm on vacation.

I pinched the bridge of my nose and rubbed my eyes.

I have to make it through this weekend. Then I can go back home and hide from Greg.

I wasn't going to let the Debbie Downer take away the view of the sunset. As I called the boys over to watch it with me, they wrestled to get close to me. At least I had my babies here to enjoy the trip with, and I kissed the top of their heads and basked in the orange and red colors dipping behind the Italian green mountains.

"The chef said dinner is ready, Jas," Allison yelled from the open door of the dining room.

The boys heard the word dinner, and they flew into the dining area. Luckily, I had gotten the best chef in Italy for the weekend. As I hurried up to change into something warm, I ensured the boys washed up since they told Greg they wanted me to do it.

At least I was trying.

Everyone sat in the makeshift dining room for our Thanksgiving dinner. Allison and Wayne, her husband of three years, were there. My mom, Greg's parents, and a couple of friends. Well, his friends, I should say. They were like him. The boys sat with my mom while I sat between Greg and his parents.

Yay, for me... not.

"Everyone's ready!" Chef Russo yelled as she came through the door with her assistant, pushing the cart filled with food. She was beautiful, with long midnight hair, delicate features, and a thick figure like me. So, I knew the food would be good.

"We're ready for fooooodd!" the boys yelled together. My mom gave them a look, and then she kissed them. I shook my head. Back in the day, she would have pinched me for that type of behavior.

"Oh!" Bethany turned and stared at the boys.

I looked at her, and she had a funny look on her face. "Is something wrong?"

"It's... nothing." She cleared her throat and said, "I hope everyone enjoys tonight's meal."

She didn't wait for a response as she turned on her flats and headed back to the kitchen.

I didn't like that at all, but no one else seemed to notice the strange interaction but me, so I let it go.

The boys danced while they ate their food, and I had to scold them. Afterward, the food and conversation flowed throughout the night's courses.

The chef glanced at the boys several times throughout the night. I chalked it up to the boys appearing more like their dad than any of us. I made a mental note to ensure we didn't hire her on our next trip.

I was already writing the email to Allison in my head when I heard my phone ding and Greg knocked on the glass, simultaneously, which signaled he had a speech to make. I wondered what the hell he was up to.

"Attention, everyone. I, we, have an announcement to make before we head off to bed."

We had an "announcement". Okay. Everyone's eyes turned to us. The boys raised their dark eyebrows.

"My fiancé and I have set a date for September of next year.I thought it would be really nifty if we celebrated Jasmine's birthday and our wedding together."

Oh, fuck me sideways!

I was perturbed. My fingers found comfort in rubbing my temple, and it felt like my brain was going to break through my skull.

"And we plan on adding to our small family. We want to give the boys some sisters or brothers. Whichever God chooses fit for us," he beamed.

The fucker beamed. I never agreed to a date. I had been putting it off for over four years now. The boys looked on quietly with their tiny mouths agape. My mom leaped up and cheered. I had to wipe away the tears that fell before anyone noticed. I grabbed the half-empty flute of champagne and chugged it in hopes that it would calm me down.

I took several breaths so I could focus on not snapping at Greg. His mom leaned over and hugged me from her chair. Her floral perfume burned my throat as I inhaled the scent. Finally, after five minutes, the boys were falling asleep at the table, and Allison took them to their room.

I didn't even know where to begin.

Everyone, minus Allison, congratulated me and prayed that I got pregnant quickly. Welp, thank God, Dr. Jones, and I finally found a birth control I tolerated. I happily told her to give me at least enough refills for the year. Being stuck with him beyond the boys turning eighteen made me want to scratch my eyeballs out.

But my night couldn't go out with just one bang. Nope, that would have been too easy for me. Once I got sick of the congratulations, I glanced at the unread message, and my heart sank into the pit of my stomach.

Mr. Brine

Good evening, Jasmine. I'm so sorry to bother you during your vacation. But I wanted to let you know that you've been outbid, and I went with the other buyers for the label. But I know you'll love the new owners.

My vision became blurry, and my lungs threatened to explode. If I didn't leave this room now, I would have a panic attack in front of everyone. I excused myself while everyone chatted and headed to the kitchen for a bottle of wine. The chef was cleaning up, and she looked like she wanted to speak but must have seen the twisted look on my face and decided against it.

I headed to the bathroom tub and drank straight from the bottle. That was where I took my birth control pill and washed it down with the wine. I fell asleep in the tub. It was the second best place to sleep besides with my babies.

Except for the backache and the stiff neck, I could have lived without that.

Chapter 10

Jasmine

It'd been a week since we got back to LA. Initially, I'd only wanted to stay the weekend but ended up prolonging the stay until the following Friday. Greg wasn't too pleased with it because he didn't want to be away from work too long. He griped about it until I snapped at him, and he grabbed me by the arm so tightly it left small purple bruises on my upper arm. The boys noticed, but I played it off like I usually did.

I wanted to forget everything, so I spent my days lounging in the sun.

I tanned, the boys burned, and Greg stewed.

You would think he would be nicer to someone who took him out on her yacht.

I had a part to blame in Greg's miserable mood since I cursed him out when everyone returned to the mainland to go home. It wasn't until everyone was asleep the following night that I remembered him pestering me about a date and kids. I shooed him off and told him yes, whatever. My mistake for not taking him seriously or paying attention. I unloaded all my frustration from his announcement and the disappointment of not getting the deal that Mr. Brine preached I was practically a shoo-in for my poor luggage. I was nervous about what this new owner would do when I demanded my masters back. Sometimes, people would rather bleed you dry than give you what you deserve.

I shouldn't worry because one thing about me was that I was a survivor. Even if I had to fight the fuckers for what belonged to me. I deserved what was mine because of the hard work, the pain, and the struggles. They'd see me in court if it came down to it.

Fuck them.

So, I focused on Tris and Teo to get my mind off things. They wanted to go to the science museum downtown, and I almost said no because the thought of me with a wig and all my disguises always annoyed me. I wore them before so I wouldn't be forced to leave anywhere because I was recognized, but that didn't mean I liked wearing them. That's why I left Bruno, my bodyguard since my career started, home —well, didn't mention I was going out is more like it. But I couldn't say no to the boys as I looked into their little faces with their long black eyelashes, and my heart melted. They knew how to get me to say yes. We spent the whole day at the museum. I spent the entire day sweating buckets, the boys running around wildly, and I huffed and puffed around the museum behind them. *The things I did for those boys.* They loved anything technical. I guessed they got that from their dad, too. Me, not so much. I got hives thinking about troubleshooting anything other than my phone.

On our way home, I stopped at the pharmacy for my birth control refill. I kissed the plastic container before slipping it into my purse. Most recently I'd caught Greg trying to slip inside me without a condom. It wasn't that I didn't want any more children, especially when I looked at my sons. I wanted a whole football team, if possible, but I just didn't want them with Greg. I brought up adopting, but Greg said, "My seeds work. So, we don't need to adopt." That was the joke, and he laughed like a goofball afterward.

It was crazy that someone who looked that good had the personality of a squid.

As Friday night approached, I had finished plastering my face with makeup. We had agreed to a double date with Allison and her husband, Wayne, at their favorite restaurant here in the Hills. La Rosa was the Hills' favorite Italian restaurant. Everyone and their mother ate there weekly, and snagging a table was troublesome unless you had some weight to your name.

Allison wasn't too fond of Greg, and she made it known from time to time that my reason for being with him was wrong. I can hear her voice almost like it was yesterday when she told me, "Greg is going to be the death of you." That was right after I worked up the courage to tell her about the engagement. She was right, but I was too invested to turn back by then. So, tonight would most likely be another messy dinner date.

I sighed and entered my custom walk-in closet. I hadn't dressed up in a while, and my closet overflowed with outfits from pre-twins Jasmine and post-twins Jasmine. No longer a size four with my thick thighs, I wore a twelve, and my thick thighs rubbed together. My voice had gotten deeper—I surprised myself when I spoke or sang. I sounded like Barry White at times. My hips were wider, and my breasts grew from barely a B cup to a D cup.

My cup runneth over.

I had the perfect dress for the night. It may have been a bit snug, but I didn't care. As I reached for the white strapless dress, my eye caught the scar from the little bite mark that stayed slightly indented on my skin. It was barely noticeable, but if you looked at it, you could see the teeth marks on the valley of my breasts from Wren, on my thigh from Tony, and one on the shoulder from Gabe. Luckily, the one on my shoulder was covered slightly by my locs and heavy-duty performance makeup. I still couldn't believe I told Greg I got bit by some friends in elementary school during a school play.

I fought to get the little white dress on and zipped it up. After five minutes of contorting my body, I had the dress on. I looked in the mirror and loved it. It fit like a glove. Simply put, they made this dress for me. I applied more makeup to my bite marks to ensure Allison didn't see them. How I'd hidden it from Ms. Nosy for so long was beyond me. I gathered my things and headed to the door where Greg waited with the boys. My mom was visiting from Nashville, so I relied on her to watch the kids.

"Oh, wow, you look great, baby. But don't you think that dress is too short? And tight?" Greg questioned. I wouldn't let him get me down for wearing my dress. "I don't want anyone seeing what's mine."

"Nope, it's just right." I rolled my eyes when I headed for the door. "Come on, we're going to be late."

My mom and the boys bid us goodbye, and we drove to the restaurant with Greg complaining about the dress. He talked about how the boys might view my appearance for ten minutes and how they would misperceive women. When we pulled up to the valet, paparazzi be darned, I jumped out. Usually, I went through the back entrance, but I couldn't wait. I fixed my dress as I heard the clicking sound of the camera and my name being screamed out. As if I were a robot, I smiled, waved, and ran into the restaurant with Greg trailing behind me.

Allison started waving from the back when I entered the quaint restaurant, and I started toward her with Greg and my bodyguard, Bruno. As I drew closer, I noticed several people had their phones out. I hugged Allison and Wayne before I sat down. Wayne was in a white shirt and blue jeans. He was handsome with his dark brown skin, hazel eyes, and broad build. He was huge, but he was a soft teddy bear on the inside.

"Oh, you look hot, Jas," Allison admired. She looked gorgeous in her blue sweater dress.

"Thank you, Alli," I responded. "You look fabulous, and Wayne, you're aging backward."

"Oh, starting with the buttering, I see." Wayne leaned back and laughed. His eyes twinkled when he opened them up. "Okay, you're trying to get on my good side. What do you want now?"

Everyone laughed as we took our seats.

The night was going well after we greeted each other and caught up. Midway into the double date, I excused myself to the bathroom, and what should have been a five-minute break turned into ten as a fan stopped me to sign something.

Not even in the bathroom could I find peace.

I could tell Allison was waiting for me to come back to grill me about something. Whenever she cocked her head to the side and raised her left eyebrow, I knew she was going to get into something.

"Why do you have a bite mark on your shoulder, Jas?" she asked with her lips thinned out.

Oh, fuck. I must not have applied enough makeup to fill in the mark. She knew my body like the back of her hand, so I couldn't tell her what I told Greg. I sighed.

"Oh, you didn't know she got bit by her friend when she was in elementary school? Wait, you knew Jas for almost eighteen years and didn't know about those bite marks? I guess I have one up on you." Greg chuckled as he smiled.

Allison turned her head to him. And if looks could kill, Greg would have been finely diced into cubes.

"Oh, it must have been from her after-school program named Club Celeste. Isn't that right, Jas?" The table was quiet, and I stared at my empty dessert plate. "You remember playing basket—balls after school when you were younger."

My face burned like someone splashed hot boiling water on my face.

I'm going to kill her.

"Oh yeah," I stumbled over my words. "It's getting—"

Wayne cut me off. "Club Celeste? That's crazy. I heard of a high-end sex club around here by that name. It's where the rich folks go to get their rocks off." I would have hit him upside his head if he wasn't as tall as a tree. "What a coincidence."

My left leg lost about ten pounds because it shook under the table so violently. Wayne was nice, but he might have ruined a peaceful night.

"A sex club? That's what unholy non-God fearing people in LA do. Thankfully, Jas isn't into that stuff," Greg, holier than thou, said.

Wayne shifted uncomfortably in his chair. Allison folded her arms like she was about to curse Greg out.

"Well, we should get going. I have—"

Greg cut me off again. I just wanted the night to be over!

"I wanted to discuss something with everyone here," Greg stated, too cheerfully for my liking. "Jas lost the bid for the record label. But I wanted to be included in this business affair. You need someone outside your lawyers and Allison to speak with Mr. Brine."

"Well, I wouldn't say I'm confronting him. I still like him. He's done nothing indecorous to me. I want my masters and the business." I continued, "I think I can talk to one man alone, Greg. He won't bite me. Plus, he's never been rude to me."

"I know, but I really want to be included. I want to feel like I'm helping somehow." Greg pleaded, and I couldn't help but take pity on him. He really tried, and I kept pushing back. I looked over at Allison, and she had that damned eyebrow raised.

"Okay, fine. I have a meeting tomorrow. Supposedly, the new directors want to meet tomorrow as well. I guess we can kill two birds at once."

"Do you want me to come with you guys?" Allison asked, but she would rather not be a part of the boring part of the business.

"Nah, I'm good," I stated. Nothing would go wrong. "Plus, I can take Mr. Brine. Greg, not so much."

"Ha, you see these guns?" Poor Greg flexed his skinny arms.

We all laughed our asses off. Well, that's one joke that Greg got right. We moved to leave in our separate cars when Allison pulled me close and whispered, "I hope you know what you're doing. I don't have a good feeling about this."

"Alli, everything will be fine," I promised her.

As she pulled away from our hug, I pinched her. She yelped and slapped my arm.

"What the hell was that for?" she asked as her small hand rubbed the sore spot.

"That's for showing your ass tonight with your joke." I folded my arms.

"I'm sorry, I couldn't help it." She smirked. "You know that man-child gets under my skin."

I shook my head.

We said our goodbyes and went to our respective cars. But as we pulled off, I kept hearing her words bouncing in my head.

I should have listened to her.

My stomach turned like a cement mixer. I had all that macho talk for everyone last night, but today was a different story. Greg and I stood outside Mr. Brine's office. I debated whether I should cut my losses and go back home. That would have been a waste of my lucky Alexander McQueen white pantsuit with my silver Louboutin heels and a silver waist belt. I put my locs into my signature pineapple hairdo, and I added my silver accessories to stand out. I had to wear an undershirt to cover my bite mark because I didn't want people to think Greg was hurting me.

Hand on the doorknob, I was frozen in my spot. I looked

dressed for business, but I was sick to death on the inside. I turned to Greg, who looked lovely in the brown suit I'd bought him. He nodded and said, "You wouldn't feel good if you didn't do this. But it's your decision. I will support you either way." His words touched something inside of me, and I nodded back to him. I took a deep breath and knocked on the door.

The voices stopped when I knocked.

"Come in," I heard Mr. Brine call out, his voice laced with his Nashville accent, similar to mine.

Well, not that much since I barely had a Southern twang anymore.

I forced myself to open the door and walked in. My nerves were shot, and the hair on my arms stood at attention. But I shook away the dread feeling and made my way into the office. Mr. Brine was in his usual chair parked behind that humongous desk, and there was a gentleman with silver hair on the other side. I couldn't see his face because his back was to the door. There was another guy in the same position with long, black, curly hair down to his back, which looked overdue for a good washing. He had a light dusting of gray hair at his temples. A third chair sat empty between us.

"Ah, Jasmine. You look beautiful as always, and nice to see you, Greg. I'm glad you could make it." Mr. Brine smiled so widely his cheeks must have hurt.

"Hello, Mr. Brine. How are you?" As I reached the desk, he shuffled to come and give me a hug. "Sorry for being late."

"I'm good now that retirement is finally here," he stated and went back to his seat. "Don't worry about being late. I'd like you to meet the new owners."

The men stood, and they were taller than me. The one with the long, black, curly hair had a mustache and a beard that was as long as his hair. *Do men think that looks good? Sheesh.*

He shook my hand. When he touched me, it felt like electricity shocked me, and I pulled my hand back.

"Hello, Ms. Grant. My name is Gabriele Sabino. It's a pleasure to meet you. Mr. Brine spoke highly of you." He took off his sunglasses, and if he felt that shock, I couldn't tell. Dark green eyes that could read everything in my mind and under my clothes roamed over my body. His unwavering gaze unsettled me, causing me to squirm.

And I knew without a doubt I was going crazy as I willed myself to believe that this Gabriele wasn't my Gabe from six years ago.

I turned to the other guy with the silver hair. He wasn't friendly at all. But the muscles and his chiseled jaw made up for his grumpy ass.

Well, maybe.

"Hello, my name is Wren Costa." He took my hand. I knew my nipples would poke his grumpy ass if I weren't wearing my heavily padded bra.

"N-Nice to meet you, Mr. Costa." I stuttered like a fool. His silver eyebrows poked out of his sunglasses. "This is my fiancé, Gregory Simmons." They shook hands, and we all sat down.

I knew I was being delusional, but it was the only thing keeping me from fleeing the hot and stuffy office. I couldn't help it. I like to run… It's second nature to me. I mean, green eyes are common—right? We never exchanged our full names. I wouldn't allow it, and I never asked if we were being honest.

But Wren is a common name, right?

I rubbed the back of my moist neck and shifted in the black, itchy chair. At this point, I felt as if I knew how my menopause felt as I began to sweat in places I forgot could sweat.

"… They bid two billion in cash, and they won. Now, I know you wanted your masters. Mr. Sabino, Mr. Costa, and Mr. Russo will be more than reasonable in your request. They're good, decent men," Mr. Brine droned on.

"Oh, there's three owners?" Greg asked. He had been like a church mouse since we stepped in.

"Yes, there's three of us. The other gentleman should be here soon," Mr. Sabino stated, who hadn't stopped staring a hole into me. "So, you wanted to buy the label to have your masters? That's a lot of work to go through just to obtain your masters."

I tried to keep my face neutral because my body shook with nervousness as his deep voice washed over me. The voice that sounded like the one that warmed my soul, but I was unsure—okay, I'm lying, but I had to save face. My fingers itched to run themselves over his cheek, where I knew I would find those deep dimples I would trace late night when he was asleep. It wasn't until I looked down that I noticed I had gripped the chair arm so hard that my knuckles were white. The bravado I once had was gone out the window.

"Well, I would have liked the passive income as well." That earned a laugh from everyone. "Plus, I know the business. So, I could guide young artists instead of them being railroaded by their families or other industry folks."

Gabriele had already undressed me several times when I watched his eyes stop on my chest and return to my eyes. The air left my lungs. I didn't have to look at Wren, who sulked in his chair, to know his eyes were glued to my chest flat out.

"How about having a more in-depth conversation about this when we're settled?" Gabriele said. That drew a snort from the other guy.

"Sorry, I was thinking about something," he mumbled.

They clearly had some type of spat going on, and we were getting the tail end of it.

"Anyway, see, they will work with you on your masters, and once you have them. You're good." Mr. Brine chimed in. He had always been like this since I met him. He loved to please people.

"Okay, sounds good, Mr. Sabino and Mr. Costa. We should get going." I hurriedly tried to get up.

"You should stay. When they're in the mood, they love to talk.

Today not so much." Mr. Brine shrugged as he looked at the pair. Wren removed his sunglasses and rubbed his abnormally gray eyes.

My heart nearly dropped out of my ass, and I felt a scream threatening to rip out of my throat. Oh my God. I couldn't even hear Mr. Brine droning on about whatever he was talking about now. I couldn't even look at them as they stared at me like they knew me.

This was a sick joke. This was just my luck.

One thing was for sure, I had to leave.

If they found out about the twins, I couldn't even fathom what they would do. I should have listened to Allison. Oh God, was I really this dumb?

I jumped up and dropped my bag. Luckily, Greg picked it up. "Mr. Brine, I need to go. Thank you. Goodbye, everyone. We will talk soon."

My pantsuit clung to me like a second skin as I turned around and tried to hightail it out the door. But of course, God wanted to see me suffer after all this time. The door burst open, and in walked Tony like he was the king. I stood there and watched as the man who was the carbon copy of my twins strutted over to me.

My eyes were wide as he reached for my clammy hand. Time stood still as he touched my cold hand, leaned toward my face, and kissed me on both cheeks. I was as rigid as a metal pole and stuck in place. I felt my panties become moist with my arousal. When he pulled back, his eyes flashed something indescribable.

"Ah, Tony! There you are, right on time. This is the talented Ms. Jasmine Grant," Mr. Brine boomed.

"Bellissima, it's nice to meet you, Jasmine Grant." He beamed as he sported the smile that always made me weak. That half-cocked smile that stated, "I'm a special type of cocky." The one I saw every day on our kids' faces.

I needed to run before I made a fool of myself in this damn office.

I nodded, and the heat from the other four sets of eyes that lasered in on my ass was enough for me to shove him out of my way and walk out of that office.

I didn't even stop to check on Greg. He'd better keep up with me and deal with it. When he hit the passenger seat, I peeled off, and when I stopped at the entrance of the complex, I looked up to see Gabe, who stared out the window at my car.

Fuck! Now I got to go home and masturbate.

Chapter 11

Tony

For five minutes, I stood in the middle of the office. Shocked? No, that was too calm. I was baffled that this petite beauty had the gall to push me. I didn't even have time to cop a good feel of those glorious mounds Jasmine had, well, on both sides, to be honest. Her breasts strained against her suit coat, and her ass jiggled as she bounced out the door when she left. If I hadn't been so shocked by the disrespect, I would have followed her to see her run from me. That would have been a wonderful sight to see.

It wasn't until we got home that night that my tongue finally returned to my mouth. I walked into Gabe's room, where he was holed up because he was in a bad mood. I burst through the door and found him deep in his hockey game on the television. He didn't even notice I'd walked in. I pulled on my hair, which needed a cut.

"We need to talk." I shuffled to the open chair in his room.

He sighed and rubbed the straggly ends of his beard. "Okay, shoot."

"First, you need to shave and cut your hair. You look like something out of the backwoods. We have a woman to seduce," I teased, but I meant every word.

"What are you talking about?" Gabe finally gave me the full attention I needed.

"I want her."

"Want who?"

"Ms. Jasmine Grant." I sighed and smiled for the first time in what seemed like years. "I want her to suffocate me with those thick thighs or her ass. Did you see her ass? I would die a lucky man with my tongue inside of her and my face smothered in her cheeks. Don't even get me started on her breasts."

Gabe stared at me like I'd grown a dick out of my forehead. But I was unfazed by it. He could be grumpy all he wanted, but I wouldn't take no for an answer.

"Wait, you're not joking, are you?"

"No, all kidding aside." I tilted my head. "Doesn't Jasmine seem familiar?"

"There's something about her. She's beautiful, smart... and engaged," Gabe specified. "But I agree with you."

"But do they have children?"

"Tony!" Gabe yelled. "Cazzo[1], do you hear yourself sometimes?"

"Sorry, Gabe, but he looked more like her pencil pusher than a fiancé." I closed my eyes and smiled. "I've been hard since I kissed her cheek. She smelled like heaven opened up and poured oranges and vanilla on me. Just like Kitty. Did you not feel something?"

"No," Gabe stated as he turned back to his game.

I narrowed my eyes at him. Yeah, he was affected. I shook my head and played with my lip rings. Ms. Grant had my full attention, and one thing I was good—no, great at—was finding out information

---

1   Cazzo- Shit

about people. If you had something to hide, I could find it and use it against you or let you get away with it. I knew I came off as egotistical, but I had the track record to back it up.

I sighed, walked out of Gabe's man cave central, and headed to my wing. My little slice of heaven. I knew what most people would expect: a black section of the house with rock band posters. Since I looked like a model for an emo magazine, but on the contrary, I'd painted my area light gray. The walls held paintings I collected on trips from around the world. The two extra rooms I had were simple for guests when they came over. Then there was my room. I had floor-to-ceiling windows around the walls that faced the hills, giving me a view of the Hollywood Hills as my daily portrait. My white California king bed invited me to sleep, but not before a bath. I entered my walk-in closet, dumped everything in the laundry basket, and retreated to my mini spa. Usually, I would chill out in the four-person spa until I was pruney, but not tonight. I had a monster boner from Ms. Grant that I needed to handle.

I stepped into my shower and turned on the water. I looked out the window that was opened to the Hills. The metal piercings, my best investment, made my hard cock extremely sensitive. I thought about Jasmine as I stroked my hard shaft with my soapy hand. What if she lived close enough to see me? Would she watch me as I thought of fucking her from behind as she screamed my name? Would she wrap those pretty plump lips around my cock and stare at me like Wren taught our Kitten so long ago? After a couple of fast strokes, I shuddered as my hot cum ran over my hand and covered the window. I stood there for a minute with my hand on the window, and my head bent back. I should have felt embarrassed about how quickly I'd come, but I didn't.

It had been six years since I found a girl that could get me hard as a rock.

But Ms. Grant had a familiar air around her that had me itching to find out more about her. What was it about this woman that had me in my shower coming all over my window and not deep inside her or Wren?

Fucking Wren.

I finished up in the bathroom and headed to bed. I couldn't get Jasmine out of my mind. I knew I had been missing in action for a while, but something tugged at my core when I saw her. It was like a familiar tug that kept her in my mind. That and she was pretty strong for such a small woman. I sighed. Kitty was responsible for this. I had known from how her eyes stared down at me that it would be the last time I saw her. That was the second time in my life that I had ever told a woman I loved her, and look at what she did. When she kept repeating the same "I love you" back, I thought she meant it, but she didn't.

That was six years and a stint in Alcoholics Anonymous later. Sometimes, I had good days, but then sometimes, I got that little voice that echoed I wasn't good enough to love or that she found me repulsive for my sexual proclivities. I knew it was a lot to ask, but it was worth it. I was worth it.

I sighed and threw myself onto my bed.

When my phone rang, I cursed myself for not putting my phone on *Do Not Disturb*. It was my sister, who didn't understand we slept at night here in the States anymore.

"Did you find her yet?" I sighed. She was worse than our mother.

"Gee, hello to you, Bethany. I'm doing wonderful. Oh, what, you miss me? Well, I miss you too, big sis." I rolled my eyes in the dark.

"Yada, Yada, Yada. I love you, too. Did you find my nephews yet?" She had been on this "You have lost kids" shit for almost two weeks now. She claimed she saw two twins that looked like me. I rolled my eyes.

"Bethany, the only nephews you have are in my ball sack, and some are now plastered on my bathroom window from where I jacked off in the shower," I yawned.

"Oh God, disgusting! I didn't need to hear that, Tony." I heard her gagging through the phone. "I promise you I had a dream about—"

"I'm stopping you right there. You're turning into Mom now." I pinched the bridge of my nose.

"Listen, did you find the woman with the long brown braids yet?" she asked, and I sat up in bed.

"What did you say? And what do you mean the woman with the long brown braids?" Bethany hadn't told me anything about that when she called me two weeks ago to tell me about the singer she was hired to cater. Honestly, this wasn't the first time my sister suggested I had some kid out there.

"I think she owned the yacht, so she must be rich. But she wasn't the one to hire me. It was someone with the initials A.J.," she continued. "Listen, Tony. She had long brown hair in braids, she was shaped like a real woman, and breasts I wouldn't mind sleeping on. I haven't had the time to look her up since I had back-to-back events since then, but I know you can find her, Tony."

My sister was a notorious lesbian, and I loved that for her, but I didn't like her slobbering over random girls. She was married to the nicest woman in Italy, Stephanie Bianchi. She was a pediatric surgeon in one of the top hospitals in Italy.

I rolled my eyes. "Okay, I have a long day tomorrow if you're done with the dramatics."

"Fine. I'm going to tell Mom then," she rushed out as she hung up. I dialed my mom's number, and it was busy.

Fuck my life.

I knew I might as well stay up until my mom called. When she did, she wouldn't end the call until I promised her that I would get to the bottom of things because she had dreamed of fish about five years ago. I breathed deeply and rolled my eyes. My mom and sister knew every old wives tale you can search on Google.

I didn't mention that she once dreamed my uncle would be married to a woman with five kids. My uncle was gay.

Cazzo, someone help me.

I thought I would just fall asleep once I got into my sleeping position, but that was better said than done. I lay awake for hours racking my head of how I would gain more information on my new interest, Jasmine Grant, until I finally felt the hard lull of slumber calling me as my eyes closed on the imprint of Jasmine Grant.

As crazy as it sounded, my mom's and sister's words followed me throughout the following day and straight into the next day. Even though I tried to knock their silly superstitions out of my head, I couldn't quite shake the nagging voice in my head.

As a member of the board, I should research every one of my artists, right? The answer was yes. I was just being my brother's keeper and finding out the information. I walked through the office and greeted everyone. The employees in the office were already running around as they prepared for their Christmas party and other upcoming events.

I opened the door to our temporary office, formally Mr. Brines, and saw Wren, grumpy as usual, slumped in the big office chair behind the desk. I knew his current mood was about Rose, but whenever we gave an opinion on anything Rose-related, it was met with an attitude or his favorite complaint, "You hate Rose," which may hold a little truth.

Rose was like nightshade; the flower looked beautiful but had a deadly touch. Rose had been nice initially, but I could see the ugly truth once we peeled away her layers. But Wren, my loveable dope, was convinced we could make it work, which wouldn't happen now or ever.

"Wren, what are you doing here?"

"Nothing. I came here to clear my mind."

You would think having your own wing in a mansion would be enough room for someone, but I guessed not. I walked over to Wren and grabbed his face lightly. This was probably the first time in months we had been alone together. This Rose situation had put a wedge between us, and it'd been weeks since we shared anything. I missed him. I closed the distance between us, kissed him, and devoured him in the office on our big-ass desk. He pulled back with tears running down his cheeks. My thumb reached out to wipe them away.

Seeing Wren like that triggered a long-forgotten memory of how I met him.

I strolled into my new high school English class. I'd finally gotten my parents to allow me to get my eyebrow pierced, which was easier said than done. The black stud stood out against my warm ivory skin. Inquisitive eyes watched me as I turned to walk to the only free desk, which was conveniently next to my eye stalker. I pulled my baggy black hoodie tighter, and my black leather pants stretched when I sat down. I watched through the side of my eye as my stalker's face turned red. I was the brave one. So, I kept staring until our eyes finally met. His eyes were so silver they almost looked unnaturally white. I winked and smirked when I finally stopped drowning in his silver pools.

"Well, thank you for joining us, Mr. Russo." The English teacher's mouth thinned out, and his eyebrows shot up. Mr. Long hated any of his students being late.

"You're welcome, Mr. Long. The pleasure is all yours." I grinned so widely I thought my mouth would split in half.

Mr. Long huffed and turned back to the board and his lesson. Since the room had given their attention to Mr. Long, I glanced back over to... Wren, which I caught from his open notebook. He caught me staring at him again, and my tongue peeked out to lick my lips. My tongue piercing must have scared him because he snapped his head back to the desk and muttered a curse. Midway through our lesson, my pen died on me, so I leaned over and asked.

"Hey, do you have a pen I could borrow?" I whispered.

"S-Sure," he stammered. I couldn't fathom why he was so jumpy around me. When he shoved his hand in his backpack and took out an extra pen, I wrapped my long fingers around his. It was as if time had slowed down, and my heart sped up. I stayed rooted to that spot until I felt myself shiver and maneuvered the pen from his hand. I smiled and gave him a break as I turned back to my notebook.

Something about Wren kept my eyes wandering over to the seat he occupied throughout class. It wasn't until the bell rang and Mr. Long was gone that I noticed I was hard to the point I couldn't hide it. I didn't care if anyone saw it either. I'm proud of what I got. But before I could move and gather my things to leave the classroom, Wren jumped up and scurried down the small aisle to leave the classroom. But he only made it halfway before a kid twice his size stopped him. Wren's biggest fan, Jimmy Lavine, grabbed his backpack. I wanted to intervene, but I stayed back and watched. Unfortunately, Jimmy was bigger than Wren and ended up winning the tug-of-war they had going on with his bookbag. Jimmy threw Wren's bag across the room. He became vaguely aware that I was in the back of the classroom watching when he glanced around the room for help.

"Aw, look at little WeWe. He's hard. Dude, what are you ten?" Jimmy laughed with his two friends.

"I-I'm not… I just have to pee… I," he stammered.

"What cat got your cock?" Jimmy heckled.

From my angle, Wren looked like he was about to cry as his eyes turned pink and sweat marks formed on the back of his shirt.

I decided I had seen enough.

"Quit being a douchebag and leave him alone, Jimmy," I demanded as I grabbed the bag from the floor. "I would hate for my father to cut ties with your dad. That will put you in the poorhouse."

I heard two of Jimmy's friends snickering behind him. When

Jimmy turned to them, they stopped immediately. Jimmy, never one to back down, said, "Please, your dad needs my dad's business."

"Jimmy, even you know that's not true." I threw my head back and cackled. "I was there when your dad came groveling to my dad because he needed money. Now, move along before I make my dad send you to the poorhouse."

"Fuck you, Russo." Jimmy turned and walked away with his friends.

"You're not my type," I taunted him, and several students turned their heads to look at Jimmy and his friend's retreating form.

Until then, I only had one friend that I would stick up for. Everyone else could fend for themselves. But as I walked slowly to Wren, I felt bad because I knew about Wren because of our dads' businesses. But between helping my parents with their separate business and perfecting my computer skills, I never made the time to meet Wren, and boy, was I upset at myself now that I'd met him. He wasn't the typical kid at Mount Woods Academy, which was filled with arrogant assholes like Jimmy Lavine and his friends. He was better than everyone there, including myself.

I stood there with his bag and its torn strap in my hand. I quickly gave it to him, and I watched as he fumbled to say something, "Thank you for helping me out," he said as he stared bashfully at his shoes.

"You're welcome, sexy." And when he finally turned those silver pools to me, I wept a little inside. He was beyond beautiful.

I wanted to jizz in my pants in the middle of Mr. Long's classroom as he licked those plump pink lips of his.

"I'm not gay," he whispered.

"Oh, okay, sure." I winked at him.

"I like girls," he said with his back squared and arms crossed.

"So, you're bisexual then?" I asked, with one eyebrow cocked.

"Yes, I—"

I cut him off as I touched my lips to his, and I was enveloped in his cinnamon scent. His lips were like a stamp on my soul, marking and ruining me for anyone else. My hand found his crotch as I palmed his dick through his jeans. As I moaned into his mouth, I felt the warm rush of his release seep out of his dick. I removed my hand, and when I pulled away, he was as red as our uniform. I looked down to see the crotch of his jeans was wet, like he'd urinated on himself. Mine were damp from where I leaned on him. I lifted my face to his, which caused my eyes to meet his, and said, "Mmh, Bisexual. Want me to help you clean up?"

"Earth to Tony!" Wren shouted, and flailing his arms in front of my face brought me back to the present.

I blinked twice and refocused my attention.

"I'm sorry, Wren. I'm tired." A smile touched my mouth. "We have been fighting more lately, and it's not right. Our little family is all that matters."

"You're right." He sighed loudly. "What are you doing up here?"

I rubbed his favorite spot behind his ears.

"Doing some research."

"On?"

"Our leading lady."

"Huh, you're talking in riddles."

"Ms. Jasmine Grant, our feisty, petite songstress."

"I don't like that. It's invading Jasmine's privacy, Tony. Why don't you try to get to know her?" Wren asked.

He was right. I did struggle with what I was about to do. I never had the desire to seek information on anyone except for Kitten. But I couldn't because the club had all of its documents on lockdown. There wasn't any internet trail that could connect anyone to the place. Whoever owned that place was someone you didn't want to mess with. I begged the front desk for any information on Kitty, but nothing. I wished I'd run out after her, no matter if my balls would have been out in public.

"Let's meet up for some 'us' time tonight." I caressed his cheek.

"Sounds like a plan."

I kissed him, but those stupid glasses were in the way this time. I snatched them off before he could move to block my hand. My lips thinned, and I instantly saw red. The red nail mark looked like someone had tried to claw his eyes out. My eyes narrowed, and my face was flushed.

But before I could speak, Wren held his hand up and protested, "It's not what you think. I frightened Rose, and she accidentally scratched me."

I bit my tongue and kept my hand stiff at my side so I wouldn't say what I was thinking because I couldn't trust what would come out of my mouth. Rose was one step away from being on my bad side. Wren took my silence as a sign he could leave. As he left our office, I stood rooted in the same spot, almost like I was glued to it.

Finally, after a couple of minutes, I got to work. I searched through the paperwork at the office. Mr. Brine was old school in some ways. He still had paper copies of the artists' information in his office. I was confused when I found the file on my mysterious queen. The other artists had their information on file, but not Ms. Grant, which, to be fair, could have been because she was retired. She had a post office box as her address, and her phone number led to her voicemail in the office.

So, I dug deeper into Jasmine. I took to the internet, and it was too easy for me to get her information. When you're famous, no matter how careful you are, there will always be someone to catch you. So, I was an hour deep into my research, and I gathered our little princess went missing in action after her retirement for a little over two years and only showed up to one or two interviews. She also has a public company with her mother, but I didn't see any revenue noted for the company.

By the time I called it quits, my eyes were dry and itchy. My stomach cursed me, demanding I feed it. That was when I got the idea of inviting Ms. Grant to lunch. I wondered if she would accept my invitation to lunch.

No, she wouldn't.

So, I hacked into Mr. Brine's phone and sent a text that read he had returned early and wanted to meet her at my favorite restaurant, La Rosa. I could go for some gnocchi with swordfish. Jasmine texted she would be there in twenty minutes. My hands rubbed together, and I smiled.

My plans always turned out nicely…. Well, this time.

I was out the door and in the parking lot with a minute to spare. I waited until I saw the voluptuous Jasmine slide out of her car and run into the restaurant with her guard. Mesmerized by how her ass jiggled in her white dress all the way to the door, I watched her get seated. I ensured I looked presentable and tied my long hair into a bun. I walked in, and luckily, they'd placed her in a seat facing away from the door.

I glided in and greeted the staff since I knew the family and everyone who worked there. As I sat down, she looked up with those wide brown eyes.

God, they looked like my Kitty's.

"I-I," she stammered.

I smiled at her. "Cat got your tongue?" I teased and watched as a slight pink color arose on the tip of her small ears. "Ms. Grant, or can I call you Jasmine?"

"J-J-J," she cleared her throat and drank some water. I noticed her hand shook slightly. "Jasmine is fine."

Is it weird that she's so nervous? It's like we did something to her.

Had we? And I had forgotten about it? No, I would remember her. Her voice was like deep velvet. I would remember a voice like that, even though she'd barely mumbled two words to me. The warmth from her voice washed over me like whiskey.

I reached out and grabbed her soft, small hand. She tried to get her hand back, but I had a firm grip on it. I kissed it and let her pull it back. I stared at her as I tried to piece her together. She noticed and straightened her back, and stared back at me.

Fuck, the little defiance act alone was a massive turn-on.

"I didn't come here to spook you or harass you. I wanted to get to know you better." As I surrendered, I held my hands up.

"Why? I'm not an active artist. Once in a while, I perform, and I go home. So, again, I ask why?" She folded her arms under her breast, which made them push up more. My eyes were drawn to them like magnets.

"You seemed fun to be around, and I'm looking for some fun friends since I'm lonely." She cleared her throat. Heat rose to my face, and I could have sworn I saw a smirk on her face.

She tilted her head and smirked. "Does that line work on ladies?"

"Well, it works on both ladies and men." I winked.

She squirmed in her seat. "Oh," she smiled.

"Let's talk like two friends." I smiled. "I just want to get to know you better. Is that okay?"

She raised one of her perfect eyebrows and chewed her red-painted lip. "I guess that's okay."

"How did you get into singing?"

She chuckled. "My best friend made me audition for music camp, and I won over the talent scout. The rest became history."

"She's a really great best friend. Are you guys still in contact with each other?"

I may have put my foot in my mouth because Jasmine turned slightly ashen.

"No, she passed away shortly after I signed with the record label." She averted her eyes to the silverware on the table.

I instantly felt ashamed. I wished I'd kept my mouth shut and just stuck to the typical how's the weather question.

Stupido[2], Tony!

"I'm so sorry for your loss and for bringing it up." She didn't yank her hand back this time when I reached out to grab it. "I can't even imagine if I lost Wren or Gabe. They're my family, and I love them."

"It's okay. It was a long time ago, and luckily, I had help coping with the loss," she said with a sad smile.

The waitress, right on time, took our orders. I let her guide the conversation, and it took no time to get her to relax. With our hands still glued together as if they belonged that way, we talked about vague topics. Her love for beauty, my goals for our business with record label, and other mundane subjects. When she laughed, it reminded me of Kitty. I savored how she threw her head back and her shoulders shook. I don't even think she realized when she reached over with a clean napkin to wipe the sauce from my cheek. I wanted to grab her wrist and pull her into my lap.

I knew it'd been six years since I desired a relationship with a woman, but I couldn't shake the feeling that drew me to her. She seemed to realize I had stopped laughing and was observing her when she stopped.

"What? Why are you staring at me like that?" She squirmed again.

"You're gorgeous when you smile. Do you know that?" I asked.

She bent her head, but not before I saw a small smile creep up on her face.

"Thank you," she whispered. "This was nice. I wasn't expecting any of this."

I continued to rub the middle of her palm.

"You remind me of someone I used to know," I muttered out loud.

---

2   Stupido- stupid

I looked down and smiled. But when I looked back up, Jasmine's chest heaved quickly, and her eyes darted from side to side, avoiding mine. The sudden change in her mood threw me for a loop. I wasn't prepared when she snatched her hand away, stood up, and gathered her belongings.

"So sorry. I'm late for an appointment," she huffed out.

"Hey, I'm sorry if—" I commented quickly because I hadn't meant to run her off since I was enjoying the conversation with no agenda for the first time in years.

"It's not you. This was a bad idea. Sorry. Bye." She rushed off as her bodyguard chased behind her.

I sat there and enjoyed the sway of her wide hips and the jiggle of her ass and sighed. I thought this date would have tampered down the voice in my head, but it made me want to chase after her.

I paid for our food and got up to leave.

It's going to be a long night with this hard-on.

Chapter 12

Gabe

I lied… and it was eating me up.

I couldn't stop thinking about how Jasmine's ample breasts slightly swayed as she walked into the office. The soft skin of her tiny hands when I took hers in mine. Her citrus and vanilla scent hugged me like a warm welcome home. When she leaned over to sit down, I watched as her pantsuit stretched to accommodate those wide hips. Like the sexually deprived man I was, I watched as her breasts jiggled as she shook her leg. Her voice was deep and warm as it traveled from my ears to my cock.

I imagined loosening her hair and massaging my fingers through her scalp until she moaned my name. I would push her down onto that big ass desk in our office as I ripped off her pants and fucked her until her throat was hoarse from screaming my name.

Fuck, I'm hard as shit. I don't even know this woman. Plus, she's engaged.

"So, Gabby Baby, we should talk about me moving in to be

closer to you guys," Rose said.

I shifted to ease the discomfort from my erection. I desperately needed to get out of here so I could cum in peace. I was still beating myself up for letting Wren trick me into this setup date. But I should have known when he came into our kitchen with my favorite tiramisù from La Rosa. One bite and I was in dessert coma and wasn't responsible for my actions. With a sigh, I tapped my feet to the beat of the restaurant's upbeat tempo. The thought of Rose wandering around our home would have been enough to have me committed to the psych hospital.

"No."

"Why Gabby? I want to be near you guys every day-"

"No."

She huffed and folded her arms under her fake breasts. She pouted her mouth like she was about six years old.

"You're so unreasonable, Gabby. Wouldn't it be great for us? I can be with you guys every day," she asked as she reached over and grabbed my erect cock. Her eyes went wide. "See, you want me as much as I want you."

Well, there went my erection. I thought as I felt myself go soft. So, I guess I could thank Rose for something.

"It's not for you, Rose!" I grunted, and I knew I was an asshole. I took her hand and placed it on the table.

Smack!

My cheek heated at the abused area as I looked at her with my mouth agape. Luckily, my massive beard and long hair covered the imprint from her slap on my face. But I couldn't hide the look of pure hatred in my eyes. I looked around, and a couple of patrons all looked at us.

"Gabby, I'm so sorry. I'm a bit drunk," she stated.

"I think we should end the night. I will take you home." I declared as I grabbed my things. I watched as she stumbled over herself to get her things together. Nobody disrespected me like that, let alone in public.

We marched to the valet to retrieve my car. I gave the valet a tip and drove her home. She started crying when I turned the radio up. It was a long drive to her home as I fought not to break the car wheel. I didn't even notice that she drank so much. She probably didn't mean to hit me, so I immediately felt remorse for her the closer we got to her house.

As I pulled up to her home, she turned to me and apologized again. "I'm so sorry. I didn't mean to do it."

I sighed and told her I had forgiven her. She gave me a kiss on the cheek and turned to leave. God, this was becoming intolerable. Wren had to come to terms with this relationship. We decided in college that we wanted to share our lives together since we were basically sharing everything, and it only felt right to share a woman together. And we had shared our fair share since college.

As I drove off, the fifteen-minute ride home only took about ten. As I pulled up to our house and ran inside, I walked into Tony's room without knocking. My mistake. I yelled so loud as I heard Tony grunt and moan his release. That was the fourth time I'd walked in on Tony and Wren going at it like bunnies.

Well, at least somebody was getting laid.

"Ah, sorry, guys. I should have knocked." I chastised myself. My cheeks were on fire and not from the slap earlier on.

"Welp, we got to cum. That's all that matters," Tony remarked as he smacked Wren playfully on his ass. I heard them kiss and shuffle to get dressed. I turned around and sat in the empty chair next to the bed.

I unloaded on them about the situation with Rose. They listened while I went on more than a rant about being publicly humiliated.

"She pinched me because I didn't want to massage her feet," Tony continued. "I'm on the very last straw I can tolerate with her. She even scratched Wren."

Wren frowned, and I knew he was about to say some bullshit. "It was a mistake, and she apologized."

I rolled my neck and was about to give Wren the bitter truth when the doorbell rang. It was after ten o'clock. Wren ran downstairs, and I looked at Tony. We both shook our heads, and it confirmed our suspicions when her signature nasal voice traveled up the stairs. It hadn't even been thirty minutes since I dropped her home.

I closed my eyes.

"This is irritating, Gabe," Tony sighed and flopped on the bed.

"I second that. Now, Rose is probably going to stay here tonight." Tony moaned.

She busted into the room and yelled, "Hey, guys."

She stumbled on the way to jump in Tony's lap, and I heard a slight huff from the collision. Rose was as skinny as a pole, so when she jumped on him, her bony appendages connected with Tony's. Tony, who would usually be in post-orgasm heaven by now, had a scowl that showed his dwindling patience. He nor I signed up for this torture. Wren could pretend all he wanted with Rose, but the fact of the matter was his connection with Tony and me should've trumped what he thought he had with Rose. Tony put Rose on her feet and stated he wanted to rest because he had an early morning tomorrow.

Now, to anyone else, that would make sense. We're used to hard work, including being up at dawn. But that was when we were younger. Nowadays, we are up at nine or ten a.m., depending on what we did the night before.

"Okay, I was thinking about your record label company," Rose said, breaking the silence, and I felt some bullshit, for the second time tonight, would come next.

"Why would you be thinking about something that doesn't involve you?" I asked.

"Ha, Gabby, baby. I think you should let Jasmine Grant go. She's dead weight… literally. Everyone talks about how she let herself go since she's retired." She picked at her nails.

"Rose!" I saw red. "If I ever needed someone to make business decisions, you'd be the last person on earth. As I told you before, we don't need or want your unsolicited advice."

"Wow, I was just trying to—"

I cut her off. "No need, thank you," I replied as I moved to get up from my seat.

"Wait, I just dropped you off. Why would you drive over here if you were drunk?" I asked her.

"Oh, I felt better afterward, and Wren invited me over," she said casually as she gave her nails the utmost attention.

Wren was going to say something in defense of Rose, but I held my hand up. I didn't want to hear any of it.

Wren and Rose tried to sleep in Tony's bed, but Tony stood his ground and was adamant about sleeping alone. I almost snickered at them going back and forth, but bit my lip from the smile that threatened to creep up my face. Wren looked like someone kicked his puppy, and Rose pouted when he wouldn't budge. I was about to leave when Tony told me to hang back for a minute.

That was when he told me about his lunch date with Jasmine and the little voice in the back of his head. I rolled my eyes and chalked it up to his infatuation. We had been through this even before Kitty deserted us when I told him she'd slipped up and told me she had fans. We deep-dived into several celebrities' social media, but we couldn't pinpoint anyone. We could only speculate who we may have thought she could have been, but nothing more.

One thing I knew was that I rued the day I suggested going to Club Celeste.

I always had a plan for us. I was the leader of our small pack, so it was up to me to figure shit out. So, when I'd heard about Club Celeste, which was so exclusive that you had to be vetted even to gain access, I'd wanted to jump at the opportunity. The plan would help us get laid until we found someone we could all agree on. It almost seemed like yesterday that I came up with the plan…

Entering the house, I heard Tony and Wren in the pool. Since I had a knack for catching them in the act, I announced I was coming into the room.

"You guys blowing your backs out, are you?" I yelled.

Tony snickered, and Wren humphed. "No," they said in unison.

I walked in and over to where they floated. "So, I have a proposal—"

"Oh, shit, not more business crap—"

I cut Tony off. "No, Princess Tony. I came up with a solution for us to get laid."

Wren perked up at the mention of getting laid. "What pyramid scheme do you have now?"

"Ha, no pyramid scheme. There's a place here in LA only known to the Crème de la Crème of LA. It's where they can go in full secrecy, and the clientele are tested and vetted."

"So, a brothel, then?" Wren asked.

"No. From what I gathered, it's a club with rooms where clientele order what they desire, and they're matched with other people who fit their description or needs," I said.

"I don't know," Tony said. He'd been skeptical about everything lately.

"How about we try it for two weeks and go from there?"

Tony squinted his eyes. "Why?"

"Because," I said back.

"Because why?" he challenged.

I sighed. "Because I'm horny and need to get laid by someone who doesn't want to trap us."

They peered at me. "I could just help you get your rocks off," Tony said, and I wanted to submerge him under the water.

I gritted out, "Tony, quit fucking with me—"

"I haven't fucked with you…yet. I'll be a good best friend and let you put the tip in."

Losing my patience, I walked out of the poolroom before he could finish. Sometimes I wondered about my best friend. I wasn't opposed to having him give me a blowie—a mouth is a mouth. But I wouldn't be able to get it up if I tried for anything else.

I shuffled to my makeshift office and was about to close the door when Tony shoved it back.

"Okay, let's try it out. We have been hard up for some top-grade pussy. How sure are you of this place?"

I pulled out the silver encrusted invite I received when I told our personal assistant to get the information from Roy Lee's assistant, which took about three days. I handed it to Tony, and he gawked at it.

"Shit, this is real silver in the invite. Who the hell runs this place?"

"I don't know, but I got the information from Roy Lee," I stated.

"Roy Lee?!? Married Roy Lee? The elusive Roy Lee?" he said, dumbfounded.

"Yep, I had dinner with him the other night, and he said they keep everything hushed. No real bank accounts, no names, and you can wear a mask, but he said they go the extra mile to prevent leaks."

He sighed. "Okay, but we have to make a promise first."

"Okay, shoot."

"If we find someone we're interested in, we stop this at once."
He looked at me.

"I promise we will give it up if we find our girl." I lifted my right hand.

"Okay, fine. I will tell Wren. When can we start?"

"In a week, once we pay our three million dollar annual fee, one million for each of us. Mr. Lee said that's how long the background and medical check will take," I said.

"Can't we choose our own doctor?" he asked.

"It gets even better. Our doctor is their go-to for the club." I watched as his eyebrow piercings almost touched his hairline.

"Dr. Haddad is their doctor?" he whispered. *Our doctor was one of the top physicians for people in our circle. His clients were in the upper echelon of Los Angeles.*

"Yep, so they're legit then," I said.

"I hope so."

"I mean, I'm not surprised there's some sex dungeon club for the top of the top, but to have it right under our nose and not notice is baffling. I think our dads knew about it, though," I said.

"What?"

"Yeah, I mentioned it to my dad the other day at our Sunday dinner, and he slightly turned red and changed the subject."

"And if your dad knows, then so does my dad. They're two peas in a pod." He stared out the window.

"Yep, shit's crazy."

"You don't think—"

"That they cheated on our moms? Honestly, I don't know if they did or if they all went together and—" I felt my stomach bubble and acid rise in my throat. *"Let's not. I don't even want to imagine my parents doing anything other than talking."*

"I agree... to both things. Set it up, and let's get started. I've wanted to get my dick wet for a while," he said as he walked out of the office.

When Tony finished, I could only sigh. Tony, like me, had clung to the hope that we could find someone to complete us. I sympathized with his need to adhere to hope or find something better than our current situation. But I couldn't agree with his intrusive method of invading her privacy. Jasmine could file a case against us for stalking her, and we wouldn't come out on the winning side.

And I honestly wouldn't be mad.

I couldn't even deal with this right now. So, in my authoritative voice, I told Tony to stop stalking her. Either do it the right way or don't at all. We were many things, but stalkers was not one of them. I sighed.

Why can't life ever be easy for me?

It was a quiet Sunday night, and the guys ditched me to sulk in their own respective wings of the house. Wren had had another falling out with Rose. Tony was locked up in his room, either masturbating to whatever picture he could find of Jasmine or finding whatever he could on her.

I hated to admit I'd spent the last two nights beating my meat like I was back in middle school when Joan Pho showed me her glistening pussy.

Right now, I couldn't imagine anything that didn't pertain to Jasmine. I didn't need to be around my parents with a boner the size of California. I wouldn't be able to look my parents in the face. I pulled up to my childhood home and sat in the car. The grand white colonial home fit right in place with the other massive homes in the gated community. My parents, like most of the neighbors, had fenced their home in and used the arborvitae and palm trees to keep out noisy neighbors. I mentally prepared myself for the mass questions from my parents. Every Sunday, it seemed like more and more of them came up. Not that I didn't want to answer them or that I thought they were annoying. It was because I came up short on how to answer them.

I walked through the expansive foyer and was instantly greeted with the smell of chicken cacciatore and panzanella, my favorite dishes that my mother had perfected. I found my mom splitting the food among our plates. Her "Kiss the Chef" apron was tied on, her brown hair was in a messy bun, and she had dots of red sauce on her shirt. Our dinners were usually quick, but I made the time and effort to come every Sunday. I kissed her and found my pa at the dining table. He was already in his favorite spot and reading from his phone, probably some gossip news. Since we'd bought the record label, he had kept an eye on our artists. He hated not working.

I smiled. "Pops, how's it going?"

"I'm good. How are you? When are you cutting that thing off your face? You look like a Vecchio bavoso[1]. How does Rose put up with that thing looking like that?" my pa chastised.

My mom walked in with our plates and set them on the table. She brought out the drinks on her little cart as well. She shook her head.

"Oh, love. Stop harassing my baby. He's under a lot of stress already," she coddled.

"Thank you, Ma. At least I know you love me," I denoted as I stared at my pa, and he just shook his head. I smiled as she rubbed my head and kissed me on my forehead.

"But I would love to see my handsome son's face. So, your papà is right." She sat across from me.

"Maybe I will." I shrugged. Every Sunday, it was the same argument.

She smiled at my pa and me. We laughed at this because Ma could never stay mad at Pa or me. She always folded and gave in to us. We dug into our meal, and the conversation flowed into our chocolate panettone dish my ma bought from La Rosa. The chef and my mother were very close, and she could get anything from the restaurant if she wanted.

"I've been thinking about you guys record label. You need to get all of these artists on a one-on-one meeting and figure out if you can skim some of the fat," he said out of the blue.

I decided to hear him out, not that I had a choice. "You have, huh? Okay, let me hear the rest of it."

"I think you can trim the two lowest performing artists like this one, Lady J. She hasn't had a hit single since two thousand and two.

---

1   dirty old man in Italian

We can let her go quietly unless she has something cooking that can bring her back into this decade. I mean, even the retired singer Jasmine Grant makes more money and still has fans and is charting songs six years later." He finished.

Honestly, I had looked into it but never thought about cutting someone until our new CEO stepped in, and now that Pa mentioned it. My mind wandered to Jasmine, and I shook my head as I felt the blood rush to my cock.

We polished off our desserts and retreated to the massive black and gold family room when my mom asked me how Rose was working out for us. When I told my parents about our desire to share a woman, they gawked and had so many questions. Our parents questioned whether any woman would want three men. They didn't and couldn't understand it, but they tried not to get too far into our affairs. I told her the truth about Rose—she was only in our lives for Wren's benefit. Of course, that led to other questions of why he was the only one benefiting from the relationship when we were all supposed to be in it together, and I sat there for a minute.

"Well," I sighed. "I can't see myself with Rose. She's good for someone, but that person is not me or us. But Wren won't let her go."

"So, what happened? And don't tell me any bullshit!" my mom threatened, which made my pa turn his attention away from the television.

"We were in love with a girl we met at…." I never stumbled over my words nor lied to my parents, but I didn't want my parents to know about our Club Celeste days. I rubbed the back of my neck. "…a networking event, and we hit it off and dated for about six months, and then she decided she didn't want us."

There was a pregnant pause, and I squirmed in my seat. One thing I struggled with was how to satisfy my parents. We'd always had a great relationship, and I never wanted to disrupt that, not with any of my business ideas or personal relationships.

"So, she left you guys a while ago, but I can tell she hasn't left your mind." My ma peered at me with her pensive brown eyes.

"Yes, I still think about her." I wanted to lie, but she was right. "I know it sounds pathetic, but I opened myself up to someone I liked and thought it was enough, but it wasn't."

"It doesn't sound pathetic, and she's crazy to leave three amazing fellas like you guys. You need to forget her and move on with Rose or someone else. If you need any therapy, then you know your uncle is always there for you," my pa droned on.

"Honestly, we're okay. We don't talk about it anymore, and it was a blip in our past." I tried to convince myself.

"I can't tell you what to do, my love, but if you want your ma to sniff out someone for you, let me know. I won't let anything happen to my boys," she came and kissed me again.

"I know, Ma. Someone new has been occupying my time. I only met her once, but there's something I can't shake about her. Tony feels the same way, and Wren as well."

"So, ask her out, Gabe. I didn't raise any wimps. You go up to her and tell her like your nonno told your nonna. 'We're going out, and I won't hear anything otherwise,'" my pa stated.

I shook my head and smiled. That was his favorite story to tell about my late grandparents. My pa could be old school sometimes. He couldn't see that I had more obstacles facing me with Ms. Grant, like that pesky fiancé of hers. I wondered if Tony was right about him being a beard for her. I took a deep breath. There I went back to Ms. Grant, but I knew once I got home, I would have a long fucking time in the shower to think about how I would love to tell Ms. Grant about her relationship.

"I wish it was that simple, Pa, but she's taken." I averted my eyes to the bay windows.

"Well, it's never too late," my pa humphed as he turned back to the television. "What's meant to be will be. Remember that, son. Don't give up hope yet."

Ma clicked her tongue. "I don't agree with your Papà." She frowned at the back of his head. "But I think you should be upfront with her, and if there is a chance, then take it, but if not, cut your losses."

I just nodded, as for once in my thirty-one years, I was confused and lost about what to do.

By the time I pulled into my driveway, I texted Jasmine to invite her to a one-on-one meeting three times, and she denied me all three times. I sighed and wanted to chuck my phone out the car window.

This is more frustrating than I thought it would be.

Chapter 13

Jasmine

If someone looked up the word dummy in the dictionary, I was pretty sure you would see my name and picture as a prime example. I should have known that the text from Mr. Brine was fake because I thought it was weird that he would come back early from his vacation. But I took my ass down to La Rosa because free food was involved.

I didn't care how rich I got. I would never turn down free food. That was why I couldn't lose these extra pounds.

I had been on edge since my lunch date with Tony. I was so startled by how much the twins looked like him. Technically, I knew they looked everything like him, but seeing it up close was shocking. When he sat across from me at the restaurant, I thought he would serve me child custody papers, and I freaked out. But when he said he just wanted to talk, I looked into his eyes and was a goner. I should have gotten up and left, but deep down, I craved his companionship. It reminded me of our time together. We would hang out while eating and talking about the most random things. I missed that the most.

Also, the years had been good to him. He'd become even more muscular than I remembered. Was that even possible? His hair skirted his shoulders, and from what I noticed, his facial piercings were still there except for the tongue ring. My hands itched to find out if his dick piercings were still in place. Like Gabe, he still knew how to command a room.

I wasn't ashamed to admit that when I got home, I abused my dildo. It was the third time since that meeting with Mr. Brine. Ever since then, I couldn't stop masturbating when I thought of them, which was entirely too much if we're being honest. It was worse now than it was when I left all those years ago. When I thought of their names, I got so wet and frustrated that I snapped at anyone who distracted me while I was zoned out.

Now, I was paranoid, and every time I stepped outside, I thought it was the day they'd catch me and drag me to court. That thought alone kept me cemented in the house. After I dropped the twins off at school, I headed home. I got Allison to run my errands and spent my days like Greg, holed up in the house. I worked out like I was back in my performance days to burn off the extra energy. But somehow, it didn't help me at all. I would end up being frustrated and going to take a scorching shower that involved dropping my dildo on the floor several times until I finally got my release.

The things I go through for some me time.

Greg and I irritated each other because we were always stuck in the house together. The feeling may have been on my end alone. Since he worked from home, he was always around, and the littlest things set me off. Like when Greg would clip his long toenails in the living room and leave them there for the housekeeper. I was so appalled when I walked into the living room barefoot and felt the sharp bite in the bottom of my foot. When I looked down and saw his toenail clippings on my carpet, I nearly blew his head off when I confronted him. He shrugged and noted the maid would clean it up and not to worry about it.

Surely, his parents taught him better than that.

I thought I was losing myself between Tris and Teo starting first grade and Greg's lackadaisical personality. When I saw the text come in from Gabe, I nearly dropped my phone. A million and one questions ran through my head. Why did he want a one-on-one with me? I already went on a lunch date with Tony. I wanted my masters so I wouldn't have to show my face back at the office. No more run-ins with Gabe, Tony, or Wren.

Business-wise, I would be free… physically and mentally, not so much.

So, I did what I do best. I ignored the first text and then the second one. After the third one, I turned off my phone and turned it back on after an hour of agony. Every time the phone pinged, I jumped up and checked my phone – for what I didn't know. I knew I was being irrational because I did agree to a one-on-one with them, but I hadn't built up the courage to face them again.

I sighed as I pulled up to Tris and Teo's new school. I grinned as I saw the wide smiles on their little faces as they ran to the car. They busted into the car and started unloading about their day. I couldn't piece any of it together, so I let them talk while we pulled off to go to our Friday after-school date, The Tarte Café. The gray and black café was small, with only five small tables and a display of Paris treats that took up half the tiny store. They kicked their little legs when I pulled into the parking space. I fixed my signature curly weave, and when I got out, I fixed my clothes. I'd lost a couple of pounds from the workouts, so my clothes fit a little looser than usual.

We got our pastries and sat at our favorite table. I smiled as I listened to the boys talk about a new subject every two seconds. They were garrulous when they weren't tethered to their electronics. I watched as their eyes twinkled when they laughed, which caused me to laugh as well. We'd been finished with our pastries for about thirty minutes, but the boys were enjoying themselves, and I didn't want the fun to stop, nor did I want to go home to Greg.

An older white lady walked by and stopped right in front of our table. I looked at the strange woman as she stared at Tris and Teo. She had long brown hair and light brown eyes. Her skin was the color of sand, and her body was toned for someone her age. She had on light pink spandex leggings and a Led Zeppelin t-shirt.

I instantly got perturbed by her presence. I was kind of tired of people gawking at my children.

"Hello," I barked out to the lady. "Can I help you?"

She looked at me and back at my kids. I instantly straightened my back and was ready to give her the business. The boys stopped talking to peer at the lady.

"I'm so sorry, but your kids look exactly like my son's best friend," she stated.

"Oh, well, you know the saying. Everyone has a twin." I shrugged, not giving it much thought.

"Yeah." She finally drew her eyes away from the twins and saw the aggressive look on my face. "There must never be a dull moment at home." She smiled, and I instantly felt terrible. I was judging her without knowing what was going on in her life.

"Yeah, they keep me on my toes." A smile touched my face. "Would you like to sit with us?"

She smiled and nodded. "I'm sorry. I didn't mean to invade your privacy. It's just me and my husband. So, it gets lonely from time to time."

It was hard to explain why I allowed this lady to sit with us. But it seemed like the right thing to do after our aggressive standoff.

"I totally understand. What is your name?" I asked.

"Rosa Marino," I shook her hand. "What is your name?"

This woman doesn't know me from Adam. I chewed my bottom lip and hesitated. I didn't have time to speak when Teo blurted out, "My mommy's name is Jasmine Grant."

It be your own kids!

A warm smile touched her face, and you could call me crazy, but something told me I could trust her. I didn't know why, but the woman looked familiar. I sighed. As I sat there and watched her speak with the boys, something clicked like a light bulb in me.

"Wait, you're Rosa Marino. *The* Rosa Marino!" I gawked. Then I was the stalker who couldn't stop staring at her. "I attended your last runway show for Yves Saint Laurent."

"Yes, that's me," she smiled sadly.

"I'm sorry. I didn't mean to make you uncomfortable. Your career was inspiring. I love fashion shows." I held my head down shyly. "I hope I haven't scared you off."

"No, it's just that sometimes being recognized and still famous is a con for me," she smiled weakly.

"I get it. That's how I feel now that I'm retired." I gave her a weak half-smile.

I must have been star-struck because it explained why I told this woman my business. Teo scooted closer to me and used his hand to beckon me closer.

"Is this our grandma, Mommy?" I laughed nervously. If there was one thing my babies didn't know how to do, it was to whisper. Ms. Marino turned red and giggled.

"I'm sorry, Ms. Marino. Kids say the darndest things." I turned to Teo and continued, "This is a friend of Mommy's. Why don't you finish your drink, and we can get going? You guys have chatted enough for all of us today."

Teo and Tris returned their attention to their drinks and talking about their friends at school. Rosa and I continued to chat about different things. It wasn't until I glanced outside that I noticed the sun was setting. I got so caught up talking with Rosa that I forgot we were not at home. It'd been a long time since I conversed with anyone outside my little circle. I didn't realize how much I needed it.

"Do you mind keeping this between the two of us? I-I'm a private person."

She made the mouth shut sign. "Mums the word! And I'd appreciate the same as well."

I nodded yes.

We said our goodbyes, exchanged numbers, and right before we left, Rosa asked if it was okay to sit with us if we met up again. I told her I would love that. It was the closest thing I would get to a normal life, and I was eager for next Friday.

What a coincidence that another Friday had changed my little, quiet life.

When I got home, I received another text message from Gabe, but it was a bit more forceful this time. It stated all artists needed to have a one-on-one meeting. It made the hair on my neck stand up. My temperature rose a couple of degrees at the thought of being close to Gabe, Tony, or Wren. I was overthinking things, as I had been lately, but I'd rather be careful than find myself in a situation I couldn't control.

I changed and got the kids washed up. I shuffled them off to eat dinner in the dining room, where the chef set up the table for us with our food already plated for us. The boys took their usual seats next to me, and Greg came lumbering in like he'd had a hard day at work. I mentally sighed because he would take off once I opened the lid, and we wouldn't hear the end of it. I hoped he would have worked later, but that was wishful thinking.

He kissed me and greeted the boys.

"Hey baby, how was your day?" he asked.

"It was good. Tris, Teo, and I visited our favorite café and got some pastries."

"Nice," he beamed. "Tris and Teo, did you guys enjoy yourselves?" he asked.

"We did, Mr. Greg!" They broke into giggles like they had a secret between themselves.

Tris said, "We met this lady today."

"A lady?" He quirked a bushy eyebrow at Tris.

"Yes, some older lady. She seemed lonely and needed someone to talk to. So, I chatted with her for a while," I quickly added.

"Oh, Jas. That was very reckless of you. Did she talk with the boys?" he asked. I bit my tongue. I knew he was just being protective, but I could protect my kids.

"Yes, but the boys told her about their games and school. Nothing detrimental." I tried to smooth it over.

"You need to be careful since your mom mentioned," he pointed with his eyes to the boys, "their father was a dangerous man."

Now, I was confused about why my mother would have told Greg that Tony was a dangerous man. Fuck, now I had another thing to add to my growing list of things to straighten out. The list was like a vine. Every time I snipped some off, another grew back quickly.

"He's not dangerous, Greg. Anyway, how was your day?" I changed the subject.

That quieted the accusations about Tony. I was beyond pissed that someone would have the audacity to speak about him, especially my mom. Even though I couldn't really blame her, she could only assume since I never told her anything about the guys. *Rightfully so*. I wouldn't because I didn't want her putting anything into the twin's heads.

My life had become a mess if we were being honest.

"… So, I think you should attend this meeting and demand your masters. Tell them you'll do whatever it takes to get them back, or you may have to act like you would take serious action against them. You might even want to be a little persuasive." Greg said as he wiggled his bushy eyebrows and chuckled.

Again, for the second time tonight, I was taken aback. Greg basically wanted me to pimp myself out to get my masters. He wanted me to offer myself up to them for what was already mine. The kids had left sometime between me zoning out and Greg's fussing with his cell phone. My mouth twisted, and my eyes narrowed at him.

What type of man would say something like that?

I never in a million years expected to hear anything like that from anyone, let alone Greg. He had been really showing out and doing things that gave me pause about him, not to mention his love of chastising me for every little thing. Now I would have to add on being my pimp to my list. I saw what Allison said, what she feared of him. That he was an opportunist, he wanted to marry someone to control.

"I will meet with them then since it's necessary to get my masters," I spoke through my clenched teeth as much as I wanted to be contentious and not give in to his demand. I settled because I didn't want negative energy to follow me into this meeting.

I got up and left the room as he called my name. But I pretended like I hadn't heard him. I went to get ready for bed, and instead of sleeping in my bed, I made my way to the boys' rooms. Greg stopped me while I headed for their room. He begged me to sleep with him. But I couldn't stomach the idea of his leech-like hands groping me in the middle of the night. The acid churned in my stomach at the thought. He finally let me go when I told him I had my period. Even then, he said it would have been a perfect time to try for a baby.

I blanched at the suggestion as I hightailed it past him.

When I settled down, I received a text from Gabe that our meeting was the next day at noon. I fell asleep with that warm sensation in my stomach at the mere thought of being in a room with them again.

The sooner this is done, the better!

I didn't know what to expect from the meeting, but I dressed like I meant business—What type of business? I didn't know. I had on my red Balmain high-waisted pencil skirt and a white crop top that covered my bite mark on my breasts was tucked into the waist of my skirt. I let my fresh, retwisted, and bleached locs down. I added extra makeup on the bite mark on my neck. My white stilettos and red Telfar bag finished out my look. I thought I looked spectacular. Tris and Teo told me I looked beautiful, making me glow. Greg noted this outfit was made to get whatever I wanted. He shut up immediately after he saw the distasteful smirk on my face.

On my way to the office, I practiced what I would say if something should come up. I had the amount I wanted to offer them for my masters. Fifty million and not a penny more, or they would see me in court. I banked on them being reasonable with me so I could be in and out within twenty minutes or less because I didn't know how long I could hold up the façade without leaving a wet trail from their office to my car.

I won't picture them naked or with their cocks in their hands as they position themselves at my...

"Hello, Ms. Grant. Nice of you to join us," Gabe announced first as I walked into the room.

I didn't realize I had opened the door. Was I really that in my head? Sheesh.

"I'm sorry for not knocking. I was rushing because I thought I was late." My face grew hot. I cursed the stupid watch that I'd been meaning to fix for a while now.

Well, I'm off to a terrible start.

I sat down in the seat across from him. They'd brought a new glass desk for the office, so I guess I couldn't hide behind it. I crossed my legs and noticed Gabe's eyes follow the movement, and it shouldn't have, but it made me sit straighter. I met his eyes as he finished eye fucking me. My eyebrow cocked, and I saw the red color peeking out from his beard. But his eyes held something I couldn't quite place in them before he blinked, and it went away.

Two minutes in, and I'm already squirming in my chair.

He fixed his shirt. "No worries, I just got in myself. The others will be here shortly—"

"Ciao, Amor Mio[1], Jasmine," Tony hollered as he burst through the office like a ray of sunshine.

He wrapped his arms around my waist and lifted me into a bear hug. His hand slipped and ever so softly grazed my ass. Tony's hard cock dug into my stomach. He placed me on my feet, and thankfully, he held onto me because I thought I was going to topple over. I never would have thought in a million years he would have been able to pick me up, but I guess I was wrong.

"Ah, hello, Mr. Russo." My treacherous core clenched and throbbed. "You're in a good mood."

"Always when I see you, and you look amazing. Red looks great on you," Tony stated. "And it's Tony. Mr. Russo is my dad." He kissed me on my hand.

"Ah, t-thank you," I blushed.

"Hello, Jasmine," Wren came around. He kissed my cheek, and his eyes dipped to my shirt.

I glanced down and fixed up my shirt since Tony had pulled out the tucked shirt, and a bit of the makeup had rubbed off when he hugged me.

Great idea to wear a white shirt. My nipples were at attention like they were soldiers, and not even my bra was keeping them at bay.

"H-Hello, Wren. Glad you're in a better mood today." I

---

1 Ciao, Amor Mio- Hello, my love

stumbled after I found my voice.

He chuckled and said, "Yeah, I'm sorry for our last meeting. I was having a rough week."

I realized he was still holding my hand and rubbing circles on my wrist, which fogged my head. It was as if someone had grabbed my head and shook it. Then he placed his hand close to the bite mark on my shoulder, and I jumped back. Our eyes met, and I couldn't read them, which was a first since Wren wore his emotions on his face. I used to be able to read him like a book, but not anymore.

Clearing my throat, I said, "No problem. We all have bad days or weeks."

"Some more than others," he said. "How was your lunch date with Tony?"

I choked mentally. "It was good, actually. I had a great time."

I spoke the truth. I didn't have to, nor did I want to lie about that.

"Did you make it to your appointment on time?" Tony asked.

His question, although innocent, made my heart speed up more than it should have, and I stumbled over my answer. "Y-Yes."

"Good. I was worried you didn't make it." He smiled, and I melted into my seat.

They sat down and started a light conversation, but I couldn't stand it. My panties were so wet, my essence was dampening my inner thigh, and my nipples were painfully erect. I was wound up like a jack-in-a-box toy that was ready to explode.

So, I cleared my throat and cut the small talk.

"So, I would like to buy my masters. I'm willing to make an offer for them." I told them with as much confidence as I could.

"Okay, and we have a proposition for you. Would you like to become a talent scout?" Wren asked.

Wren and Gabe had been most talkative, but Tony's eyes

hadn't left my breasts since we sat down. It was like he was having a private meeting with them. I wished he would stop because they were so sensitive that when my shirt shifted, I had to bite back a moan and had a come to Jesus moment with myself for behaving like a teenager.

"I would have to think about it. I'm not looking for an active role. Now that I have done my part, I just want to collect what I deserve," I explained truthfully.

"Okay, how about we give you until the end of this month to think about the position?"

"Yes, that will work. I would have to talk with my fiancé about it, but don't get your hopes up." I cringed, and I hated that I even had to speak it.

Tony's mouth thinned into a straight line.

"Do you have children, Jas?" Gabe asked.

I was sure I looked ghastly because it felt like all the blood had drained from my body. The air in the room grew colder as it felt like I would die at any moment.

"W-What do you mean?" I stammered as my heartbeat to the rhythm of their clock.

"I mean, I understand if you and your fiancé have kids and you don't have the time," Gabe inquired, and he looked honest. He didn't know the magnitude of his question.

"No, I don't," I lied quickly. I'd never wanted to slap myself more than I did right then. It was definitely time to go. I needed to run fast. "Listen, I have to go. I'm offering you fifty million for my masters. Please think about it and get back to me at the end of the month as well. You fellas have a blessed day."

I was out of the office without hearing their goodbyes. I looked like a coward, but I couldn't stand it anymore. It'd been almost thirty minutes, and my juices leaked down my thighs. A long shower session with my new rose was what I needed. Soft footsteps followed me, or so I thought, but when I turned around, no one was there.

I must be going crazy.

I was almost to the elevator, to freedom, when I heard a soft voice.

"Konnichiwa[2], Ms. Grant!" Ms. May called from down the hall.

"Hello, Ms. May. How are you?" I loved Ms. May. Over the years, she'd become more than the office cleaner. She was like family.

"I'm wonderful," I smiled. "How are you and the family?"

"We're good, Jasmine. I got something for the boys. I have been waiting for you to come in, but you haven't been by in a while." She reached her dainty arms into her purse and pulled out the gifts for the twins.

"Oh, Ms. May, you didn't have to. They're spoiled rotten already."

"I saw these cloth tigers when I returned from back home and thought the boys would love them."

They loved tigers, and they loved to collect traditional toys from wherever we traveled.

"Oh, they will love them. I will give it to them. Did you get my holiday card?" I inquired.

"Yes, thank you for the money. We really needed it." She bowed slightly. "I won't keep you. Thank you for everything. Mata Ne[3], Ms. Grant."

She turned to return to her cleaning cart, but I got an idea of how I could use her help.

"Ms. May," I called, and she turned back to me. "You know we have new owners, and they seem nice. But I would like you to keep an ear out in case they plan on chopping me. Do you mind keeping an ear out for any gossip or news? I'd rather be informed than be blindsided."

Ms. May took a moment to think about this. Her pensive dark

---

2 Hello in Japanese

3 Goodbye in Japanese

brown eyes tried to figure out my angle and replied, "I will keep an ear out. We have to look out for each other." She winked.

"You still have my personal number. So, you can text me or call me whenever you hear anything."

She nodded yes, and we said our goodbyes. I turned to walk back to the elevators and nearly collided with Wren. My boxes flew to the floor. He grabbed me by the arms to steady me, and I almost melted in his hands. I had cooled down from being locked up in that room with them, and now, with him holding my arms, my body was threatening to faint. He bent to pick up my boxes when I was steady enough. He peered down to read them, and I snatched them from him.

"Seems I can't keep my hands off of you, Ms. Jasmine," Wren declared, and he smiled. "Who are Teodoro and Tristano? They must be lucky guys to get gifts."

"Right, I'm sorry. I didn't see you there. Oh, they're cousins of mine," I rushed out.

"Mm, interesting." He smiled. "What were you up to? Hiding in the cleaning closet."

"N-No, I was talking with Ms. May." I pointed to her cart which was now down the hallway.

"Oh, gossiping about us, huh?"

My face was feverish, and before I could respond, the elevator chimed. I jumped into the elevator, and to my surprise, Wren stood in the doorway and stared at me, which made the sweat on my back slide down.

"I should walk you to your car, Jasmine." His eyes pinned me to my spot against the elevator wall.

He had a gleam in his eyes that told me he was up to no good or that he could see how his touch wound me up. He pushed the lobby button and stood so close the hair on his arms grazed mine. A pool of warmth headed straight to my saturated panties, and I knew my juices would wet the leather of my seat.

We exited the elevator, and I tried to tell him I was okay to walk to my car, but he wouldn't take no for an answer. We had armed guards in the building and in the parking lot. I would be okay physically, but mentally, probably not. When I reached my car, I jumped in and turned it on. But he wanted to talk more when all I wanted to do was to get home and masturbate in peace. He tapped on my window, and I stupidly rolled it down.

That was my mistake.

"How tied are you to this fiancé?" he asked.

Wren was never this ballsy when we were together. That turned me on more than it should have. I guessed he'd changed. The heat from his gaze rendered me speechless as his silver gaze waited for my answer. But of course, I couldn't choke out the words.

Lost in my turbulent thoughts, I didn't see when Wren's hand gravitated to my breast and pinched my taut nipple. He roughly caressed my bud through my shirt and bra. You would think I had enough self-preservation because I was in a parking lot, allowing a man to grope me, but I didn't.

"W-What are you doing?" I stumbled out and grabbed his hand, stilling his movement. Not that it helped since he just cupped and squeezed the tender appendage.

"Shh, I'm giving us both what we need," he noted as I let go of his hand and it descended.

I should have stopped him, but I didn't.

"I-I can't. I-I'm engaged." I stammered, but I said it more for myself rather than Wren.

His hand disappeared under my skirt, and I greedily opened my legs till the fabric couldn't stretch anymore to give him better access as he found his way to the warm soaked center. His eyes lit up when he felt my wet folds. He smiled so widely I thought he'd split his face. *I should stop him!* I thought, but I didn't—couldn't. Instead, the deprived woman in me scooted into his open palm as I fought for purchase to my sanity.

I was down bad.

"Are you wet for me?" he asked, and I almost yelled out a duh, but my voice caught in my throat when he swiped his finger and dipped inside my folds. He plunged two fingers, knuckles deep, into my hot core, and his thumb found my engorged clit. All the while, we stared deep into each other's eyes. He moved in closer like he would kiss me but held back as I rode his fingers. Each time he thrust into my wet pussy, I matched his strokes by lifting my hips. His fingers curled and hit that spot that had my back arching away from the leather seat. My Tesla swayed with our intoxicated dance. I was drunk on his sandalwood scent that filled the car and the soft caress of the kisses he placed from my earlobe to the corner of my mouth.

"Please, Wren," I moaned in my raspy deep voice.

"Please, what?" He taunted me while still bringing me to my apex. "Tell Daddy what you want?"

"I need to come, Daddy," I absentmindedly whimpered out.

I was a needy mess as I clung to his arm, digging my fingers into him.

His free hand found my nipple and pinched and rolled the forgotten sensitive peak without mercy. He leaned over and sucked my earlobe. My body tingled from his soft breath as he whispered for me to come on his fingers. And you know what my treacherous body did? Came so hard that the Los Angeles blue skies lit up with stars. I let my head hit the headrest and closed my eyes shut to help calm the pounding in my ears.

Wren's chuckle made my eyes pop open. I looked over at him as he took his wet fingers and sucked them off slowly, and he moaned. I felt myself grow warm again.

I sat there and stared into his eyes as we wordlessly spoke. My body was still warm, and my bottom lip quivered in my post-orgasm state.

Wren winked and smirked. "You taste very familiar, Jasmine Grant." With that, he turned and walked back to the office.

All the way home, I banged my head on the headrest. I cursed myself all the way to my house and straight into my bedroom with Greg hot on my heels. I slammed the bathroom door in his face because I couldn't stand to look at him.

I stood in the mirror like I was standing before a judge. The tip of my nose and ears was a slight pink color. My breast was still sensitive as it rubbed against the cotton shirt. Shame, disgust, and anger were what I should have felt.

But I felt more alive than I had in years. The silver glint in Wren's eyes, his sandalwood scent still stuck in my mind and if I squeezed just right, I could still feel his thick fingers that touched the place inside me that had been abandoned since I left them in room seven.

I'm in big trouble.

Chapter 14

Wren

Have you ever felt as if you had to follow someone? The prickling sensation of someone or something that edged you hightail it behind them. That was how I felt when Jasmine got up and swayed those curvy hips out of the office. Granted, I tried my hardest not to ogle her breasts, unlike Tony, who was salivating over her nipples that stayed erect the whole time. Okay, I glanced a bit too much on the couple of occasions that Gabe wasn't eye fucking her from his seat.

So that's why he replaced that enormous desk Mr. Brine had in here.

It wasn't until the soft click of the door that something snapped inside of me. It was like Jasmine was metal, and I was a magnet. This was quite fitting since I now had silver hair. I digress. I was up and out of my chair before Tony or Gabe could reel me back in. Even when they called my name, I didn't listen.

I dipped and followed Jasmine's hips as she sashayed down the hallway. One minute I was watching her ample ass, the next, I had dodged into the empty office space near the cleaning closet. It was wrong, but I overheard everything she told Ms. May. So, our little Jasmine wanted to spy on us. She was playing with fire, and if there was one thing we knew how to do, it was to put them out.

I hadn't meant to disrespect her or Rose, which I did. When I got to her car, I had too much of her vanilla and citrus perfume in my system, which led me to want to know if the inside tasted as good as the outside smelled. And it did. One taste and I recognized she was our stray Kitten.

Well, maybe.

Okay, to be fair, I was ninety percent—okay, well, sixty percent—certain that she was Kitty. But I needed proof, or Gabe and Tony wouldn't believe me for even mentioning it without concrete evidence. Could it be that she was living right under our noses?

I chewed my bottom lip as I entered the office with Gabe and Tony. They looked at me like I had grown a horn out of my head.

"Ms. Grant is interesting," I dreamily stated, and I smiled.

I didn't have to look over to know that their eyebrows were near their hairline.

"She is, isn't she? Did you see her nipples were hard the whole time after I hugged her?" Tony sighed. "I've never been a breast man, but I wanted to slip in between those pillows and suffocate in them."

That was the first time I'd seen Tony in love with breasts. He was always the ass man. I guess he'd changed since he was sporting a woody. He had a blissed-out smirk on his slightly pink face as I peered at him. His pink tongue peeked out to wet his plump lips. I'd missed his tongue piercing, which he removed out of spite, and the opening closed in a week.

Tony took it out once Kitty left since it was one of her favorite things, and he needed time without it. He did it to punish Kitty in his own sort of way, which backfired on him because the tongue repairs itself quickly.

The crack of my neck helped ease the slight pressure that gathered in my neck. I knew I was stalling on telling them about my incident. So, I bit the bullet, and I got down to telling them everything I overheard and how I accidentally finger fucked her in the parking lot. It pissed Tony off that he wasn't there, and Gabe pinched his nose, a sign he was losing the last bit of patience he had for us—well, anybody.

"Wren, I expected this from Tony because he has no common sense sometimes, but not you," Gabe huffed out.

"Hey, I'm right here." Tony waved his arms and rolled his eyes. "I'm so proud of you for taking the bull by the horns." He smiled and slapped my back, and Gabe glared at him.

"This could cost us millions, Wren, if Jasmine says you sexually assaulted her. The shit would hit the fan. Our families' names and businesses would be ruined," Gabe commented, and he was right mostly. But I didn't think she would. She was as eager as I was for the release.

Too bad I was the one with blue balls.

"I don't think she will," I thought out loud. I rubbed my hand through my hair. "Fuck, now I'm not sure, but I'm definitely sure she's hiding something. She tastes like Kitty-"

"I'm going to stop you right there because, for one, you can't go off of a taste from six years ago. Second, Kitty is long gone, and it's time we moved on," Gabe declared.

Being defiant, I turned to Tony. "Tony, baby. We agreed to leave it in the past, but I promise you it's her… well, I think it's her. Okay, honestly, I'm sixty percent sure it's her."

Tony stared out the window. "Gabe's right about one thing. You can't just say that because Jasmine's arousal reminded you of her. Plus, aren't you head over heels in love with Rose?"

"I-I," I stammered. "I wouldn't say love."

I forgot about Rose in all of this. My stomach violently churned at her name because even despite her irritating me most of the time, I knew she was still in our lives.

I remembered when she first hit me. It took me by surprise because I'd accidentally slipped up and told her I didn't like her dress. That was about a month ago, and ever since then, it'd been rocky with us. I secretly despised being around her, but I grew weary of us finding anyone else.

That was why I put up with the bullshit because I hated the endless dating cycle we had become accustomed to. The first date frustration when we have to explain our relationship. The blatant look of disgust and judgment on some of the dates faces when we told them our preferences. It became like a job requirement checklist whenever we had to start over. Instead of enjoying meeting new people, it became more of a task.

I changed the subject to something I could control at that moment.

"She told us she didn't have kids, right?" I asked as I walked over to Tony and hugged him from behind. "But Ms. May gave her gifts for her 'boys'. When I asked her, she claimed they were her cousins. Is it me, or is that weird? Who calls their cousins her boys?"

"What were their names?" Tony asked.

"Don't even go there, Tony. I'm not having you track down kids and hospital records," Gabe forewarned.

Tony and I rolled our eyes.

"I mean it, Wren." Gabe continued. "You're becoming like Tony. You can't be in 'love' with one girl and want another one. It's not right for either of them. Even if Rose is like a thorn in our ass, she doesn't deserve to be cheated on. You, of all people, should realize that because you had a similar experience."

I sighed. Gabe was right. I hated to admit it. He always brought up the girl I thought I was head over heels in love with during my freshman year of college. Melissa Santos was hot and bright. She had long, curly hair, a fantastic smile, and beautiful blue eyes. We did everything together to the point where everyone thought seeing one without the other was weird. It was midway into the second half of the school year when I walked into her dorm room and found her bent over her computer chair by Joseph Graham, the captain of the robotics team. To add salt to the wound, when she saw me, she told me to get the fuck out and close the door. We never spoke after that, not even for an official breakup.

Dating in college wasn't for the faint of heart.

But that was then, and this was now. What I did with Jasmine was wrong, but I still held firm to what I believed—that she was Kitty—and Gabe was grumpy and horny.

"What you did was fucking reckless and irresponsible. You owe Jasmine an apology for that and Rose, as well." Gabe looked like he was either going to burst a blood vessel or strangle me.

"Oh, so it's okay for you to look up pictures of her and masturbate to her, huh?" I chided. I thought he was joking, but he rounded the table before I could blink and was a mere inch from my face. He was so fucking close that the short strands of his messy beard tickled my face.

He looked like a barely hinged person, and then he grunted—sorry, he growled, for me to get the fuck out of the office before he bashed me into the glass table. Tony had his hands between us when I grabbed him. Gabe had been full of himself lately. I didn't care how much shit was going on. I wouldn't be spoken to like that. My bullying phase happened a long time ago and I didn't plan on it returning.

When we got home, Tony headed to his room. He had been eerily quiet during the car ride, and I decided he'd had enough for the day. One thing about Tony was when he was quiet like this, it was best to leave him alone. Unlike Gabe, Tony wouldn't unload on you. He wasn't as aggressive as Gabe but could be a hard-ass like him.

Two peas in a pod.

I was headed to the bathroom when a knock on the door got my attention. I thought it would have been Gabe coming to apologize, but it was Tony. He asked if he could sleep in my room for the first time in months. I told him yes, and he got naked. He didn't even have to ask me. I undressed and brought my lips to his as we devoured each other in a kiss that left me breathless. Working out our frustration in our fiery kiss. It was as if we hadn't seen each other ten minutes ago. He grabbed my neck and released me from his brutal kiss. Tony's minty, warm breath caressed my face. We stood like that having a stare off, for a few minutes, which reminded me of earlier with Jasmine.

It did not prepare me for the next question, which should have grossed me out, but instead, it turned me on.

"Let me smell it." He demanded, and he didn't have to explain further. I should've been disgusted, but I held my finger that was soaked with Jasmine's juices to his nose, and he sniffed the barely present scent. His jaw twitched as he picked up the faint smell.

"Turn around," he grunted. I got shivers down my spine for what was to come.

I did as I was told and got on all fours, waiting for my punishment. When Tony groaned, I looked back to watch him as he lubed up his enormous cock. He would not be forgiving today. I knew that for sure as he slapped me on my ass cheek hard, and the sound ricocheted through the room. He didn't try to soothe the sting either. The second slap drew me back to reality. I went to tell him off, but he thrust his cock into me in one stroke.

I heard his deep groan and he found his footing behind me.

He gave me just enough time to adjust before he started to thrust deeply. He pulled all the way out to my entrance and thrust back in. He reached around me and took my sensitive cock in his hand. His pace never wavered as the light scent of his Baccarat Rouge 540 fragrance filled my nostrils. The piercings on his cock branded me as it rolled over my walls. My balls were already tight and drawn from earlier, but now it felt painful as I felt my thick cock grow in his hand. But he didn't relent when I said I was going to cum. He just sped up his strokes as he followed in his pursuit to finish with me. I tried to cling to my sheets, but I failed as my body began to tremble from my impending orgasm. I cried out my pleas because I needed it after Jasmine left me aroused to the point I nearly came on myself. Tears fell from my eyes and onto my bed, mixing with the sweat that dripped from my body. Tony, the sadist, with one hand keeping its pace on my cock, the other found my neck, his latest favorite position. He leaned over and started fucking me faster, tightening his hand around my neck and his grip on me. The pressure on my throat made me woozy as I felt myself getting close to the edge. A couple of long, even strokes from the base to the tip of my already painfully hard cock, and I came all over my bed and his hand.

His unyielding strokes kept me withering on the bed as my shaky knees barely held my lower half up. I was hot, clammy, and thoroughly spent. I exhaled when I felt Tony collapse on top of me, releasing the chokehold he had me in while his hot cum filled me up. He slipped his soft cock out of me and sat against my headboard. I don't know how, but I crawled between his legs and rested my head on his chest. From this angle, I could see the wet spot our cum made on my green sheets.

Tony held me in his arms, rubbing my forearm for what seemed like hours before he sighed.

"I think I believe you," he whispered softly. It was almost as if he was saying this for himself.

"You think?" I said, confounded.

"Yes, but I can't be sure, Wren. That's the God's honest truth." He switched me over so he could get up. He paused at the bathroom door. "Let's not discuss it tonight. I have so much brewing inside of me emotionally that I wouldn't make a sound decision, especially if it turned out to be true."

With that, he walked into the bathroom. As I sat there, I

wondered what I would say or do, even if it were true. The hurt from everything we went through to Tony's alcohol addiction, The grumpy madman demeanor Gabe had picked up, our trio almost breaking up, and my desperate need to start our little family.

The betrayal would be the most fucked up thing.

The following two weeks were strange. They were the longest Gabe and I hadn't spoken or interacted with each other. It was worse because our family reunion had passed. Each year my family, the Russos, and Sabinos get together for a weekend. The three-day event was usually filled with lots of food, the squalling of children in our families, and laughter. But not this year. Gabe avoided me, us, and our families made several attempts to figure out the problem between us.

Our little tiff lasted so long that it affected our weekly family dinner, which was uncomfortable for our families during our standoff approach period. Tony had tried to intervene but was unsuccessful in taming the Hollywood Hills Yeti. We just went on avoiding each other, which was becoming exhausting.

We threw a party for our employees at both businesses. Even though Gabe still had spoken nothing other than a hello or goodbye to me. At first, I didn't let it bother me because I figured he was grumpy. After all, he hadn't had sex in a while. But little by little, he chipped away at my brick wall. Now I felt so mentally spent, so much so that I sulked in my room and had not even tried to go out with Rose—well, to be honest, that may have been the only shining light in this whole debacle. I hadn't noticed how Rose suffocated me until I had spent some time away and really observed my time with her.

I was about to drag myself to the gym to at least work out since I had all of this pent-up energy, and I couldn't fall asleep when Tony barged into my room. His black hair framed his wild shoulders. He was dressed in black shorts and a white sleeveless shirt.

"I can't take it anymore!" he exclaimed. "It's driving me crazy, sitting and waiting around for the shoe to drop."

I tilted my head at him. Tony was locked away in his office for almost three days after we returned from our office party. Jasmine attended in a silver mini dress that drew us like moths to light. Of course, when we tried to get close to speak with her, she slithered away, as we watched the sway of her ass in her departure. Gabe liked to say he wasn't affected, but I saw him bore a hole into her anytime she inhaled.

Poor old grumpy horny Gabe!

"What are you talking about, Tony? Have you been drinking again?" I mentally slapped myself for the joke.

Tony's eyes turned dark with anger, but he shook it off in a blink. "No, I haven't had a drink in almost five years." He cleared his throat. "I have a plan to find out about Jasmine. I know she's hiding something, and it's been killing me for the past two weeks."

"So, what are you planning?" I asked because I was confused.

"We're going on a brief trip to Ms. Grant's house." He smiled as I gawked at him. "What? Don't look at me like that!"

"Are you okay? Like seriously, okay? Or have you bumped your head?" Because what he was thinking was beyond incomprehensible.

"I might be slightly going crazy, but that's beside the point." He jumped on the bed. "It's a foolproof plan, and we will be in and out with no one noticing."

"No."

"Come on, Wren. Don't you want to know?" He pleaded, "I mean, I'm doing it without you. So, either you come or don't. But I won't let you know what I find if you don't."

"Tony, please don't. You don't even know—" I stopped mid-sentence. "Wait, that's what you've been doing all this time in your office. How did you find her information?"

"Well, I found more than that—"

"What do you mean?"

"Well, I did some digging and asked around the office. It seems our little Jas went MIA for over a year, and when she finally made an appearance, she was withdrawn. Doesn't that seem odd for one of the most famous artists to go MIA for so long?"

"I'm pulling a page out of your book. Where's the proof? And not some office gossip. Plus, if Ms. May found out you were asking questions, she would tell Jasmine."

"And that's where we come in." He rubbed his hands together and grinned. "I will hack into Jasmine's security system. One of us will go in and gather the information on her and leave. Easy peasy. It will be like that one time we broke into the frat house."

Yeah, except I did all the work since I was the only one who knew how to pick a lock. I got us in and out without bumping into anyone. I pushed the short bangs out of my face.

"Fine, but I'm only doing this because I don't trust you to get in and out without messing shit up," I retorted. "And we're not telling Gabe, or he will have a stroke."

"Deal." We shook hands. "Be ready in the next thirty minutes. All black attire and a hat for that silver hair."

My mouth dropped open. "Tony, you didn't tell me it would be right now!"

He winked at me. "Come on, the sooner we get the information, the sooner you can be deep inside Jasmine's tight pussy, getting her pregnant."

I tapped my foot. Tony could be a lot sometimes. "I don't want her to get pregnant, well, not only for that reason. I don't care who goes first, I just want us to find the right one for us."

"Okay, come on, Shakespeare, we have a home to raid. It's already midnight," he stated.

I rolled my eyes and tapped my foot lightly against the hardwood floor. Tony had the craziest ideas, and I sometimes went along with them.

Love will make you do the craziest things.

I pulled on some black gym clothes and a hat because how easy would it be to catch someone with silver hair and pale skin? I really didn't remember why I dyed my hair this color. As I ran down the stairs, I almost fell over Gabe. He had on his typical pissed, gloomy face when he looked me over. I opened my mouth to speak, but he held his hand up and stated, "I don't even want to know."

Well, fine, I wasn't telling your grumpy ass, anyway.

I hopped in the car, and Tony was already driving away before I could put the seatbelt on.

"You don't need it, Wren." He grinned as I looked at him. "She basically lives in our backyard. She's five minutes away."

I stared at him. Could Kitty have been living only five freaking minutes away, and we were here like some newbies with our dicks in our hands? Could life be that cruel?

It took Tony four minutes to get to her home, which shook me because he sped down the hill so fast that the gates and the trees were one big blur. I felt my heart rate triple when he pulled up in front of her massive brown electric gate.

"I have to jump that fence?!" I exclaimed warily. Even though I knew the answer, I still had to ask.

"Yes, my fit stallion." He grabbed my face and kissed me. "Just kidding, I will shut down her security, and you can push the gate in. After that, it's a quick jog to her house."

"Define a quick jog," I asked.

"I think a minute or two. Jasmine's property is one mile in."

"A fucking mile? Tony, that will take me ten minutes to run," I yelled.

"Take one for the team, Wren."

I sighed. "Couldn't you at least drive me up a bit and then wait?"

"No, you got this. Plus, I have to stand guard."

I rolled my eyes. "Whatever! Can I go now?"

"Yes, you're good to go."

I rushed out of the car, wanting to get this over with. The gate, to my surprise, was heavier to push open than I thought. My muscles rippled under my black hoodie as I pushed the gate wide enough for me to slip through. I can't believe I got myself into this, I thought as I jogged to Jasmine's house—excuse me, mini-mansion. It was beautiful, with a white brick exterior and huge windows that must flood the home with natural light during the day. Her lawn to the house was immaculate and nothing short of what you would see here in the Hills. She had lots of flaky juniper shrubs and cedar trees to keep her privacy. The front of the house had tons of lilacs and rose buckwheat fragranced the air.

As I reached the house, I leaned against the brick wall to catch my breath. My thighs burned slightly, and my lungs demanded that I suck in fragrant air. I closed my eyes, still leaning on her home away from the windows, even though it was dark inside, cursing Tony for getting me in this mess.

I used the time to text the knucklehead Tony and told him I was there. He gave me the green light. I cursed as I looked at the digital and traditional lock combo. Tony handled the digital lock, but the deadbolt was engaged. So, I got my lock pick items I'd had since college and got to work. It had been a minute since we'd had to pick anything, so I struggled as the lock kept slipping from the tool. I cursed Tony, Gabe, and everyone from here to New York. They said old habits die hard, but that didn't apply to lock picking. Second, who doesn't have a fully digital lock in this century?

My back was wet with my sweat, and just when I was ready to give up, I heard a click and twisted the door handle.

Fuck YEAH!

If I'd been anywhere else, I would definitely have celebrated and shouted about my success, but not now. I did a victory dance, and I heard a buzz from my phone from Tony telling me to quit goofing around.

I rolled my eyes. Tony couldn't let me have this one victory dance moment.

I pushed the door and stood inside the vast open space foyer. The back of the house was all floor-to-ceiling windows. The formal dining area, living room, and kitchen flowed into each other. There was a long off-white hall to my right, so I started there. She had black marble flooring throughout, and I felt bad for walking on it with my sneakers. I could hear my ma screaming in my head that I was being disrespectful. I opened the first door. It was an office. But it looked like a stuffy old man's office, not Jasmine's. The smell of old molded books made me close the door quickly as I moved on to the next one.

I was at the last door when I pushed in, thinking it would be a dead end. Nope, I found a lilac office that mirrored Jasmine's space at the label, overlooking the pool and a kid's play area. I would file that away for further investigation purposes. It was pitch black in the office, and I was so nervous that someone would see the light and investigate. So, I used my flashlight on my phone to search her closet and file cabinet. I found some paperwork for a company in someone else's name, Stephanie Johnson. I took a picture of that and kept moving.

It wasn't until I got to the last drawer of her desk that I found an album. I saw pictures of her when she was young, maybe fifteen, and a variety of other photos. I couldn't pinpoint which one I should take. So, I took pictures of most of them.

I would have gotten to search some more if I hadn't heard the door open and shut. Luckily, I ducked under the table just in time. I listened to Jasmine's deep feminine voice as she cursed her fiancé. She called him a lazy big dick and I almost snickered but held it back. She didn't even turn on the light as she opened one of the locked drawers and took out something. I couldn't see what because it was way too dark, and I had hidden under the desk.

So, I dared to poke my head out and saw her silhouette. She had on a long t-shirt she probably wore to bed—I knew it wasn't meant to be sexy, but seeing her bent over while the purple t-shirt rode up her ass had my cock straining against my gym pants. I squinted from my position and saw that she didn't have any panties on, and I felt my cock weep.

Shit. Don't let me cum in my pants from a peep show.

When she found what she was looking for, she popped up, and the shirt gathered on top of her ass. She pulled it down, and I almost groaned, but I held my hand against my mouth. She sighed, muttered something about her need for the real thing, and rolled her neck. Almost like a trance, I heard her close the door behind her, and I was up and out the door before I could lose her. She walked past a couple of doors in the long hallway and turned into the one room I thought was a guest room. I followed behind and pressed my ears to the door but couldn't hear anything.

I knew I should go, but wouldn't I have been a total ass if I didn't check to ensure she was okay?

Yeah, I needed to make sure she made it to her destination. That was my story.

I cracked the door to the plain room that was void of any warmth. I crept in and locked the door behind me. There was a silent, puttering sound of something going off in the small room. It drew my attention to the bathroom. I admitted I should be out of her house and halfway down her driveway, but I was nosey. As I poked my head around the corner, I heard a soft sigh.

I thanked God I hadn't turned around.

Jasmine stood near the sink with the inside of her right leg pressed flat against the counter and the oversized T-shirt hiked up over that glorious plump ass. She threw her head back and slammed her eyes shut. Her small hand pushed the dildo in and out of her wet pussy.

The sound of the dildo and her juice as it entered her made me jealous of the red toy. Jasmine's full lips were slightly parted, and the most hypnotizing moan flowed out, followed by my name. I thought I had control over my body, but one minute I was at the door with my leaking cock, and the next, I pulled her hand away from what was mine.

Her eyes popped open, and I watched from the mirror as terror replaced disbelief. Her bottom lip trembled. I paused to allow her to send me away because I didn't want her to do anything she wasn't comfortable with. As I stood there, we had round two of our stare off, and then she opened her sexy little mouth and said the magic words, "I need you, please."

Without hesitation, I did it. I wrapped my hand around her neck and plunged the toy right into her. I thought she would fight me on it, but she reveled in it. As I drove into her with long, fast strides and a slight squeeze of her neck, she moaned my name as I tightened my grip on her neck. Her free hand found her clit that peeked out, ready for her to circle and stroke it. Jasmine turned a subtle shade of pink but never stopped meeting my thrusts, and I didn't ease up. I was about to cum in my damn pants as pushing the dildo into her tight cunt became harder. She slowed down her thrusts, and I tightened my hold on her neck.

I leaned in and whispered, "Come for Daddy, Gattina". She shook like a leaf, her eyes snapped shut, and she yelled my name as I let go of her neck. Her head dropped to the sink's marble countertop, and I removed the dildo. She was the same height as Kitty as well. Perfect for me. It wasn't until her breathing returned to normal, she spoke.

"What are you doing in my house?" she asked breathlessly.

"The better question is, why are you here in a house with someone you don't love or can't please you?" I challenged back, and she shocked me as she whipped around and stared at me.

Bang! Bang! Bang!

"JASMINE! Baby, are you okay? Open the door," Greg wailed

like a bitch.

I started for the door. I don't know why because I didn't know what I would do. But Jasmine stopped me before I could make it there.

"Please don't cause any trouble for me," she pleaded.

"Baby, open up, or I'll call the locksmith," Greg wailed.

"I'm coming, Greg. Go back upstairs. I'm okay," she yelled.

I smirked and shook my head.

"Don't even make a joke!" she whispered and ran to the window. "I don't know what you guys are up to but stop it. I mean it."

I knew she meant to be serious, but she was too adorable when she was mad. She stood with her hips cocked to the side. Her small, dainty finger pointed at me while she scolded me.

"Okay, baby. Whatever you say. Just remember you're ours."

"I'm not yours or anybody else's!" she hissed.

I smirked. "Sure."

She stood wide-eyed, and her mouth dropped open slightly. I took that opportunity to kiss her before she could come to her senses. She allowed me to place her hand over my crotch. I thought she would protest, but she stroked me through my pants. Her hand never left my crotch, even after our lips parted ways.

With that, I took the dildo I was still holding while Greg continued to bang on the door. Her eyes widened even further when I popped it into my mouth to suck off her release. Her hand, absentmindedly still applying slight pressure with her slow strokes, had me wishing I could tear it off of my hot body. My back stiffened, and the warmth in my stomach flooded out of me along with my release. I wasn't embarrassed—Well, maybe just a bit. No point in denying it. I struggled to regain my breathing. Her eyes bugged out, and I kissed her again as I hopped out the window and ran down the driveway.

It took me half the time to get back because I was hopped up on endorphins, and I jumped in the car before Tony ruined the moment. I kissed him, and we shared the best kiss. We sucked and moaned as we lapped up our Kitty's juices until nothing was left. We sat there breathless.

"I hate you! Twice in a month, and I get the leftovers," he muttered. He pulled off as I recounted every single second of our encounter.

"Who is this Wren, and what did he do with my loveable softie? Wait, you mean to tell me you gave her a hand necklace?" He turned to look at me when we finally parked in our driveway.

"It was just a feeling," I shrugged. "Your spirit possessed me. Like, all jokes aside, this is Kitty."

"What did you get that's proof?" Tony questioned. His arm tapped the wheel lightly. He was just as anxious as I was.

I showed him the pictures and my other observations. He sighed. "What am I supposed to be looking for, Wren?" He seemed confused.

"She has a business under a different name, Stephanie Johnson," I pointed out.

"That's not proof, though, Wren. You and I know that."

"Fuck, you're right. I didn't have enough time."

"Yeah, 'cause you were thinking with your dick. Which, by the way, did you cum in your pants?" He looked at my semi-wet crotch.

I gave him a droopy smile. "Yes, when she stroked me through my pants. I felt myself jerk and explode from kissing her."

"How the hell were you so lucky? I can't believe I'm jealous of my own damn boyfriend."

"Don't be a hater. Okay, you remember Kitty had a honey birthmark under her breast?"

"Yes, shit. Did you check for the bite mark? Or the birthmark?"

Oh fuck! I had my chance to check, and I missed it because I got hypnotized. He didn't have to look at me to know the answer to the question.

"You're the worst spy partner ever." He shook his head. "Let's see what this business tells me and hope this is enough.”

Damn, I really fucked that up. I worried, biting my bottom lip, and tried to figure out how I would distract my love from our current predicament when the perfect idea to help relax Tony popped up in my head. We made our way towards my half of the house. My wing was simple, with gray walls and white accents that always uplifted my mood. Light hardwood floor throughout my area. I had the same wall-to-ceiling windows in my corner, but I had light green sheer curtains that covered them. We stumbled into my room and started getting ready for bed. We usually slept naked, and tonight was no different, as I made my way to stand in front of a naked Tony.

“Koibito[1], I think you should be rewarded for all of your hard work. Don’t you think so?” I asked, not taking my eyes off the light green eyes I have come to love.

“Yes, I deserve to be rewarded for all the torture I’ve been through,” Tony said with a smirk.

“Lay on the bed, Tony. Knees to your chest and hands on that masterpiece in between your legs,” I commanded. “I think I earned a taste of you, Koibito. Don’t you think?”

Tony’s black eyebrows raised to his hairline as a half-smirk appeared on his beautiful face “Yes, you have, my sweet love. But are you asking me or telling me?”

“Both.”

Tony all but jumped in the bed as he threw off my decorative pillows. His back on the bed with his legs spread and lifted to his chest. His beautiful pink tight ring of muscles was within a mere inch of my face, and both of his soft hands on his long cock. I looked up to the man that I would do anything for and saw nothing but love shining in those marvelous light green eyes. Every day, I wondered how I was lucky to find my better half.

____

1   Sweetheart in Japanese

Spreading his small cheeks a bit more gave me enough space to work, I worked the spit that had gathered from me salivating over seeing Tony in this vulnerable position. Tony hates this but I guess with everything going on with our Jasmine situation, he needed to step back. I puckered my lips and let the glob of spit drop in his puckered entrance. He shuddered when it hit his entrance and gripped his dick harder. My finger touched him as I used my spit to tease and coat his rosebud. Slipping a finger into him, I knew he was tense as my poor finger barely made it past the opening.

"Relax, Koibito," I said. Using my finger to massage the muscles some more, Tony began to relax more each time my fingers made a complete loop around it.

I helped ease some of the tension from his legs by holding him at the crook of his knees. Glancing up, Tony was using both hands to stroke himself while his eyes narrowed, and the pupils overtook the light green of his eyes. Without breaking our connection, I kissed the heavy ball sac that lay between us and removed my finger, which was still massaging the puckered muscle. My pink tongue flattened as I ran it over it, causing Tony to shudder and stiffen slightly. My tongue made work of his tight hole as I licked and buried myself inside of him. Tony lifted off the bed as he arched his back. His hands squeezing and stroking his massive dick, from the looks of his dick, he wouldn't last long. Tony's breath hitched as I curled my tongue inside of him, rubbing at the thin walls.

"W-Wren…Fuck…Shit," he said, and I couldn't help the smile that was placed on my face.

Over and over, I swirled and worked over the rosebud. My own grunts joined Tony's. His earthy taste coated my tongue as I continued to wring out his orgasm. Looking up at my love's face, his eyes were barely open. Some of his pre-cum dripped on the smooth skin in and around his belly button. The legs I held started to tremble and shake as he drew nearer to coming. I removed one of my hands from his knee and placed his knee in a bent position. Tony had sweat dripping off his body and a red flush to his olive skin.

"You're almost there, Koibito. You've been so good. Keep stroking our cock like that."

Tony only whimpered and shuddered as his strokes slowed on his cock. One hand shot off his heavy, angry dick and plunged into my hair as he tried to get me back onto his needy hole. But I didn't bulge. Instead, I plunged my two fingers into him. My thick fingers searched for the little elastic button that would give me what I wanted…what he wanted. I curled my fingers and found the spongy spot.

"I'm going to make you cum all over yourself. You've been so good, Daddy," I heard my gruff voice call out.

I massaged the little treasure spot. His body started to tremble, and my mouth latched onto his ball sac as I teased him with my mouth. Tony grunted out, "Fuck!" as ribbons of cum splattered his abs. Tony went limp as his sticky hand dropped to his side. His breathing slowed down as he rode out his orgasm. I pulled away and smiled at my handiwork.

Tony was still muttering shit in a daze when I leaned over and licked his sweet cum off of him. Looking at Tony, he had nothing but love and admiration shining in his lust-filled eyes.

"You…I love you, il mio tutto[2]."

"I love you too, Koibito. We'll get our girl and complete our family. This I promise you." I reassured him with a chaste kiss as his eyes closed.

I went to get a washcloth to clean Tony up while he rested. After I was done, I lay next to my love. I couldn't be sure, but I hoped what I promised Tony would come true, or I would have failed two people I loved.

---

2   My everything in Italian

Chapter 15

Tony

I wished I had never sent Wren in because I was jealous.

I had every right to be mad as I stewed in my shit. I was the one that made the plan. All I needed was a chance to ride that glorious ass like the Metrolink. I spent umpteen days and nights beating my poor meat to her, and Wren got a taste twice. I huffed. It was okay because I knew I'd have the last laugh in all of this. I felt it in my spirit.

I didn't know how, but I would.

I walked out of my wing and to Lord of the Grump's wing. His wing was always a bit depressing. He had black and white everything. No color lived there except the paintings he had purchased. His black hardwood flooring started in his hallway and wove throughout his wing. He'd painted the walls white with a black accent wall. His furniture was black and white with a hint of gold. It was a shame neither his mother nor I could convince him to change his design. But to each his own.

I flung open the door with my tools in hand.

"LUCY! I'M HOMMMME," I shouted. Gabe sighed and turned back to watching his hockey game. "None of that grumpalumpagus. I come bearing gifts and gossip."

Gabe groaned, and not the good type of groaning. I placed the trimmer and shaver down and set up shop for my impromptu barber shop. I was going to get my brother back to his sexy self even if I died while trying.

I mean, that may happen in this case.

Gabe had been moping like me, and I knew it was because he hadn't had a sample from the Jasmine fountain. Come to think of it, he hadn't asked me for "help," nor had I seen any ladies leaving his wing recently.

"No."

"Yes, and I'm willing to die on this hill." I stood with my arms crossed. "Plus, when we get Jasmine, do you want her to be near this mess?" I asked as I picked up his greasy beard. He looked like something off those hunting shows.

"I don't want her. You guys can have her."

I turned and watched as he folded his arms. Those green orbs didn't even flinch when his team scored. He just grunted.

Okay, bratty, I never thought I would see the day.

"Yeah, that's why you're locked up in your room, beating your meat to her almost every day."

Gabe gave me a look that would kill anyone, but I knew he was a big softie, like Wren. But he hid it better. He always had to put on the macho Italiano shit, like he was the godfather. He needed to leave that to his uncle who was in that lifestyle.

I turned on the equipment, and after wrestling with Gabe, he finally allowed me to take it off. I have never been so relieved to see my brother's face. I almost kissed him, but I knew he would punch me in the stomach. He looked at me after I chuckled. I trimmed and chopped his beard until there was nothing left but stubble. Then I got to the thing he called his hair. His inky black curls were wild and slightly greasy. I had to wipe my hand with the towel that was thrown over him.

My poor brother was down for the count.

I gave him a low cut to bring back the Gabe we all knew and loved. I chopped inches of curls and some knots from his head. No more of this grumpy sex-deprived hunter. Of course, I would never have told him that.

When I finished, I stepped back and marveled at my creation. I was Picasso with a trimmer and shaver. Finally, I could see the old Gabe with his chiseled jaw, high cheekbones, and those dimples. Now, all we had to do was get him laid. I didn't mind going last since I was going to wear Jasmine's ass out when I got a hold of her.

This time I...

"Why are you looking at me like that?" Gabe asked, his mouth pulled into a frown.

"What do you mean?"

"You looked like you were two seconds away from bending me over the chair." He folded his arms.

"If that's what you want, Gabe. Your wish will be my command." I rubbed my hands together, bowing in my middle.

He rolled his eyes as he moved to the bathroom and stood in the mirror.

"Shave your face now, or I can do it for you—"

He cut me off. "No, I'll do it."

After he finished shaving, I finally got a cleaned-up glimpse of my brother. He looked like he did before Kitty left us. Sane and civilized, ready to take on anything. Too bad it was nighttime. Even if he was back to looking like the normal Gabe, his attitude and grumpy frown still marred his face. I tried to get him in a better mood, but he wouldn't budge.

Honestly, I was scared to tell him about our little adventure because he would probably blow up. That was why I'd been sitting on our "escapade" for two days. But I guess I couldn't hide it anymore from him. I decided it would be best if I told him instead of Wren since they were still not on speaking terms.

When Gabe returned to his throne, aka his monstrous black barrel chair, I waited a couple of minutes until he was absorbed into his game. He wouldn't go off like a bomb if he was distracted. *I hoped.* I took a deep breath and unloaded about the plan, the photos, the company, and Wren lending a hand to Jasmine—in hindsight, I should have left the last part out. But I babbled a bit too much to backtrack. It wasn't until Gabe turned to me and I saw the flash of jealousy replaced with anger that I knew I'd probably spilled too much.

One minute, Gabe was sitting in his chair. The next, he moved that tall, wide frame down the hall to Wren's wing. Gabe moved so fast I barely kept up with him as he barreled down the sage hallway. He busted through the door, and Wren was in bed asleep. He stomped over and shook him until Wren woke up with a deep grunt.

And that was when shit hit the proverbial fan. All of his anger and frustration were unloaded on Wren. He blamed him for my plan to go to Jasmine's house and to spy on her, even though I thoroughly remember telling him it was my plan. He cursed us out for being stupid and said we acted on impulse and not common sense, which I'd give him. But he wasn't right. I redirected him to place his anger on me every time because this was my fault. He somehow linked it back to Wren. But of course, he found some way to string the Rose problem in there as he roped in that she made him compliant and was docile about things that made little sense.

I took offense to that jab. I told Gabe we got enough information and that I could look the person up and find out more about the business and its owner. But that made him even madder as he turned and almost barreled into me. He left Wren and me in total silence after he told us off.

Poor Wren looked fed up and humiliated.

"I'm sorry, Wren. He's becoming intolerable. I will try to talk to him."

Wren, who'd been staring off into space until now, turned to me. "It's okay. I think some part of me knows he's right—being with Rose has made me compliant. But not anymore," he sighed.

I went to sit on the bed. "What's up?"

"It's time for us to move on from Rose. Since we returned from Jasmine, I have been thinking about it, and it's not right to string her along. I texted her to meet us at La Rosa tomorrow at noon. I was able to reserve one of their private rooms for us since we will most likely be in and out in ten minutes."

I had never been so happy. I was almost sure Wren would leave us for Rose. Not that I would make it easy for him because he was mine first, and no one outside of our group and Jasmine could have him. My smile was genuine. It was as if someone had lifted an anchor off me, and I could finally swim to shore. It was overdue, especially when she knocked the hell out of me a couple of weeks ago. I hadn't seen her since then, so there wasn't any emotional attachment.

After I put Wren back to bed, I got up and whistled to my room. I went to bed with peaceful dreams of blowing out Jasmine's back on our la Barca del Sesso, which translated to "the sex boat"—yes, I named our boat. I smiled in the darkness as I fell asleep.

The following day, we walked into La Rosa in a feverish mood at noon. Even the grumpy Gabe was over the moon when I told him about the meeting with Rose today. So, here we were, Gabe with his new fresh-cut hair, black jeans, and a black and white button-down shirt. Wren wore his typical silver gym outfit because regular clothing was foreign to him. And me, the piece de la resistance, I had on my best pink Tom Ford tailor fitted suit and white Louboutin shoes. I changed out my black piercings for some pink-colored pieces with silver gems.

I looked good enough to fuck if you asked me.

We all sat around the table as I carried the conversation among us. Wren looked like he wanted to run for the hills, and Gabe was back to sulking. Granted, he looked like a handsome sulking giant. The waitress we knew tried to flirt with Gabe, but Gabe didn't even bat an eye at her. He just nodded and chugged his Campari and soda, extra light on the soda, like it was the last drink he'd ever have. After the second refill, I told the waitress not to bring any more. She nodded, and Gabe glared at me.

"When we get Jasmine to finally see reason, then you'll be back to normal." And it earned me a whack to the back of my head.

"Anyway, where is she?" he grumbled. "We have to wait—" He was cut off when we heard the stomping of Rose's heels. I swear, for someone her size, she walked like an elephant in a stampede.

"Hey, guys," she shouted as she entered the room. Good thing the rooms there were basically soundproof. "Traffic held me up, but I am here."

She sat down, and her sunny disposition almost threw me off, but I rebounded quickly. No one wanted to speak. So, I took the reins, and at first, I was nervous because I'd never actually broken up with anyone before, but I was tired of dragging it out. So, I cleared my throat and rolled my shoulders.

"Rose, we wanted to speak with you about our relation—"

She cut me off before I could even get started. I sighed.

"Yes, same here. I think we should break up. I had enough time to think, and it would be for the best."

My jaw hit the floor as I gawked at her. I was pretty sure everyone's face resembled mine. Gabe's grunt captured my attention, and when I turned to him, our eyes met, and we laughed our asses off. I turned to Wren, and he was laughing as well. To think I wore my best suit to get dumped on a date by Rose. *The universe is funny as hell, man*. We laughed for at least a few minutes, and Rose sat with her arms crossed.

"I'm sorry, Rose. I must be honest. We called you here to break up with you. Just for you to turn around and dump us." I wiped away the tears from my face. "It's crazy."

"Well, I had no choice. My childhood friend I had lost contact with over the last couple of years is back, and we have reconnected over the past couple of weeks since I hadn't seen or heard from you guys."

"That's great! We wish you nothing but the best. You deserve it," I said honestly. "But we have to be honest with you, Rose."

We told her everything about our time over the last couple of weeks. Of course, we left out the name of the person. We wouldn't want to cause any trouble between them. She looked upset about the events that occurred, but she had a feeling that something was up. She took her friend coming back into her life as a sign that it wasn't meant to be. And she noticed that Gabe and I were not connecting or trying to connect with her. I apologized, and so did Gabe. We all apologized to Wren because he was genuinely invested until the past couple of weeks.

I sent a prayer to God, thankful it went over so smoothly. I had come prepared for the uphill battle we usually had with her, but it worked out in our favor.

Is this the start of our luck coming around? I hope so.

We ate our food and ended up staying back for some drinks, well, soda for me, but you get the drift. When we left, Rose said her last goodbye and wished us luck.

When we got home, I was so amped up about the prospect of finally going after Jasmine, I got hard thinking about it. Tomorrow, I had painters and designers coming to paint Jasmine's wing of the house. I decided on a lilac accent wall with white walls. We had a couple of paintings in our storage area that I picked out. I loaded up on vanilla-scented candles and aromatherapy diffusers. Also, I searched for everything to take care of her locs and body products she might need. I brought a year's worth of everything.

I stared at the ceiling as I thought about the possibility that she would be here soon. I could imagine her walking around the house naked, swaying that fucking perfect ass around as I followed her like a lost puppy around the house and did whatever she wanted.

I noticed my hand had taken a mind of its own as I pulled out my heavy cock. I shuddered as I stroked over the metal piercings. I used fast, short strokes as I imagined my dick stuffed inside Jasmine's mouth until I hit the back of her throat repeatedly. I squeezed lightly while my cock twitched. My back stiffened as I tried to edge myself, but Ms. Grant, on her knees in my head, got the best of me, and I shot my load all over my pink suit and my hand.

God! What would I do to have cum all inside of Jasmine?

As I wiped my hand on my suit, I rolled my neck. I texted my connection at the Tom Ford store and asked if they had another pink suit in my size, and they did. I told them I would swing by their shop tomorrow.

I did my victory dance—I am up to two lucky moments for the day. I cleaned up, threw the soiled outfit away, and went to bed after that euphoric release.

It wasn't until the next day that I worried I may have counted my blessings too early. I woke up to Gabe arguing with the painters and the designers. He told them it was a mistake that they were there, but the painters and the designers insisted I called them. I had to unglue Gabe from the door and tell him I did indeed call them. The designer took one look at Gabe, twisted her red lips, and rolled her eyes.

"Before you say anything, King of the Unlaid," I teased, and he narrowed his eyes at me and stuck his hands in his pockets. "I called them because I was decorating for when Jasmine moves in. Wren told me her office was in lilac, and I told the designer the colors, and they've come up with the perfect design."

Gabe stared at me, mumbled something unintelligible, and walked off with his hands in his pockets. He had a big case of morning wood, and I knew he would run away to masturbate. I would have chuckled, but I felt he would come back down and shut me up. I gave the designer the key code and left refreshments for the crew on my way out the door.

With that done, I jumped into my car to head out to pick up my replacement suit. When I turned my car on, I received a ping from my phone, letting me know my search for Stephanie Johnson had returned. So, Ms. Johnson was an alias name, that was for sure. I shuffled through the documents I'd gathered on her. It took me a couple of days because whoever buried her information was good, but not better than me. I smiled as I continued looking through the company's documents. It was a real estate company that was killing it with a net worth of over two billion and over two hundred properties.

Okay, I'm impressed, Ms. Grant.

I kept searching through the endless files from her real estate portfolio. I scrolled so fast I almost missed when the documents changed to a birth certificate for twin boys, Teodoro and Tristano Grant. The mother listed wasn't Jasmine, but it was under Stephanie Johnson's name. Our girl must have good connections in the Department of Health. I scrolled some more until I found hospital records for Stephanie. She stayed in the Cedars Sinai maternity ward for a week.

Why would she lie about having kids?

The more I learned about Jasmine, the more I got pulled into her web. I sent everything in a secured email to Gabe and Wren before I pulled out of our driveway.

My mind traveled to the birth certificates filed one year after our time at Club Celeste. I worked the kink out of my neck as I pulled up to the Tom Ford store. Jasmine didn't have to tell us about her life before us, and nor would we ever judge her for it. Maybe being with Greg, she had to act differently, but with us, we wanted her just the way she was—Well, that was me speaking.

After finding parking, I hopped out of the car and ran into the store. My connection, the personal shopper, Henry, got the suit, and he picked out some new items for me. I stood there chatting with him for a minute when I got a glimpse of the sexiest person on Rodeo Drive.

I hated to be rude, but I apologized and quickly told Henry goodbye. Something had come up. I flew out the door and followed her down the block. She ducked around the corner while I had parked on the main road. I watched as she hopped into the backseat of her car.

Shit.

After I hightailed it back to my car, I dumped the bags in my back seat. I jumped into the driver's seat and the car shook when I slammed the door. I could hack into her GPS and find out where she was going, but I saw her black Rolls Royce with her driver and her guard speed by me. Common sense would have told me to go home, but I was out of patience and common sense. I was hungry for a taste of Jasmine—for God's sake! It was my turn to dive into her, but this time, I wouldn't be like Wren. I would confirm if our suspicions were correct.

What the hell will I do if it's true?

Shit, I really hadn't thought that far. Would I be furious if she hid from us? Shocked that she lived five minutes from us? Or would I be disappointed if we ran her off into the arms of her stiff librarian? So many unanswered questions swirled around my head when I realized we had pulled up to a store entrance.

I watched as her guard jumped out of the front seat and opened her door. Jasmine came out of the car and stood there as her guard closed the door. I noticed she was in full disguise mode today. She traded her locs out for long, curly brown hair. She wore some black gym outfit that would make Wren's dick harder than steel. The clothes dwarfed her tiny petite size. She pulled the hoodie over her head and turned to walk into the mall. I was so damn mesmerized by how the pants, even though big on her legs, held onto her wide hips. Hips her twins gave her. Something about her being a mom made me hard as a rock.

Great way to learn you have a MILF fetish.

I parked my car and jogged into the Robertson Boulevard shopping district in West Hollywood. The boulevard looked slow, and that wasn't typical for this area. The fan palm trees and the small rustic buildings made the area seem deserted when there weren't tons of people lounging around. I looked around, and she hadn't made it far until I saw her hurry into the black stone Chanel store with her bodyguard. Luckily for me, not so much for her. I had a way into the store when they locked it down for special guests.

Jasmine was far away from the front door when I approached. I knocked on the door, and my favorite older lady, whose family works for our company, came rushing to the door. Jasmine's guard tried to stop her, but he took one look at me when I lowered my glasses and pursed his lips.

"Bonjour, Mr. Russo. How are you?" She batted her eyes.

"I'm well. I saw one of my stars and wanted to say hello." I turned to Jasmine's guard, Bruno, and winked. He frowned. He'd been a hard ass, but he would have to adjust.

"Yes, of course, Mr. Russo. I ask that you don't make any trouble." She wagged her wrinkled finger at me.

"Me? Trouble? Ms. Dumont, I would never do such a thing." I had to lay it on thick. "Especially to a beautiful young woman like yourself."

"Oh, stop, Mr. Russo. You go talk to the lovely Ms. Grant. She's been one of our favorite customers since she was fourteen."

"She is my favorite as well." I winked at the older lady and turned to walk toward Jasmine.

I playfully tapped Bruno on the back as I passed, and he grunted.

She had her back turned to me, and the sales associate rushed to the back to retrieve whatever she came for. From where I stood, I could press her into the counter and let her feel every inch of my hardened cock that threatened to burst any time. But I had to think smart. Wren had messed up his opportunity twice, and I wouldn't make the same mistake for the third time.

So, I leaned close to her ear and whispered, "My sneaky Jasmine."

She jumped and nearly toppled over the bags she had in front of her as she spun around to face me.

"What the fuck? Why would you sneak up on me like that?" she squeaked out.

"I wanted to see if the old saying was true."

"What the hell are you talking about?"

"You know the saying. Cats have nine lives." I smiled.

Jasmine went on the defense. She didn't know, but I noticed when she was confronted she stuck her chest out as if she wasn't trembling inside. Her full bottom lip quivered ever so slightly. I saw the thin sheen of sweat line her upper lip.

"Oh, how funny." She quirked her eyebrow at me and turned around to hide. But I grabbed her and turned her around. I was a mere inch away from those pillows she called lips. She gasped, and her mouth formed a small O. I could—no wanted to—smash my lips onto hers, but I leaned against her front. Not close enough for her to be smushed, but close enough for her to feel my hard dick against her stomach and for me to touch her nipples that strained against her hoodie, begging me to suck them.

Her lip trembled, and I pulled away. As I was about to leave, I turned and gave her the last clue I was on to her.

"See you around, Stephanie Johnson." I looked her in the eyes and winked.

I didn't have to stay to know she had heard me.

She gasped so loud I thought people in New York had heard.

Count your days, Jasmine!

Chapter 16

Jasmine

Holy fucking hell! I thought to myself as I paced my home office.

It was the one place where I could scream, cry, or let my anger out. It'd been a week since I'd dared to go out and pick up the custom Chanel items I got for the boys and me, and I'd been hiding at home since then. I knew that was cowardly of me, but I didn't give a shit. The only thing I cared about was the boys. I watched as they played outside with Greg, laughing and swimming.

Greg had been super quiet and avoided my questions about what he was up to when he locked himself away in his office after work. I would never go into his office and disrespect his privacy, but the thought made me itch with a need to know. With Greg, I didn't want any surprises. Ours was strictly a business relationship. I needed something, and he offered a service I needed. That was it; nothing more, nothing less.

I went back to pacing the floor like a crazy person. Back and forth. My plush white carpet had a trail going around my desk. I'd probably lost ten pounds already. Nothing came up when I watched the footage from when Wren broke into my house. I figured Wren got into my office, and Tony was there to erase the footage. That was the only way they would have known about Stephanie Johnson. The thought made the hair on my neck stand up, and a drop of sweat formed on my temple. I contemplated fessing up to the guys, but I could hear my mother's voice almost like it was yesterday.

"Jasmine, you're going to do what? They will take them away because that's what rich men do. Those men don't want you! They only wanted what you were dishing out freely to them. Now you're left with the responsibility of your actions. You made your bed. Now it's time to lie in it."

"GOTCHA!" my assailant screamed as they wrapped their arms around me, yanking me back into the present.

I screamed and kicked my way out of the person's arms until they let go of me. The light sweat felt like someone threw a bucket of water on my skin. I turned to see Allison holding up the surrendered sign with her arms.

"You scared the living shit out of me!" I knew I sounded crazy, but I have had enough scares in my life. "Alli, I'm already on edge. I don't need you adding to my problems."

"Sheesh, a sista can't even play with you anymore." She plopped down in my office chair.

I looked outside to ensure the kids hadn't heard me, but they were too busy playing with their water guns.

"I'm sorry, it's just that I'm scared, Alli." She knew about everything since she was the only person I could trust.

"I don't even know what to do—I mean, I know what you should technically do, but…" She stopped when I raised my eyebrow.

She always was the liberated one in our friendship. I was the one who lived vicariously through her, hoping some of it would rub off on me soon.

"I don't have much time since Wayne and I are going to Phoenix for the weekend. But like I said, if they haven't made a move, then they were probably pulling your leg. Plus, there aren't pictures of the twins anywhere on the internet."

"You're right. I'm just tripping. You and Wayne have a great time at your parents' house." I gave her a hug and a sloppy kiss.

"You know I want to see you happy, and Greg turns my spirit. He's not right for you. It's not right to be with someone just for your kids' sake." I turned to watch as Greg played with the boys. They were torturing poor Greg, but he seemed to not mind it.

"T-They need a father, plus my mom likes him," I said as if it would make matters better.

"The fact of the matter is that they have a father already… I mean three fathers."

I knew she was correct, and I was being hard headed.

Allison sighed and went to hug me. "Just think about it. I've got to run. See ya later." She turned around at the door. "Oh, I forgot I got the information you asked for. They live five minutes away. I sent it to your email. Ciao."

With that, she left me wide eyed as I gaped at the door. Of course, I knew they lived close by because they'd mentioned it several times, but I never thought it would be in my backyard. My mind raced at the implication that they could show up at any minute and turn my life upside down—well, more upside down than usual. My stomach threatened to regurgitate my breakfast.

See, the guys weren't the only ones with resources. If it wasn't for Allison, I wouldn't have been able to keep the boys out of the paparazzi. I asked her to use my alias name, and she got her connection at the health department to list the boys' birth certificates underneath it to protect Tris and Teo. Now that they knew about the boys, or at least I thought they did, the once normal, quiet life I had worked out was crumbling around me slowly but surely.

I held my head as the warning signs of a migraine reared its ugly head. I pinched the bridge of my nose, hoping to end the pounding in the back of my eyes. The boys ran to the window and sprayed the water gun at me as they laughed. I held up my arms and acted like I got shot. They ran away, and I smiled. I couldn't imagine anyone removing them from my life. As I looked on in a trance, the phone rang, and I almost didn't pick it up, but I did.

"Hey, Jas."

"Hey, Mom." My voice broke. The pressure got to me, and the sob bubbled in my throat.

"Hey, what happened? Jasmine Grant! Do I need to come out there and kick someone's ass?"

I snorted at the thought of my mom going to the guys or Greg and confronting them.

"Nothing, Mom. I'm missing you." I mean, it wasn't really a lie. During the past five years, we'd built a good relationship.

"Why don't y'all come back home? The boys have a four-day weekend, and I'm free. You and Greg could spend some time alone." She had me until that last part. But honestly, I thought it was the best plan for me at that moment. Some time to breathe and to replan was what I needed.

And that's how you found yourself in the crappy mess you are in now.

I didn't think twice as I hopped on my plane and found myself on my mother's doorstep, squashed on my old queen-sized bed with Greg's sweaty body flopped over me. Even though the air conditioner was at seventy degrees, he was baking. I didn't even want to move because I knew once I did, he would want to have one of his five-second humpathon. I should have stayed at my damn house and suffered whatever fate awaited, but nope, I had to learn the hard way. We had been here for two days, and he had been in and out of the house. He didn't want us to stay at his house, either. It was odd that Greg wasn't following his routine, even for him.

Greg flopped to the other side, and I breathed a sigh of relief. I smiled because I'd dodged him again—or so I thought. He grabbed me by the hip and pulled me over.

Oh, God! Why are you punishing me?

"Greg, I told you, no sex in my mom's house!" I whispered. "These walls are paper thin, and everyone could hear."

"I can't wait until we get back home. I need to cum inside of you." His hot breath whispered in my ear.

"No." I had begged Greg to wait until we were married before I fulfilled my end of our deal. He agreed, but I would get a hysterectomy before that ever happened.

"Let me put the tip in. I promise I will pull out," he pleaded.

"Absolutely not. If you don't have a condom, you're not doing anything. Plus, this is not very Christian-like, is it?"

"You're right," he sighed.

I felt sorry for him because maybe I was being too bitchy. I sighed and grabbed his cock in my hand.

He shuddered. "What are you doing?"

I ignored him and pumped his cock. Greg went stiff, and it wasn't from an incoming orgasm. He grabbed my wrist, and I tried to move my hand, but he gripped it while his nails dug into my skin.

"What are you doing?" He had a bewildered look on his face.

"I was helping you relieve yourself!"

"No, that is a form of masturbation. That is unholy, and only whores need to use their hands like that."

It was as if someone had slapped me across my face with coal. Did Greg basically call me a whore? I was beyond pissed. I got up to wash my hand in the bathroom. As I stomped down the steps, I didn't care if my mother or Greg woke up. The boys wouldn't budge if I did. I grabbed my yoga stuff and continued to the backyard before I ended up with a knife from the kitchen and some new form of sausage for the neighbor's dogs.

I rolled out my mat and got to work doing the yoga stances I had imprinted in my mind since I was sixteen. I contorted and stretched my body until I was covered in sweat, and my heart was racing. Not wanting to stop there, I hit the road with Bruno for my morning run, with him trailing after me in the car. Poor Bruno, I thought, if you weren't used to the hills in Nashville, they would kill you. The sun was beginning to peek out from the horizon as I reached the house's brown front steps. Sitting on the steps, I huffed and puffed until I got my breathing back in order. It'd been a month since I started working out again, and I'd lost ten pounds from stuffing my face with grass, lean meat, and water. It had been hard, but as I looked at my shrinking thighs, I was overjoyed. Luckily, my stomach had returned to almost normal from Allison and my mom kicking me in my butt to get back into the gym.

I headed straight to the shower and prepped for this event my mother wanted us to attend. Tris and Teo came bouncing off the wall and ran toward me.

Tris looked up through those long lashes and mumbled, "Mom, when can we go home? It's boring here, and we miss our friends."

Teo came up and hugged my arm and mimicked his brother's look. "Yeah, Mommy. We want to go home."

They planned this little setup. I imagined them in their room with their little heads bowed together as they worked on their "Mommy's a sucker" look. I looked at the two mini Tonys, knowing they hated my mom's home. Even though it was perfect for her, it was neutral, with nothing really for the kids but pictures of a family that no longer remembered us and better times. I watched them mope and sigh while I put on my other accessories.

I struggled to tell them that Greg wanted to leave LA and return to Nashville. The boys would hate it here. It's something we fought over because, as much as I loved Nashville, I couldn't see myself living here again.

"Well, my spoiled babies," I rubbed their little cheeks. "Let's get through grandma's event, and we can see tomorrow."

Luckily, that settled their inquisitive little minds because I had run out of things to tell them. After spending the next couple of hours watching movies with me, they scurried to the other room, terrorizing their grandmother with their happy squeals. I smiled.

When I was done getting ready, I returned downstairs to where everyone waited for me. My stomach churned like I was on a roller coaster. It was most likely a prelude to the night's events.

I noticed my mom was dressed in her infamous silver skirt suit. Her hair was wrapped in a silver scarf and white shoes. She looked good. The kids' babysitter, my mom's church sister, Ms. Carolee, gathered Tris and Teo in her chubby arms and shooed them into the kitchen for dinner. My suspicion spiked since my mom said she would drive separately because Ms. Carolee had to leave early. I wanted to protest, but like my mother always does, in her country accent, she hushed me up and told me "to get". I held in an eye roll because I didn't want to be disrespectful.

When we hit the road, the urge to upchuck the small salad that I had eaten before I got dressed doubled. I couldn't determine why I felt that way. It might have been Greg's hand on my thigh since we left the house. Every time I removed it, he placed it back. Bruno, who was driving behind my mother, kept shooting Greg murderous looks in the rearview mirror.

When we arrived at the venue, a small dark seafood restaurant, the hairs on my neck stood up, and I needed to use the bathroom. The restaurant had the weirdest Turkish blue shade painted on the exterior that was chipping in some areas. The dark windows were covered in stickers and neon signs. It was a small local business that had seen better days. The parking lot only held six cars, and that was being generous. Before he could grab me, I was out and into the restaurant. If

I thought the outside was odd, the inside took the cake. They had white curtains that covered the windows. The furniture was well-worn, with cracks in the chairs. The owners used tablecloths from the nineties to dress the tables.

Something about tonight didn't sit well with me, and the faster I could get it over with, the better.

Greg, my mom, and Bruno kept calling my name behind me, but I didn't listen. Everyone in the small restaurant looked surprised at me bursting through the small restaurant. It took them a moment, but they eventually came to and shouted surprise as if it were my birthday, which it wasn't. My birthday was September twenty-fifth, and it was nowhere near September.

I looked around the room to see Allison, Wayne, Mr. Field, Mrs. Field, Greg's parents, and some of Greg's awful friends from our Thanksgiving vacation. Everyone stood as I gawked at them from my position at the restaurant door.

"Hello, everyone. I'm glad you made it to our dinner party," Greg announced as he saddled up to my side.

"Yes, thank you for coming to our event!" My mom said bubbly.

I looked at them wordlessly. *Our dinner party?* If this was one of his crazy ideas of announcing something, I needed to stop him immediately. But of course, I didn't get the chance as everyone swept me up in embraces and congratulations. Mr. and Mrs. Field looked terrific and hadn't changed much since I'd last seen them. Allison and Wayne looked fresh-faced and nervous as I pulled Allison to the side to grill her. She stated she did not know what the party was about and that my mom had said it was her dinner party.

I promised Allison and myself that my mom would hear about it when we got back to the house.

After thirty minutes of me giving Greg the evil eye and him ignoring me by speaking with his boring friends who thought I needed more time to work out my "heathen" ways, mentally, I rolled my eyes and stewed in my seat. My mom all but gloated and walked around like she was on cloud nine. When I saw Allison worriedly look over at me, I chided myself. I needed to stop fretting and accept my fate. I straightened myself up and decided to fake it until I got home.

Twenty minutes later, Greg knocked on his champagne glass, signaling he wanted to make an announcement. My mom and everyone, besides Allison and I, looked at him with stars in their eyes.

"Thank you, everyone, for coming out tonight. I understand this was last minute, but I wanted to do something for my wonderful fiancé. I know we decided on Jasmine's birthday for our wedding, but I think with all of our family here, maybe we should bump the wedding to the end of this month instead. So, what do you say, love?" Greg turned to me.

The fucker! Before I opened my mouth to say anything, I glanced around the table and watched as my family and friends peered at me as I sat there, my sweaty dress clinging to me. Perspiration lined my forehead, and I thanked God I put on deodorant because my armpits were drenched.

This man had put me in a tough spot again, and I…

"I'm so excited! What a blessing from God." My mom said, breaking the strained silence.

"Baby, come on, everyone is waiting," he goaded as his claw-like hands touched my shoulder.

I opened my mouth, but it was as if someone had ripped my vocal box out of my throat. I looked at Allison as if she could save me, but she had her watery eyes fixed on the glass of champagne in front of her.

I held back the tears that threatened to fall and, in a voice so low, I thought no one would hear, I whispered, "Yes."

Everyone cheered except for Allison and me. My mom beamed, said a prayer for our union, and took a turn of pictures with my strained smile. After she decided she took enough she left us in the tiny restaurant to go back home.

About thirty minutes later, I couldn't stand the smiles and the cheery voices anymore, so I excused myself, ran to the bathroom, and emptied my dinner into the toilet. I was a big sweat ball when I leaned on the bathroom door. The walls were boxing me in as I willed myself to take a couple of deep breaths and finally pushed myself off the door when I was in control. It wasn't until I forced myself from the door that I realized I had my phone in my hand. I leaned against the sink and checked my text. I had one from Allison that said it was time to nip this in the bud that was sent a minute ago. The other was from Rosa Marino. She asked if I wanted to meet up with her for a lunch date.

I couldn't even think about having lunch with Rosa with everything that was going on.

Less than two weeks, and I'd be locked in for thirteen years. I pushed off the sink and nearly stumbled, but I caught myself and let the tears fall from my eyes again. It was my fault, and life was coming back to bite me on my big ass. I snorted and wiped the tears with a paper towel from my face. I put back my fake smile and returned to the table. My temper got the best of me when I tried to engage with everyone, so I ignored the conversation. But after twenty minutes, I'd had enough. I told everyone I needed to go home because I felt sick.

Bruno was up and out while I walked to the door. The car waited while I stumbled out into the cold Nashville night and dropped into the car. A little bratty, but I didn't care. The bottle of champagne I guzzled down had turned me into a raging bitch.

Thankfully, Greg caught a ride with his friends, so I had enough time to get to the house and discuss this little party. When Bruno pulled up front, I jumped out and stumbled inside. My mom was in her room. It was the perfect location because it wasn't close to the boys' room.

"You knew he was going to push me to get married sooner. Didn't you?" I folded my arms.

"Well, yes! Aren't you happy? He can't wait to get married to you."

"No, mom. I'm not happy about this or that you tricked my friends into coming to your 'dinner party'."

"Wait, tricked? I asked everyone, and they agreed to come out because they wanted to see you. Mr. and Mrs. Field were elated when I told them the news."

The champagne I guzzled down was working overtime because I couldn't account for the words that slipped out of my mouth.

"I'd rather slit my throat than marry that boring, disgusting man! He clips his toenails all over the house and wipes his dick off with his boxers. I have been with him for five years and haven't been pleased with him even once! He's a waste of a man and a waste of space," I yelled.

"Jasmine Grant! I don't know who you think you're talking to, but you better fix yo' attitude and take your drunken tail to bed," she scolded. "You would give up a good man because he's unkempt? That's why he has you there to help build him up. Your job is to take him from being a bachelor to a married man! That's the role of a woman. You should be grateful he wanted you. Your past isn't squeaky clean either."

"Fuck you!" I swayed a bit. "Fuck you, and fuck Greg. You guys should fuck each other and marry each other."

I looked at her through my blurry vision, and it was coming before I could react. I tried to stumble to the bathroom but fell short and threw up in the doorway between my mom's bedroom and the guest bathroom. Greg stood on the stairs across from the bathroom and watched as I looked up. I couldn't even talk as I held the wall and made my way to my old room. I wobbled and fell onto the full-size bed.

I didn't wake up until noon the next day, and everything smacked me in my head when I did. My brain was fighting with my skull. I sat up slowly, hobbled to my bathroom, where I had pain medicine, and swallowed it with a handful of tap water. I laid back down until my headache subsided.

When I was able to open my eyes again, I knew for a fact we needed to go home. I contacted the pilot and told him I needed out of there as soon as possible. He told me he could fly out in two hours.

I'd overstayed my welcome, and when I made myself go downstairs, my mom left early and told everyone but me goodbye.

"Tris and Teo, get your stuff ready. We're leaving soon. Greg, are you coming back with us or staying?"

Tris and Teo both screamed yes and ran upstairs to get their things.

Please say you're staying. Please say you're staying.

"Nah, let me get my things, and we can go. I cleaned up the mess you made last night. Your mom was mad about something. She left early this morning and kissed the boys goodbye."

I suppressed my sigh and turned around to hide the eye roll. "Fine. Be ready in the next ten minutes."

It was the first time since I'd met Greg that he'd been this quiet, and it was music to my ears. He said nothing, not even when we pulled up to my house. It made me wonder if he'd overheard us or not. Either way, I didn't care. Luckily, Tris and Teo knew how to keep me company. Greg shuffled into his office and stayed in there for hours. The weight of his silence was heavy, and I was kind of sorry for him having to clean up my vomit.

I walked past his door about ten times before I sighed and went in for the kill. The stench of old books, mold, and something else permeated the air. I almost gagged but held it together.

"Hey, is everything okay?" I asked.

"I'm good." He smiled, but it didn't reach his eyes.

"I wanted to apologize and thank you for cleaning up my mess. You shouldn't have to do it."

"It was no problem." He turned back to the computer, and I turned to leave now that I'd said my piece. "No, I'm not done."

I jerked back and asked, "What's up?"

"You embarrassed me in front of my friends and my parents. I was so ashamed and disgusted by your behavior." He said as he crossed his arms.

I reeled back like someone slapped me. "I have no clue what you're talking about."

"You turned our party that was peaceful into an awkward mess. You're supposed to be a Christian woman, but your morals." He shook his head. "I had to apologize to my family and friends because you were drunk and rude to them."

"Wait, I didn't even speak to your friends, and I was very nice to your parents." Almost too nice since his mother always turned her nose up towards me.

"A woman is not supposed to get drunk. You should only have one or two glasses, and that's it. Anything else is a loose woman's behavior...Whore like behavior" He pinched his nose like this conversation frustrated him. "I blame Allison. I should talk to Wayne about putting her in her place. She acts like a w—"

"If you say anything about Allison, I will fucking kick your ass back to Nashville. I'm going to step out so you can get some sense." As I turned to leave, I slammed the door as hard as I could.

So many thoughts ran through my head. The kids went back to school tomorrow, and how to get away with murder were the main ones my mind kept going back to. After I got them ready, I locked myself in my room and had a self-care night, which wasn't a good one since all I could think of was the word whore thudding in my ears. Greg banged on the door when I climbed into bed, but I didn't answer him. I turned my back to the door and felt like I was at my last string before I snapped.

I thought I would be in a better mood after I slept like a log for the first time in ages without someone being in my bed or without taking the Ambien I was prescribed. I got myself together to get the twins off to school. After I dropped them off, I texted Rosa that I couldn't make it but could possibly meet up with her at a later date. Mr. Jackson sensed my mood, rolled up the partition without another word, and all I could do was cast my eyes down.

Not wanting to go home, I told Mr. Jackson to take me to the label's office. It took us twenty minutes, driving down the green, manicured, hilly back roads to get there, as I gripped the armrest like I was going to break it. When we approached the brown building, I told him to wait in the car. I didn't stay for his response as I was out and on my way.

I avoided everyone, ran into my office, and locked myself in. I hit the rolling blackout shades so no one could see me. Luckily, it was the middle of February, and Mr. Brine had always given the staff a week off during the kids' extended weekends and holidays. *I guess the guys upheld that rule.* Almost everyone worked from home, so there weren't many people there. Except for Gabe, not that I was looking for him, but I saw his car parked in the lot. Not that I was looking for it.

Once in my office, I washed out a glass tumbler and opened the hundred-year-old cognac that I had saved for when I bought the record label, but since that was moot, I might as well enjoy it.

One glass of the sharp, bitter alcohol led me to drink three glasses. I knew I shouldn't indulge since I was technically drunk within the last forty-eight hours. But fuck it.

That was when I thought if they wanted me to be a whore, I was going to give them a whore. Stumbling to the bathroom, I brushed my teeth and made myself not smell like a distillery. Before I could think it through, I was down the hall and opening the door to Gabe's office, hoping he was still there.

He looked up, and his eyebrows raised. As I stopped in the middle of the office, my legs became like lead as I became rooted to the spot. It was like he'd done a whole three sixty. He looked exactly like how I had left him. His curly black hair was back to its short cut. He'd shaved off his grotesquely long beard. I could see his sharp jawline and those deep dimples I loved to kiss.

"He looks so fucking hot." Inadvertently, I muttered the words out loud.

He chuckled and replied, "Well, thank you. I haven't heard that in a while."

Fuck, his chuckle had my thighs crushed together. Quickly, I walked over to his desk before I could talk myself out of it. I shouldn't have been in there in hindsight, but I wanted to feel free and not judged. I also wanted to feel powerful by taking control of something in my life.

I marched around the desk to a confused Gabe and turned his desk chair towards me. I expected some resistance, but he allowed me to control the moment, which made me wetter. His eyes were unreadable, but I didn't care. I was a mere inch from his lips, but I knew that was dangerous, and since I had on a long turtleneck, he couldn't see anything. My hand reached out and circled the shell of his ears and gently tugged on his lobe before I could think about what I was doing.

He hadn't moved an inch since I'd turned him around. It was almost as if he was holding his breath. My knees landed on the carpeted flooring, and I placed my hand on his crotch. It should have surprised me he was hard already, but it didn't.

I looked up to see if I had the green light to proceed. Gabe nodded, and my tongue glided over my bottom lip. His dark, lustful eyes followed my pink tongue. His clove and grapefruit scent made my head spin. My nipples were already sensitive from the friction of my bra, and when my breasts rubbed on his leg, it made me moan. I opened his zipper and took out the prize I'd been waiting to win.

His huge thick dick was heavy and angry. I forgot how fucking big he was. But I didn't back down. I grabbed as much of his dick as I could by the base and ran my tongue along the underside of his cock straight to the big red tip. I watched, his eyes narrowed, and his jaw clenched. His struggle to control himself made my pussy drown in its own juices. I ran my tongue over the slit of his tip, tasting the salty pre-cum that pooled there. He tasted like heaven when his cum hit my tongue. *I missed this! I missed him.* I thought as I spat, sucked, and stroked his cock with my two soft hands. One pulling and teasing to the left and the other to the right as I worked to bring him over the edge. Gabe's eyes were closed to the world as he groaned and grumbled his pleasure. His muscular arms bulged and relaxed as he held onto the handle of the desk chair.

His hand shot to my head.

I pulled back before he made contact and declared, "No touching, keep your hands on the armrest," in my deep, aroused voice.

When he complied, I sank down on his cock, taking him as much as possible into my mouth. His cock twitched as it glided over my tongue. I continued to suck him down as I let my spit from my strained mouth roll down to where I was stroking him. Gabe groaned, and when I came up for some air, he had his head thrown back. I smiled and returned my mouth to his weeping cock. Hollowing my cheeks, he hit the back of my throat. He wasn't even halfway in, and he was making me gag. I removed one of my hands and used it to tug and tease his heavy ball sac. His gruntled moan filled the room, he twitched again, and I knew he was so close. I drew out to the tip and sucked him back in.

"Fuck Kitty," he grunted, and it was as if cold water washed over me, and I came to my senses at that moment. I pulled off while he was coming. Some of his salty and sweet cum landed on my tongue, but I pulled out too fast, and his cum flew all over my face, and some landed in my hair. But I didn't feel it or care.

"W-What did you call me?" I stammered.

"Shit, I'm sorry, Jasmine, I called you Kitty. It was someone—" he said, but I held up my hand.

I was clammy, and my mouth ached from his cock. But I was in shock. He called my name after I turned and left the door open. I punched the elevator like it was my lifeline, and when it opened, I flew in. Gabe's voice came closer to me. I hit the close button and held it until it locked me in. When I got to the lobby, I walked like a zombie into the car. Mr. Jackson peeled off, and I stared out the window. I closed my eyes and banged my head on my headrest.

Fuck, Fuck, Fuck! Why do I keep fucking up?

I left a massive tip for Mr. Jackson, and I trudged into the house. Greg was there to greet me. But I didn't have the strength to speak.

"Hey, I'm sorry. I overstepped my boundary," he pleaded. He kissed me and made a face. "Hm, kind of sweet and salty. Did you have bacon and doughnuts? Or something new today?"

I opened my mouth, but nothing came out.

"And you have some dried white stuff on your face and hair," I heard him call out as I walked to my bedroom.

It was only then that my shock turned into laughter, and I laughed until it turned into a sob. What I did was stupid and reckless— but I felt so fucking empowered on my knees, and when Gabe gave me control, it turned me on even more. I locked the door to my room and prayed for forgiveness that I didn't deserve.

Shit! Maybe I was a whore.

Chapter 17

Gabe

I didn't know who I was more upset with, myself or Jasmine. I meant to retrieve my file in the office and go home. What was meant to be, at most, a five-minute trip turned into a waiting game. The soft stomping and cursing of someone outside the office drew my attention. I ignored it and let whoever it was take it out on the floor.

That was the initial plan.

But then I walked out into the hallway when I heard a door click shut and was enveloped in the scent that made my cock jump to life. It had been in a semi hard state all day. That was, until she blew in, and then my cock was painfully hard, and I got angry and returned to my desk.

I was about to take care of my little situation after going back and forth on whether jerking off in the office was appropriate. Of course, it wasn't, but I was past the point of what was morally right and wrong. When I was about to unleash myself, Jasmine flew in like a hurricane of vanilla perfume and determination in her eyes. I saw her falter, but she regained her strength after she gave me a compliment.

Then she blessed me with the best head I'd had in six years. I'd almost wept as much as my cock did. I should have been embarrassed when my cum splattered all over her beautiful face and locs. But it made me hard again when her blown brown eyes turned up to me in shock as she looked on in disbelief that she had done something so bold.

But I wasn't.

It made me want to throw her over my shoulder and take her home and have her beg for forgiveness for torturing me with her ample ass and those full breasts. It seemed my brain had left me on a one-track mindset.

I had almost zipped my cock up, rushing out to catch up to her. But sadly, it was too late as the elevator door was closed by the time I got there. I was going to use the stairs, but one of the employees stopped me to approve the project he had been working on.

I clutched the steering wheel and sulked all the way home. As I stumbled in and stomped to the kitchen, I grabbed the water and went to find Tony and Wren in their usual spot, but they weren't there. So, I had to search for them all over until I found them in Wren's small gym, which was located next to the pool.

I entered and didn't care if I caught them in the middle of their "me time."

To my surprise, they were actually working out.

When I stepped in, they were both on the treadmill and looked like they were on their fifth mile of running. They stopped and shared a look of dread. I couldn't blame them at all. My attitude was nothing less than repugnant, and I'd said some hurtful things that I wished I could take back over the past years. I guess I wasn't as good at coping as I thought I had been when I came back from my extended self-care vacation.

"Can I speak with you guys for a minute?" I asked.

They hesitated, and I paused. My feelings were hurt, but I couldn't blame anyone except myself. They sat on the bench and gave me their undivided attention.

I blew out a bundle of hot air and rolled my neck, which sounded like someone's eighty-year-old grandparent's knees.

"Yeah, what's up?" Tony asked, "We haven't done anything crazy recently."

Wren nodded.

"I'm not here to unpack on you. How I've been acting toward you guys is unacceptable. I'm big enough to admit when I am wrong, and I'm here asking for forgiveness from both of my best friends." Before anyone interrupted, I continued. "I was in a dark spot before Jasmine rolled into our lives, and then when she came into our lives, it multiplied. I should have managed it better. It took me a long time to figure it out, and it's because she reminded me of what we lost."

"You forgot to mention that you were very horny," Tony uttered, and I frowned.

"It's her fault I have been in a terrible mood lately. She came in here—"

"Made your dick hard?" Tony pointed out.

"Made you masturbate too much?" Wren tagged along.

I pinched my nose. I could lie, and Tony and Wren would never be the wiser.

"Yes, to both," I said as I sighed. "I have been walking around with this hard-on for almost two months."

"Yes, we saw that gigantic cock of yours that nearly poked our eyes out. It's surprising it didn't fall off." Wren chuckled.

My lips thinned out, but I rolled my eyes.

"Just like now. It's ready to stab someone. It's really unnatural, Gabe. Maybe that's why Kitty ran. She didn't want you to burst through her throat anymore."

Wren's mouth dropped to form an O. Tony's hand flew to his

mouth as he realized his mistake. I couldn't help myself as the bubble rose in my throat, and I laughed so hard I had tears in my eyes. Wren and Tony joined in, and a warmth poured over me, and I felt like I was almost back to my old self.

Once we gathered ourselves, I apologized. "Thank you, guys. I really needed that, especially after today."

"What happened today? I thought it was your day off," Wren said.

"Ms. Grant strolled through and nearly sucked the skin off my dick," I smiled.

I rendered them both silent. I can think of only two times my brothers have been this quiet. One was when we held our breaths and hoped Tony passed his English finals. The second was when Kitty left us with our dicks in our hands.

"I hate both of you!" Tony huffed. "I only kissed her cheek, and we felt each other up."

That sent us into another laughing spell.

"How are you, Gabe?" Wren asked.

"I'm annoyed that Jasmine has disrupted my life and that I can't even do anything about it because she's engaged," I shook my head. "To be honest, my life was in shambles before then."

"Fiancé smian—"

I cut Tony off. "Don't even try it!" I bellowed, and Wren snickered.

Wren and Tony told me about their latest run-in with Jasmine. I shook my head when I discovered Tony called her out on her alias name. Some things they'd done were outlandish, but I wasn't totally surprised by their antics. They'd never change, and I wouldn't have it any other way.

"In all seriousness, did you go over the information I sent you?" Tony asked.

"No, I haven't had the chance—" I replied. "No, sorry, that was a lie. God's honest truth is that I'm scared to find out."

Wren sighed. "Do you think—" he started, but he stopped and shook his head like he couldn't fathom what he thought.

"What were you going to say?" I asked.

"Nothing," Wren replied. "Look over the information, and let's discuss it later."

I nodded and turned to leave them. I had so much stuff running through my head that it would be best to go for a drive. I entered my second oasis, our six-car garage that held some of our most beloved cars. The others were in storage. I walked into the tan wall garage and decided on my first baby, my red nineteen-fifty Ferrari one hundred sixty-six.

My Ferrari purred to life, and I started my trip up the winding hills of LA. The homes lined with metal gates of the who's who in Hollywood. As I passed through the blurred neighborhoods, I wondered which one belonged to Jasmine. I climbed higher up the hill, close to the glaring Hollywood sign of LA, and hit the area's apex. The air became thinner, but as soon as my body reacted to the change of the thin pressure, it was gone because I was hitting the downslope.

I didn't want to face reality. So, I took about three more rounds around the Hills. An hour later, I was back in my office to face the music.

Some would have called me a coward because I avoided examining the pictures. But just like earlier on, when she touched and tugged on my earlobe, that brought me back to Club Celeste. I chose to ignore it. I didn't even attempt to look through Tony's documents because I was afraid to find out the truth, and the best way to save myself from being hurt was to ignore them. The thought that the woman we fell for was right under our noses as we'd fumbled and wasted our time with others that we weren't interested in was beyond hurtful.

I wasn't ashamed to admit that I was still head over heels in love with Kitty. I wanted to worship the ground she walked on and give her the world.

I gripped the edge of my desk hard. The wood desk edge dug into my palm. A dull pain greeted me, but I welcomed it.

Moment of truth, I thought, as my hands shook like a leaf. I pulled up everything on my Mac and read through the files first. Twenty minutes later, I was pretty sure, not a hundred percent sure, that Jasmine was Kitty. If we were going by the information in front of me, then that would mean there was a possibility she was cheating on Greg with us during our time at Club Celeste, and she never loved us.

It was all a lie. The late-night talks, the dinners, etc., were lies.

I couldn't even believe that someone would be that cruel.

Then I looked at the photos, and I should have paid attention to them when Tony gave them to me. It was the last photo that everyone barely looked at, but it was when I zoomed in so close that if you didn't know what you were searching for, you would have missed it because it was extremely blurry. It was the brown birthmark that was shaped like a crescent moon under her right breast that confirmed it. I knew it like the freckles on the back of my hand, from all the late nights of tracing it repeatedly, committing it to memory.

It wasn't until my phone rang that I realized my tears were falling. I was never one to be too masculine to cry. The person hung up after I let the phone ring. I wanted a drink, but we agreed with Tony not to store alcohol in the house. I looked at the once-filled mini-cart and sighed.

I guess I was right when I read that note from the front desk she had stuffed in her purse. I had been a fool for believing Jasmine. She gave us false hope when she had someone else waiting for her at home. She used us to cheat on her boyfriend, then turned around and had his kids.

Poor naïve Gabe.

It felt like the carefully built wall I'd erected had come tumbling down with each tear. The walls I kept in my mind dropped and flooded with the memories of our time together.

After I gathered myself enough, I sent a text to Tony to confirm it was her. My phone weighed heavy in my hand. I knew I should just leave it alone, but I had to hear her voice. Maybe I'm a masochist because I hit her number to call her without thinking.

On the third ring, she answered in a breathy voice.

"Hello?" she said for the second time. "Gabe, is that you?"

I choked. The words lodged in my throat. What could I say to her to make her reconsider her plans? Why should she leave her fiancé to be with us? Why were we better for her than Greg could ever be?

"I'm sorry we weren't good enough," I said in a voice I wasn't entirely sure was my own. It sounded small and fragile, like my voice could break, if it went an octave higher. Jasmine didn't hear it though because she had hung up a couple of seconds ago.

I dragged myself to my bedroom, which was hard since my body felt like lead, and lifting my legs was a chore. But I found I couldn't sleep as I tossed and turned. So, I did the next best thing. I packed a bag filled with the essentials and texted the guys that I would be back soon and that I needed to clear my head.

In thirty minutes, I was inside the Sodo condo I purchased after Kitty—Jasmine— left. It was where I'd holed up for two months until I was ready to face the world with the help of my Uncle Vincenzo. My uncle was my therapist. I knew it was unorthodox, but he helped me during my life's pain points and would drop everything to help me. I sent him a text, and he said he would meet me at the house.

I promised I would leave when I was ready to take on Jasmine. But for the moment, my mental health needed attending.

Chapter 18

Tony

Gabe had been missing in action for about a week. He hadn't even called us, only a simple text to let us know he was okay. But I was not surprised because when Kitty left, for about three months, we didn't hear from him until he magically reappeared. As for our Jasmine situation, we had one measly text and a couple of blurry pictures we hadn't even looked at because we couldn't make out anything in them.

I pushed down on Wren's back which made his ass poke out more as I continued my deep strokes. The prickly heat of my orgasm threatened to rip through me like it wanted to take my soul. Wren had already cum twice, and I was punishing him at this point. He moaned as I repositioned myself and fucked him into the bed.

It was what I wanted to do to Jasmine.

I sped up my pace, and Wren cursed. His sheets were damp from his sweaty body and cum. That was how I liked Wren. Nothing but a bucket of sweat and cum. I could imagine Jasmine underneath Wren with her own sweat and essence mixed in with ours. That was all the restraint I had left as I came so hard my eyes crossed, and I dropped all my weight onto Wren.

"You want to kill me?" Wren asked breathlessly.

"Sorry, I'm a bit frustrated and worried," I huffed truthfully as I rolled off Wren, still semi-hard.

He slowly rolled to his side to face me. He looked down and took me in his hand. His soft hands glided over my piercings, which made me sigh with frustration. I wanted to stop him and tell him it wouldn't work. It wanted that tight little pussy Jasmine kept hidden from me.

After a minute of him working out his wrist, I stopped him.

"I appreciate the effort, but Tony's stairway wants a one-way ticket to Jasmine's womb." I sighed.

"What are we going to do?" he asked. "Has Gabe contacted you yet? Do you think he's going to be MIA like last time?"

"Well, I hope not because that would be too long to wait. I think I would kidnap Jasmine before that happens."

We chuckled over my joke.

"I would like to invite her to dinner again, but I doubt she'll come willingly." I faltered.

"Do it, Tony. You never know. I'll bet you five thousand."

My love knew I could never turn down a chance to win money. If it was one thing I would do, it was win that bet.

I jumped up from the bed, and my semi-erected cock slapped my thighs when I walked. I grabbed my phone and texted Jasmine.

Kitty

Ciao Amore!

We have a lunch date tomorrow at eleven in the morning.

No.

Yes!

NO! Not today nor tomorrow.

Okay, I will be over at your house tomorrow then.

Absolutely not.

I'm serious, Tony!

Tony! You better answer me.

Damn, I want to hear you say my name like that.

-__- Fine! Where and when?

La Rosa. Come to the private room.

I returned to the bedroom from the closet, a huge smile plastered onto my face, and I jumped back into bed. Wren was hooked on the reality show on the television, but I turned it off.

"Time for round two, and I would like you to Zelle me the five thousand." I grinned.

"Shit, how did you get her to say yes so fast?" Wren looked pleasantly surprised.

I kissed him, slipping my tongue into his waiting mouth. It was days like this I missed my tongue piercing. Wren was breathless when I finally released his pink, swollen lips.

"Baby, you doubt my persuasive nature all the time."

"Well, technically, the last time you met up with Jasmine, you were supposed to get evidence, and you didn't," he challenged.

"You say potato. I say potatoes." I shrugged. "Plus, you didn't get any evidence either."

He humphed. "Fine, let's go to bed then since you're going to be up at the crack of dawn."

"Uh, we're going for round two." I held his arm.

Wren laughed as he pulled from my soft hold and turned to cover himself. He reached over and turned the little light off, and darkness flooded the room.

Wren dared to ignore me, and he didn't pay me any attention when I tried to slide between his luscious cheeks. He swatted me away.

Like, who swats someone away in this century?

I sighed. I knew I was right that Jasmine was our Kitty. But I couldn't shake the conversation I'd had with my mom and my sister a couple of months ago. I hadn't told anyone yet, but if it was true, then there was a possibility we were fathers. The mother was somewhere struggling alone.

The thought didn't sit right with me.

The other part Gabe mentioned to us also kept coming back. That Kitty was most likely cheating on Greg with us. She found out she was pregnant and fled.

Whatever the case, I'm ready to sort this shit out.

As promised, I was waiting for my petite queen at eleven at La Rosa. I didn't have any concrete plans, and if I were being honest, I just wanted to be near her. The way she smiled made everything seem insignificant. The citrus scent that seemed to be embedded into her skin and locs. But I couldn't help but grow tired of the runaround. I wanted her to quit playing around so we could have some closure.

Yes, I knew that was unreasonable, but I was entitled to my opinions. I could only be so patient. I was going to call lunch off when I heard the soft click of heels down the hallway, and the door opened and clicked closed. I got up and turned to greet Jasmine, but I stumbled back. She had on a yellow sundress that highlighted her curvy body and made her honey-brown skin glisten. She wore white high heels, making her seem taller than she usually appeared. Her hair was in a half updo.

I hugged her and kissed her cheek. Rose and jasmine scents clouded our space. I wanted to dig my face into her neck and just inhale her essence. The tips of her ears turned a slight pink. It made me smile a bit that I had that effect on her.

"Here, let me pull out your seat." I dashed to the other side of the table.

She hesitated for a minute and then took the offer. When she gave me her back, I saw the dress get swallowed up by her ass. Either she didn't have underwear on, or she wore a thong.

I shifted my hardened dick in my pants and sighed.

"Thank you for accepting my invite," I said with a smile.

"Accepting." She cocked her eyebrow. "You sure have a funny way of inviting people to lunch."

"Would you have said yes otherwise?"

That earned a smile, and she quickly sucked her bottom lip between her teeth.

"No, I wouldn't have," she answered after a minute passed.

We started off by being polite and asking about our different business affairs. I planned on taking it easy and not torturing Jasmine with twenty-one questions. I finally got her to crack a smile twenty minutes after our food and drinks came.

An hour after we finished eating and the small talk ended, she cut the pleasantries.

"Okay, now tell me why you asked me here, and no, I don't want your job offer," she asserted with her back straight and arms folded under her ample breasts, pushing them up.

I could see her nipples fighting to get my mouth around them. I couldn't see between her breasts because she had a backless halter-style dress that covered her chest.

"So, Jasmine Grant. We both know we have been dancing around this topic."

Her eyes narrowed. "What do you mean, Mr. Russo?"

Damn, even the way she pronounced my name made my dick twitch.

I tapped my foot against the tile floor of the room as I reached for my research. I pulled it out and placed it in the space between us. Jasmine hesitated and collected the papers. Her eyes widened, and her chest rose heavily with each document.

"So, Jasmine Grant or Stephanie Johnson?" I folded my hands together. "It's clear you have amazing connections, Jasmine. You had your kids' birth certificate filed under your alias name. That's big time."

She looked ashen under my observation. "H-H," she stammered and cleared her throat. "You dug up information on me. Why?"

I looked her straight in her eyes. "Why did you lie about having kids?"

"T-That's not any of your business!" she squeaked out.

"Is it not? Did you cheat on Greg back then?"

"W-What, no!" she stammered out.

"You told us you loved everything about beauty and fashion in club celeste." I tilted my head. "Is it not true, Kitty?"

Her eyes shifted between the door and me.

"Did you find out you were pregnant with Greg's babies and

run from us that night?" I asked.

The look on her face was nothing short of fury. Her heart-shaped lips pursed together, and she narrowed her eyes at me.

She got up, and instead of leaving, she charged into the private restroom.

I shouldn't have unloaded on her, but I was tired and wanted answers. With Gabe gone and the possibility—well, about everything had worn me thin.

I approached the bathroom and knocked, but luckily, she hadn't locked it. Jasmine leaned on the sink and popped up when she saw me enter.

I walked up behind her, grabbed her chin, and tilted it to suck and kiss the tender area of her neck. When I reached her ear, I whispered, "Do you want me to make you feel better, Kitty, like before?"

In the mirror, I could see the emotions flicker on her gorgeous face and the lone tear that rolled down her face. My thumb snaked out to swipe the tear away. I waited, my dick in between her glorious ass cheeks as my teeth continuously grazed her earlobe.

In the smallest voice, she whispered, "Please."

That was all I needed. I lifted that sundress and nearly creamed my pants at the sight. Jasmine's glorious ass was spectacular with clothes, but it was heavenly without them. I noticed she'd lost weight recently, and I disapproved of that.

By some miracle, I managed to put on the condom I had stored in my pocket with one hand.

My hand grabbed her throat as I angled my cock at her entrance. She tried to push down, but I tightened my grip on her neck and loosened it when she stopped moving.

"Don't you lose any more weight! I've waited so long to feel those thick thighs wrapped around my head," I grunted out.

She groaned, and I pushed into her soaking wet core in one sweep. Her pussy was like a furnace as she tried to burn me alive. A small gasp left her mouth when she felt me slide home.

"Oh god, I'm so full!" she exclaimed, and I chuckled. "Please, Tony!"

Not one to deprive my waiting lady and my poor straining cock, I fucked her like I was on death row. My strokes were erratic, and she moaned, her face turning a slight shade darker from my hand on her neck. I grew hungry and more frantic with my strokes. Jasmine clung to the sink for dear life, and her hands tightened until her knuckles were white.

Our moans and my grunting ricocheted off the walls.

Her deep voice sounded heavenly when she whimpered out, "Please, baby, fuck me harder," which I obliged.

Each stroke and slap to her perfectly rounded ass cheek brought the punishment I wanted to inflict on her. Her walls squeezed the life out of my dick, and I let go of her neck right before she broke into pieces around me. She looked like a queen with her tear-soaked face and heaving full breasts. I leaned over, placing kisses on her intoxicating skin. I gave her five seconds, and then I returned to fucking her even more frantically than before as I chased my orgasm.

Every time I hit her spot, Jasmine whimpered, "Yes, right there." My whole body stiffened as Jasmine clenched down on me, causing me to lose the battle to stay in her as long as I could. A sound I would only assume was animalistic released from me, and Jasmine shook and whimpered through her current orgasm.

Fuck! That was one of the best releases I'd had in ages.

We stood together, connected, my soft cock still inside her, begging me not to pull out of our home. The mirror was slightly foggy from the hot air circulating between us. It pained me to slip out of her, but I did and helped her clean up and covered her before tucking myself back in my pants.

Jasmine turned to me, and I saw her eyes filled with unshed tears. The tear streaks from her earlier tears lined her face.

"I-I'm sorry," she whimpered.

I opened my mouth, but nothing came out. But Jasmine leaned in and kissed me. The kiss was nothing short of a needy kiss as she explored, nipped, and lapped at my mouth. I pulled away after a minute or two because I was two seconds from throwing her over my shoulder and taking her back to our place. She held my face with her two hands and kissed the tip of my nose as she racked her hands into my hair, like she'd done so many times before.

"I'll wait for you outside," I muttered, and I went out and took my seat, knowing that, right then, I had to let her go, and if she wanted to come back, the ball was in her court.

Five minutes later, Jasmine crept out of the bathroom. She gathered her things quickly and said goodbye.

Fuck it!

Right before Jasmine left, I grabbed her wrist, which made her turn back to face me. She wanted to protest, but she opened her mouth and then shut it.

I kissed her wrist and drew circles around her pulse point. "I will let you go for now. But I'm coming back for what's mine, and in case you didn't know, that's you," I proclaimed as I gave a last kiss on her wrist, and I watched as her plump bottom lip trembled.

She nodded, gave me one last kiss on my cheek, as I watched her leave the room.

And it was a glorious sight to watch.

She didn't know it, but I touched the bite mark I left on her right thigh when I was deep inside her, even though I didn't have to because she all but confirmed our suspicions when she didn't deny any of it.

I should be angry, sad, or even mad. But the prospect of

Jasmine, our Kitty, returning to us, even if it was a sliver of hope, had me feeling revitalized.

I sent a message to our family group chat.

> Jasmine is, in fact, Kitty.

> I felt my bite mark on her, and she denied nothing.

Wren Babes

> Our Kitty has strayed back home like we suspected.

> Yes, indeed.

> The ball is in Jasmine's court now,

> but I will take it if she makes the wrong choice.

Wren Babes

> I like how you think.... sometimes.

> *rolls eyes* Okay lol

I waited about five more minutes until I gave up hope Gabe would reply.

It was when I was tucked into bed with Wren and I heard the door creak open, and Gabe popped his head in. I struggled to open my eyes, and when I did, I looked at the clock.

"Gabe, what the fuck! It's three in the morning. Where have you been?"

"I needed to get away and clear my head. After reading those documents and seeing the pictures, I wasn't in a good place. Did you not get the picture with her tattoo? Don't you remember when she ran out, you said you saw a peace tattoo on her hip? That was hidden under some bandages? How about the crescent moon-shaped birthmark that was under her right breast?"

"Now, how was I supposed to know what that blurry picture was? It was so grainy, and I couldn't blow it up on my phone. A simple text explaining would have sufficed."

Gabe sighed, and Wren stirred but didn't wake up. He slept like the dead.

"I'm sorry, Tony. I had to have some me time with my uncle." He looked downcast. "I feel horrible for running out on you guys again."

I knew he would be more level-headed if he went to visit with his uncle. I wouldn't have wanted to be Greg if Gabe didn't get his shit together. One thing about Gabe is if he gave you a piece of himself, he would paint the Hills red to get you back.

"Everything is good, Gabe. I'm glad to see you back and in one piece. That's all that matters. Go get some rest, and we'll devise a thorough Jasmine-proof plan later."

He nodded and left the room. Wren hadn't budged a bit, and I returned to sleep with all the ways I would make Jasmine pay.

Handcuffs, swings, oh my!

Chapter 19

Jasmine

I will let you go for now. But I'm coming back for what's mine. And in case you didn't know, that's you.

Those words had circulated in my mind since I'd had my lunch date with Tony. Every chance I got to masturbate, those words brought me over the edge… one too many times. It made me feel shameful because I wasn't some gotdamn object, but I couldn't help it. It struck some fire in my stomach to know they still wanted me.

Plus, when his piercings hit my spot…

I sighed heavily as the words ricocheted in my head as I stared off into space. A gentle voice with a hint of accent spoke my name, which brought me back to my dull reality.

"Earth to Jasmine! Come in, Jasmine." She flailed her arms in front of my face.

I was embarrassed to be seated there, in Rosa Marino's home, with my thighs clenched as I thought about Tony's words. Heat spread to my face.

"I'm so sorry. There are a lot of things on my mind right now," I uttered. My mind and body almost seemed to wait for the guys to swoop me up like Cinderella.

Pathetic really!

I should have stayed home, but my conscience got the best of me. So, when she called to invite me over, I said yes because I didn't want to say no to her, and I really needed to get out of the house.

"It's no problem. I totally understand. Do you want to talk about it? I have been known to be a great listener." She wiggled her eyebrows as I giggled.

I thought about it some more. I needed someone to talk to who wasn't aware of the situation or anything about the guys. From the beginning, I told her everything. Everything about Samantha, Sage, the club, and the guys fell out of my mouth.

I watched her face go from disbelief to shock and everything in between. When I was done thirty minutes later, she pinched the bridge of her nose and shook her head. She didn't have to say anything as an icy chill ran through me. I felt berated and scolded without words. Telling her was a big mistake. I sat there and wondered why I had agreed to this mess of a lunch date.

"First, I'm truly sorry about your best friend. I lost one of my twin brothers in an accident. It was ages ago, but you still carry scars from those traumatic events. So, I understand what you went through."

"T-Thank you." I peered at her to see if she was being honest. "I hope you don't look at me differently because I paid for sex, technically."

She smiled and declared, "I wouldn't dare. I don't blame you, especially since you didn't have anyone else to take care of those needs. We're only human."

I still felt ashamed, but I placed a smile on my balmy face.

"I should tell you that—"

The bellow of a male voice cut her off. "Rosa, have you seen my golf gloves? I can't play without them!" the person yelled out.

I turned to smile and to ask Rosa if that was her husband. But when I did, she looked as if the blood had seeped out of her body. She tried to get up before he came in.

But it was too late. I looked over to see someone who looked like Gabe but was older and rounder. My mouth flew open, and my eyes popped out.

"Oh, hello, I didn't know you had a guest, my love," the man noted as he grabbed my hand. "My name is Giovanni Sabino."

I sat there and gaped at him.

"Well, my good looks have stumped you." He smiled.

"H-H," Rosa stammered. "This is Ms. Grant, one of Gabe's new artists."

"Ah, yes, the retired artist. I have read and heard so much about you," Mr. Sabino mentioned cheerfully.

Say something, you twit!

"W-Why thank you, Mr. Sabino. I should get going anyway. It was a pleasure to meet you," I stammered. It was a miracle I made it through that sentence.

It was stupid, but I felt blindsided. If I wasn't embarrassed before, I was mortified now. My face was warm, and the pressure in my chest was unbearable. I told this woman her son paid to have sex with me. I told her, and she had seen the twins.

Great fucking job, Jasmine.

I didn't give her time to reply. I was up and out before she could stop me. She called my name as she rushed to keep up with me. I made it out the front door. I thought I had enough ground to escape her, but nope.

I got to my car, and she snatched me like a child.

"Listen, I'm sorry I didn't tell you about who I was. I remembered Gabe and my husband talking about you. When I saw Tris and Teo, I knew something was up. So, for being underhanded, I apologize. But I was honest when I told you I wouldn't tell anyone. I was being a mother first and foremost. You can understand that," she pleaded.

Some of me could sympathize with her, so I nodded because I didn't trust myself to say something practical.

The sound of a car pulling into the driveway and parking beside my car drew my attention. A pink Cadillac was very out of place for the hills. The driver flung her thin arms open at Rosa.

Rosa looked at her watch, and her head popped up. I almost thought her head would snap off from how quickly she looked up. She cursed, and before I could ask her what was wrong, her new guest spoke.

"Ciao, Rosa." The older woman with midnight hair and light green eyes stood in front of us. At that moment, something deep in my spirit knew shit had hit the fan.

"Ciao, Stefani." Rosa was red. "This is my client. She was just leaving."

"Hello. I'm sorry I have to run. It was nice meeting you," I responded quickly.

"Ciao, Aunt Rosa!" A lady came up beside Stefani. She took one look at me, and she cursed. "Oh my God, it's you! I never forget a face and a body like yours!"

"E-Excuse me. You have the wrong person." I shuffled to my car.

I tried to sit, but she wrapped her hand around my arm. She used her weight to stop me from leaving.

Fuck me sideways! I stumbled as I tried to remember where I had possibly seen her.

"No, I wouldn't forget a banging body like yours. Nope, you're the woman—" she said, but Rosa cut her off.

"Bethany, you have the wrong person. Now, my client has a sick family member at home. She needs to leave now," Rosa lied.

"But Aunt Rosa—"

"Ho detto di lasciarlo andare ora[1]," Rosa spat out in Italian.

Bethany dropped my arm finally. I should have fought her, but something told me she would have laid me out cold.

As I pulled away, I saw Rosa give me a sad smile and wave. But Bethany stared at me like she knew the depths of my secret. Even as I pulled away, her face drew a blank. I got to the gate for their community, my heart still pounded against my ribcage, and I gripped the wheel like I wanted to break it off and smash someone with it. It felt like everything was crashing down on my carefully planned normal life. So, you would have thought I would cry? But no, I wanted to hit the next person who fucked with me.

I was so mad my throat throbbed painfully.

My mother called. I cursed and wondered why the fuck she was calling me.

"Hey Jasmine, I'm here early, but no one's answering the door. Are you close by?" she stated.

"Hey, Mom, what do you mean you're here early?" I asked, confused for the second time today. Yes, my mom and I made up after the Nashville trip, but we were still on a rocky road. I would have remembered if she was supposed to visit us because I would have prepared for her arrival.

"Oh ha, Jasmine. You expect me to believe you forgot your bridal shower party was tonight?"

Oh, fuck me! I *had* forgotten about that stupid shit my mom guilt-tripped me into having. I guess that was right since the event was two weeks from tomorrow. That made me even madder than I was before.

"I will text Greg and let him know you're waiting outside."

"Okay, bye, love. See you soon."

I told her goodbye as well. When I stopped, I texted Greg, and

---

1   I said let it go now, Italian.

he responded immediately. I wondered why this fool never wanted to answer the door.

When I reached home, I thought I would have cooled down by then, but nope. The decorations and the steady stream of the event planner's employees coming in and out of my house multiplied it. Stomping through the house, I plastered on the fakest smile and made my way to find my mother.

I didn't have to look far because she and Greg were huddled together in his mold-encrusted office.

The smell pissed me off.

"Mom," I gritted out. "Greg."

Greg had been strange since we returned from Nashville. He was holed up in his office, and when he wasn't, he played his new game, asking Jasmine twenty-one questions to piss her off.

My mom looked up, and her eyes had hurt written in them. I folded my arms because, not to be mean or anything, I didn't give a shit right now.

"Jasmine, I-I," she looked down at her hands. She never had done that in my entire life. "I thought we were supposed to break into Real Estate together. We were going to do it as a mother and daughter business."

Fuck. I wondered if it's too late to change my name to Fuck because if you looked the word up, you would find my name and picture underneath it as a prime example.

"Mom, I'm really not in the mood right now. I'm sorry I withheld that Allison and I have been buying homes since the beginning of my career. We shouldn't proceed with that idea since sometimes we don't work well together. I still love you very much, though."

That was the actual truth. At least I could get that off my chest. One less lie I had to keep up. To my surprise, my mom came over and hugged me.

"I love you too. I understand, and it's best if you and your husband start that journey together."

"How did you find out?" I asked, puzzled.

"You told on yourself." Greg finally spoke. His nostrils flared at me, and I was sure if my mother wasn't there, he would have hit me. "That's why you weren't rushing to get your masters. It was because you were sitting on a shitload of cash."

Okay, just when I thought I would never physically harm Greg, he proved me wrong.

"Listen, I worked my ass off for what is mine. I don't need you to tell me what is and what isn't essential. And if I decide not to tell you about my affairs, that's my business."

With that, I turned on my heels to leave, but he wheeled me around. I didn't know Greg could move that fast. His fingernails dug into my skin. My mom jumped up and tried to get him off of me. If it was any other time, I would say it was hilarious to see her beat at Greg's sinewy arms as she yelled for him to let me go. But I wrenched my arm out of his grip.

"You're disrespectful, Jasmine." His eyes told me he wanted to say more, but he stomped back to his seat.

"Jasmine, are you okay?" my mom said, but I held my hand up and nodded as I left before I heard my mom giving Greg a piece of her mind. *If only she knew it wasn't the first time it happened.*

Finally, alone in my bedroom, I locked the door. Thankfully, the boys weren't home. I rolled my neck and looked at my arm. There were angry red welts and scratches from prying my arm out of Greg's hands. I most definitely would have a couple of black and blues. I looked over at his aftershave, and the thought of replacing it with rubbing alcohol crossed my mind. But I didn't. Instead, I drew myself a bath and hoped it would help me with my temper.

I stayed in the tub until I was basically a prune. Afterward, I showered and then got ready. I was gorgeous, to say the least, in my white Valentino crepe dress and white custom-made Dior stilettos. I left my locs down because I didn't care to do anything else.

I sat on my bed until the little fists of my twins beating the door down brought me back to my present situation. I leaped up, opened the door, and locked it behind them.

"Mommy, you look beautiful," Tris cajoled, and my mood slightly turned around. I could never be mad around them. "Can we come to your party?"

I hugged them and kissed them until they begged me to stop.

"Sadly, no, my loves. This party is for Mommy and her friends," I said. "But I wish my best men in the whole wide world could join us. I will miss you."

"But we're going to be bored stuck in here," Teo whined.

"I know, and Mommy is sorry. I promise tomorrow, when we go to New York for Mommy's interview, we will do something fun afterward."

"Oh, I forgot we're going to New York!" Tris jumped up. He was usually the quiet one, but not today. "We can go to the Hall of Science!"

A smile touched my face. I didn't think Tris and Teo remembered they had been there before, but as I watched them do their little dance, I couldn't help but join in, and I forgot about everything for a moment. The party, the wedding, my mom, and the guys...

Until there was a dreaded knock on my door. It was Allison telling me everyone was downstairs and waiting for me. I instantly felt the throb in my throat return.

I yelled out I was coming, and that was enough for her. I walked the boys to their room, and Greg was already there. He fixed his mouth to say something, but he took one look at my face and turned his own screwed-up face away.

I didn't care as I hugged and kissed my babies. They were already deep in their laptops, doing what I didn't know. I turned to leave and threw Greg a pissed look.

The moment my heels hit the last step—I was right back to square one, pissed off. But what could I do? I plastered on my fake smile and greeted everyone. I thought I was in the clear until Alison mumbled for me to fix my face.

My mother and Greg's mother sandwiched me on the sofa. How fun. Not! Greg's mother basically talked right through me as if I wasn't there, while my mom just nodded and gave her a smile that didn't quite reach her eyes. I don't think I've ever seen my mother so stiff and quiet in my life. Luckily, I got everyone a bottle of champagne—better yet, the party organizer did.

It was thirty minutes in, and I could tell you two things. One, my mom, when she did speak, and Greg's Mom spat when they talked. It was like Water War One. Two, Allison sulked along with me because she opposed this union. Wait. Three things. The champagne didn't take away my anger.

It wasn't until I looked over to Sage, who I'd invited, that she announced, "You're so lucky you've found someone like Greg to care for you."

I knew it was stupid of me—hey, blame it on the alcohol, but it was like an epiphany. The cold sensation of my reality washed over me and told me to wake the hell up.

I got up and looked at Sage and said, "Thank you."

"Fuck this!" I exclaimed. She looked at me as if I were crazy. Well, I suppose I was.

My mom shifted uncomfortably in her seat and Greg's mom gasped. Sage's eyes bugged out. Allison smirked like she was saying, "About damn time." Greg's friends and aunt looked dumbfounded.

"Jasmine, what—"

I cut my mother off. "Mom, I love you, and we've had our difficult times, but I would rather slit my wrists, sew my vagina up, and become a nun than live with a man that can't please me, physically or mentally." As I laughed, I sounded manic.

The wait staff for the night pretended to be busy while they lingered around.

"I thought I needed Greg for the boys or to appear normal, but you know what? I'd rather die alone than be with him. I'm sorry— Well, no, I'm not sorry. Too bad, Mom and Ms. Simmons." I turned to her. "Your son is a religious, verbally abusive freak... and not the good kind of freak, either. He's used this arrangement to control me, but I won't have it. At first, I thought I could live with it until the boys were eighteen, but I can't. On top of everything, he's boring!"

Greg's mother nearly toppled over her chair as she tried to get up. She looked like she was going to say something, but then I heard a small cry coming down the stairs.

My heart stopped as I rushed toward Teo. His little face was red, and he had tear streaks down his face.

I forgot my speech and ran over, almost knocking my mom over.

"Hey, baby, what happened?" I cooed, "Mommy is right here."

He stuffed his face under my chin as I carried him in my arms.

He whispered something, but I didn't hear him because Greg came rushing down with his face twisted and his eyes filled with anger.

"What the fuck is going on?" I gritted through my teeth.

"He pinched me, Mommy, because I didn't want him to mess with my Nintendo." Teo pointed to his little arm where a red splotchy area had formed, which would definitely leave a black and blue on him.

I couldn't even think straight. It took me a minute for my mom and Allison to pull me together. I took a few deep breaths and kissed Teo, whose sobs turned into a silent cry. Tris, who had crept down behind his brother, hid behind my leg.

One thing about me was if you hurt me, I will be okay, but if you fuck with my kids, I will make you pay.

Stay calm until the kids are in their room! Stay calm until the kids are in their room!

I repeated it three more times to calm myself, but Greg wanted to push me.

"It's Allison's fault that I had to punish Teo. You hang around Allison, who treats herself like a common whore and influences you to allow the kids to disrespect me!" he yelled.

All the women in the room went quiet.

"Now Gregie, that's—" Greg's mother started to say but got cut off.

He continued, "You dress like a slut, and you act like one, too. How are the boys supposed to have a good picture of a Christian woman? When their mother and their 'aunt' are nothing more than high-class whores."

Oh, but the bastard still wasn't finished. He turned to Allison and pointed his finger in her face. "I like your husband, but he needs to deal with you. You need to be punished for disrespecting his name."

Greg reached into his pocket and threw my birth control pills on the floor. "And she's a liar. She ruined her body and lied to me about wanting kids. But you couldn't wait to open your legs and let some strangers get you pregnant! You poisoned your body with this stuff."

My mother mumbled as she picked up the discarded pills, "Well, thank God for small favors."

Stay calm until the kids are in their room!

I turned on my heels and took my boys with me. I got an ice pack for Teo and marched them upstairs. In the distance, I heard Allison and Greg arguing, but I was on a one-woman mission.

I got to their room and told them to lock the door until Allison, their grandmother, or I returned. Their little faces wanted to protest, but I kissed them. I told them they were the best kids in the world and that I was lucky to be their mother. Also, what that man said was untrue.

Before I headed back to the crime scene, I stopped at the utility closet by the staircase and retrieved the item I wanted: my bat. Yes, I had a gun and a gun license. I mean, I was a Southern woman, after all.

But I wanted to paint my walls with his insides.

My grandmother, my mom's mother, always taught me to keep a bat and a gun nearby because a bitch would always want to try you. She was always such a good Christian woman who would curse you out and send you back to God in a body bag.

I came down the back stairs by the kitchen with the bat behind me.

Greg and Allison were still going at it. I took my bat out, and the eyes of everyone who faced me popped out their head as I raised the bat. When I brought it down as hard as I could, I aimed for his back—well, it was supposed to be his back, but it landed on his ass. Everybody gasped.

I heard Greg yell and spin around. I lifted the bat to hit him again, but he stopped me.

My face probably looked possessed, like my grandmother's spirit merged into mine because my mother yelled at me.

"Jasmine Grant, stop it. Let's talk about this like adults!" she pleaded, and I understood she didn't want me to go to jail. "Think of the boys! You have to be there for them. Not in jail!" she yelled.

Allison grabbed the bat and stated, "She doesn't need to go to jail, but I deserve a hit." And she hit him in the stomach so hard he doubled over in pain.

I smirked.

"Get your shit and get the fuck off of my property. You're a worthless piece of shit. Your mother raised a bitch, and your father made you an even bigger bitch. If I ever catch you around here or in the Hills, I will find you, and I will greet you with something worse than a bat next time, and my mom won't be able to save you."

"Y-You can't kick me out of the house! It's ours!" he yelled as he regained his strength to stand up.

"Excuse me?" My Mom, Allison, and I spoke as one.

"I built this home with *my* hard-earned money! I toured eleven months and two weeks of every year during my entire career." I woosahed and meditated before I continued. "You have until the count of three to get out of my house and my life before I land this bat right on your useless dick and render you nutless because they'll be stuck inside you. It will be a well-deserved nonsurgical vasectomy."

He stared at me like I was crazy, and maybe I was.

"I was foolish to think I needed someone like you or anyone to care for my children. When in reality, all I needed was my own gotdamn self. Thank God, I have seen the truth. Goodbye, Greg. Hope you find someone else's life to ruin."

He looked around the room and hesitated, as if I was joking. So, I took a step towards him, and he ran out the door. I followed him to make sure he got my message.

"Could you give me my wallet and phone? Or could someone give my family and me a ride?"

"You can call an Uber," I stated, "from outside of my gates."

"B-B-But," he stammered.

"B-B-But you better get to walking. It's a long road to the gate." I mocked him. "Allison, could you drive behind them and make sure they get the fuck off my property? I have two little men to put to bed. Plus, we're heading to New York tomorrow."

"Sure thing, boss lady." Allison smirked and jumped in her car, but not before she yelled out loud enough for everyone to hear, "Thank God you came to your damn senses before you married him."

I smiled.

"For the first time in five years, I feel light as a feather. Sage, sorry for the entertainment tonight. There's a guest room down the hall, the third door to your right. You are more than welcome to crash here if you like."

"I have to leave super early, so I will go back and pack. But girl, that was kick ass. Glad you didn't shackle yourself to someone you couldn't stand for the sake of your kids. Trust me, been there, done that." Sage shook her head. "Now, go hug those babies. They're probably still shaken from everything. I wanted to punch him, girl, but I can't go to jail."

We laughed at that. I waited until Sage got to her car and went to my babies.

I had to knock three times before they opened it up. They flew into my arms when they saw it was me. I'd already experienced the most incredible love there was from my babies.

I told them that what they heard was to stay in this house and that they wouldn't see Mr. Greg anymore.

I know, petty as fuck, and I didn't care.

After I tucked them in, I promised them I would be back. I threw some stuff together for the next day's trip and got their things packed because I knew the sneaky sneaks would pack their laptops and games and nothing else. I told my mom, who looked worn out from tonight, that she could stay until Sunday night.

Before I could make it to the twins' room, my mother asked to speak with me in private. I folded my arms and geared up for the tongue-lashing that was sure to come. She pulled me into the room I'd dedicated to her when I had the home built.

"Jas," she called even though she averted her eyes. "Something has been bothering me."

"Is it about earlier? About the business?"

She kissed her teeth and smiled. She sat on her bed. "No, that's water under the bridge. I'm worried that maybe I caused this fiasco. I caused you to probably hate me."

As I looked at my mother, I saw that the last few hours had taken a toll on her. Her brown skin looked ashen, and she had dark circles under her eyes. She sat with her shoulders slouched. There was a lot I could say that would probably break my mother, but I wouldn't be that person.

"Mom, I understand you wanted the best for me, and you were

only doing what you thought was right. Yes, you were a part of the problem, but I don't blame you for Greg. I blame myself for not setting boundaries or believing that I wasn't enough for my kids. I blame myself for not putting myself first and losing what really mattered in life."

"Can you ever forgive me? For Greg? For playing some role in tonight's events?" she asked.

I supposed I could tell her to leave my life and never come back. But as I looked at my mother with tears in her eyes, I knew I couldn't hurt her, because, despite everything, I still loved my mother.

"Yes, Mom, I forgive you, but I won't forget. I think we need to keep some things separate in order for us to have a healthy relationship."

"I agree," she nodded. "I want us to work on our relationship, and I want you to find love your way."

It might have been everything that had happened, but I let out a sob, and I tasted the salty tears that cascaded down my face onto my dress and into my mouth. I couldn't see my mother, but the warm embrace let me know she was still there. We stood like that, swaying back and forth until we had no more tears. I kissed her and told her to go to bed with a promise that we would fix our relationship after I got back.

Before I headed back to the twins, I asked Allison to call the one moving company for tomorrow. I wanted Greg's existence erased from my home. She had everything confirmed in our last phone call after she got back home. I booked her and Wayne a last-minute vacation to Mexico for tomorrow afternoon. I sent everything over through text and told her to cut her phone off and enjoy being away from the craziness after Greg's stuff was gone.

I decided to take my own advice and put my phone on Do Not Disturb. I found my way into Tris and Teo's room through the dark because I was too tired to turn on the light in the hallway. *Sad, I know!* By the time I made it to their room, I had just enough energy to push the beds together and slip in between them. That's where I fell asleep in bliss, between the two people who mattered the most to me.

Chapter 20

We waited and waited for Kitty to come to her senses. But of course, she was stubborn like Tony. I stayed at the office to see if she would show up by some miracle. But nope, nothing. I drove by her home, even though it made no sense, as her house was too far from the street to see. I rode past the school where most of the highly affluent parents sent their kids. It wasn't my best decision, to be honest. I looked like a creep, waiting to catch a glimpse of Jasmine.

I was sitting in my car after going for a drive because I couldn't fall asleep. I wished I could have said her unwillingness didn't bother me, but it did. I wanted to believe Gabe was wrong about Kitty cheating on her fiancé with us. But what proof did we have other than she hid her life from us? Nothing.

Each day that passed, I became more and more convinced that she didn't love us like we loved her. It was all a lie to use us. I sighed and hopped out of my car.

I entered the house, and I knew something was going down.

Tony was pacing the floor, and his arms fought with the air while he spoke to Gabe. Gabe, of course, sat listening with his blank face and his arms folded across his broad chest. The only way I knew it remotely affected him was the tick in his jaw and the big vein that ran up his neck that popped up when he was deep in thought. His green eyes stared off into the distance.

"Hey, I'm back," I yelled, but it was as if I were talking to myself. "I said, Hello, I'm back!"

Tony stopped pacing and snapped his head up. "Oh, hey Wren, I didn't even know you were out."

I shook my head. We'd tried to take our minds off our current Jasmine problem by going out on our weekly date night. But we'd both cut it short because we were in foul spirits. Tony called me Jasmine twice, and I was barely present during our conversations.

Love sucks sometimes.

"Gee, thanks, I guess." As I flopped down, I sunk down into the groove I made in the dark blue couch.

"... So, we should stop this wedding. If Jasmine will not do what's best for her, then we should decide for her," Tony went on, utterly ignoring me. "If we leave tonight, we can be there on time for the wedding. It's only ten pm. We can call the pilot, be there early tomorrow morning, and nip that wedding in the bud."

I looked at him like he had told me he had seen a flying pig. Tony could come up with the craziest ideas, especially when he wanted something. He would move mountains and the earth to get it. That was why I loved him so much.

But this may be a bit too far. Who were we to disrupt Jasmine's life if she didn't want to be with us?

As much as I hated the idea, it was possible that she didn't like us. We were totally different in every way possible, culturally and personality-wise. But that made us work well when we met. Sometimes I wished life wasn't so freaking complicated.

"Tony, I—" I started but got cut off by Gabe, who seemed to have come out of his trance-like state.

"Wren, call the pilot. Tony, make sure you book a hotel. I'll grab the invite and pack a bag," he demanded, and I sat there wide-eyed and shocked because, usually, Gabe was the first to say no to Tony's crazy ideas.

"What?" I asked, still in disbelief. "Look, I understand that—"

"Listen, Wren, hold whatever you're going to say because I've had enough, and I won't allow Kitty or Jasmine to prevent me from at least trying to get her back. I don't care if I have to destroy Greg in the process."

He spoke so calmly that it stirred something deep in my soul.

A possessive Gabe!

I've only seen Gabe act this way once, and it was over a hockey game. But never about a person outside of our family. Jasmine must have gotten under the big bear's skin more than he let on. I remembered asking him his whereabouts after the three-month "vacation" after our last night at Club Celeste. He'd replied he felt like going away, and so he did.

Yeah, vacation, my ass.

It wasn't until Tony pestered him enough to find out he was holed up with his uncle for three months. But then he shrugged it off as "life problems." I shook my head.

"What are you shaking your head for? Get going and call the pilot," he repeated.

I sighed.

Tony yelled from somewhere in the house, "I called the pilot because Wren is too slow! He said to be there in the next thirty, and we're good to go!"

I shook my head. "What if this doesn't work out in our favor, Gabe? I can't handle being rejected again."

"Well, if it doesn't, we can't say we didn't fucking try our hardest." He sighed. "I want to try... Have to try, Wren. I-I loved her—still love her. It sounds crazy."

"No, it doesn't. We would be crazy not to fight for Jasmine. She's worth it, Gabe. As hard as it may sound, I think we were meant to go through this situation."

I turned and walked up the stairs to pack a bag. Honestly, I wouldn't sleep at all until we concluded whether we wasted our time going to Nashville. I wanted to know.

Love sucks sometimes.

I could tell you many things I knew for certain. One, Japan has an area called Rabbit Island, which is located in Okunoshima. Second, avocados are fruits, not vegetables. Last, the average Italian consumes twenty-five grams of pasta per year. Maybe triple that for our family.

But in this situation, I didn't understand anything.

Gabe, Tony, and I ended up arriving late to the venue by ten minutes because Tony, the diva, had to look impressive to "capture" Jasmine. I tried to get it into his giant head. We were not capturing anyone, but I failed. When I turned to Gabe, he shrugged his shoulders. I'd definitely crossed over to the Twilight Zone. There was no feasible explanation. It was the invasion of the body snatchers.

When we arrived at the church, New Life Pentecostal church. Oversized blue prairie windows lined the massive white building, and the parking lot could hold at least two hundred cars. We quietly shuffled into the church's wooden auditorium. On the bride's side, a handful of people came for Jasmine. But there were over a hundred, I guessed, people sitting on Greg's side. We sat on Jasmine's side, of course, and waited.

Almost thirty minutes had gone by, and nothing. I heard someone tried calling Jasmine, but she wasn't picking up. Someone called Jasmine's mom, and it was the same thing. I texted her to see what was going on, but she read the text and never replied.

"She read it and didn't reply?" Tony repeated when I mentioned it.

"Yeah, do you—"

Greg cut me off as he stumbled in, sweat stains circling his armpits and the back of his shirt stuck to him. He had a baseball hat on. His clothing looked crushed, and his eyes were bloodshot red. He was either high, drunk, hadn't slept, or a combo of all three.

I watched as he sulked to the altar.

"I'm so sorry, everyone. Because of unforeseen circumstances, we canceled the wedding for now. I meant to update everyone, but it slipped my mind." He scrambled off to his family's side. They had a lot of questions and were upset because some came from out of state to attend the wedding.

I would be pissed as well.

"That's odd. They must have known because Jasmine's mom isn't here," I guessed out loud.

"So, we came here for nothing then." Tony tapped his foot on the wooden floor.

"Something isn't right, and I want to get to the bottom of it." Gabe shook his head.

"Okay, you're scaring me, Gabe. Who are you? And what did you do with my Gabby?" I grabbed his shirt, being dramatic.

"Ha, I'm serious. Now I'm itching like Tony to find out." Gabe continued.

"Hey, I only do the good type of itching." Tony winked at Gabe.

I snickered but stopped when Gabe hit me with the side eye of death.

That was when I got a crazy idea, and I worried I may have hung out with Tony a bit too much lately. I chewed on my bottom lip from the church to the little condo we'd rented. It was in downtown

Nashville. From our condo, we had a view of the Batman Tower and other office buildings. The streets were buzzing with a mix of tourists and locals. Although it looked nice here, I missed home and my vegan sushi.

Gabe parked the car, and we sat there until the steam from our breath fogged the windows. I couldn't tell you why I was nervous, but I bit down on my lip hard enough to taste copper in my mouth. I decided just to shoot my shot.

"I have Ms. May's number. She gave it to me when I told her my ma made the best mapo tofu in LA," I whispered. I thought no one heard me because we sat silently for five minutes.

Finally, Tony broke the silence. "Are you thinking what I'm thinking?"

Oh shit, I had a feeling what he was going to say, and I did not like it at all.

"Which is?" Gabe inquired.

"Nashville is the home to two things. One, it's the birthplace of Jasmine Grant. Second, it's the home of Jasmine's dear mother." Tony tapped on the window.

"Okay and?" I was lost.

"How about we pay a visit to our future mother-in-law?" Tony asked while his mouth cracked from his smile.

Gabe and I sighed.

"I will not be sneaking into her home. We're too old for that stuff, anyway," I asserted.

"You mean you're old, me not so much." Tony smiled, and I humphed.

"I think that is a brilliant plan, actually. We will go there as concerned employers and wedding participants," Gabe remarked.

Holy hell, I think I reached the middle section of the earth. That's twice he agreed on a Tony-type plan.

If I were religious, I would have prayed then. "I'm literally lost for words right now." I was astonished.

Gabe shrugged. "Tony, you have her mom's information... actually, how did you even get an invitation?"

"Now, Gabe, you know I'm a genius? You should never underestimate me," Tony mentioned. "As a matter of fact, while you two were busy sulking and pouting, I gathered information for our next move."

I mentally slapped myself. The plan could go two ways. It could be the breakthrough we needed, or we could land ourselves in jail for harassment. I wasn't too fond of the latter.

Before we went about our mission, Gabe stopped me in the hallway before I headed to my room to change.

"Wren, did you get the package?" Gabe asked.

"Yeah, it's safe and sound at home," I replied, as I remembered the little plan we had for when we got home.

Chapter 21

Wren

The devil, aka Tony, made us go to Jasmine's mother's house right after we fed our depleted stomachs. Because, according to him, we couldn't be good detectives on an empty stomach. Sometimes, I wondered how we'd stayed together for so long.

We pulled up in front of a tiny home on a hill. You could tell the older home needed a bit of TLC from the outside. The brown bricks that were once red had a slight black film over them. It seemed as if it hadn't seen a power washer in a while now. The small shrubs had turned brownish, and some fell off the branches when the wind blew. I guess that was more due to the season than neglect. The driveway had cracks, and a newer Toyota SUV was in the driveway.

"Okay, Tony, you're the watch out because, for one, you can alert us if Jasmine comes to visit her mom. We don't need her running scared," Gabe asserted.

"Absolutely not," Tony replied. "I'm going, and that's that."

I agreed with Gabe, but when Tony was determined to do something, he would do it. We were an intimidating group of men, especially since Gabe and Tony are well over six three. Plus, we were three white men—well, two and a half.

"Uh, Let's get this over with. The faster this goes, the faster I can return to my vegan sushi," I sighed happily.

"You just ate!" Gabe declared.

"Yeah, and?" I uttered as I rolled my eyes.

I got out of the car to get it over with. I had an evil little voice in my head that said we would end up in some Nashville jail. That would be my luck. A vegan LA boy starved to death because of his unwillingness to eat slop. My ma would say, "Look what my itoshigo[1] went and got himself into because of a girl."

I approached the door and looked back to see if Gabe and Tony were still in the car with cold feet. But they were right behind me. I hesitated to knock on the door. Every time I lifted my hand, I felt like I was going to upchuck the dinner I had eaten. I wasn't even sure why I felt that way. It wasn't as if we were breaking into her home.

Gabe sensed my hesitation and told me we would ask her some questions. Nothing more, nothing less. But I begged to differ. Nothing was cut and dry with my brothers.

Gabe knocked and then rang the doorbell. From my position, I could make out the loud creak of the old home's floors. Right before she approached the door, Gabe leaned over to us and stated, "If you see anything interesting, take a pic or grab it."

I sighed and rolled my eyes. Of course, I would have to do the dirty work.

The door swung open, and Jasmine's mother stood before us. She looked suitable for her age. Her brown skin held a few wrinkles, but she still looked young. She wrapped her hair in a beige headscarf. Her head only reached my stomach and she had to crane her neck to look at me. She and Jasmine shared small brown eyes.

____

1 Beloved dear child in Japanese

She openly gawked at each of us, but when she got to Tony, her eyes got big like she'd seen a ghost. I looked at Gabe and Tony. We had the same cocked eyebrow, wondering what was up with this lady. She stood there—mouth agape at Tony.

He must have harassed her in a past life.

I found my common sense first, cleared my throat, and smiled.

"Hello, Mrs. Grant. My name is Wren Costa, and my business partners and brothers are Gabriele Sabino and Antonio Russo. We were wondering if we could come in and talk?" I gave her my best friendly smile.

"A-Are you with the IRS? Am I getting audited?" she asked, her eyes still glued to Tony.

We chuckled. "No, we're your daughter's new employers. We were invited to the wedding, but it got canceled. So, we were concerned and thought we would stop by." I tried to smooth it over.

"Oh, s-she invited y'all?" Her eyebrows bunched, and her narrow eyes became narrower as if she wasn't buying it. "Can I see the invite? And some credentials?"

Gabe's eyebrows were so high they almost blended in with his hair. He pulled out his phone to show her the website with our pictures and our photo identifications. She still looked skeptical, even with proof.

I liked her.

"Let me confirm with someone first. I can't have anybody come up in my house all willy-nilly," Mrs. Grant stated.

Tony was quick to react. He grabbed her hand and turned on his charm.

"Mrs. Grant, I'm so sorry. We must have frightened you. Here we are, three strange men, coming to the house of this beautiful young lady. I would have thought you were twins if I didn't know you were Jasmine's mom," he insisted, and she chuckled and told him to stop it.

She chuckled! I really loved this man.

"Here, let me call Allison, her personal assistant for you." Gabe, the clever bastard, showed her his phone. "See, is this not Allison Johnson's number?"

"Y-Yes," she stammered.

"I'm going to dial it and ask her to verify me. Would that ease your concerns?" She looked up at Gabe, and I swear it was the same expression Jasmine gave him when we met with her and Mr. Brine.

She nodded her head.

Gabe called her and placed her on speakerphone. Allison sounded suspicious like we were up to no good.

I mean, she was right.

I had to bite back my laugh when she asked Gabe if he had sniffed that Hollywood snow. Tony laughed, and Ms. Grant's face turned ashen.

She muttered about something being unholy, and finally, we entered... grandmother heaven. If the outside was old, then the inside was prehistoric. Her kitchen hadn't been updated, but the appliances were new. The living room was stuffed with pictures and an old tube television with a light coat of dust over it. Jasmine lived in a ten-bedroom custom mansion, and her mom was stuck living in the eighties.

"Wow! A tube TV. Does it still work?" Tony voiced.

She stopped fussing with the papers she was moving to make space for us to sit and looked at Tony. "You sound like..." she started but stopped right in the middle of her sentence.

"Like whom?" I asked.

"Nothing. You reminded me of someone." She chuckled nervously. "You guys have a seat. I'm sorry about the mess. I've been occupied lately with some family issues and health issues. So, I haven't had much time to clean."

"It's okay. It's cozy here, and It's not as bad as you think, Mrs. Grant." Gabe worked his magic. "Have you thought about moving?"

"Yeah, but this is the home my husband, Jasmine's father,

passed away in, and I couldn't leave this place." She sighed. "Jasmine bought me a place near her, but I don't feel right moving and giving up my home. Even though I would love to be closer to my gra— my daughter."

She smiled like we didn't hear the almost slip up. Jasmine had her trained well. It was almost laughable.

"So, you guys came, and they canceled the wedding. I owe you guys an apology. I was supposed to send out a notification about the wedding being canceled, but I got caught up in some things." She offered us a weak smile. She quickly turned her face, but not before we saw her brown eyes become watery and her lips turned downwards. I felt sorry for the older woman and whatever she may be going through.

"Yes, we were worried because she hadn't told anyone they had canceled it, and we couldn't get in touch with her," Gabe stressed.

"Yes, she had an interview last week, as you know." We nodded. "She took some me time afterward. I was supposed to contact everyone, but I got overwhelmed and sidetracked by personal things."

"I can totally understand," Gabe replied. "Mr. Brine mentioned after she retired, she took about a year and several months off. So, I guess that's not out of the norm for her, right?"

Mrs. Grant plastered on the fakest smile I'd ever seen. Her mouth stretched so wide across her face that I thought she might split her face open. Her eyes shifted from right to left, and she nodded.

We all jointly smiled and told her we understood, like they made us in a factory. We spoke for a few minutes about unimportant things, making conversation. I studied the pictures she had around the tiny room. There were a couple of photos with a man who looked to be Jasmine's late father. A couple of photos of a little girl that had to be Jasmine when she was young. I didn't know she was serious when she stated she was as skinny as a tadpole.

Well, look how far she'd come.

I gave Gabe a look, and he picked up on the clue.

"Mrs. Grant, I'm so sorry for being pretentious, but would you happen to have some tea? My throat has been itchy since we arrived," Gabe claimed.

"Oh, yes, of course. Sorry. I got so caught up in the conversation. Would anyone else like some tea or something else to drink?" Mrs. Grant offered.

"No, thank you, but I would love to see your kitchen. I've always loved a vintage kitchen," Tony mentioned.

Boy, that was the biggest lie I'd ever heard from Mr. Russo. "Does it have a subzero stainless steel refrigerator?" I rolled my eyes.

Their looming presence blocked her view from me snooping, as the trio moved to the small kitchen, where Gabe blocked the kitchen entrance with his broad shoulders. Mrs. Grant wouldn't be able to see me.

I sighed and looked at the thousands of pictures that were stuffed on the old fireplace. I made a mental note to speak with Jasmine about her mom. As I scanned through the photos, I made quick work of it as nothing seemed to be from this century. I was about to give up when I saw some in a China cabinet along with her fine China. What an odd combo, but who was I to judge?

I combed the ones in the cabinet and found a picture of two newborns. They looked like they had just entered the world. I snapped a photo of them. I thought her kids would have come out with more Melanin because Greg had a darker tone than Jasmine. But that was before I started learning about babies and birth a while back.

I heard a light laugh flow from the kitchen. I was about to give up when my eyes caught the picture wall in her hallway. I played with just going back to the old red sofa, but something drew me to the semi-dark hall. I flipped the switch on, and the hallway was flooded with lights. These pictures were current as I walked the hall. I looked at the kitchen, and Gabe was still stuck there, but not for long as the kettle whistle sound died down. There was a collage frame with pictures of

Jasmine's career in them. As I browsed the medium frame, there were teen pictures of Jasmine and some of her backstage images. But it was the last photo that caught my attention.

There stood Mrs. Grant with two boys who looked like the photos in Mrs. Russo's home. I could spot that smile from a sea filled with mouths and knew it was Tony's. I held my hand to my face and noted the wetness that stained my hand when I wiped the tears away. My heartbeat tripled, and the burning flame of anger licked my stomach. I wanted to throw up and cry.

We had kids.

So, my suspicions were almost correct.

I mean, *we* have kids. We were dads and didn't need a DNA test to prove it. They were the spitting image of Tony. The trio came back, but I dodged getting caught snapping several photos of the picture. I pretended to notice the photos on the mantle, but my mind was on the twins. I quickly wiped the tears from my eyes and hoped I didn't seem like I was having a mental breakdown, even though I was currently in the middle of having one.

Something cold snapped inside of me. I wanted to curse Mrs. Grant and tell her to bring our boys to us now. But I stopped as her chuckle brought me back into our current reality. When I turned around, the naive Wren was gone.

Gabe was the first to see my stony stare, and he raised an eyebrow at me.

"Mrs. Grant, I hate to be rude. But why were you gawking at my partner?" I asked.

"Excuse me? I don't know what you mean by that?" she scoffed.

"You stared at him like you knew him from somewhere." I tilted my head at her. I felt the burn of the stares from Gabe and Tony on the side of my face. "Can I ask you another question?"

"I'm sure you're going to ask, anyway," she remarked grimly.

"We heard you have grandkids, but you don't have any pictures of them on your mantle.”

She choked on the sip of tea she took. I went over to tap her on her back to help her out. As I rubbed the spot, I continued my questioning.

“It's weird not to have pictures of your grandkids out here,” I continued. “Greg must have been overjoyed when Jasmine got pregnant. Would you say they look more like Jasmine or Greg?”

Mrs. Grant looked as if all the blood had left her face. “Do you think they look like their father? Except for a few minor details here and there?”

“I-I think, um, I have to go to an appointment soon. I think maybe it's time you should leave. It was nice meeting you, fellows. I've tried to stay out of Jasmine's affairs since she retired,” she noted, and I knew it was a double entendre, but I believed she didn't believe her own words.

I smiled sweetly. “Of course, we wouldn't want you to miss your appointment. Thank you so much, Mrs. Grant. You opened my eyes to what secrets a vintage home can hold.”

As we headed out the door, we were halfway to the car when she yelled for me specifically. As I turned back, I wondered if it was a last-ditch attempt to get us off of Jasmine's tail.

“I hope you know that I had nothing to do with anything,” Mrs. Grant articulated as she turned on her feet and marched right inside. She slammed the old wood door shut.

I turned because I would never let her or anyone see me crying. I felt like burning up her tiny vintage home. How it made me look wasn't important to me. I wanted blood.

I slammed the car door closed. Before saying anything in the silent car, I sent a text to Jasmine.

Kitty

Congratulations, Mrs. Simmons.

I hit send. I didn't want to give away too much of what we knew until it was time.

After fifteen minutes, we pulled up to the home we'd rented. No one moved like we did earlier today.

"So..." Gabe faltered.

It wasn't until then I felt the last single tear drop from my eye. Gabe gave me a worried glance in the mirror. I couldn't think right then. I needed a bath and sleep.

"Congratulations to us," I mewled, almost absentmindedly.

Gabe and Tony gave each other a look.

"We're fathers of twin boys." I sent the text of the photo in our family group chat and slipped out of the car, leaving a stunned Gabe and Tony.

Chapter 22

Tony

Bethany was right.

My Mother was right.

And I looked like a fucking fool!

I should be pissed off, angry, murderous, etc. But as much as I tried, I couldn't be. Instead, I felt the harsh sting of sadness and failure. I'd failed my kids by not being there for them. I'd missed out on all of their milestones. They didn't even know me or their family, which was the hardest pill to swallow.

Another man got to raise them.

Greg got to be there with them through their first steps and words, and they probably even called him dad.

I was wrong. *That* was the hardest pill to swallow.

After I told Gabe I needed some time alone, I sat in the car. I needed a drink as badly as I needed air. I needed the burn to remove the throbbing sensation in my throat. My chest felt heavy, and I clutched it as another sob wrecked through me.

I wanted to call Jasmine and ask her why she hated me so much, enough to keep my flesh and blood away from me. Were we really that bad, or were we her side pieces? We told Jasmine almost everything about our lives, at least the things she allowed us to tell her, which wasn't a lot.

I should have hated Jasmine, but my damn heart and soul wouldn't allow it. She had already sunk her perfectly manicured nails into them and wormed her way into me. It was too late for that. I sat there as the Nashville orange and red sunset died and turned into a dark night with stars lighting up the sky.

That was when my mind took a wrong turn. I became hooked on my phone as I fumbled through my contacts to find the person I needed. I should have taken my ass to bed, but I couldn't let it go.

I found the number and hit the call button. On the third ring, my uncle picked up.

"Hey Tony, how's it hangin'?" my uncle, Lorenza Russo, my father's brother greeted me.

Uncle Lorenzo was what I called the non-licensed, off-the-books, ultimate finder. I was good at finding people who had the slightest trace on the internet, but my uncle had connections outside of that. He didn't work for the upstanding citizens of the world. He worked for some of the unsavory characters that needed to get shit done. I had already checked reservations under her name and her alias in New York but couldn't find anything. Nor could I find anything on the gossip blogs I followed.

And I couldn't thoroughly search since I didn't have my equipment.

"Uncle Lorenzo, it's not going well, to be honest. How are you?"

"I'm fine. What's going on?" he asked.

So, I poured out my heart to him, leaving nothing out, even about the twins. After I was done, I made him promise not to tell my mother. She would have a heart attack knowing she had grandbabies out there and she couldn't spoil them.

"I'm so sorry, Tony. I couldn't even imagine what I would do if I were in your shoes. Do you want me to find out where she is for you? And this Greg guy would have some information as well. I can get his information?"

"Can you get me Jasmine's information? I already have Greg's information. He wasn't hard to find. It's my slippery lady friend I can't find," I stated.

My uncle grunted.

"Give me an hour, and I will have the information... maybe less if I can get ahold of a friend that owes me a solid."

"Okay, if you call me and don't get me, just text me the information or leave a voicemail. I'm going to visit Greg."

"Hey, take Gabe and Wren with you—"

I cut him off. "No, I promise I won't do anything but talk to him."

He blew out air and told me to be careful as we hung up. I had to do this on my own. I usually depend on Gabe and Wren for most things, as they were my support anchors. But this one I had to see about on my own.

It took me twenty minutes to get from downtown Nashville to Brentwood, Tennessee. The gritty streets and lights from stores and buildings turned into lush green estates. The little older homes with their eclectic range of houses turned into mini mansions. It was clear I wasn't in the city anymore.

I pulled up to a home that was on a slight hill. It was a modest two-story brown brick home. It looked as if Greg had recently built it. The lawns were well maintained, a big contrast to Mrs. Grant's tiny home.

I jumped out of my car and jogged up to the dark house. I had never been the guy that goes inside. I was always the one looking out.

But that didn't mean I didn't remember how to pick a lock and ask an associate of mine to help cut the alarm for the night.

After ten minutes, longer than I wanted to admit, I was in the door. I held back the choke that threatened to strangle the breath out of me. The house was pristine on the outside, but holy shit. It smelled like mothballs and mold and—I took a big sniff and covered my cough—whiskey.

If there was one thing I knew, it was alcohol, which told me someone had indulged in the harsh drink a little too much. I walked through the small foyer and looked around the home. It wasn't tiny, but it wasn't huge.

I opened a couple of doors and didn't find the bastard there, so I proceeded up the stairs to the bedroom area. The stench of whiskey was so alluring that I could have gotten drunk just by breathing. My mouth watered because it reminded me of the past when I used to toss it back like it was water. But, of course, the moldy scent mixed in soured the longing for it.

There was rattling from a room on the other side of the short hall. I followed the sound, and the moldy scent turned to a sweaty, stale combo. It was as if the mold had soaked up the sweaty body scent. I opened the door to the room where I'd heard the noise.

The smell alone made me gag before I saw Greg. Whiskey bottles surrounded him. There were too many to count. Greg sat on the chair in his office. Gone was the outfit from this morning, replaced with his boxers, a whiskey bottle, and a stained whitish shirt. He didn't have his bifocals on, and I could see the dark circles and the reddened eyes as he stared straight into the plain white wall.

I almost felt sorry for him, but then I remembered he'd gotten to enjoy my sons before I had.

I snapped into action as I opened the window to let the fresh air in because it smelled like ass and alcohol. The alcohol smell wasn't as bad as the unwashed ass scent. I stuck my head out the window and checked my phone. I had twelve unanswered text messages from Gabe, Wren, and, most importantly, my uncle. I would read them later.

"Have y-you come to kill me? Has she sent you?" he slurred.

I was offended. Just because I was Italian didn't make me Tony Soprano.

"No, you're doing a fine job of that yourself. Did you drink all of that by yourself?" I asked because, well, I didn't know why. It made me feel good that he was doing so miserably.

I glided over to the desk and stood in front of him. It was the first time we had looked at each other face to face. I looked at the drunken Greg, and my anger for him faded. He looked at me, and something in his drunken mind clicked.

"So, you're the one she was whoring around with and defiled her temple for?"

Okay, the moment of sorriness was gone in an instant.

"How did I not see it before? You look like them." He was talking to himself more than me. His mouth pulled into a frown, and I wanted to sock him in the face for even frowning about my bambinos.

And before I could stop myself, I came around the desk and punched him. I wasn't the best fighter, but when push came to shove, I would get your ass. The crunching sound of his nose filled the dank room. Radiating pain started from my hand to my wrist as I shook out my hand.

He didn't react to the punch. He just took the end of the white shirt and added blood to the mix of stains. I shuddered as I watched him stick the end of the shirt on him over his nose.

Ew!

"Listen, you pathetic fucker, don't you ever go near Jasmine or my kids," I gritted through my clenched teeth. I grabbed Greg by his shoulder and wanted to head butt him, but his following words made me pause.

He laughed like a lunatic. "No worries there. You can have the whore. She dumped me anyway. Our agreement is done, nullified. It was for the best since her ways will send her straight to hell.”

Okay, the guy was a religious nutcase. Even though we were only together for six months, Jasmine didn't appear religious in any type of way. That gave me pause, and my need to protect Jasmine grew even though she'd hurt me.

“She hid money from me and properties, and it seemed she had a whole other life.” He took a drink from a half-full bottle of Tennessee Whiskey. “Then that whore Allison convinced her to leave me. She's a veritable demon. Jasmine was a good Christian woman who fell on hard times. But I thought with our arrangement, I could still save her. If I could get to her and cleanse her of her sins.”

“Greg, I'll be nice and leave after this, but mark my words. If you ever go near Jasmine and my kids again, you'll meet God and his disciples much sooner than you originally planned, and that's not a threat. It's a promise.”

I turned to leave, but something nagged at me. “Did they ever call you Dad?” I asked. I hated myself for asking him, but I had to. It scratched at my soul.

“No, those mutts called me Mr. Greg. Those disrespectful abominations should have been wiped from the earth. I tried my best to be a father to them, but I couldn't stand—”

He screwed up his face, but I didn't give him a chance to continue as I rocked back and punched him again. Greg's putrid body slid from the old office chair and onto the floor. The outline of piss seeped from his boxers, and I jumped out of the way. Grabbing the half-empty bottle, I poured the whiskey on him and wanted to light the fucker on fire, but I didn't. I couldn't risk going to jail when I hadn't even met my sons yet.

With my throbbing hand, I left that miserable dump. The last time I punched someone was in high school, and the asshole was harassing me for being Bisexual. But it felt amazingly therapeutic for me to end Greg's fucking disgusting babbling.

As I exited the moldy home, the cold Nashville night air made me clutch the suit jacket I still had on, but gratefully, it numbed the pain in my hand.

Ha! Maybe it was God blessing me for punching the religious misogynistic prick.

I quickly returned to the condo and noted it was well after eleven o'clock before I walked inside. I had expected Gabe and Wren to be dead to the world by now, but both of them were up with a drink in their hand. My eyes sought out the cold drink. I licked my lip and turned away. *Old habits sometimes die hard.*

"Where the fuck were you?" Wren demanded. He stood with his back stiff like a rod. Even though he was a couple of inches shorter than Gabe and me, the surrounding air made him seem taller.

"I went to see the fucking worthless bastard that got to be near our kids," I confided. "He was drenched in his piss, alcohol, and unwashed ass when I left him knocked out on the floor."

Everyone went silent. Gabe stared at me as if he was trying to gauge whether I was fucking with them.

"I'm not fucking with you guys. A part of me had to know," I voiced.

"Let me see your hand." I shoved my hand at Gabe as he poked and prodded it. "You didn't break anything. You need some ice and pain pills. In the morning, you should be fine."

"I barely felt it. You should see Greg." I smiled triumphantly.

Wren shook his head and smiled.

"I'm glad you're okay and safe. We were worried about you and almost called your mother to see if you'd called her."

"God, no. She would be pissed, and there would be a warpath to find Jasmine and tear her a new one if she found out she had grandchildren." I shook my head. "I mean, she already found out, but now I have to confirm it."

"What?" Gabe and Wren repeated together.

My hands found my neck as I worked out a kink. Taking a deep breath, I told them everything I had bottled up the past couple of months. It was a hard pill to swallow, but I opened up to them now. It was the longest I had ever gone without telling them a suspicion.

"I guess that's why you're taking it so well because if it were me, Greg would have died in that home of his, and I would've had to call in my uncle for a favor," Gabe expressed.

"Okay, Godfather in the making. You're following in your uncle's footsteps, huh?" I uttered.

We chuckled because even though Gabe's disowned uncle was every stereotype of Italians, we knew Gabe was all talk. He was too much of a big teddy bear.

We sat there for a minute. Gabe and Wren sipped their drinks, and I nursed my injured hand. The silence made everything come crushing back like a tide.

"We missed everything. The boys' first steps, first words, etc. We were robbed of everything," I muttered as I let the tears fall again. "I feel like a failure of a dad, even though I didn't know about them. But fuck!"

I banged my head on the back of the couch.

I continued. "Even after everything, I can't find the hate I'm supposed to have for Jasmine. It made me want to get her and lock her slippery ass up."

We chuckled.

"That, and I definitely want a drink right now. But I promised myself that I wouldn't ruin my sobriety," I announced.

Gabe jumped up, almost unaware that they were sipping their drinks still, and took the bottle and cups to the small sink in the kitchen. He drained everything.

"I'm sorry. It didn't even register that we were drinking in front of you," he replied as he returned.

"I'm sorry as well... for everything." Wren came over and hugged and kissed me on my cheek. He whispered, "I'm glad you're back safely."

Wren smiled up at me, and I knew everything would be alright.

"Does it make sense that I still want to find my special picture and masturbate to Jasmine?" I sighed.

"What?" Gabe chuckled.

"I had a special uncut photo of Jasmine from her GQ photoshoot. She's on one of those chaise chairs with her ass towards the camera, and it's the sexiest shit even though you can only see her ass." I beamed.

"So, you've been holding out on me, then?" Wren asked and chuckled.

"There was too much jizz on it to give to you." I laughed. It felt good to let loose a bit after the past twenty-four hours.

"Wren, I have a confession to make." Gabe paused. His hand rubbed his neck. "I have been asking Tony to help me... uh... relieve myself." Gabe blushed.

Wren fell back into the chair. "You what?!?"

Wren's mouth was flat-out wide enough I could stuff myself in it. His eyes were the size of saucepans.

"You asked Tony to give you head and not me? I'm hurt." He placed a hand over his heart.

"Wait, did you know?" I questioned. I knew when Wren was joking and when he was not.

"Yeah, I came home one night to ask Gabe if I could use his car. As I got closer to the room, I heard him grunting and moaning out Kitty's name... wait, Jasmine's name. I have to get used to that now. I heard you moaning, which I can spot anywhere." He shrugged. "I figured you guys would tell me in time. Does that mean we have to fight for Tony's hole when he finally decides to bottom?"

Gabe and I laughed. Gabe replied, "No, I do not want to be a top or bottom. I've always been okay with anyone giving me a blowie. It's something about Tony that reminded me of Jasmine."

He pinched his nose and rolled his neck.

"Poor Tony and Jasmine. Their jaws suffered from that monster cock you carry around." Wren shook his head.

We busted out laughing.

"Well, it's a hard job, but someone has to have the biggest dick here," Gabe smiled.

We fell into a fit of giggles as we watched Gabe pretend to lift something heavy with his arms. Once the laughter died down, I had to slap us into reality.

"What is the next step? I won't go another month without having our sons in our lives."

"All I know is I'm next," Gabe stated, and his normally dark green eyes turned stormy black.

"Alright, alpha male. She should be able to pick, and that's if she wants any of us. I'm willing to go last because they always save the best for last," Wren bragged.

We smiled.

"I have a plan. I don't know if it will work, but I think it will," Wren declared, and we sat silently so he could further explain. "Let's call Ms. May! Hear me out, please?"

We nodded, and Wren continued.

"Well, I have been getting close to her since we took over as the directors, and I have her number. Remember Jasmine asked her to spy on us?"

We nodded and answered yeah.

"Well, our Kitty loves to run. Why don't we mislead Ms. May and tell her we're headed to NY, but we stay here, wait until she shows up, and then corner her? That way, she has our kids with her." He finished.

"That's the craziest shit I ever heard." Gabe looked bewildered.

Wren sent him a look. "Oh, but crashing a wedding isn't, huh?"

That shut Gabe up, and I chuckled. But stopped when Gabe threw me a death look.

"I think it's a great idea." I grinned. "My loves, let's catch us a Kitty."

With that, Wren called Ms. May since it was only nine in California. Ms. May picked up, and they chatted for a bit until Wren told her about our plans. She rushed off the phone. This happened after he told her we would go to Jasmine's penthouse in New York to check on her, which was right up the block from our penthouse. She was less than five minutes from our home in LA and less than ten, give or take traffic, in New York. Life was so crazy.

If that wasn't divine intervention, I don't know what is.

After I extended our reservation, we held off telling our family because that would add more fuel to the flame. I didn't need them inferring when we could handle our Kitten alone.

That night, I fell asleep to the picture of the twins that was burned into my brain, hoping I could salvage my relationship with them.

Chapter 23

Jasmine

I was hiding from my problems, but for once in my life, I didn't give a flying fuck.

It had been two weeks since I'd left California for my interview with Blazing R&B, the largest R&B radio station in the New York area. I had so much fun during the interview that it almost made me miss the career. But then I stumbled outside, and the paparazzi and some fans blocked the entrance to the radio station. Poor Bruno and his team had worked up a sweat from pushing and shoving the droves of people from the door. Thank God they didn't know where my condo was. I never wanted Tris or Teo to have to deal with this mess. I could see their little, tearful faces if people tried to grab at them and snap pictures of them.

When I was done, I promised to take them out, and we spent the day in the Hall of Science. Afterward, my head was a pool of sweat. I hadn't sweated that much since my last concert, where my trainer had me run about twenty miles on the treadmill. Tris and Teo wanted to eat every single item off the menu in the cafe area. I mean, really, where did boys put that stuff? If I ate a slice of bread, I would be twenty pounds heavier the next day. Bruno and I had to haul them up to the penthouse because they were knocked out when we got home.

It must be nice!

Tris and Teo begged me to stay another day, and I ended up folding. When I looked around, it had been a week, and the kids wanted to stay longer for tech science week at the museum, so I folded again. What essentially was a two-day vacation ended up being two weeks.

Yes, it was more of me avoiding my responsibilities, but shit, I deserved to relax. It was the first time in so long that I hadn't worried about someone judging or berating me. I was free and wanted to enjoy it until I didn't have it anymore. My boys and I were having the best time with each other.

Really, I could have kicked myself for being stupid enough to tether myself to someone because I thought they needed a dad when all they needed was me. If I could have taken back the last five years, I would not have listened to my mom's advice.

I wouldn't have gotten myself into this mess.

Speaking of which, I should call her. She had been blowing up my phone for the last two weeks. But I put my phone on Do Not Disturb the Sunday after my interview, and hadn't put it back on because I wanted some alone time with Tris and Teo. And slightly because I saw that congratulations from Wren and had wanted to vomit. That was the most hurtful thing I'd read since this whole thing started. But I had no one to blame because I got myself into this mess. So, I guess I had to see myself out of it.

But when I was ready, which I wasn't.

It was a rainy day in the city, and because the penthouse was basically windows, the soft pattering of the rain ricocheted off the windows. So, we stayed in our pjs and watched movies until we passed out with me in my lounge dress that's seen better days and shorts and the boys in their last pairs of clean pjs which stopped above their ankles.

We looked like three hot messes, but we turned up the heat, got some blankets, and stuffed our faces. I had started snoring during our second movie when my phone buzzed.

Determined to leave the outside mess alone and soak up the last of our time alone, I let it go to voicemail. But after the third call, I answered it.

Luckily, I did because it was Ms. May calling me.

"Jasmine! I almost gave up," she humphed.

"Hello, Ms. May. So sorry, we're watching a movie, and I didn't hear my phone ring."

"I have news for you! The bosses are coming to New York. They were worried about you after you didn't show up at your wedding," she huffed out. "But you told me you canceled it. Thank God. I didn't like that man."

I could almost see her scrunched-up face...

"Wait, what did you say?" I squeaked.

"Mr. Sabino, Mr. Costa, and Mr. Russo are coming to New York."

I nearly dropped the damn phone. I heard Ms. May screaming my name.

"Y-Yes Ms. May," I stammered.

"Listen, I hate to pry into your business. But it's not lost on me that one of them looks similar to the twins." I heard her cough and come back to finish. "Listen, I know the situation is much more than it seems. But you owe it to the boys to fix this."

"I know, and I will," I told her, and I meant it. I just didn't want to do it right now.

I guess I didn't have a choice. I thought as my brain short-circuited, and I fumbled around to get ready to leave. I ran to take a quick shower because—well, I don't know why I just found myself in the hot shower scrubbing like a mad woman in order to get out quickly.

The towels were in the dryer, still wet because I forgot to turn it on before we went out. So, I stuck myself into the only clothing I could pick out. My old purple crop shirt and old sleeping shorts. I bypassed the flip-flops and stuck my feet into the sneakers that were becoming drenched since I was wet.

Insanity at its finest.

That was how I found myself on my plane right back to Nashville. In between my boys, with them nestled into my side like they always were. But I didn't feel good at all and knew what I was doing was wrong.

Shuddering from the slightly damp clothing and the cold air of the plane made me finally wake up. My head hit the back of the headrest repeatedly. *You're fucking this up again, Jasmine.* I thought as I finally admitted defeat.

I called the flight attendant, who I had already told to take the night off. But she came running from the sleeping area. Her wild red curls were tousled. She had changed out of her uniform and ran out of the area with a pair of jeans and a shirt on. I instantly felt bad for disturbing her downtime, but I didn't want to waste time going to Nashville.

"I'm so sorry to disturb you, Mia. You were probably asleep already."

"No, Ms. Grant, it's no problem. How may I help you?" Mia asked as she stood before me. Her normally olive skin was flushed.

"Can you tell the pilot to take us home to LA?" I asked, and my stomach churned.

"Certainly, right away, Ms. Grant." She scrambled to the cockpit.

About ten minutes later, I heard Ralph, my pilot, come on the intercom and say, "Ms. Grant, you're going to be the death of me and these last-minute switches." He chuckled into the intercom. He was always teasing me about something. After fifteen years, he'd earned the right. I was so embarrassed when I had to tell him about the wedding being canceled. He shrugged his wide shoulders and just said, "It would have happened if it had been meant to be." I saw him smile. He reminded me of my dad when I used to fuss over my toys, and he would give his nonchalant response about it being just a toy.

Thinking about my dad reminded me it was time to renew his flowers at his private mausoleum. It had been a while since I'd made my way to the little cemetery by the church I used to attend. But today wasn't the day for it.

I'd gotten so good at running that it had become second nature to me. As I made my way home to put an end to this mess, even though I wanted to cry, I plastered on a smile. I kept it on throughout the flight even though inside, I was crying because they would hate me and most likely try to take Tris and Teo away from me. But I would fight them until I had nothing left.

Six hours later, I pulled up to my home. My body grew heavy with the thought of the fight ahead of me. God, they would be dragged into the paparazzi spotlight, and every gossip blog would have a field day. I wouldn't even know how to explain that to them.

Bruno and I brought the boys to their room. They were still knocked out from the flight but whined when I let them go. It took me a good five minutes to unlatch Tris.

Finally in my room, I grabbed my phone to start this shit show. My hands shook as I wrote the text to the guys.

Gabe, Tony, Wren

I know you guys are out of town, but we need to talk.

When will you be back in LA?

I threw my phone on the bed and waited.

After about thirty minutes, I gave up and called Allison to see

339

if she wanted to go out. I needed to burn off this nervous energy, and what better way to do it than by going out dancing? She agreed and promised to drag Wayne to babysit in two hours.

A part of me wanted to break into their home and search their things as payback, but I wouldn't even know how to break into their home. Knowing Tony, he probably had drones monitoring their home.

I settled for having a mini spa day to relax my nerves and slept next to Teo until they arrived.

It wasn't until someone whispered, "Wake your tail up," and a smooth tongue left a trail of wetness on my earlobe that I knew I had to wake up.

"Ugh!" I yelled loudly, but the boys didn't budge. "Why do you have to lick my ears?"

"It's the most appetizing earlobe I've ever seen. I couldn't help myself." She winked, and I shook my head.

"Now, time to get up and party our asses off until it's time to face the little violin," she huffed out as we walked back to my room. "I'm proud of you, Jasmine. It takes guts to go into the lions' den. But you and I both know that this was bound to happen. If they try any shit, we will be there to help you."

I nodded because I was too much of an emotional wreck to say anything else. My hands shook as fast as my pounding heart.

Allison gave me room so I could dress and settle my nerves.

"Okay, time to get dressed, Jassie J," I replied out loud.

I threw on my nude-colored thong and bra first, and then I went in search of my eat-your-heart-out dress. I was deep in my closet when I found it. It was a nude-color bustier bodycon dress that had a micro mini length. Once the dress was on, I decided I wanted to go commando, as I ditched the thong. I paired it with my nude stilettos from my sold-out shoe line. My hair was down since I had it retwisted.

Okay, Jasmine. Get your priorities right! You are going to dance until you can't feel your feet!

I got a good look in the mirror and almost came all over myself from the dress alone. This dress was gorgeous. I felt powerful and in charge. That was totally the approach I wanted to take.

They can't fuck with you because you're unfuckable.

"Oh, sis! Now you pulled out that freakum dress! I've been begging you to wear it for a while," Allison scolded as I yelped and jumped from her, sneaking up behind me.

"You scared the living shit out of me!"

"Yeah, uh huh," she chided when I turned to her. "That's not something a church girl would wear, Jassie."

She smiled so wide I thought her mouth would split.

"I-I," I don't even know why I was stuttering like a fool.

"Turn around," she demanded.

"No, you already know—"

"Yes."

She cocked her eyebrow, and I rolled my eyes. I turned around and she palmed my booty. I folded my arms and turned back to face her.

"Oh, no panties, Jas." She placed her hand on her chest. "What is the world coming to?"

I frowned and rolled my eyes at her. "I would have worn it to meet the guys," I said nonchalantly.

Allison's eyebrows were sky-high at my statement.

"Fine! I'll change," I sighed.

"No, wear it. Let's go."

"So, you gave me that whole drama-filled act for nothing?" I asked.

"Well, someone has to keep you on your toes." She winked.

I folded my arms and kissed my teeth. We laughed as we grabbed our things and rushed out of the house.

We waited in traffic for twenty minutes before we arrived at the club. Bliss was a new club that opened in East Hollywood. The outside yellow décor was something unheard of for this part of town. It made the club stick out like a sore thumb, and honestly, it wasn't someplace I would have even thought to go, but there I was.

Allison got us in the back entrance, which was covered by a heavy black curtain, and into VIP. They'd flooded the section with ocean-blue furniture. The blue and white lights made the vibe in the little section cozy. It made up for the yellow eye sore outside. I was ready to let loose from the stress that coiled inside my chest. I ordered two bottles of cognac.

Allison and I got hammered and danced the night away to the latest songs in the VIP dance area. The blue and white lights pulled us to the center, where we danced under the dim white spotlight. When the DJ learned I was in attendance, he mixed in my songs. It was kind of cheesy dancing to your own songs. But I was so drunk, I didn't care. I couldn't tell my left foot from my right foot as Allison and I two-stepped on the dancefloor. We met some up-and-coming artists and took pictures, which was a typical no-no for me, but I wasn't in the right mind frame to say no.

After three hours of dancing and drinking, we stumbled into my house and crashed on my bed. I exhaled and closed my eyes as my brain was still dancing to the pounding in my chest.

I'd escaped my problems for the night, but there was no escaping what awaited me the next day.

Tony

I got up and walked over to the living room of the Nashville home we'd rented for the next two days. Everyone was asleep but me. I sat on the sofa and pulled on my lip piercing. This situation had made sleeping impossible for me. Even now, as I sat in the dark, cold living room, all I could think about was wrapping up with her in my bed after we spent the day together.

It was stupid to think we could go back and pretend like nothing ever happened. But I wanted to move forward for the sake of my kids.

That and I still wanted to fuck her silly.

I was about to go work out when my phone buzzed on the table. We had left our phones on Do Not Disturb since we were turning into raccoons from not sleeping. My eyebrows clenched together at who would text me at two in the morning.

My mouth pressed together, and I narrowed my eyes against the low light that flowed into the living room.

I looked at my phone to see a picture of Jasmine in a dangerously short dress. Her bite marks showcased like shining trophies on display on one of the major gossip sites on social media. She looked amazing as I zoomed in on her picture. My free hand found my neck and rubbed the tight muscles as I exited the photo and scrolled through the notifications that I'd missed and saw her text about needing to talk.

I laughed even though the situation wasn't funny. We were here in Nashville waiting to catch our Kitty, and she'd found her way home. Of course, leave it to Jasmine to throw us for a loop.

I shook my head and got to work. I called the pilot and told him we needed to leave soon. He groaned but promised he would be ready in an hour. I shot a quick message back to Jasmine that said we would be home tomorrow afternoon.

I gathered Wren's things since we shared a room and woke him up. He flicked me off but got up when I threatened to sell his gym equipment. We woke Gabe up last because he was an ass when you interfered with his sleep.

He stomped around but, after he was up, cursed our existence. We told him Jasmine was in LA. That put his ass into motion.

We returned home after nine in the morning because of fueling problems and traffic. When we entered our home, I did my little happy dance. My arms flared in the air, and my body moved from side to side. I liked Nashville, but nothing beats being at home.

"Let's go out!" I roared. "Nothing is going to happen today. So, let's go out. I have a feeling for a virgin pina colada."

"Okay, but I'm picking the activity for the day. I suggest breakfast at the Blu Jam, and then we can go from there... or we could bum rush her home," Wren offered.

"No, let's give her a day, and then we'll go from there. We've been cooped up in that condo. So, let's have some fun," Gabe declared.

We did just that. It was a relief to not have to pace the floor and think about what would happen next. After we filled our stomachs, we headed to the mall to shop. Like the diva I was, I filled the car with bags. We went to get our nails done, and Gabe chose bowling as our activity. I felt old in the sea of young people around us. But that soon faded away to pure bliss.

We returned home around eight after we ate dinner. Our driver helped us with our bags, and we dumped everything in the living room until we had time to sort through them. We said goodnight to our driver and decided to hit the theater for a movie.

We had just started to head that way when the doorbell rang. We thought the driver might have dropped something. So, Gabe went to open the door. As we watched him open the door, he stopped mid-speech and stood rooted in the spot.

Chapter 24

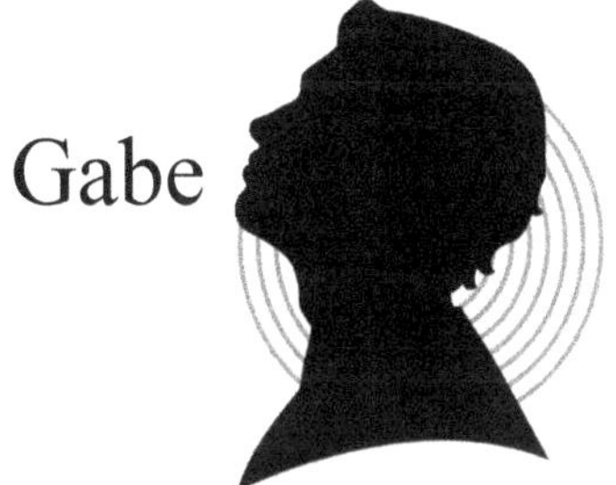

Gabe

Here I thought the night would be an uneventful Saturday night. When I opened the door, I hadn't expected to find the petite, feisty woman who haunted my dreams at night and my mind during the day. The brown goddess was dressed in a pink mini sundress with white flats. The front had a V-neck that showed off her ample chest and Wren's bite mark. I tried my best not to stare as she held her arms behind her back and lightly rocked side to side. But like a pendulum, it drew me to them, and I couldn't help but feel my cock stiffen.

I was a sucker for breasts... and ass.

She cleared her throat, which drew my attention. My cheeks flushed red, and I saw her bite back a smile. The little minx thought she was so coy. I stepped away, and when she entered, I closed the door and checked out her ass as it swayed in that short dress. When she walked, some of the dress caught in between her cheeks.

She stopped in the expansive foyer, which made her appear tiny in the room. Tony and Wren stood in front of her with lust-filled eyes. I stood behind her, not close enough to touch her but close enough to see my bite mark on her shoulder. The citrus and lavender scent hugged me like a warm embrace.

She straightened her shoulders and stated, "We should talk—"

"Strip," Tony demanded.

The command came out gruff with desire that swirled in his eyes. Tony, who always had a joking demeanor, was gone. That Tony was replaced with one who looked like he would bend her over in the foyer.

"I-I came here to talk about—" she stammered.

"Our kids," Tony finished for her. Judging by her gasp, she didn't know about our Nashville trip. "We will talk about them later. Right now, you're going to strip."

She stopped for a minute, appearing stuck, but went on.

"No, I need to apologize for my actions. I purposefully withheld our kids from you guys, and I regret keeping our kids a secret when we reunited. I cannot undo my actions, which were driven by fear, but I can promise to make up for it from now on. If you give me a second chance, I will make it up to you." She said as she took on her familiar stance. Shoulders squared and if I were in front of her, I knew I would find her bottom lip trembling.

Our little defiant Kitty thought she was in charge. It was cute. But it was late, and I was done with the impromptu apology session. I could tell Tony shared my sentiments as a slow smirk appeared on his face.

I tapped her shoulder, and she turned around towards me. She craned her neck up to peer at me. I decided I was leading the ship tonight. I swooped down and threw her over my shoulder. She yelped. My arm was tight around the back of her knees.

She punched and slapped my back, and I giggled at her failed attempt at stopping me. Her tiny hands grabbed onto the hooks in my pants when she wasn't hitting me.

"Let me down, Gabe!" Jasmine yelled.

I slapped her on her ass, and she squeaked as I walked toward the stairs.

But Tony stopped me and smirked. "Our little kitty is soaking wet, and she didn't wear any underwear," Tony smirked as he ran a finger from the back of her thigh to her drenched lips. "Why would you walk into the lions' den with no underwear and a drenched little tight cunt?"

She lifted to look at Tony. He ran a finger down one of her folds, and her thighs clenched. He popped the tip of his finger into his mouth and moaned at the slight taste of her juices.

I continued up the stairs and into my room. Jasmine hit my back again in an attempt to get down, and I threatened to slap her again. She pinched me, and I slapped her on the ass again. This time she wiggled, bumping her ass in my face.

I could have cum just from her ass being so close to me. My dick was heavy as I fought the urge to readjust myself. I put her down in front of my bed, and she readjusted her dress.

Her hair was slightly skewed as she ran her hand over the long locs and dress. She cleared her throat and said, "Who told you I wanted to be with you guys?"

Tony, Wren, and I started laughing like madmen. After a minute, I wiped away my tears. Jasmine's lips were pursed, and she crossed her arms under her breast.

"Baby, you're not leaving this house tonight or ever," I stated. "Strip for us."

Jasmine was always good with a neutral face. I guess showbiz would do that to you. But her eyes always gave her away. I saw the struggle in them as uncertainty gave way to wanton lust.

She slowly unraveled herself from her pink sundress, standing before us naked, almost like the day she left us. I thought she would shy away like when we first met, but she stood boldly with her hand cocked on her wide hips. Her pink tongue slid out to wet her plump bottom lip. Her stomach was smooth and held the telltale sign of stretch marks and a slight pudge, which made her even sexier.

I couldn't stand it anymore. I thought my heart had dropped into my cock at the way it throbbed.

"Get on your knees, baby. I want you and Tony to share my cock," I grunted out.

Jasmine's eyes widened, and her mouth dropped. Wren took that time to grab her hair and pulled her into a searing kiss. She arched her back, and Tony bent down to take one of her brown buds into his mouth, lightly biting and lapping at the tender brown peaks. I watched as she moaned against Wren's mouth, and Wren's free hand sought her neck. He squeezed her neck, turning the tip of her nose and ears a soft pink.

Wren released her, and she let out a greedy little moan that made me clench my fist. Placing a soft kiss on her lips, he turned her head to Tony.

"Do you deserve my kiss?" Tony questioned as he took her face in his hand.

"Tony, I'm sorry," she whimpered.

Tony kissed her, which wasn't the soft kiss he usually dished out. It was fueled with anger and lust. He nipped her bottom lip when he withdrew, his mouth was slightly swollen from their kisses. Tony leaned down and whispered something in her ear. She looked at him when he came back up. She nodded to him and got onto her knees.

I walked over to the trio naked since I'd undressed while they were wrapped up. My cock slapped me on my stomach, begging for the squeeze I knew would come once I was deep inside Jasmine.

I turned her head with my hand in her locs. I held my cock in my free hand. My cock hit her on her cheek playfully as I got lost in her big brown eyes.

"Wren on your knees. I want all of you to get my dick wet," I grunted. "Open your mouth, my pretty Kitty. Share this cock with your fiancés."

I didn't give her any time to reply as I stuffed my angry cock into her wet, warm mouth. It was just how I remembered as I fought the urge to cum down her long throat. The soft velvet of her palate hugged and warmed my hard appendage. Jasmine's tongue slid under the sensitive side of my dick. I could feel myself twitching each time I hit the wall in her throat. I was lost to the warm heat that spread throughout me when I noticed she removed my hand from her soft locs with ease and slid me out of her mouth. Her lips and hand found my heavy balls as she squeezed and sucked on them. The act made me curse out loud, leaving me breathless. Wren grabbed my cock and took me deep into his mouth as he sucked and swallowed the pre-cum and Jasmine's spit. He gagged, and a small moan left Tony's mouth as he pumped his stiff cock. It was the most beautiful sight to behold.

Jasmine pulled Wren off of me with a pop. I watched as Jasmine greedily took Wren by the hair and took command of his mouth. She sucked and licked whatever Wren had left of me with a moan.

Tony joined the duo. Their sweet song of love had me weak as they enjoyed themselves. It was the hottest thing to watch, and I was jealous. I pulled my painful cock straight and cleared my throat. As they pulled away, the little minx sucked Wren's tongue.

Jasmine wrapped her tiny hand around my cock and looked up at me. I wordlessly removed my hand and gave her this one time to have control. I watched as they continued to share my cock. Jasmine's mouth captured one side and Tony's, the other. Their spit gathered and dripped onto the black hardwood floor and all over them. Wren sucked the tip of my cock in his mouth as he rolled his tongue over the sensitive slit of my head. Which almost made my knees give out as I stood there trying to steady myself. Jasmine, who demanded control, took my cock from them and swallowed me whole. When she hit the back of her throat, her moaning became erratic. The vibrations drove me crazy and made me almost lose my footing. They continued their punishment on me until I couldn't take it anymore and pulled away, eliciting a firm grunt from all of us. My cock, wet and heavy, bounced with a slap on my stomach.

The heated sensation that ran through me pinned me to the spot until I decided what I wanted to do next. I moved back to sit on my wide black barrel chair. I wanted to watch while they prepared her for me. I wanted her ready to squeeze me while I was deep inside her.

"Open her up for me," I grunted, and I didn't even recognize my harsh voice.

Wren lifted Jasmine and placed her on the edge of the bed. There she sat with her pretty pink pussy wide open and dripping wet with her arousal. We didn't even have to tell her to open up wide. She played like she didn't want us, but the little minx knew what she was up to, and if she thought she was leaving us again, she was sadly mistaken.

I sat back and stroked my cock, and bit my lip. The pain helped to keep me from coming all over myself. Jasmine's dainty hand slid down her core as she played with her clit, all while her eyes stayed trained on me. The sweet melody that came from her mouth made me choke my dick and bite my lip harder.

She'll be the death of me.

"Let's get her ready for Gabe's enormous cock." Tony smirked as he pulled his eyes from Jas' hand. "Let's give him a show. What do you say, Kitten?"

She bit her plump lower lip, still wet and swollen from kissing and giving me head. She turned those glossy brown eyes to Tony and removed her soaked fingers from her core. She stuck the two digits into her mouth and sucked her juices off of them. It made my cock twitch at the reminder of how her lips wrapped around me while she sucked me in.

I tilted my head back and moaned as I stroked my cock. From my angle, I saw Tony and Wren on their knees as they sucked, licked, and bit at her wet pussy and swollen clit. Tony and Wren each had a finger in her velvet center and were knuckles deep into Jasmine's core, fingering her while they took turns torturing her clit with their mouths. Jasmine's full breast called to me as she arched her back. Her head was thrown back as she bit into her bottom lip. Her legs shook as she reached closer to the edge, and they removed their fingers from her warm core. Wren stuck his tongue deep inside her cunt and tongued fuck her while Jasmine rode his tongue until she screamed her release. Wren leaned back and showed me her juice as it flowed out, soaking my black silk sheets. Not wanting to miss out, they returned to lapping, sucking, and fingering her to her next orgasm.

Jasmine's weak legs were limp, and she tried to close them, but Tony grabbed them and kissed her inner thigh. She rose on her forearm, sweaty from her multiple releases.

"Pl-Please, no more!" she whimpered weakly as I saw Tony wipe the sweat from her lip.

Tony turned back towards me and winked. I nodded for him to continue. Wren helped Jasmine turn around with her head hanging off the edge of the bed, facing me. I got a glimpse of her breasts and her hardened buds from my spot.

She met my gaze, and I winked at her. She was beautiful.

Tony kissed Wren while helping him put his condom on, then guided Wren to Jasmine's entrance while Tony straddled Jasmine's stomach and leaned down for a kiss. Her face was flushed from all the blood rushing to her head. When Tony released her, she was breathless.

"I have been dreaming of fucking these big, beautiful breasts. I want you to push them together," Tony requested.

Jasmine gasped and threw her head back, the only sign that Wren had entered her.

"Shit," Wren grunted out. "You're so fucking tight, baby. I don't think I can last long."

We all groaned.

Tony slipped his pierced, lubed cock between Jasmine's breasts and grunted when he slid between her valley. Her eyes closed, and her mouth hung agape as they relentlessly fucked her. The rush of blood had her holding her head up for relief. Her hands pushed her breasts together as Tony glided between them. Every time the bulbous tip of his dick peeked out from her breast, Jas pink tongue sneaked out to lick the tip, and Tony shuddered when she did. I gripped the chair like my life depended on it. She moaned, and her words became erratic when Wren sped up. She choked out an "Oh God" as I watched her descend. Her hands slipped from her breasts, but Tony grabbed them, then her head and pulled it up.

"Open up for your dessert," Tony grunted out as he stroked himself.

Tony's breathing became erratic while Jasmine cried out as her release made her go limp. Their release was cataclysmic as Jasmine's sweaty hands dropped to Tony's legs. He held her head, grunting and milking his cock while he fed his cum to her. Tony moved to the side, allowing her to view Wren. He kissed her and gave Wren the reins.

Wren leaned over her, sinking her into the bed. He wrapped his hand around her pretty little neck and pounded into Jasmine. It was pure ecstasy as Jasmine's face flushed and Wren grunted, telling her she was his "good little whore." I almost came in my hands from how tight I was fisting my cock when Jasmine responded.

"I am your little whore." She stiffened and wordlessly shouted as she came, which triggered Wren, who let out a curse as they fell together. Wren fell on top of Jasmine as they shared a lazy kiss. He slipped his soft cock out of Jasmine and cleaned Tony's cum with his mouth until nothing was left. He leaned in for another kiss, taking her breath when he pulled away.

Their chemistry left me breathless as I watched the heaving of Jasmine's breasts slow down and her eyes slip closed.

"Bring her to me," I commanded as I sat there, ready to explode from watching them together and edging myself.

Wren picked up her limp body, her back pressed against his front. He placed her in a straddled position, and I grabbed her as she was unsteady. If I didn't get inside of her soon, I would explode.

As soon as I had control of her, I grabbed her hips to steady her. Tony grabbed an extra condom and was going to roll it on me when Jasmine stopped him.

I cocked my eyebrow and tilted my head at her.

"I want to feel all of you," she whispered, and I had to wonder if I made it up in my mind.

"You know what this means, right?" I asked her to give her another way out.

She nodded. My smile turned dark, and I heard Wren say, "We're planning for baby number three already."

I didn't respond as Jasmine and I stared at each other.

"You're going to be a good girl and take this dick, aren't you?" I commanded.

She sighed weakly and nodded.

I gave her the green light, and I let go of her. I knew I was the biggest of us, and my cock could be intimidating. That's why I gave her control. Either way, I won because her wet, tight pussy sucked the head of my cock in. It twitched. She made it halfway in before she slowed down and started cursing.

"God, I-It's been a while since—" she stammered.

"You're taking my dick perfectly. It was made for you, my good girl," I praised her while my hands massaged her round cheeks. "I know you can do it again."

I kissed her until her worries went away. Tony and Wren started kissing and nipping at her skin. Tony moved to the back to watch us as my tongue and mouth nipped and explored what she had deprived us of for six years. Once I heard her moan in my mouth, I knew I had her. I grabbed her hips again, spreading her ass cheeks wide so Tony and

Wren could see, as I thrusted the rest of myself into her wet core.

"Fuck! You bastard," she pulled away and yelled out.

"Fuck," Tony groaned, "I'm sorry, Kitten, but watching your little tight pussy suck down Gabe was so beautiful."

I knew she didn't mean it because she would have clawed my eyes out if she had.

She moaned and leaned against my forehead as she adjusted to my size. I could stay like that forever. Deep inside my favorite place, the only place for me.

It was a while before she felt ready to ride.

With her hands on my shoulders and my hands on her hips, she found her pace. Jasmine lifted as far as she could and sank to the base. Her body trembled as she ground herself at the base of my dick. She complained but handled me like I was made for her as I leaned back and watched my beautiful other half use me for her pleasure. *Yes, ours.* No other woman could make me feel this way. Leaning over, I kissed and licked the piercing marks that Tony made earlier. Her hands raked through my hair, pulling me closer like she was afraid I would leave her. Her riding became sloppy, and her breathing was shallow as she slowed when she got closer to the edge. My other hand traveled down to her clit as I gently stroked the sensitive bundle. A grunt left my hoarse throat, "Come for me, baby." She squeezed around me, and I gritted my teeth. She shouted her release and fell limp against me. Her body was slick with sweat. Jas' breathing grew shallower and uneven as she came down her high.

I kissed her forehead and whispered, "I'm not letting you go again. Your mind, body, and soul belong to us," in her ear. Her breathing hitched as I wrapped my arms around her waist and told her to wrap her arms around my neck. My feet rooted to the floor as I plunged into her. Crazed, frantic, and almost demon-like strokes followed suit. My mouth became my heart as I told her I loved her repeatedly with each stroke I had made. I watched as her breasts tempted me, and I took one of her large nipples into my mouth and lightly bit, sucked, and lapped at it. She cried out as another orgasm hit her and slumped over me. She was so tight that I felt myself slip and obliterate into a billion little pieces.

The slick sweat felt like our bodies were baptized and born again. I was still semi-hard inside Jasmine as I stroked twice and emptied the rest of my cum into her. She sighed and buried her face in my neck. I forgot Wren was still in the room, and Tony had slipped out without me seeing.

"She's sleeping with me tonight. If you want to stay, you can, but she won't leave my side until she's pregnant," I told Wren.

"A breeding kink, Gabe?" His eyebrows shot up. "I never knew you had that in you."

I didn't either, but I was finding out that when it came to my Jasmine, she'd changed me.

He shook his head, and I slipped out of her, missing our connection as soon as I did. I carried her to my bed—our bed and laid her down. Wren returned with a warm cloth and cleaned her up while he handed me a spare one. I cleaned up and dumped our washcloths in the hamper.

When I returned, Wren had slipped out but had already tucked her under the sheet. I smiled and got in next to her. She immediately found me, and I wrapped my arms around her. This was where she was supposed to be, with us.

Not with anyone else.

Not with Greg.

Not in Nashville.

Not in New York.

But here in our home. Spending her days and nights with us and making memories with our kids.

I sighed and let it go. Jasmine wiggled and continued to lightly snore. I smiled because some things never changed. It'd been almost seven years, but one thing that ran through my mind was Jasmine was home.

Now, we just have to convince her.

Chapter 25

Jasmine

Is this what heaven feels like?

After what seemed to be an orgasm marathon, I gradually came to life again. I stirred and stretched my limbs and winced at the slight discomfort from when Tony's piercings glided between my breasts as I lazily woke up. I chuckled slightly as my arm wrapped around Gabe and threw my leg across his waist. The sun was high over the hills and warmed our bodies. I looked to see Gabe still lightly snoring as I watched the sun's rays highlight his beautiful features. I missed the way his dark curls shined in the light. Taking a loose curl, I twirled it around my finger and watched it bounce back. From this angle, his morning wood nudged at my entrance.

I didn't think I could fit him inside of me today. I was so sore, even from the position I was in. A slight ache between my legs as I stretched my lower limbs made me hiss. After I initially fell asleep, Gabe woke me up three more times with his dick at my entrance ready to go. During the last round, I didn't even think he was aware his body sought me out in his sleep. And what did my greedy body do?

Opened up and gave him what he sought… willingly.

I tried to get up without waking Gabe. As I remembered, he was always grumpy when he was awakened. I raised up, and he pulled me back to his chest and rolled over on top of me. He placed kisses along my jawline until he reached my lips. I had to do a double take because he kissed me so gently. He reached down to place himself at my entrance when the enormous head of his cock pushed into my tender core. I winced and bit down on his lip.

He withdrew, and my passion pent-up body cried out.

I may be going crazy.

"I'm sorry, love," he croaked out and frowned. "I didn't realize you were that sore."

He slipped off the bed, smiled, and kissed me. "I'll be right back."

With Gabe gone, I finally got a good look at his room. It was black and gloomy like his prior mood bled out into this living space. That was the exact opposite of what I had seen today. Gone was the hard glint of the wild man I had seen in the office a couple of months ago. In place was Gabe's smile, the one I'd loved seeing late at night and in my dreams.

I sat up and went to find my phone when Gabe walked back in, still naked as the day he was born. His cock bobbed angrily at me.

Sheesh, even when he's semi-hard, he's massive.

He picked me up like I weighed nothing and carried me to his impressive bathroom.

"I didn't know you were a romantic, Gabe," I joked as I peered at him.

"Did you forget we used to spend half our time in that spa tub at the club?"

"No, I hadn't forgotten." My face heated at the memory of them cleaning me until I came all over myself.

How embarrassing.

He placed me in his tub, which was more like a small pool. Each side of the tub had a seat for at least four people and a headrest.

"God, this is massive," I gawked around the room. It was bigger than my bathroom at home. He got in a seat next to me.

"Well, you know there's nothing small about me." He winked at my fiery face.

We chuckled. I took a deep breath and sat back. It took me a minute, but I recognized the scent. I turned to him. "You got the rose chamomile and vanilla bath bombs I like?"

He smirked and nodded.

"Gabe, I, uh," I stammered.

"Spit it out," he teased.

I looked down at the soft bubbles of the water. I was so sure of myself before I'd come to their home, but I was choking.

Today is about sorting my shit out. I've had my fun, and now it's time to right a wrong.

"I'm sorry—"

The door swung open, and Tony and Wren stepped through with what looked like mimosas for all of us.

"Did you guys think you could continue the party without us?" Tony teased. His smile touched his sparkling eyes.

"Especially since we had to listen to Gabe destroy our little Kitten all night! While I had to resort to Wren," Tony joked. He was rewarded with a smack in the back of the head.

Wren handed us our drinks and joined us in the tub. I was surprised to find it was plain orange juice, but I downed it anyway. The conversation flowed even though there was an underlying tension, or maybe it was me who was counting down the ticking time bomb.

I placed the empty champagne flute on the side of the tub. I took the deepest breath I could imagine and rolled my neck.

Everyone stopped talking after I cleared my throat. All the

guys' intense eyes fixed on me. I squared my back, hoping the jets would give me some confidence.

"Listen, I owe you guys an apology. That Friday, I did plan on having sex with you guys and saying goodbye afterward. I admit to that, and it was a shitty thing to do." My foot tapped the tub floor lightly. "I folded under pressure and my mom's judgment to end the secret trips to Celeste. But it wasn't all of their fault. I listened to that little nagging voice, and I doubted myself.

My mom and I's relationship has been strained since my father passed away from cancer when I was ten. I think—I know that catapulted her dependency on me. The only time I felt free from my mother was when I was at school or with my best friend, Samantha, and even then, she stayed in the back of my mind. Then we switched roles when Sam committed suicide. I became a lost sheep without my mother. At the time, the best thing was to lean on my mom, or so I thought. I lost myself until my therapy sessions finally hit home, and I decided to take control of my life. When I met you guys, I was obsessed since day one. It became more than just sex for me as time went by. I realized I just wanted to be close to you guys because, with you guys, I felt like I could be my true self. My whole self, without anyone judging me." I stopped to catch my breath and clear my throat.

"See, up until Club Celeste, the only other freedom I experienced was being retired because my mom didn't have anything to control me with anymore. Instead, I foolishly made my fear of losing my mom, the only other family member I had besides Allison, drive my life. I hid our relationship from both of them because I was too afraid to stand up for myself and for us. I was a coward and thought I could just coast through the twins' life just being with Greg because I didn't have any faith in myself to stand up to my mother or stand up for us." I continued.

I looked into Tony's eyes, who peered at me from across the tub. I was never great at reading people, but Tony's eyes held something that made me want to run and hide. It was a disappointment. The one thing I feared more than being hated. It cut like a knife lodged deep in my chest.

I opened my mouth to say something, anything, to break the silence.

"Why?" he asked. The question was simple, but it felt like the knife dug deeper, and the little strong bravado I once had faltered.

I sighed and focused on the empty champagne flute in Wren's hand.

"I hadn't planned on keeping the twins away from you guys but then I deleted everything, got a new phone, and changed my number before I found out I was pregnant." I turned back to Tony and almost stopped, but I kept on. "It shook me to my core. I cried, laughed, and cried again. Imagine my face when I found out I was having twins. God! Allison had to damn near scoop me up from the doctor's floor. I was scared and ashamed. Scared because I was going to embark on this journey by myself. Ashamed that I didn't reach out and contact you guys."

I gave them a pitiful smile. I drew my legs to my chest even though the tub was warm. The action comforted me.

"It was such a scary time. I went through a hard time with hyperemesis gravidarum. Even if I didn't eat, I was throwing up. I lost weight and became dehydrated. I had to spend so much time in the hospital and at home. But I made it through with Allison's and my mom's help. When they were born…" A smile touched my lips. "I looked into their little faces and knew I would do anything for them. I suffered from postpartum depression, and it was rough going through it by myself full-time. But I got help."

"Did Greg help raise the boys? Do they consider him their father? And..." Wren asked, seeming to pick up from Tony's question. Tony's eyes were glued to the wall-to-ceiling window in front of the spa.

I chuckled out of nervousness, which drew Tony's attention to me, and my face burned.

"Yes and no, honestly. My mom arranged for Greg and me to meet. She insisted the boys needed a father, and I was still going to therapy for my postpartum depression, which she chalked up to not having a man around." I rolled my eyes hard. "I went with it, but they weren't responsive to Greg in the beginning. After they turned one, I decided the twins needed a father figure in the house, and I realized he made my mom happy. So, I would live with my decision until they were eighteen. Now, they wouldn't go to Greg or allow him to do anything with them until they were two. I guess by then they figured he was there to stay. He was there for them, but they just knew he wasn't their real dad."

It was silent in the bathroom until Tony shifted. "Did they call him dad?" he whispered.

I laughed, and my hand flew up to my mouth. "No," I bit back my smile as they stared at me. "They called him Mr. Greg. They knew he wasn't their father, and I didn't want to force them to call him dad. But they appreciated him."

"Oh." He looked relieved.

I nodded, and they looked around. The guys, except Tony, laughed. When the laughing died down, Tony continued.

"I should hate you. Feel upset and want to lash out at you. But as I sit here looking at you, I feel nothing but regret and sadness." He rubbed a wet hand in his hair. "I love you, and you tormented us for six years. We tried to replace you, but no one can hold a candle to you, Jasmine. I've thought about this repeatedly. I struggled with whether to file for full custody, but I'm not evil. Plus, I couldn't take my kids away from their mother. So, we want to give you another chance."

Okay, a totally different direction than how I thought this would play out.

"I don't mind trying again, and I'm not running this time." I smiled. "It was like I had a mini epiphany during my farce bridal shower party to get it into my thick skull that I deserved better than Greg. I deserved you guys, and what I needed—no craved, was right here in this room all along. So, no matter what's in store for us, I'm in it for the long haul."

I never knew how good it was to confess my sins out loud. Even though the wet trails on my face weren't from the tub water, I still smiled at the thought of finally being free.

Wren excused himself to run to use the bathroom in his room. Tony pulled me over to sit in between his legs, and I immediately sunk into his warmth as my body returned to where it belonged. He reached over to grab a bottle off of the tub. I was about to ask him about the bottle when the scent of lavender filled the area as he poured the liquid into his hand. He began to massage my scalp until I was putty in his hands. Overwhelmed with his skillful hands in my hair and the fact that he still remembered my favorite oil, I let out a small moan as my mind slipped from reality. It wasn't until Tony spoke that I remembered where I was.

"So, with that being said," Tony continued, "I had all your personal things packed and moved into your wing here with us."

"Excuse me?" I let out something between a laugh and a moan because I thought he was joking, and he was still massaging the hell out of my scalp.

He had a wicked pair of hands, and when Tony stopped, I nearly cried and wanted to throttle him in a loving way, of course.

"He's serious, Jasmine. He's gotten movers to pack up your belongings so that you can move into the wing we made for you," Gabe stated calmly while he lightly ran a finger up and down my neck. *I don't remember him moving to this side of the tub.* He knew I couldn't think when he did that. I'm like putty in his hands.

"Y-You can't do that," I said as I made my failed attempt to stand my ground. My heart tripled a bit but not from fear.

He leaned in and kissed me from my jaw to my ear, and my

swollen clit throbbed with each kiss. He whispered, "Kitten, we can, and we will."

I wrestled myself from Tony's legs and turned to see his mischievous smirk.

"If you think we would let you run off again, you've made a sad mistake. If I ever have to chase after you again, Jasmine, you better pray because if you thought Tony was bad, you have another thing coming." Gabe stood up with his cock still semi-hard.

I licked my lips, and I felt my thighs clench as if I was face-to-face with his cock. I could almost hear Allison jokingly scream "whore" in my ears.

"Do you guys still want a house full of kids?" I wondered as the thought ran through my mind.

"Of course," Gabe winked. "And I'm willing to bet you'll be pregnant after last night or the next couple of months."

My mouth twitched as I tried not to smile at the revelation. The thought that maybe I could be pregnant right now made my heart speed up. My mouth won our little battle as I felt my lips widen into a smile.

He held his hand out, and we got out of the tub. Wren came back, bouncing, when Gabe grabbed me in a bear hug and kissed me. I pushed him away because I forgot I hadn't brushed my teeth. He shrugged when I told him that.

"Jasmine, we have something for you first," Wren said as he rubbed the back of his thick neck, his face was beet red as he shifted on his feet.

There stood the men that made my heart swoon. Tony, Wren, and Gabe looked at each other apprehendingly until Gabe cleared his throat.

"So…right," Gabe paused. The scene before me would be laughable if I wasn't scared of what they might say. This was the first time I'd seen him unsure of himself.

"Listen, Jasmine. We have done a lot of thinking about this

situation we've found ourselves in, and we decided that even though our circumstances may have changed, we still want to be with you and be fathers to our children." Gabe said, picking up from where he left off.

"My ma always said that you'll find your better half when your spirit collides. Before meeting you, I've only ever felt that with Wren and Gabe. But when I saw you, that familiar something clicked inside of me like it did when I first met Gabe and Wren." Tony ran his now dried hand into his hair, making pieces fall out of place. I had to fight the urge not to go and run my hand in it and fix it like I loved to do. Tony continued, "We knew you were the one for us since the moment we left our room at Celeste the first night. When you left us, you took a part of us and gave it back to us every Friday night."

The thick sensation of the sob that was stuck in my throat burned. I wiped the fat tears that fell from my eyes while my lips trembled.

"Jasmine, I won't lie to you and say that our road will be filled with diamonds and gold, but we're willing to try because we love you today, tomorrow, and the rest of our lives," Wren said. "You are the only other person that I want to wake up to outside of our family. As Tony mentioned, you complete us in every shape and form. I-We don't want to live without you."

I don't think I've cried that much since I gave birth. I stood there before them, soaking the white towel with my tears and snot. I couldn't be certain, but I may be having a mini-stroke because my heartbeat tripled, and the sob in my throat broke as I saw them get on one knee.

"W-What are you guys doing?" I asked even though I knew the answer.

"We're proposing to you, Jas," Gabe said with glassy eyes. "We couldn't decide on a ring that would convey our commitment and love for you, so we got a custom-made ring with our favorite stones that reminded us of you and your birthstone, of course. We were lucky that our jeweler was able to pull some last-minute strings for us to get you this ring."

My eyelids were burning from the way my eyes stretched when Wren opened the little gold box.

"The vintage blue sapphire for your birthstone," Wren said as he pointed to the color-changing gem on the right of the ring. "My gem was the alexandrite, rare and color-changing, like you, Jas. Inspired by all of your colorful attire and hair from Celeste."

"Mine is the Red Beryl," Tony touched the red gem on the left of the sapphire, "Inspired by that hypnotizing red mini dress and mask you wore the first time we met…and the red lingerie at your great escape…actually do you still have it? Because I've had lots of-"

Tony earned a slap to the back of the head from Gabe. He narrowed his eyes at Gabe, and Gabe ignored it.

"…and this," Gabe continued as he took the ring from Tony, "Moldavite gem represents me the night you fell asleep after muttering how much you loved us."

"I-I what?" I said with my voice thick with emotion.

Gabe cracked a smile that had my shaken body weak, "Yes, I didn't think you were aware, but I kept that secret since then."

My mouth dropped open, and some of the tears slid from my top lip into my mouth. All I could do was nod like I lost my voice.

"You said you were committed to us and wanted to give us a second chance. Well, this is the second chance. We don't want second best when we have the best already, and that's you, Jasmine Grant, if you haven't noticed. We want you and our children in our lives permanently." Gabe continued.

"No more running and hiding or letting others dictate your happiness," Wren said.

I didn't know what to do with myself as I stood there in the middle of the vast bathroom in the white towel they gave me, staring at the three men I loved…three half-naked men as the white towel did nothing to stop them from giving me a peep show.

"Jasmine Grant, will you make the ultimate commitment to us? To have us and truly give our family a second chance at love? Will you marry us?" Tony asked.

A thousand questions ran through my mind at this very moment. Would I make a decent wife? Would I be enough for them? Would I survive this if things go south? But as I looked at them, my heart waiting patiently on their left knee, my mind had already made up its mind and screamed "yes" as if we didn't have a long road ahead of us.

"Yes," I said as I mustered up the strength I could. "I love you, Wren Costa, Gabe Sabino, and Tony Russo."

Their nervous faces were gone the moment the words left my mouth as they jumped up, dropping their white towels to the ground, as they each scooped me up into a bear hug. I couldn't help the crazy wide smile that broke out on my face. My heart was overfilled with so much joy and love that if I died right now, I would be content.

I knew I didn't deserve them or this moment, but I vowed then and there I would do everything and anything to keep them in my life.

The soft buzzing sound filled the room breaking our little celebration.

"I think our time is up, and we definitely need a shower," I said as I wiped my face clean of the fresh tears on my face. "You guys couldn't wait until we had dinner or at least until we had clothes on." I chuckled.

I knew I was fussing and talking just for the sake of it. But I was all out of words with a bundle of emotions swirling in me. The soft buzzing rang in the room again, but this time, it caught Wren's attention.

"Oh shit! I forgot that I brought your phone in here. You dropped it in the hallway," Wren said, as he handed me the phone from the countertop.

"Oh my God! She must be so worried, and my babies!" I trembled as I looked at the notifications on the phone. "Oh God, it's three in the afternoon. Shit."

I dialed Allison's number as I moved into the bedroom, and she picked up on the first ring.

"I'm so sorry, Allison. I didn't realize I slept the whole day, basically."

"Yeah, yeah, yeah. One-third of your boyfriends called me already. Right before twenty colossal-sized men came stomping through your house, packing everything up. I was going to call the police, but they mentioned one of the big bosses' names." I heard the click of her seatbelt. "They've been there since eight and left around an hour ago. They should have arrived already. Did you not hear anything?"

"No, I-I just got out of the tub," I stumbled out.

"Oh, you slut, you got your back dislocated last night?" She laughed.

I sighed and shook my head. "Allison!"

"Alright, alright! I'm going to take the boys to get a snack and drop them off at the sex palace." She snickered.

I sighed, and we said goodbye after confirming she'd be at the house in twenty.

That was all I needed to kick my still naked ass into gear. I got in the shower, and Gabe, Tony, and Wren accompanied me. I hopped in, and what was supposed to be a quick shower turned into Tony eating me out from behind. After another shower and Gabe's shorts and Wren's shirt, I was ready.

I finally made it out of Gabe's room. There was a wing on the other side of the home that held everything I owned. I thought my house was big, but this place was huge. The area upstairs had four hallways. Each one had its own decor. The main room had neutral colors and was cozy. It was where I guessed they gathered to hang out.

"We were waiting for a special someone to fix this area." Wren crept up behind me.

I yelped, and he hugged me. Gabe and Tony followed behind him.

"Listen, I should talk with the boys before introducing everyone. They can be super shy sometimes, and it takes some time for them to warm up to people. Especially since their lives were uprooted in less than a day."

They didn't get a chance to respond as the doorbell rang, and I flew down to get the door. I smelled the remnants of someone cooking in the back part of the home, which I figured was the family room and the kitchen area. The smell of food made my stomach grumble, but I ignored it.

I rushed to the door, and my face lit up. I'd never been away from Tris and Teo this long. I instantly felt the hot heat of shame for being away from them. I kissed them until they were giggling.

"Well, do I get a hello kiss, or am I chopped liver?" Allison smirked.

"Oh, Ha." I hugged and kissed her. "Thank you so much, and again, I'm so sorry."

"It's no problem," she shrugged.

"Aunt Allison got us pretzels, Mom!" Teo smiled.

"I see. I'm jealous! You didn't get me one." I kissed his little nose.

"I guess you had a different type of protein to fill your stomach, huh?" Allison snickered, and I gave her a look.

"Listen, I have to go. You know how Wayne gets when I'm gone too long." She smiled.

"Go on, and I will call you later. I have to talk to the boys." I kissed her goodbye, and she was gone in a blink.

I took the boys in. Their little eyes wandered the strange house and found the first empty room.

I spent the next few minutes explaining some of what was happening. Of course, I didn't go over everything, just enough so they understood what to expect. Their little eyes shined as I told them they had daddies.

"This is our dad's house, mom?" Tris asked. His little eyes were full of wonder.

"Yes, and you have three dads," I stated firmly.

They looked at each other and smiled.

"We have three dads?" they asked jointly.

My lips quivered as I tried to hold back the laugh at their little surprised faces.

"Yes, and they are waiting to meet you guys. So, are you ready?" I smiled.

"What if they don't like us?" Tris held his hands in his lap, which he did when he was afraid.

"Baby, if they don't like you, then we're leaving as soon as possible. How does that sound?" I smiled at him.

"I guess it's okay, Mom." He gave me a little half smile as I hugged him.

They looked doubtful but grabbed my hands. I led them up the stairs, away from all the aroma in the back of the house. I made a mental note to ask what was being made down there.

Wren, Tony, and Gabe were all pacing the living area. Tris and Teo stopped walking and tried to hide behind my legs. With a whine, I pulled them to my side again, and they shoved their faces into my legs.

The guys stopped pacing, and they all had shaky smiles plastered on their faces.

"Hey, Teodoro and Tristano. I want you guys to meet your dads." I spoke in my best motherly voice.

Tris and Teo's shoulder-length black hair fanned their faces. I pushed it out of the way and repeated myself. It wasn't until Tony came over and bent down to greet them that they took their faces out of their favorite hiding spot.

"Hey, I'm Tony, your dad," Tony said. His eyes filled with unshed tears. "I know this is all new for you, but your other dads and

I would love to get to know you. Would that be okay with you guys?"

Teo and Tris both looked up at me, and I nodded for them to speak up. Teo, the outspoken twin, was stuck.

"I think I don't mind… If Mommy doesn't," Tris mumbled.

I tried to bite back the smile. It was rare that Tris would speak up for the both of them. I looked to Teo, who was stuck on Wren and Gabe, who had snuck over and tried to get the now shy Tris to speak.

"Yes, sweetie. I don't mind at all." I said absentmindedly as I turned my attention to the trio.

Gabe and Wren were at eye level with Tris. Teo went to stand next to his brother as they spoke to them.

"You can call me Pa," Gabe said. He cleared his throat and continued, "So that us old guys don't get confused."

"And you can call me either Babbo, Poppa, or Oton," Wren said. "I will let you choose, and you let me know which one fits, okay?"

Teo and Tris gave each other a look. Their eyes were wide, and looked unsure of themselves as they stood there side by side.

"I think it will be okay to call you Babbo, right Tris?" Teo asked.

"I think so as well," Tris replied with his voice filled with wonder.

Tony, Gabe, and Wren finally got Teo and Tris to open up after that, and I stepped away so they could start bonding. Seeing them together brought tears to my eyes. I watched all of them cry, including Gabe. I stood there with my stomach cursing, but I couldn't stop thinking about the scene in front of me. It reminded me of my dad and me whenever he left to travel for his job and came back. It was as if he were gone for five years and not just a week.

The boys were telling them about their games and their laptops. So, they were in seventh heaven.

"Guys, let's get something to eat before I pass out," I begged while swaying slightly.

"Yeah, I'm hungry, Mommy," Tris tagged along.

I looked at them. These kids could eat the whole pantry and still be hungry. I shook my head. They gave us a brief tour of the first floor, and Tris and Teo oohed and awed through the tour. We had the same things at home—well, the old house, but theirs were on steroids.

We were all huddled in the kitchen, eating the food that Gabe reheated for us, when I stopped to look at the scene before me. Tris and Teo were so deep into their conversation with their dads. Their little faces lit up when they spoke. They loved the attention. Their dads cut their food, gave them way too much money for the Nintendo online store, and planned a tech museum road trip around California. It hadn't even been a full day already. I shook my head. They already had them wrapped around their tiny little fingers.

I didn't notice when Wren had slipped up next to me.

"Hey, what are you grinning about over here?" he chided as he playfully bumped my shoulder.

"Nothing… I'm just admiring how well the boys have you guys twirled around their fingers already."

We chuckled at my joke.

"Well, they had a great mother to help raise them. So, what's not to love?" Wren smiled. "In all of this, I think we forgot to say thank you."

Now it was my turn to look perplexed. "Thank me for what?"

Everyone's attention turned to our conversation. "Thank you for raising our kids and keeping them safe and loved," Gabe said from across the room.

I was so thrown off by their gratitude that I fumbled with my words.

"I-I… you're welcome," I got out. "Thank you for giving me— us another chance."

"We would be crazy not to. Plus, remember what I said the night everyone fell asleep except us," Wren said.

I stood there and tried to rack my brain. He saw me struggling and helped me out.

"We were speaking about our relationship when you said," He stopped to clear his throat and put on an accent that I guessed was supposed to be mine. "I'm attached to you guys in such an unnatural way that I can't live without you guys."

I instantly remembered the night he spoke of. I was tipsy, and the liquid courage was flowing through my veins. It was the first time I opened up and gave them a piece of how I felt about them.

I blushed. "You remembered that?"

"Yeah, that and that darn mask." He smiled as I playfully hit him.

He grabbed my hand and kissed my palm.

"We felt the same way. It's a shame we had to lose time together just to find our way back to each other."

"What do you mean by lose time?" Tris asked.

I forgot the boys were still up as I turned to their little beady red eyes that cried out it was bedtime.

"Well, Mommy had to step away for a bit to think about stuff," I answered half truthfully. When they were older, I would tell them the truth.

"Oh, okay, but no more stepping out," Teo yawned out. "We like our dads."

That earned a chuckle from me and the guys.

"Of course not," I said as I looked at each of the three men I ran from. "I'm never leaving again."

As I looked around the expansive kitchen, I knew with all my heart that I meant every word I said then and now with every fiber of my being.

Tris and Teo decided the answer was good enough. They crawled into my lap and fell asleep in my arms as I showered them with kisses.

We cleaned up the kitchen, which was littered with our food containers. Gabe had slipped off to take a phone call with his parents, and Wren and Tony helped me take the two spoiled boys upstairs. When I entered my wing, aka Queen Jas' wing, as Tony called it, I was stumped. Everything seemed copied and pasted into their home. The lilac, silver, and white decor made me fangirl. That was my favorite color combo. They laid out all of my personal items from earlier.

We took the boys to a room across from my bedroom. They'd decked it out in the same theme. I made a note to have my interior designer come and change it because the boys wouldn't like it.

"Tris can sleep here and Teo in the other room," Wren offered.

"No, they will get up and raise Cain if they're not together," I explained. "How about they sleep with me for the night?"

"You're going to be sleeping with us tonight," Tony stated.

"You know we're going to have to change our schedule. Kids are in the house now." I gave him a pointed look.

"Yes, mama bear," Wren called out. "How about we all sleep together?"

"So, I will have to fight for my life because you *and* the twins sleep like you're fighting?"

"At least we don't snore!" Tony yelled out.

I threw a pillow at him. Luckily for him, he had excellent reflexes. He chuckled at me.

"Hey!" Tony shouted. "Remember when I had to wake up because I thought you were dying from your snoring? You told me to just turn you over and to leave you alone."

"I remember no such thing," I chuckled. "Fine, but if I don't sleep well, I'm blaming you."

We made quick work of getting ready for bed. I almost pleaded with them to let me sleep in the giant tub, which looked larger because the bathroom here beat my old one tenfold. Tony showed me the loc products he brought me, and I kissed him until we were panting.

Gabe returned, and we all tucked in for the night.

I was definitely fighting for my life tonight with the twins' legs or arms skewing over me already. I could already see the black and blue marks I had somewhere on my body from where the twins kicked me while they were sleeping. The guys took their spots next to the twins. The purple comforter tucked everyone in as we said our goodnights.

When everyone was snoring, I looked around at the dimly lit room. I noticed the portrait that Samantha had drawn. It might have sounded crazy, but I knew she had something to do with this situation. She was probably upstairs on cloud nine, laughing her ass off, happy as a lark.

And if I could have, I would've thanked her for being there for me and pushing me. If not, I wouldn't have had anything close to this moment.

I kissed Teo and Tris's heads and fell into a deep slumber with my last thought.

From this day on, my life will change for the better.

Epilogue

Jasmine

4 years later

And I was right...

To think, I ran and hid for six years. When I could have been living in bliss, that word was not enough for what I had presently. It exceeded my expectations. If I could, I'd roll back the time I'd wasted with all the unimportant people in my life and start afresh. But alas, that would have been too easy.

I thought back as I prepared the table for our family dinner.

Tris and Teo became like sponges and absorbed everything of their dads'. It was scary, to be honest. I sometimes called them by their dads' names. Their mannerisms and statures were identical. Tris had stepped out of his shy spell, and he couldn't wait to meet new people. Teo was still the same but wanted to follow in Tony's footsteps.

We got a private tutor specializing in computer informatics, and Teo was like a sponge, soaking up everything from his tutor. I found the little hacker breaking into my iCloud account once. His explanation was he was helping me out. I laughed. But Tris? He wanted to follow Gabe. He became Gabe's shadow, much to Gabe's delight. He even brought him to work when they had a day off from school.

Wren, Gabe, and Tony decided they would dial down their days at work, which wasn't a lot, but they were looking for an excuse not to get involved in the daily business affairs. So, we took family trips and made up for lost time. We would sometimes spend weeks in a different country. Thankfully, the boys switched to an online classroom when that happened.

The guys' parents, especially Mrs. Russo, had been unhappy about the situation. There were many arguments expressing how they felt I would run off with the kids again. It took me a long time to convince them I was there to stay, and no amount of running would help me because Tony promised he would hack into my cellphone so I wouldn't have a place to hide.

That should have turned me off, but it didn't. It made me want them even more.

We worked on our issues through couples' therapy. I think the therapist saw us cry so much that she had a brand new box of tissues ready during our weekly meetings. Luckily, we started therapy before the triplets arrived.

Yes, triplets, as in three babies. When I discovered I was pregnant with triplets, I almost told the doctor to sew me up after giving birth. Everyone laughed, but I didn't. But it was all made up when I saw the tears of joy and trembling hands as each of them cut our babies' umbilical cords. At that moment, I knew I couldn't wait to replicate this moment again and again.

Gabe went around on cloud fifty. He claimed "his" boys, aka his sperm, were blessed by God himself. We laughed at him every time. We decided to continue the tradition of naming the boys after their biological father's first initial. I didn't care what they called them, to an extent, as long as they were healthy.

When Geovanni, Giannino, and Gianni turned three, and boy, if I thought the twins were rambunctious, the three of them took the cake. They copied everything their older brothers did as if they were their parents and not us. One day, we came home and found them helping the twins with their chores. I couldn't stop laughing. Of course, we placed the twins on punishment after that event. But that didn't stop me from picturing their little skinny selves picking up the clothes from the floor. Their midnight curls were a mess, stomping their tiny feet and narrowing their dark green eyes while they worked. Even thinking about it made me chuckle.

I wiped the sweat from my brow and rubbed my back as I called Teo and Tris to help me finish the table. I yelled and got no reply.

They're probably glued to their computers or games.

I tried to keep the boys out of the paparazzi's sight, but sadly, they snapped a picture of them at a closed-off event. Several entertainment shows called me every day until I gave in and went with the one that paid me the most. My fans were over the moon from the interview, and I shared the one photo of us from Christmas with the guys, me, and our five kids. I couldn't even imagine the amount of gossip that circulated after that. But I came out and explained my relationship and asked for privacy. I had been able to avoid them recently, so there had been no slip-ups.

Now I spent my days being a stay-at-home mom. That didn't say much since I did that before, but now I had my best friends to share my days with. We had a union ceremony after the triplets were born because I wanted to show up to my ceremony and celebrate, not huff and puff. Wayne and Allison attended with her little pregnant stomach. I was so happy for them that I bought them a home closer to us.

I tried my hardest to get my mom to move to LA, but she stated she wasn't ready to leave, especially when she now had Maxwell Hurst. Maxwell was a tall, handsome, salt-and-pepper man in his late sixties, perfect for my mom. He knew how to handle my mom when she got one of her messy ideas.

I liked that for myself.

He reminded me of my dad, which was crazy, but that was my mom for you. She eventually moved from that old home to a condo in Nashville about six months after the guys and I got back together. Her simple explanation was that it was time to move on, and she needed to stop leaning on me because she feared losing me. I agreed. When we went to help her move, she and I had another heart-to-heart, and she apologized for keeping me from my true happiness.

"Jasmine, I never meant to take over your life. I was doing what I thought was best for you…Sorry, best for me and my loneliness," She smiled as Geovanni came over and jumped into her lap, and she kissed his cheeks. "I kept you from being truly happy. Seeing you with your partners opened my eyes. I haven't seen you this happy in a long time."

"Mom, again, it wasn't all your fault," I said as I tickled Geovanni until he ran off to destroy something with his brothers. "It was my fault as well. I knew I should have worked to find them and correct my mistakes, but I didn't. I had plenty of time to correct it after they reappeared in my life, but I chickened out. But I think I was supposed to go down this path so that I can truly be the best me for everyone."

My mom looked as if she was going to cry. We hugged and got to moving her stuff to the condo. Everything was done and placed within the weekend. I can safely say that she will still keep her condo filled with pictures and her old electronics, but I digress.

Now she was in town with Maxwell because I was about to birth my second set of twin boys. This time it was Wren's turn, not that the kids differentiated whose father was whose. We clarified to them they belonged to all three of their dads. Of course, there was the occasional kid at school who told them it was impossible, but my kids had grown to ignore them. On the other hand, I had to deal with the ladies at the PTA meetings who couldn't decide if I was lucky or couldn't imagine having three men. I shrugged.

To each their own.

I took out the plates and placed them on the table. My Mom, Maxwell, and the guys' parents would arrive any minute. I had worked months on this last family dinner before the twins got here.

Tris finally came down and hugged me. "Do you need help with anything, Mom?"

I smiled and told him I was already done, but he could help get his brothers ready. They were suspiciously quiet.

With our home almost filled to the brim with kids, toys, and love, I thought getting my tubes tied would be the best as we approached seven kids. But the guys put up a fight until I agreed to make it to ten. Which was reasonable since I wanted more kids, and we could afford them.

After this set of twins, they wanted to leave the last three up to chance. I shook my head.

Leave it to them to make everything about a game.

Before I couldn't travel anymore, I made a trip to Nashville. I refreshed my dad's mausoleum with fresh flowers and had it cleaned out. It devastated me to see the dust and dirt caked onto the private mausoleum. I couldn't blame my mom because I knew it was hard for her to come out here, but I wish she had told me. Mr. and Mrs. Field moved out to Florida to be close to family. I paid their home off and had Samantha's casket moved so they could visit her whenever. My guys brought them a new boat as a thank you to them for being there for me. They were so thankful, but we didn't need any thanks because I knew if the shoe was on the other foot, Sam would have done the same for me.

"MOM!" one of my many kids called.

"I'm coming!" I shouted back.

My kids didn't understand that I had too much load to be hauling ass anymore. I made it to the kitchen. The pantry door was wide open, and I watched as the triplets ransacked the pantry. My three adorable little boys were covered in flour and syrup.

I groaned because they were also about to have a field day in the tub. After I wrestled them out, I called Allison and my mom to see if they could come earlier to help me with them. I made Teo and Tris help clean up, much to their dismay.

If their fathers hadn't stepped out to gather the cake and a couple of other things needed for the dinner tonight, they would be livid, and the triplets would be on timeout, their favorite hobby nowadays. I hated it because they would cry the whole time and call out for me from their perspective corners and if there's one thing my boys knew how to do, is to get me to rescue them, especially when they turned those big green eyes to me as they pleaded for me to help them.

I let out a deep breath as I thought about the tedious job of going up the steps. I wasn't supposed to be doing anything but lying down, eating, and watching movies, according to my husbands, even though my past pregnancy and my current one were a walk in the park compared to my first pregnancy.

As soon as I gathered the strength, mentally and physically, to go up the stairs, the front doorbell rang.

I was on my way to answer the door when the urge to pee hit me like a brick, and the warm liquid ran down my thigh, not even two seconds later. I cursed through the pain. I was scheduled to have my twins by cesarean next week.

I guess these two can't wait.

"Mom, I think you peed on yourself." Tris pointed as he came down the steps with the triplets in tow.

I looked down at the pool of liquid on the floor. I hadn't reached the door when another contraction knocked the sense out of me. Luckily, Tris rushed to answer it.

One minute I was cursing the kids' fathers, and twelve hours later, I was holding my six-pound twin boys, Wolf and Wynn Russo

Costa-Sabino. Yes, we all changed our names to match. It was a mouthful, but I loved it. They had my eyes, for now. My doctor stated it could change, but she shut up when I looked at her. She was supposed to be on my side. They had my features, but they had dark blonde hair, Wren's skin color, and chubby little cheeks. Simply put, I was in love again.

I looked around the room and smiled. Allison, Wayne, my husbands, the guys' families, my babies, and my mom were all around me. They all were dressed up for the missed dinner, but I didn't care. I quietly thanked God I came to my senses and stopped running from love.

La Fine

Enjoy the book?
Don't forget to leave a rating and review!

About Author

Teal Rose is a Why Choose paranormal romance addict that took her wild ideas from her hippocampus and placed them into her writings. She typically loves writing romance with a Why Choose, paranormal, and fantasy sub-genre. Teal's main goal is to share her vision of seeing Black Females being loved, heavy on the love, in these spaces.

She's Pro-queer, and everything she writes will have a representation of the LGBTIQA+ community. Hence her tagline, "Smut for EVERYONE."

When she's not writing, we can find her in front of her TV, watching movies and shows about witches, vampires, and things that go bump in the night. You can also lure away her from her books with any Grand Theft Auto, The Last of Us, and any other multiplayer games she can get her hands on.

Come stalk me!

Social Media

Instagram- https://www.instagram.com/author_teal_rose/

Facebook- https://www.facebook.com/TealRoseAuthor

FB public group - https://www.facebook.com/groups/492026645843692

TikTok- https://www.tiktok.com/@authortealrose

Goodreads- https://www.goodreads.com/tealrosewrites

Website- https://www. teal-rose.com

Newsletter

Stay up to date on what's next!

https://teal-rose.us11.list-manage.com/subscribe?u=ea13bed4a5f498000c4d65c51&id=9273a181f1

More Books by Teal

Ruined

Second chance at love? Or a second chance at failure?

<u>**Kyndall**</u>

Ten years ago, I made the mistake of falling in "love" with someone who didn't share my sentiments. It left me broken, homeless, and hopeless until my cousin came in to save the day. Now, that person is back, along with three surprises, after I worked diligently to move on from the damage they had done to my life and determined by hell or high water to make me a part of their family.

But what happens if I don't want to play by her rules? Or will I crumble as I did ten years ago?

<u>**Melissa**</u>

I am the quintessential wife to my partners, and I have a perfect life, except we're missing the right one to complete our family. But how can I find the perfect girl when I still think about the girl I abandoned to follow my dreams and help my dying aunt so long ago?

A second stroke of luck has brought her back, and I won't fumble as I did before.

Will my possessive and controlling personality ruin the only chance to recapture my lost love? Or will it help me?

I can't control the future, but I'll make her forgive me, and she will be mine whether she likes it or not.

387

www.ingramcontent.com/pod-product-compliance
Lightning Source LLC
Chambersburg PA
CBHW040852010826
48978CB00013BA/985